"NOBODY TOUCHES MY GUNS, MISTER."
HER VOICE CAME OUT IN A LOW,
BREATHY WHISPER.

He lifted one brow as a slight grin curved his lips. "Nobody?"

"Nobody."

Ignoring her protest, he slowly unfastened her gun belt and set it across her bed. "You don't need them, darlin'. When a woman's dressed the way you are, she's got a whole different set of weapons to use against a man."

"Like what?" she asked, her eyes locked on his. Her lips were ripe with invitation. The scent of her skin drifted around him, as heady as any home-brewed whiskey, and every bit as intoxicating. The air felt heavy between them, thick with sexual curiosity and erotic potential.

Don't do it, his instincts warned him. *Find another woman.* But Jake didn't want any other woman. The woman he wanted was Miss Annabel Lee Foster, and she was standing right in front of him, just waiting to be kissed.

He slipped his arm around the small of her back and pulled her to him. "Like this," he said.

Chasing Rainbows

Victoria Lynne

A Dell Book

Published by
Dell Publishing
a division of
Bantam Doubleday Dell Publishing Group, Inc.
1540 Broadway
New York, New York 10036

ISBN: 0-440-22328-8

Printed in the United States of America

Published simultaneously in Canada

October 1997

10 9 8 7 6 5 4 3 2 1
WCD

For my husband, Bob,
the man who brought
Swee Pea and Ju-Ju Bean
into my life.
I couldn't have wished
for more.

Chapter 1

Colorado Territory
October 1866

A hanging was never an easy thing to watch. If a man was lucky, his neck snapped on the drop, killing him instantly. Jerked to Jesus, as the saying went. But not all men had that kind of luck. Plenty of victims slowly choked to death at the end of a poorly strung noose. They died gasping for air as their tongues turned black, their bodies jerking and heaving until the bitter end. It wasn't fair and it wasn't pretty, but that was the way life worked. Some men died quick and some men died hard.

Jake Moran reined in at the outskirts of Stony Gulch, Colorado. He hadn't intended to stop, but the spectacle unfolding before him seemed to demand acknowledgment. An ancient oak—the hanging tree—stood silhouetted against a brilliant autumn sky. As a crisp breeze lifted the rich carpet of red and gold leaves scattered beneath its limbs, a minister droned on over an open Bible, reading last rights. The sheriff stood guard with a group of deputies. The condemned man, visibly trembling, awaited his fate with his head meekly bowed in prayer.

Jake's dark bay tossed his head and sidestepped skittishly. Jake stilled the motion with the gentle pressure of his thighs. "Easy, Weed," he soothed, stroking the bay's silken neck. Glancing back at the proceedings, he noted that his action had drawn the attention of the town sheriff. After a brief word to one of his deputies, the sheriff edged his mount toward him.

"Afternoon, Jake."

"Sheriff."

Sheriff Roy Cayne was large and rawboned; his ruddy complexion appeared wind-whipped. He matched Jake in height for they were both tall men, but that was where the similarity ended. The sheriff's blond hair had long since gone gray, and he moved with the lumbering stride of a man whose girth had settled around his belly.

The two men sat for a moment in companionable silence. "Ain't seen you around these parts in quite a while," the sheriff finally commented.

"Been working the tables out in Haggerty."

"Any luck?"

A grim smile crossed Jake's lips. "I've had better."

He returned his attention to the hanging, scanning the crowd that had gathered on the grassy knoll beneath the ancient oak. Women, dressed in their best calicoes and sunbonnets, strolled arm in arm with their husbands and sweethearts. The succulent aroma of salt pork and roasted sage hen drifted from open campfires. High-spirited children scampered between the wagons, laughing and shouting as they conducted mock hangings among themselves.

"Looks like quite a party you're throwing here," Jake commented.

Sheriff Cayne scowled in response, regarding the citizens of Stony Gulch with the pained air of a parent whose offspring were misbehaving. "Folks just couldn't stay home, could they?" Shaking his head in disgust, he leaned over and released a long, dark stream of tobacco. He wiped the juice from his chin and continued, "You'd think this was some fancy shindig the way folks are carrying on. Hell, we've even got some big-shot reporter from back East here taking notes, interviewing folks and whatnot. Says he's gonna write a story on the hanging."

Jake followed the sheriff's gaze toward a dapperly dressed man who moved through the crowd with a notepad and pencil in his hand. He looked the reporter over without much interest, then returned his attention to the prisoner. "Who is he?"

"Part of the Pete Mundy Gang that holes up in Blackwater Canyon. Gang robbed the stage a couple of weeks back, shot up the driver and his men pretty bad."

The Mundy Gang. That explained the celebratory mood of the crowd, as well as the presence of an East Coast reporter. Jake carefully eyed the condemned man. He was too short and scrawny, and Jake realized that the prisoner wasn't the man he'd been hunting. Jake sized him up anyway, looking for traits that would identify him as a member of the gang.

He was dressed in an oversized, faded flannel shirt that had been tucked into rough denim pants that had seen better days. His face was shadowed by a sloppy felt cap that had been pulled down tight over his brow. The man's head was no longer meekly bowed. Instead he stared boldly out into the crowd, as though trying to face them down. The result was neither menacing nor intimidating but a rather pitiable mixture of both anger and bravado. The prisoner looked more like a skinny, worn-out miner than a hardened criminal.

Jake silently cursed his luck and timing. Had he arrived in town just a few hours earlier, Sheriff Cayne might have let him question the man. Clearly it was too late for that now. "What about the rest of the gang?" he asked.

"Got away. Posse tracked them a bit, then lost their trail."

"Any idea which way they headed?"

"Nope."

Damn. Jake bit back an impatient sigh and tightened his grip on Weed's reins.

Sheriff Cayne eyed him speculatively. "You interested in the Mundy boys?"

"I'm interested."

"That a fact?" The sheriff mulled that over in contemplative silence. "So are a lot of folks. A lot of folks. 'Specially since the money from that stage robbery was never recovered. Twenty-five thousand dollars in federal greenbacks just sitting out there, buried somewhere in those hills." He shook his shaggy head and let out a deep sigh. "No telling where them boys stashed that money."

Jake nodded toward the prisoner. "Wouldn't talk, huh?"

"Not much. Admitted to being part of the Mundy Gang but claimed not to have had anything to do with the robbery or the killings. Claimed to be just riding by when it happened."

"Now, there's a fresh alibi."

Sheriff Cayne shrugged. "Things ain't always what they seem."

Jake arched a brow, mildly surprised by the sheriff's apparent defense of a convicted felon. "You think he might have been telling the truth? He might be innocent?"

"Guess it don't matter what I think. Jury voted guilty, that's good enough for me."

The reply took Jake completely off guard. Sheriff Roy Cayne had ruled Stony Gulch with an iron fist for nearly twenty years. He was tough but fair; Jake would have bet his last cent that the sheriff wasn't someone who would sit idly by and watch an innocent man hang. Looked like he'd have lost his money.

As though reading his thoughts, the sheriff raised his shoulders in an indifferent shrug. "Just doing my job, Jake, upholding the law. Jury wants a hanging, they'll get a hanging. Can't say I like it much, but the people in this town don't pay me to like it. They pay me to keep the streets safe and obey the rules of the court. That's what I aim to do."

"Can't ask a man to do more than that."

Sheriff Cayne nodded in agreement, but his expression remained troubled.

Jake tilted his head toward the prisoner and made a guess. "Young?"

"Too young." The sheriff looked as though he wanted to say more but resolutely tightened his lips instead. "Hell, maybe I'm just gettin' old." He pulled his watch from his pocket, flipped open the case, and glanced at the dial. "Reckon I oughta get on with it," he said, raising his arm to signal his deputy.

The deputy stepped forward, bringing the condemned man with him. In Jake's estimation, the sheriff couldn't have picked a worse man for the job. Despite the desperate air of self-importance he tried to project, it was obvious that the deputy was little more than a store clerk with a tin badge. He was stoop-shouldered and rail thin, and clearly unnerved at being the sole focus of the crowd's attention. The deputy fumbled with the rope, barely managing to fashion it into a noose before he tossed it over a sturdy limb of the hanging tree. That accomplished, he assisted the prisoner into the saddle. With shaking hands, he caught the noose and adjusted it around the condemned man's throat.

A hushed, anticipatory silence fell over the crowd.

The deputy wavered for a moment, as though paralyzed by the enormity of his task. Visible beads of sweat glistened on his forehead despite the cool air. He swallowed hard and set his hand on the horse's withers, only to have the animal skittishly shy away from him. As the animal moved, the rope jerked hard around the prisoner's neck and forced a strangled moan from his throat.

The gruesome sound was enough to goad the deputy into action. Resigned to his duty, or perhaps just anxious to have it ended, he tried again. He raised his hand and brought it down hard against the horse's hindquarters.

The horse shot out from beneath the condemned man.

Jake held his breath, waiting for the bone-shattering crack that indicated the man's neck had snapped on the drop.

Nothing.

The rope ran taut as the prisoner plummeted toward the ground, then sprang back. Instinctively the man began to thrash about in a vain struggle against the noose. Frantic gagging sounds emerged from his throat.

He was still alive.

A collective gasp rose from the crowd and filled the air. The deputy turned an unnatural shade of green and backed away, clearly horrified at the consequence of his botched job with the rope.

Anger tightened Jake's gut. He had been to hangings where it took over twenty minutes for the life to run out of a body, and had hoped to never see it again. "You might have shown your deputy how to tie a noose," he said.

The sheriff shrugged. "I did show him. Maybe next time the damned fool'll pay attention and get it right."

Jake shifted in his saddle, disgusted by both the spectacle and Sheriff Cayne's stony indifference. The prisoner was a member of the Mundy Gang, and perhaps, for that reason alone, he deserved to die. But not like this. Not gasping and choking for air before a titillated crowd. As for Jake's own interest in the proceedings—well, that had expired the second the noose had dropped. Since it was too late for him to question the man, he figured he might as well ride on. He'd seen enough death in his time for it to limit its hold on him as pure entertainment.

Just as he urged Weed forward, the prisoner writhed in a violent, painful spasm against the rope. The man's hat tumbled from his head . . . releasing a long mane of pale-brown hair.

Jake Moran had spent a lifetime reading other people's faces, judging the cards they held by the expression in their eyes. The vital necessity of that skill was matched only by the importance of keeping his own features carefully neutral. He'd become a master at hiding his emotions, for his profession demanded it. But at that moment, astonishment struck and left its mark on his face.

The condemned man was a woman.

Without any clear goal in mind, he urged his mount forward, but the sheriff caught his reins before he could move. "Easy," he murmured, his eyes focused intently on the prisoner.

"Hell, Roy, you're hanging a *woman*?"

"I'm doing what the court says I gotta do. Now, you just stay easy, Jake."

Jake shook his head, sickened. This certainly wasn't the first woman to be hanged in the Colorado Territory, but such hangings were rare indeed. They generally only took place if the crime was exceptionally violent—or the woman exceptionally notorious. Jake pieced together the information he had collected on the Mundy Gang of Blackwater Canyon. They were infamous for their sharpshooting, their ruthless brutality, their contempt for the law . . . and for Outlaw Annie, who rode with the gang.

Outlaw Annie.

A woman with a reputation nearly as wild and wicked as that of Calamity Jane. A woman who had faced down savage Indians and angry lawmen with equal aplomb. A woman so good with a knife she could skin the belly off a rattler before the snake ever felt the blade; so good with a gun she could knock the feathers off a migrating goose with a single shot. A woman who liked her whiskey rotgut, her bear meat raw, and who could bed the devil himself without even scorching the sheets.

Jake had never really believed she existed. To him, the legend of Outlaw Annie had merely been one of many tall tales of the frontier, stories that were swapped from trader to trader at night as a way to pass time in front of a lonesome campfire. But she was real all right, and now he'd seen her—choking at the end of a noose.

Annie continued to thrash against the rope, but her motions were getting weaker. It wouldn't be long now, he thought. But just as that notion formed in his mind, the noose, poorly tied as it had been, began to pull apart under the combined strain of the woman's weight and her desperate struggles.

The buzzing whir of fraying jute was immediately followed by the dull thud of a body hitting dirt. Outlaw Annie collapsed in a motionless heap at the base of the ancient oak.

The crowd strained forward, breathless and excited, transfixed by the grisly spell death holds over those who get to stand back and watch it descend upon somebody else. Jake tensed, waiting. Was she alive or dead? Sheriff Cayne peered anxiously at his prisoner, clearly absorbed by the same question.

Finally, after endless seconds of agonizing suspense, Annie moved. She was still alive. Jake felt his muscles slowly unclench. Beside him, Sheriff Cayne let out an audible sigh of relief. Jake glanced at him sharply.

The deputy who had tied the noose reluctantly stepped forward and helped Annie to her feet. A chorus of boos and hisses greeted her.

"String her up again!" shouted a voice from the crowd. The bloodthirsty cry was immediately taken up by the rest of the assembly. "String her up! String her up!"

Sheriff Roy Cayne waited, indulging his taste for drama. Once the shouting had reached nearly a fever pitch, he raised his pistol and fired off a round. As the echoing blast ripped through the air, a hushed silence fell over the mob. The sheriff wordlessly nudged his horse forward. The crowd parted as seamlessly as a river around a rock, allowing the big man and his mount to glide through the masses.

Once the sheriff reached Outlaw Annie and his deputy, he turned to face the citizens of Stony Gulch. "It's finished," he stated flatly. "Judge Carter ordered a hanging at noon, and that's what you got. You folks can all go home now."

Howls of protest instantly rose from the crowd.

Sheriff Cayne greeted the noise with a fierce scowl. "I said, the hanging's over. Go home, all of you."

The court had ordered a hanging, and the sheriff had given it to them. But Jake knew that if Sheriff Roy Cayne had really wanted the woman dead, he'd have tied the noose himself. Instead he'd depended on the incompetence of his deputy, and the bumbling fool hadn't let him down. Jake's respect for the sheriff's cunning doubled; he had obviously been planning this from the beginning.

The townsfolk, however, clearly had a different feeling on the matter.

"A hanging means killing, Sheriff, and she's got it coming!"

"String her up!"

"You don't want to do it, we will!"

The sheriff stared down the mob for a long minute. "That a fact?" he drawled. He spit out a long stream of tobacco juice, then unpinned the battered tin badge from his vest and held it up. "In that case, you can have this too. I want nothing to do with a town that goes vigilante."

The townsfolk fell silent, weighing the threat. Before Roy Cayne had taken the job of sheriff, Stony Gulch had been a haven for rustlers, thieves, outlaws, and renegade Indians. With Cayne gone, it would be only a matter of weeks before the town slid right back into the same lawless morass. Faced with that possibility, the righteous steam that had driven the mob quickly evaporated into the bitter gloom of petulant defeat.

"If we let her go," a voice demanded, "what's to stop her from bringing the whole gang back to town looking for revenge?"

"She says she has property out in Cooperton," the sheriff answered. "That's a good hundred miles from Blackwater Canyon, and a hundred miles again from here."

"How do we know that's where she aims to go? How do we know she ain't lying?"

Sheriff Cayne frowned. He tipped back his hat and scratched his head, mulling the problem over as though he hadn't considered it before. "Now, there's a good point," he said. "Appears to me the only way to see that she gets there is to take her there personally." He paused and surveyed the crowd. "Who's gonna volunteer to do that?"

"That's your job, Sheriff," a voice answered immediately. "You and your men oughta go."

"Fine. We'll just do that. Then you all can go against the Pete Mundy Gang by yourselves if they do come to town looking trouble."

"We got families of our own to protect," answered a voice from the crowd. "We can't go off halfway across the territory, risking our skins for the likes of her."

The sheriff stared at the citizens of Stony Gulch for a long, shameful minute. "So that's how it is," he said. "There's not one man here willing to see this woman as far as Cooperton."

Jake Moran hesitated only briefly. He had learned long ago that the secret to winning wasn't luck but knowing how to play the cards that he was dealt. This might just be the break that he had been looking for. He had already wasted three months on the trail of the Mundy Gang. Not once had he been able to get close to them.

Riding side by side with Outlaw Annie might finally give him the edge he needed to close that gap.

He paused, considering the task he was about to volunteer for. In all likelihood, it would be nothing but a lengthy ordeal and a major pain in the ass, but even a pair of deuces was better than a handful of nothing. In any event, how much trouble could one woman cause?

With that thought in mind, he nudged Weed forward. "I'll see that she gets to Cooperton."

A shocked buzz swept through the crowd as all heads immediately swung toward him. Jake ignored the townsfolk's excited voices and prying eyes, focusing instead on the prisoner.

Hostile. There was no other word to describe her. Annie's gaze snapped toward him, responding to his words like the play of gunfire. Her hands dropped to her hips and balled into tight fists, as though she'd been seeking her revolvers and came up instead with only empty air. Undeterred by her lack of weapons, she boldly gave him the once-over, surveying him from head to toe. Her lip curled in naked contempt as she finished her appraisal.

Jake dismounted and returned her stare. The woman's clothes were filthy, her face smudged with dirt, her hair lank and flat. Her brown eyes burned with scorn. She was young, just as the sheriff had said, probably not much older than twenty. Despite her relative youth, she exuded a cool confidence that she could handle anything or anybody. A confidence that was ridiculously unfounded, Jake thought, given her present circumstances.

So this was Outlaw Annie.

He had heard that she was six feet tall and weighed over two hundred pounds. He had heard that she had once wrestled a grizzly with nothing but her bare hands—and won. He had heard that she once swam *up* the Niagara Falls. But the truth belied every rumor he had ever heard. The legendary female gunslinger looked neither immense nor intimidating. She looked like a scrawny pup who had been kicked around one time too many and was determined to fight back.

He watched as she lifted her hand to brush her hair from her face. Her fingers, he noted, were surprisingly long and sculpted; her wrist was fine and delicately molded. It was difficult to get a read on the rest of her body. She was about average height for a woman, that was all he could tell. There may have been curves beneath her baggy clothes, there may not have been. Not that he gave a damn one way or another.

The bottom line for him was that she looked manageable. Rough, stubborn, and pure hellion through and through, but manageable.

"I'll see that she gets to Cooperton," he repeated.

The sheriff studied Jake, as though weighing his words, then looked to the crowd. "Any man here object to Jake Moran seeing Outlaw Annie out of town? Speak up now if you do."

Uneasy silence answered him.

"It's done then," the sheriff pronounced decisively.

Sheriff Cayne reached for his rope. As he pulled it from her throat, Annie flinched and closed her eyes. Then, as though shamed by her show of weakness, she opened her eyes and threw back her shoulders.

The sheriff gave no sign of noticing either her fear or her bravado. Instead he towered over her, saying in a tone capable of intimidating even the toughest outlaw, "I'm giving you a second chance, missy, but this is the last one you'll get. I ever hear you're in trouble with the law again and I'll hunt you down and hang you myself. Is that clear?"

Annie simply stared at him, her expression mutinous.

Sheriff Cayne waited. "You can thank me if you want to."

She swallowed hard and, in a raw voice, choked out, "Go to hell, lawman."

The sheriff studied her for a long moment, then let out a weary sigh. He turned and drew Jake forward. "Jake Moran, meet Miss Annabel Lee Foster." He gave Jake a hearty clap on the shoulder.

"Congratulations, Jake, she's all yours."

Chapter 2

𝒜nnabel Lee Foster shook her head in stunned disbelief. It had to be a trick. They were just trying to fill her mind with hope, to make her believe them, then they were going to string her up again. The fact that they had left the hanging tree and returned to town did little to ease her fear. That was nothing but a low-down, dirty lawman's trick. She was going to be hanged again, no doubt about it.

Annie swallowed hard and forced the thought out of her mind. Her stomach was tied in a thousand tight knots, and her knees shook so badly she could barely stand up, but she'd be damned before she would disgrace herself and let her fear show. If it was time for her to leave this earth, she would go the way Doc Mundy had taught her: proud and tall, not cowering and begging for mercy.

But no matter how hard she tried to turn her thoughts away from the hanging she couldn't ignore the burning ache that filled her throat. With each breath she took, it felt as though a nest of angry hornets was buzzing around inside her neck. The painful sensation served as an inescapable reminder of the dry, searing sting of jute. As if she could ever forget the feel of a rope digging into her neck. With shaking fingers, Annie touched the tender, swollen flesh. No real damage there, she supposed. Not yet, anyway.

Realizing that her thoughts were only serving to fuel

her panic, she turned her attention to the goings-on in the sheriff's office. Sheriff Cayne stood a few feet away, speaking with his deputies. Although she did her best to eavesdrop, their discussion was carried on in tones too low for her to hear. Occasionally they glanced her way, but mostly they ignored her. That was just jim-dandy with her. She'd had more than enough of their attention for one day.

Standing slightly apart from the others was the stranger who had volunteered to escort her to Cooperton. He stood with one broad shoulder propped against the window frame, his long legs firmly planted, his arms crossed over his chest. He gazed out the window, looking bored and removed from the business going on around him. And though he didn't appear to be paying the slightest bit of attention to either her or the sheriff and his men, Annie's instinct told her that he was alert to even the smallest movement in the room.

Jake Moran. That's what Sheriff Cayne had called him. Annie searched her memory, but the name meant nothing to her.

He was a gambler, that much she could tell. He was dressed in black, like a minister, but without any of the shoddy sacrifice so often seen in men of the cloth. His jacket and pants were cut from fine wool serge and emphasized the broadness of his shoulders, his narrowly tapered waist, and his long, powerful legs. Beneath the jacket, he wore a vest of gray silk brocade, with a perfectly starched white linen shirt and narrow black string tie. On his head, he wore the finest silver conch band that she had ever laid eyes on.

The men Annie had known never wore anything so clean or new, but Jake Moran wore his clothing casually, like a man used to the finer things in life.

Annie frowned as she studied him. The man had more money on his back in wearing apparel than she had ever spent on clothing in her entire life. That fact alone should have made him the most dandified city slicker ever to fall out of a stage and trip over a pile of mule dung. But, despite the fancy trappings he wore, the gambler was lean, muscular, and all male, no doubt about it.

Her grudging appraisal of his body finished, she turned her attention to his profile. Beautiful. That was the first word that came to mind. Annie qualified it immediately. Fact was, he was too good-looking, she decided. His cheekbones were high and lean, his lips smoothly sensual, his skin bronzed from the sun. He had a firm chin and a straight nose with a bump or two that might have come from gambling with the wrong hombres. His hair was thick and curled slightly about his collar; the color reminded her of the rich brown-black hue of a strong cup of coffee.

But it was his eyes that captivated Annie the most. She stared at him and thought before finally deciding on a color. Framed by impossibly thick, spiky black lashes, his eyes were the color of a frosty winter sky just before snowfall. They charged his gaze with a hint of danger and the promise of storms to come.

Annie considered him carefully. The man had been given the kind of looks that would only lead to trouble, she decided. And Annabel Lee Foster had already seen enough trouble to take her to the end of her days. The last thing she needed now was to get tangled up with the likes of him.

As if reading her thoughts, Jake turned toward her, moving too abruptly for her to avert her eyes. It wouldn't have mattered even if she had. His expression told her plainly that he'd been aware of—perhaps even slightly amused by—her scrutiny.

A wave of embarrassed heat spread through her body as his satisfied gaze locked on hers. The gambler studied her in silence, looking as pleased as a hog that had fallen into a mud puddle. Obviously the man was well aware of his appeal and expected women to just fall to pieces if he so much as glanced their way. Well, he had another think coming if he expected her to act like a goose-brained ninny just because God gave him more than his fair share of good looks.

Refusing to give him an edge of any kind, she immediately took the offensive. Using a tone that the boys in the Mundy Gang would have instantly recognized as a danger signal, she demanded, "What are you looking at, Mr. Fancy-Pants?"

"I'm looking at you," he replied, completely unaffected by her barb. He shook his head, not bothering to hide his amusement. "Outlaw Annie."

Annie let out a snort of disgust. "Figures."

He lifted one dark brow in silent question.

"Your voice," she clarified. "Sounds just how I reckoned it would: smoother than a baby's butt."

He smiled, revealing a set of perfectly straight pearly-white teeth. "I'll take that as a compliment."

"Suit yourself. I damned sure didn't mean it as one."

His smile widened. "You don't waste your bullets, do you, darlin'?"

Annie eyed him levelly, her fists planted firmly on her hips. "Never," she answered. "And I don't miss, neither. 'Specially when I aim for the heart."

"Then we ought to get along just fine." Although his expression didn't change, an icy frost returned to his eyes. "I believe you'll find that's my least vulnerable spot."

In that instant, Annie knew why his eyes had looked so familiar, and felt like a fool for not recognizing it earlier. Jake Moran had killer eyes. She'd run with the gang long enough to recognize eyes like that when she saw them: charming one minute, hollow and deadly the next. The eyes of a man who had killed before and would kill again.

Bearing that in mind, Annie regarded him in silence, sizing him up. He talked like a Southerner, she noted, catching a slight, lazy drawl that clung to his words. Interesting. The information didn't serve any immediate purpose, but it might come in handy later. Despite the man's relaxed posture, there was a predatory feel about him, a shadowy darkness that reminded her of a hungry cougar lurking in a cave. He was hunting for something, she'd bet her best pair of buckskins on it.

Their standoff was finally broken by Sheriff Cayne. "Listen here, missy, you oughta be grateful to Jake," he interjected. "He's the only man in town who volunteered to take you. If it weren't for him, you'd be swinging from that old oak right now."

Annie spun around to glare at the sheriff. "So?"

"So maybe you shouldn't go looking a gift horse in the mouth."

"Why not?" she shot back immediately. Her attention returning to Jake, her gaze moved over him in cool disdain, then her eyes locked deliberately on his. "What do I want with a stable full of useless, fancy-footed mealymouthed old nags—even if they are all free?"

Jake gracefully inclined his head, apparently not the least bit offended by her words. "That's mighty flattering, darlin'."

The sheriff sighed and shook his head, tacitly admitting defeat by changing the subject. "Here they are," he said, tossing a burlap sack on his desk. "All your worldly goods."

Annie reluctantly shifted her attention from Jake to the bag. "Less what you and your men stole," she muttered beneath her breath, moving to inspect her belongings. Meager though they were, everything appeared to be in order. With one major exception.

"My guns, Sheriff. What'd you do with my guns?"

"Ah, that's right," Sheriff Cayne exclaimed with a smile. "I can't forget those, now, can I?" He passed her an empty set of holsters.

Annie slung them around her hips and waited impatiently. Without her guns to fill them, the holsters were about as useless as a milk bucket under a bull. When the sheriff still didn't move, she prompted, "Colt .45's, walnut grip, snub-nosed barrel, the initials *A.F.* carved into the stock."

"The way I figure it," the sheriff replied, "Outlaw Annie wore guns, not Miss Annabel Foster. You're turning over a new leaf, don't forget. Besides, with Jake along to protect you, you won't be needing those guns."

So that's where this was heading. Annie took a deep breath, barely managing to hold on to her temper. "I don't want protection, Sheriff. I want my guns."

The sheriff frowned as he considered her statement. "Tell you what I'll do," he said, withdrawing her Colts from a locked cabinet. "I'll let Jake hold your guns. He's a reasonable fella. If you're a real good girl and don't cause him no trouble, I'm sure he'll give 'em back to you. Ain't that right, Jake?"

Jake shrugged.

Annie clenched her fists. She was as angry over the gambler's cool disinterest as she was at Sheriff Cayne for his high-handedness. Without her guns, she felt as naked and defenseless as a newborn cub. "That's my property, you hear me?" she said tightly.

"Appears to me," Jake said slowly, "that's my decision now. You planning on acting like a real lady?"

"What the hell would you know about real ladies, you no-account, thieving, hustling—"

"You can keep the guns, Sheriff."

"No!"

Jake slowly smiled. "Does that mean I have your word that you'll be good, darlin'?"

He held the upper hand in the argument and they both knew it. Any more words from her would just strain her throat, and Lord knew that had already had enough wear for one day. Annie swallowed her rage and choked out an answer.

"Yes."

She watched in impotent fury as the sheriff passed Jake her guns.

"Don't worry, darlin'. I'll keep them warm for you," he said as he tucked them into his belt.

He was deliberately goading her now. The smartest thing for her to do would be to shut up. But Annie had never been one to back down from a fight, even when she was on the losing end. "That's about all you'll do," she spit out. "Bet you can't even fire them. You look like a palm-gun man to me."

Thrown as it was in the heat of anger, the insult fell way off the mark. Annie was referring to the derringer pistols most gamblers hid beneath a ruffled sleeve or tucked within a vest pocket. Surprise was the key factor in determining the gun's effectiveness. The dainty pieces fired just one round at a time and were accurate only at close range. Jake Moran obviously didn't waste his time with them. He wore his six-shooters in plain view, one on each hip, and he looked like he knew how to use them. The lower ends of his holsters were lashed to his thighs with rawhide thongs to give him that extra speed on the draw that might make the difference between life and death. Something told her that precaution was a product of years of gunplay.

Undaunted by her mistake, she continued recklessly, "I'll get my Colts back, and you better watch out when I do. You just wait and see what happens then." Rather than the ferocious growl she'd intended, her words ended in little more than a rough whisper.

Without her voice to back her up, she glanced away in an attempt to underscore her threat. It was a tactical error on her part. Before she could guess his intention, Jake covered the distance between them with two long strides. One large hand came to rest on her shoulder while the fingers of his opposite hand brushed lightly along the base of her throat. Annie instinctively jerked from his touch, but the wall pressed against her back, leaving her no room to maneuver.

"Get your hands off me," she hissed.

Except for the slight increase of pressure on her shoulder, presumably meant to steady her, Jake ignored her words. A slight frown drew between his brows as he studied her throat, then he glanced over his shoulder at the sheriff. "You have anything for this?"

Sheriff Cayne lumbered toward his desk. "Might have some liniment somewhere in here."

"I said," Annie whispered in a low growl, "get your hands off me."

Jake paid her no mind, his attention focused instead on Sheriff Cayne as he fumbled through a desk drawer. Well, Annie had given him fair warning. Twice. A sharp knee in the jewel sack might be just the thing to convince him that she meant business. She jerked up her leg, but Jake guessed her intention before she met her goal. He twisted to the side, pinning her body against the wall with his own. With one fluid move, he captured her wrists and held them above her head, effortlessly immobilizing them with just one hand.

Annie struggled against him, her breath coming in short, furious gasps. But the harder she tried to break free, the closer he leaned into her body. Her breasts were crushed beneath his chest, her thighs trapped beneath his. The heady scent of his body seemed to wrap around her, draining her of all strength. Even as she fought his grip, she was uncomfortably aware of the ease with which he held her captive. The man was a towering mass of steel and muscle. Unwilling to concede defeat, she glared up into his icy blue eyes and shot him a look so full of unleashed fury it would have sent a lesser man running.

Jake Moran simply smiled. "Enjoying yourself, darlin'?"

"You son of a bitch."

"You hear that, Sheriff?" Jake called. "She's trying to sweet-talk me into letting her go." He turned back to Annie, his gaze locking on hers. In a silky voice low enough for only her to hear, he said, "You want to play rough, Annie, so will I. I'd remember that if I were you."

Remember it? Hell, he couldn't have knocked that thought out of her mind with a stick of dynamite. Not when he was pressing his body against hers as though he were trying to mold them into one. She clamped her jaw shut, swallowed her rage, and nodded tightly. "I'll remember," she forced out.

"Good." He released her hands and took a step backward.

Annie ducked out beneath his arm, escaping to the far corner of the room. She wheeled around, her fists planted defiantly on her hips. "And here's something for you to remember, mister," she shot back. "You try that again, and I'll bash in your skull."

The sheriff held up the liniment jar, a baffled expression on his face. "Jake was just trying to—"

"I know what he was trying," Annie interrupted, glaring at Jake. "I don't like to be touched. You got that, mister? *I don't like to be touched.*" Despite her efforts to remain calm, her voice sounded tense and unnaturally shrill even to her own ears. With any luck, that would be attributed to her near miss with the noose rather than the turbulent state of her emotions.

But one look at Jake Moran's face instantly crushed that hope. His mouth tightened to a thin line as a look of grim understanding crossed his features. Fortunately the moment quickly passed. When he finally spoke, his tone was so flippant that Annie wondered if she had seen the reaction at all.

"Suit yourself, darlin'. It's your neck."

Pride brought up her chin. "That's right, it is."

The door rattled and a blast of cool air filled the room. One of the sheriff's deputies entered, hauling a drunk who looked the worse for wear after a brawl.

With the attention momentarily shifted from her, Annie sank gratefully into a chair to compose herself. That fancy-pants gambler had rattled her more than she wanted to admit. Even as her heart pounded in her veins and her stomach churned with nausea, she fought to control her reaction. It wouldn't do to show weakness, not now. But if given the choice between feeling a man's hands on her skin and sitting in a tub of cold snakes, she would choose the snakes every time.

Well, he wouldn't get near her again—that was for damn sure. She would get her guns back eventually. Just let him try that little stunt of his then. She took a deep breath, allowing the calming thought to wash over her.

Her mind otherwise occupied, she paid little attention to the conversation carrying on around her. Therefore it wasn't the words that caught her attention as much as the sudden absence of them. Thick silence fell over the room. She looked up, finding all eyes focused expectantly on her.

"What do you have to say about that?" the sheriff asked her.

"About what?"

Sheriff Cayne sighed and settled one bulky hip on his desk. He let out a stream of tobacco juice, expertly guiding it into the dull brass cuspidor near his feet. "I was saying that it was funny how Pete Mundy worked," he repeated. "I remember when he and the boys weren't no gang at all. Seems to me they were nothing but a bunch of misfits hiding out in the hills, rustling a few lame cattle and stealing gold dust from drunken miners. Then suddenly, about two years back, they smartened up and got sophisticated. Started pulling big money jobs that took brains and talent, things like holding up stages and robbing banks."

Annie shrugged. "Things change, I reckon."

"Things maybe, but not people," the sheriff countered.

She glanced over at Jake, watching as he removed a bag of tobacco from his vest pocket, rolled a cigarette, then placed it between his lips. He struck a sulfur match against his boot and raised the flame to the tip. Although his relaxed stance hadn't changed, the subtle tensing of his jaw told her that he had more than a passing interest in the subject. He didn't speak but simply regarded her with his cool, watchful gaze, as though weighing her every word.

"Where can I find Pete Mundy?" Sheriff Cayne asked.

Annie returned her attention to the sheriff. "Hell, I expect."

"You're telling me that Pete's dead?"

"He's dead," she confirmed flatly. "So are the rest of the boys."

"That a fact?" The sheriff frowned, obviously dissatisfied with her answer. "The way I heard it, you and Pete were madly in love."

"You heard wrong."

"Maybe. Or maybe you're still protecting him." The sheriff paused a beat, then continued, "Lot of women might find that kind of life exciting. A handsome outlaw, a hideout in the woods, easy money . . ."

"I'm not like a lot of women, Sheriff."

"I can't argue that, now, can I?" Sheriff Cayne rose to his feet, placing his beefy hands on his hips. "You feel like telling me where the money from that stage robbery might be?"

She shrugged. "The boys weren't exactly talkative about that sort of thing."

"And I suppose you've got no idea."

"Afraid not."

The sheriff studied her for a long, hard minute.

"You're the most contrary, mule-headed, disagreeable woman I've ever laid eyes on. You want to know why I didn't let you swing today?"

Annie brought up her chin. If he was expecting gratitude for parading her out in public and wringing her neck like a spring chicken, he had better think again. "Why?"

"Because I believe you didn't have anything to do with that robbery or killing those stage men. I believe you just got roped in with the wrong bunch of fellas. I don't care what those jurymen said. Seems to me they wanted vengeance, not justice, and that's not the way I run my town."

She studied him in silence, weighing the truth of his words.

"Problem is," he continued, "lot of folks might not be as levelheaded as I am. They might come after you, thinking if they can get you to talk, then they can get that stage robbery money for themselves. If you're lying to me about that stage money, you'd better come clean. I don't care how much money is buried out there, it won't be worth it once they're done with you. Some of them boys can get pretty rough, if you get my meaning."

Annie eyed him levelly. "I get your meaning."

"I hope so, missy, I surely do. But that's something you don't want to test. Why don't you just tell me where to find that money? You'll walk out of here free and clear, and there'll be no reason for anybody to come looking for you."

A bitter smile curved her lips as sudden comprehension came over her. "So that's what this is all about."

"What do you mean?"

"You want me to buy my freedom. Hand over that stage robbery money to you, and in return, you'll let me just ride out of town. Nice little plan. Sorry I can't help you out, but I can't tell you what I don't know."

Sheriff Cayne's ruddy cheeks darkened. "You accusing me of wanting to keep that money for myself?"

Annie shrugged. "A dog's hind legs ain't as crooked as most lawmen I know."

"That money belongs to the God-fearing hardworking folks who live in this town. If you've got a decent bone in your body, missy, you'll see to it that they get their money back."

"That's my goal in life, Sheriff, to make them happy. The same folks who wanted to string me up twice. *Cuando las ranas crien poco.*"

The sheriff's brows drew together. "What's that, Mexican?"

"I think she's trying to say," Jake translated, a hint of amusement playing about his features, "*cuando las ranas crien pelo.* 'When frogs grow hair.' "

His Spanish, Annie noted, was smooth and rolling. Just the way Diego had tried to teach her to speak, though she'd never quite been able to get the hang of it.

The sheriff let out an exasperated breath and said to Jake, "If she changes her mind and suddenly remembers where to find the money from that stage, you let me know."

Jake nodded in easy agreement. While he had remained attentive to the conversation, Annie saw none of the keen intensity that had been in his eyes while they were discussing Pete and the boys. It was subtle difference, but it was there. The gambler was clearly more interested in the gang itself than in the twenty-five thousand in federal greenbacks that was missing from the stage robbery.

While Annie mulled that over, Sheriff Cayne turned to his deputy. "Run over to Ella's Cafe and have her make up a few sandwiches for tonight. Then go by the general store and pick up some supplies. Enough to see the two of them as far as Aquio Pass." He opened a desk drawer, removed a bill from a tin can, and passed it to his deputy. "I reckon that ought to cover it." The deputy pocketed the money and swung out the door.

The sheriff turned next to Jake. Moving with an unexpected dexterity for a man of his bulk, he reached into the gambler's vest and plucked free his wallet. He let out a low whistle as he thumbed through the bills. "Not bad. Must be at least three thousand in here."

"Twenty-eight hundred and some change," Jake corrected. He crossed his arms over his chest and propped one broad shoulder against the wall. Although his tone and posture implied a calm acceptance of Sheriff Cayne's action, the simmering tension that radiated across the room was unmistakable. "You want to explain yourself, Roy?"

"Just taking out a little insurance, Jake. I made a promise that Annabel Lee Foster would get to Cooperton, and I aim to see that it's done right. I can't have you changing your mind two days out and riding off. I've got nothing to hold you to your promise."

"You have my word," the gambler answered tightly, looking like a man who expected that to mean something.

"A man tends to forget his word unless there's something holding him to it."

"Don't worry, mister," Annie cooed, unable to hide her delight at this new turn of events. "The sheriff's a reasonable fella. If you're a real good boy and don't cause him no trouble, I'm sure he'll give it back to you. Ain't that right, Sheriff?"

Sheriff Cayne reddened and muttered indignantly that that was exactly what he intended to do. "It's just a precaution, you understand. You have the sheriff in Cooperton wire me once the two of you have arrived, and I'll see to it that you get back every penny."

"Sure you will," Jake replied.

The sheriff didn't miss the implied insult. He sent

him a disgusted look. "Now, that's real trusting. Nice world you live in, Jake."

"It's the only one that would have me."

The sheriff held up the wallet. "You thinking about changing your mind, now's the time to do it. Otherwise I'm gonna hold this for collateral until you get to Cooperton."

Jake lifted his shoulders in an indifferent shrug, apparently concluding that the money was a matter of small concern. "I wouldn't dream of abandoning Miss Foster," he said smoothly. "Not when she's already developed such an obvious affection for me."

Annie turned away, pointedly ignoring his mocking words. When she glanced out the window a few minutes later, she saw the deputy returning, a sack of supplies in one hand, the reins of her mare in the other. Her heart gave a little leap at the sight of Dulcie. Until that moment, she hadn't truly believed that Sheriff Cayne meant to let her go. She'd figured the odds of that happening were slimmer than a bar of soap after a week's worth of washing. Clearly she'd been wrong.

She looked at the sheriff and, receiving his silent nod of assent, stepped outside the tiny jailhouse and into the street.

Pale October sunshine hit her face. A crisp breeze tousled her hair, carrying with it all the scents of fall: wet leaves, smoky bonfires, freshly cut cords of wood, fruit pies baked with cloves and cinnamon. Annie stood perfectly still, drinking it in. Sheriff Cayne hadn't been lying after all. This was her chance. An honest-to-God new chance to start her life over. Wary that her joy might spill over and show on her face, she moved toward Dulcie and gently pressed her cheek against the mare's mane, hiding her emotions. After a moment, she felt a slight pressure against her calf and looked down to see a familiar bundle of knotted white fur. She reached down and scooped the cat into her arms.

The scrappy feline had kept her company during the

long nights before the hanging. The cat usually appeared after midnight, climbing in through an office window while the deputy snored away at his desk. Using leftover bits of supper as bait to draw her closer, Annie had slowly earned the animal's trust. The cat had eventually allowed Annie to pet her and, once or twice, had even spent the night curled up at the foot of her cell bed.

As Annie gently stroked the cat, a shadow crossed her face, blocking out the sun. She looked up to see Jake and the sheriff towering over her, both men scowling at the furry bundle she held. The sheriff spoke first.

"That's got to be the sorriest-looking beast I've ever seen."

Annie frowned as she considered the statement. The cat had obviously clawed and fought to get by, and it showed. Her fur was matted with knots, her tail was broken and bent at a right angle to the ground. A tuft of fur sprang from a scar above her left eye like a haughtily arched brow, giving her a cynical, slightly superior expression.

Annie shrugged off the imperfections. "Has she got a name?" she asked.

Sheriff Cayne let out a choked laugh. "I don't think you want to know what the boys and I call her."

"Who does she belong to?"

"Who would want her? That thing's half-wild."

That settled it. "I'm taking her with me," she announced impulsively.

"Absolutely not," Jake said.

Annie glared up at him. "I wasn't asking." She nuzzled the cat against her cheek, coaxing a thick, rumbling purr from deep within the animal's throat. "Besides, she likes me."

Jake instantly dismissed that. "You've been feeding her."

She held the cat toward him. The unruly feline immediately arched her back and began to hiss, swiping one sharp claw his way. Annie smiled and rewarded the behavior with slow, soothing strokes. "Maybe she's just a good judge of character," she replied smugly.

Holding her new pet tightly, she slid her boot into the stirrup and mounted Dulcie. She gave Jake a long, hard look, then turned to Sheriff Cayne to make one final appeal.

"I don't need an escort, Sheriff. I can make it to Cooperton on my own. And I sure as hell don't need Mr. Fancy-Pants here tagging along and slowing me down."

"I don't reckon you've got much choice in the matter," the sheriff countered. "I want you out of the territory, missy, and I aim to see that it's done right. If Jake don't take you, I'll have to send one of my deputies, and my men are working double time as it is."

Now that Annie was actually convinced that the sheriff meant to let her go, she mentally debated the wisdom of having Jake accompany her. If she had to have an escort, she would probably be better off with one of the sheriff's men. It would be fairly simple to manipulate any of his addle-brained deputies. Jake Moran, on the other hand, looked about as easy to push around as a Texas longhorn with a case of indigestion.

"I don't suppose a man like you has a wife waiting for him at home somewhere," she suggested to Jake, offering him a reason to decline the trip.

A look of genuine amusement crossed his face at her none too subtle ploy to get rid of him. "I'm afraid that my devotion to the fairer sex is far too profound to be exhausted by a single object."

Annie snorted in disgust. "You mean you like tomcattin' around too much."

"That too, darlin'."

Jake swung effortlessly into the saddle of his dark bay. "You may as well get used to me. Until we reach

Cooperton, I'll be closer to you than a mama bear to her baby cubs."

Annie made a face that clearly expressed her displeasure.

Jake shrugged and adjusted his Stetson. "It might not be that bad. Who knows? Could be we'll even get along."

"I wouldn't bet on it, mister."

Amusement once again softened his features. He spurred his horse, easing the bay into a gentle trot.

"Neither would I, darlin'. Neither would I."

Chapter 3

$\mathcal{J}$ake Moran had been dealt some bad hands in his lifetime, but this one had to beat all. Escorting Outlaw Annie to Cooperton. Hell of a fool idea. Even if nothing went wrong, the journey would still take them at least two weeks. Jake shook his head—the odds of nothing going wrong while he was traveling with Miss Annabel Lee Foster were slim to none.

Their journey was already cursed. Weed had thrown a shoe, their supply sack had burst open and emptied out on the trail, and Annie's mangy alley cat had wandered off and gotten lost for over an hour. The miles they had covered that day had been negligible. They had made camp at dusk less than ten miles outside of Stony Gulch. At that rate, they would be lucky to reach Cooperton before the first snowfall.

Jake sat with his back supported by a flat rock, his long legs stretched out before him. He held a flask of bourbon between his legs and took slow, pensive sips as he considered his options. He could ride flat out come morning; head north, or maybe go back East. But that would still leave the problem of that damned wanted poster with his face splashed all over it. Sooner or later, the law would catch up with him. In fact, he'd taken a hell of a chance with Sheriff Cayne. If that poster had reached Stony Gulch before Jake did, chances were real good that the sheriff would have invited him to take Annie's place in the jailhouse cell.

With a murder charge hanging over his head, the stakes were too high for Jake to simply ride away. The only chance he had of clearing his name was to find the Mundy Gang—and that meant he had no choice but to play his cards close to his chest and stick by Annie.

Well, he did have one other choice, he amended silently. He could ride back to Gunpowder Falls and turn himself in. But Jake had never been overly confident of the justice process. Particularly in the ability of a tiny, one-horse town—a town known for its harshness and brutality rather than its legal sensibilities—to convene and hold a fair trial.

It wasn't that Jake had never killed before. He had done plenty of that; more than he wanted to remember. But he had never gunned anybody down in a dark alley behind a saloon. The man had been shot in the back, no less. It was Pete Mundy who had done that; Jake would swear his life on it. It had become a matter of both pride and stark necessity for him to prove it.

Jake thought back to the conversation Annie had had with the sheriff in Stony Gulch. The woman had been lying when she told Sheriff Cayne that the boys in the Mundy Gang were dead. Only two weeks ago, they had been spotted buying supplies outside of Gunnison. And if Jake knew that, he was damned sure that Annie knew it too. She was protecting the boys, no doubt about it. Although his conscience chafed at the idea of using a woman to lure out a killer, he knew of no other way to accomplish it.

He glanced at Annie, watching as she pulled apart the remains of her sandwich and allowed her cat to lick the stringy roast beef from her fingertips.

"What do you call her?" he asked, nodding toward the cat.

Annie glanced up at him and shrugged. "Cat."

Jake nodded. A bit obvious, but better than Fluffy or Sugar, he supposed.

Her gaze fell to the bourbon flask in his hand. "You planning on getting drunk, mister?"

"I hadn't thought about it. Why? Did Pete get drunk?"

"Pete did a lot of things."

She turned away, pointedly returning her attention to her new pet. So much for conversation. That was probably just as well, Jake decided, taking another swig from his flask. No sense getting to know her—either she'd lead him to the men he needed to find or they would ride their separate ways. Annie seemed to be of the same mind, for she displayed no interest in him whatsoever. They had spoken less than a dozen words to each other since leaving town.

Jake's gaze moved from the dancing silvery-black shadows of the cottonwood and scrub oak that dotted the horizon to the inky-purple mass of the San Juan mountain range. But his thoughts stayed focused on Annie. There were only two kinds of women in the West. The good ones and the bad ones. The good ones were wives and daughters, school teachers, store clerks, and the like. The bad ones were the saloon girls, dancers, prostitutes, and assorted feminine rabble that drifted across the frontier. No doubt in the world to which group Outlaw Annie belonged. But that was her business, he supposed, not his.

The solitary howl of a wolf broke through Jake's musings. The lonesome cry was answered by another and another, until the howls reached a haunting crescendo. Jake pushed his thoughts of Annie away and rose to his feet. As long as the woman drew the Mundy Gang out of hiding, he didn't give a damn about anything else.

"Better get some sleep," he said. "We ride out at dawn."

He glanced at the fire, debating whether to kick it

out. It was a cool night, without a breeze to lift the embers or spark the flames. The fire would burn itself out in a couple of hours, and the warmth would feel good in the meantime.

Annie briefly studied the flames and seemed to draw the same conclusion. She stood and moved wordlessly to her bedroll. A frown touched Jake's lips as he surveyed the small pile of rocks and sticks that sat beside her bedroll. Annie had methodically stockpiled them earlier as she had spread out her blankets.

He nodded toward her meager arsenal. "Is that meant to keep me away or the wolves?"

"I don't reckon there's much difference, do you?"

Jake shook his head. "You do know how to flatter a man, don't you, darlin'."

Annie sat down and pulled off her boots and hat, setting them both carefully beside her. "I ain't never tried," she answered with a shrug. "Never saw much point to it."

"I believe the point is flirting, courting . . ." He paused for a moment, considering. "Have you ever been courted, Annie?"

Her eyes immediately narrowed. "You better get one thing straight right now, Mr. Fancy-Pants. I ain't like them tarted-up saloon gals back in Stony Gulch. You come near me again and I'll bash in your skull. You got that?"

"I take it the answer is no."

"Did you hear me?"

Jake didn't know which was more ridiculous: her paltry threat or her fear that he might actually try to force himself on her during the night. Aware that she was entirely serious, however, he nodded solemnly. "I believe I'll be able to resist the allure of your feminine charms."

Annie didn't miss his mocking tone. She scowled and brought up her chin. "See that you do."

He shrugged off his jacket and shirt in preparation for bed. She watched him intently, displaying none of the usual signs of embarrassment or feminine modesty at the sight of his bare chest.

"You always dress fancy like that?"

"Part of the job," Jake answered easily. "Men get a few extra bills in their pocket, they start looking for ways to spend it. When it comes to gambling, most men prefer to lose their money to a well-dressed gentleman rather than a dirty tinhorn lout who looks no better than they do."

"You always win?"

"Always."

She frowned. "Why? You cheat?"

He overlooked the insult. "Maybe I just get lucky." He paused, treating her to his most seductive smile. "Or maybe I'm just that smart."

Annie studied him in silence for a long moment. "I doubt you're that lucky. You sure as hell ain't that smart."

Jake arched a dark brow. "What makes you say that?"

"If you had any brains at all, you wouldn't be here now." With that final statement, she slipped between her blankets, still fully attired, and rolled over, presenting him with her back.

The mournful cry of a wolf filled the air. Cat hissed and scratched at Jake's boot. Dulcie and Weed skittered nervously.

It was going to be a long, cold night.

Jake wondered if she wasn't right after all.

"*W*hat are you after, mister?"

Jake shifted in his saddle, stalling for time as he considered Annie's question. He figured she would wonder. He hadn't expected her to ask outright.

They'd been riding hard all morning and had finally stopped to breathe their mounts. Locating a stream that had carved its way through the rough terrain, they ambled slowly along its banks. The day was crystalline, flooded with brilliant autumn sunshine and crisp, cool breezes. Rugged canyon walls soared above them, encasing them in a chasm of earthy red clay. The subtle fragrance of cedar and pine drifted through the air.

"Well?" Annie demanded impatiently.

"Just thought you could use a friend, darlin'."

"You ain't no friend of mine."

Unwilling to debate the truth of that statement, Jake continued with a cool shrug. "Sheriff Cayne needed help, and I had some business out Cooperton way. Plus there's the matter of my money—"

"What money?"

"That twenty-eight hundred cash Sheriff Cayne is holding for me."

"That's nothing," she said. "Not to someone like you." Her eyes flicked over him in harsh appraisal, as though mentally calculating the cost of his clothing, his boots, his saddle, his horse. "I'd wager you've got at least ten times that amount waiting for you in some bank back East."

Jake hid his surprise. Her guess was uncannily accurate. Although twenty times that amount was more like it, and the bank was in St. Louis.

"So if it's not the money that's driving you," Annie continued, "it must be something else. Either Sheriff Cayne's got some other hold over you, or there's something you want from me. Maybe both. I ain't figured it out yet, but I will."

"You let me know when you do."

"You'll know, mister. Believe me, you'll know."

She lifted her canteen and took a long swig of water, wiping her mouth with the back of her hand. In an unconsciously feminine gesture, she removed her hat and tilted her face upward to receive the warmth of the sun. The movement revealed the long, smooth column of her throat and accentuated the subtle swell of her breasts beneath her coarse flannel shirt. Released from its confines, her hair tumbled in loose waves about her shoulders, shimmering with streaks of honey and wheat.

The movement also afforded Jake a direct view of her face. For the first time, he could truly see her features—unlike in the sheriff's office, with her battered felt hat pulled down low on her brow, or over the dim, smoky light of a campfire. When not brimming with anger and hostility, her eyes were rich and warm, framed by long, curly lashes and set with a mischievous tilt at the corners. The color was far from dull brown, as Jake had once thought. Annie's eyes sparkled with light and vitality, reflecting assorted shades of gold, green, and chestnut. Her cheekbones were high and smoothly sculpted, her soft pink lips were full and generous. The gentle, sun-tinged glow that warmed her cheeks struck him as far more attractive than the pallid porcelain sheen most women sought to attain.

Even more compelling than her physical features was the character revealed in her face. Intelligence showed clearly, as well as the gritty determination and strength of spirit he had first noted when he had seen her at the hanging. All in all, she presented a compelling mixture of unaffected femininity and rock-solid backbone. This was not a lady who would be easily intimidated—or easily forgotten.

Jake eyed her consideringly. If not for the regrettable circumstance of her birth and upbringing, Miss Annabel Lee Foster would have been a truly magnificent woman. He pictured her dressed in the finery of a well-bred lady rather than her customary attire of worn-out flannel and faded denim, an empty pair of holsters strapped to her hips. Perhaps a gown of rich gold velvet to emphasize her unusual coloring, her hair swept up and away from her face, an elegant strand of pearls around her throat. He saw her gracefully descending a staircase, shimmering sunlight flooding in behind her, a flock of eager suitors waiting below.

Annie chose that moment to glance over at him. Momentarily flustered by his open appraisal, she quickly reverted to her natural state of belligerence. Stuffing her hair back under her hat, she slapped the worn felt over her head and pulled the brim down low.

"What the hell are you lookin' at?" she snapped.

A small smile tugged his lips as his image of Outlaw Annie as a woman of style and elegance instantly shattered. "I'm looking at you, darlin'."

"Well, don't. I don't like it."

"What do you like?" he asked, unoffended.

They nudged their mounts away from the stream they'd been following, forging a southbound trail through a grove of aspens. Although he'd asked the question only in an effort to keep their conversation alive and relieve the tedium of the trail, Jake was surprised to find himself genuinely curious.

"I like Cat," Annie replied after a moment, scratching the ears of the mangy beast that sat curled around her saddlehorn. "And Dulcie." She patted her mare's neck.

"What else?"

She leveled him with a cool stare. "Men who don't ask a lot of questions."

Jake grinned. "You've got a style all your own, darlin', I'll give you that."

His amusement faded as Annie wordlessly turned her mare east, moving away from him at a brisk pace. Jake spurred Weed into a light canter and cut across her path. He caught her reins in his hand, bringing her to an abrupt stop. "Cooperton's the other way."

Annie frowned and tugged her reins out of his grasp. "I have some business of my own to take care of first."

"What sort of business?"

"Business that don't concern you."

He let out a long-suffering sigh. "Evidently I didn't

make myself clear. Until we make it to Cooperton, everything you do concerns me. For the next two weeks, I'll be following you closer than your own shadow."

"Only you'll be talking a lot more."

Jake ignored the remark. "What sort of business?" he repeated.

Annie studied him silently for a minute, a mulish expression on her face. Finally she lifted her shoulders in a careless shrug. "I've got something I need to pick up. You can follow me if you want to, mister. Just don't expect me to wait up for you."

With those parting words, Annie dug her heels into Dulcie's flanks, urging her little mare into a gallop. The wind lashed her face as she flew over the rough ground, leaving a trail of dust behind her. Jake took out after her, watching in admiration as she rode. She moved with a supple grace that was completely unselfconscious, her lithe form perfectly matched to her mount's long strides.

Annie didn't slow until midafternoon, when they reached an old silver mine. She dropped Cat to the ground and swung off Dulcie. Jake followed suit, hitching Weed beside Annie's mare, his reins looped around the branch of an old cedar.

"You planning on doing some mining?" he asked.

"I'll be digging, all right, but it won't be for any puny bits of worthless rock." Although she was obviously struggling to maintain an air of indifference, a glow of childlike excitement shone in her eyes.

Jake glanced around the abandoned sight, wondering at its cause. The mine had obviously been played out years ago. The mouth of the main shaft was choked with tumbleweeds and sagebrush. A dilapidated shed stood a few yards away, leaning drunkenly against the hillside. An odd assortment of rusted and broken tools lay scattered before it. Although the cooking fire had long since cooled, a battered tin coffeepot remained suspended over the ashes, swaying in the breeze. A soft wind kicked up clouds of dust and dirt and carried the faint, acrid scent of sulfur with it.

"We got anything left in that supply bag?" Annie asked, obviously intending to eat before getting down to the business that had brought her there.

As Jake was also hungry, he didn't object. He pulled a blanket from his saddle and spread it out beneath a shady cedar. Next he dug into the supplies Sheriff Cayne had provided, retrieving a few day-old biscuits, a hunk of creamy yellow cheese, thinly sliced ham, and two tart green apples.

They ate in silence, listening to the sound of the wind rustle through the cottonwoods. Once the meal had ended, Annie rose to look for Cat. In keeping with her habitual pattern, the mangy beast had wandered off once again. Jake stood and stretched. As a gentle breeze stirred the air around him, he heard the soft, rustling flap of a burlap sack. Annie's burlap sack. The sack that contained all her worldly goods—and perhaps a clue as to how he might find the Mundy Gang. Jake eyed the bag consideringly. Another stiff breeze might just spill open the contents.

For that matter, so would the toe of his boot.

He hesitated briefly, reluctant to invade the woman's privacy. But after a few moment's reflection, he realized that hanging for a murder he didn't commit appealed to him even less. He glanced around for Annie. Confident that she was still occupied with hunting for Cat, he dumped the contents of her bag onto the blanket.

Jake studied the paltry assortment of personal odds and ends with a slight frown. Torn rags, a broken bridle bit, a handful of rifle cartridges, a small velvet purse that jingled with coins, a badly worn book, an equally distressed leather Bible, and an old tintype photograph completed the collection. He lifted the book first, somewhat surprised that Annie could read. Not that she wasn't bright enough, but that she'd ever been given the schooling. *Winston's Guide to Proper Etiquette and Deportment for Refined Young Ladies of All Ages* read the gilt title on the cover. He flipped open the front jacket, noting the name that had been penned in the upper right corner in a young girl's roundly ornate cursive: Catherine Elizabeth Foster.

Next he examined the tintype. The portrait showed two young girls dressed in their Sunday best, holding hands. Jake smiled at the tiny image of feminine perfection. Looking at the tintype, he could almost hear the stiff crunch of crinoline beneath their freshly starched dresses, almost feel the satiny smoothness of their ribbons and bows. The older girl, who was perhaps eight, looked appropriately solemn at the occasion of having the photograph taken. The younger girl, however, appeared to be struggling just to stand still. An impish grin curved her lips, her eyes glowed with excitement, and her chubby cheeks were rosy and flushed. Unlike the properly sedate older child, a bit of the younger one's personality was already showing through. Her dark-blond curls were mussed and scattered. The lace edge of her skirt drooped about one ankle. A tiny smear of dirt streaked her chin.

The younger girl was Outlaw Annie.

"You don't ever get tired of nosing into other people's stuff, do you, mister?"

Jake turned to find Annie scowling at him, Cat bundled tightly in her arms. Nearly all signs of the high-spirited, adorable young girl she'd once been had vanished. Still, he was certain that it was her in the tintype. Her features hadn't changed that much: the soft curve of her lips, the small nose, the pert tilt of her expressive eyes.

"How old were you?" he asked.

She let out an exasperated breath. "Five," she answered. She released Cat and reached for the tintype, returning it to her burlap sack.

"The older girl's your sister?"

She gave a curt nod. "Catherine."

"Where—"

"She's dead," Annie answered flatly. She propped her fists on her hips and asked, "You got any more questions?"

Several, Jake answered silently. The photographer's stamp in the lower corner read *Johnston & Sons, Philadelphia.* The clothing the girls wore was obviously high quality. How did a young girl from a well-to-do family in Philadelphia end up running with an outlaw gang in Colorado? Where were Pete Mundy and the rest of the boys, and why was Annie covering for them?

Jake shrugged easily, assuming a pose of casual indifference. "None that can't keep for a day or two, darlin'."

He let the questions roll through his mind, keeping half an eye on Annie as she stuffed the flannel and denim scraps back into her bag. He frowned, his curiosity captured by her movements. "You brought cleaning rags?"

Annie stiffened, momentarily frozen in her task. "My clothes," she answered tightly.

"I apologize," Jake said instantly. "I didn't mean—"

"Never mind."

If she'd been wounded at all by his thoughtless blunder, it didn't show. She methodically continued her chore, hesitating only when she reached the small velvet purse that contained the coins. Scowling, she pulled open the purse's strings and peered inside. Apparently satisfied that the contents hadn't been disturbed, she placed it within the burlap sack and gave him a long, hard look.

"That's my money. Three hundred twenty-nine dollars and forty-eight cents. You get any thoughts about stealing it, or just dipping in for a loan, and I'll—"

"Bash in my skull," Jake finished for her, bored.

Annie tilted her chin. "Just see that you remember it." Her packing finished, she swept past him and into the dilapidated shed, returning seconds later with a pair of rusty shovels. She pressed one into his hands.

"We got some digging to do," she said brusquely. "You know how these work, Mr. Fancy-Pants?"

He arched a dark brow. "I believe I'm familiar with the concept."

Annie gave an unladylike snort. "From watching other folks dig, most likely. Bet you never been on the blister end of one before."

She spun around and marched resolutely past the mouth of the abandoned mine, industriously shoveling away near the base of an old cottonwood tree. Jake watched her in silence. After a few minutes, she stopped and glared up at him. "What's the matter, mister? Afraid you'll get your pretty clothes all dirty?"

Figuring he had that one coming, Jake let the remark go. "Do you mind telling me what we're digging for?"

"I don't suppose the words *it's none of your business* mean anything to you?"

"Not if you want my help."

Annie muttered something beneath her breath. She glanced down at the hole she'd dug, then scowled up at Jake. Finally she let out a burdensome sigh, set her shovel aside, and reached into the back pocket of her denim work pants. "Here," she said. "Since you're so all-fired curious, take a look."

Despite her grumbling attitude, Jake heard a note that sounded almost like pride in her voice. He stepped forward and accepted the worn piece of paper she passed him. It was dirty, smudged, and nearly torn through the folds, like a cherished letter that had been read over and over again until the contents had been thoroughly memorized. But upon closer inspection, he saw that it wasn't a love letter at all. It was nothing but an old advertising circular for a hotel.

Paradise! the flier exclaimed in bold, twenty-point type. *Come visit the Palace Hotel in Cooperton, Colo-*

rado, the West's most elegant resort for distinguished ladies and gentlemen. The Palace Hotel: culture and civilization in the midst of the wild Western frontier. The flier went on to describe the hotel's lobby, rooms, restaurant, and theater in gushing, effusive detail. Although the name was unfamiliar to Jake, that didn't necessarily signify. Grand hotels had been springing up all over the territory since the discovery of gold at Pikes Peak and the subsequent boom in Denver City.

"Very nice." He folded the flier and passed it back. "You planning on robbing the place?"

Annie's brows snapped together. "I own it," she shot back. "I got the deed buried right here. Now are you gonna ask any more questions, mister, or are you gonna help me dig?"

Jake removed his jacket and rolled up his sleeves. The old cottonwood Annie had selected as a marker had grown since she'd buried the deed, forcing them to dig through and around the tree's thick roots. Two hours later, they were both streaked with dirt and breathing heavily. Finally they reached the rough pine box that contained the deed. Jake lifted it and passed it to Annie, watching as she split the wood and withdrew the yellowed parchment.

"I don't suppose there's any chance that you came by that legally, is there, darlin'?"

Annie wiped the perspiration from her brow and sent him a dark look. "It's more legal—and a hell of a lot more accurate—than the piece of paper that says your mama and daddy were married the day you were born."

Jake bit back a grin. "Well, now, that does reassure me."

He crossed to where Weed stood, flipped open his saddlebag, and retrieved his bourbon flask. Then he sat down and leaned against a smooth rock, stretched out his long legs, and took a deep, comforting swallow. Annie wordlessly took a seat across from him. After a few minutes, Cat wandered over, hissed at Jake, and settled herself in Annie's lap. Whether it was a trick of the fading afternoon light or the fact that she held the deed firmly in hand, he couldn't help but notice the relaxed glow that softened Annie's features.

"So your outlaw days are over," he commented, trying once again to draw her out.

Annie nodded. "Yup."

"You'll be a high-society lady now, running a grand hotel."

A contented smile drifted over her face. "That's right," she said. She glanced down at the flier, which sat beside her, running her fingers softly over the page. "That's exactly what I'll be."

Silence fell between them once again. Realizing that he would get nothing more from her, Jake glanced at the surrounding woods, frowning as the hint of sulfur once again assailed his nostrils. "What's that smell?" he asked.

Annie sniffed, then nodded in recognition. "There's a hot springs over that ridge," she replied.

Following her gesture, he rose and went to investigate. Hot, steaming pools of water glistened a mere hundred yards away. Jake had already determined that they should ride for another hour or two rather than making camp at the old mining shaft. But the opportunity to bathe in the hot springs before bedding down for the night was all the incentive he needed to reverse that decision. Fortunately Annie readily agreed. The only point of contention was their bathing schedules.

"You're going first, mister. I ain't taking off my clothes while you're within fifty yards of me."

"I'm afraid not, darlin'. What's to stop you from taking off with both horses while I'm up to my neck in that hot water?"

"How do I know that ain't exactly what you're planning on doing to me?" Annie shot back.

The argument continued for another ten minutes until a resolution was finally reached. A dense outcropping of rocks and scrub brush separated the pools and allowed for a modicum of privacy, so they could both bathe at the same time.

With their horses stationed within easy view, Jake took off his clothes, tossed them over his saddle, and sank into the steaming spring. The rustling of the bush beside him, followed by a blissful sigh, told him that Annie had followed the same course.

Their enjoyment of the hot springs was short-lived.

Given that their compromise was based entirely on a mutual distrust of each other, without taking any other factors into account, it wasn't long before Jake discovered the error of their plan.

The cool evening air was shattered by Annie's ear-splitting scream—followed by a steady stream of curses.

Jake leapt from the spring and raced toward her, only to be knocked flat as a dark bay thundered past him. He rolled over, narrowly avoiding the animal's flying hooves. He sprang to his feet just in time to see Weed and Dulcie gallop away, a strange rider on Weed's back.

Comprehension was quick and bitter. Someone had stolen their horses. The realization that followed was even worse. Night was falling. Their blankets, guns, money, and supplies were gone. He was stranded in the middle of nowhere with Outlaw Annie.

They were both completely naked.

Chapter 4

"*Y*ou take one more step, mister," Annie warned, "and I'll, I'll—" She stopped short, unable to come up with a single threat that could be reasonably accomplished while she sat naked in a pool of steaming water.

A low rumble of laughter greeted her words as Jake easily surmised her predicament. "I take it that means you're not hurt, darlin'."

He stood only a few yards away, looking absolutely ridiculous. His Stetson sat at a jaunty angle on his head and his feet were tucked into dark leather boots. But with the exception of those two items—and the thick pine bough that strategically covered his private regions—he was totally and completely naked.

Annie took in his body in a glance. After years of doctoring up the boys in the gang, the sight of a man in his natural state was no longer shocking to her. But looking at Jake in just his boots and hat stirred a heated curiosity within her that she had never felt when tending the boys' wounds.

While his smooth manners, tailored clothing, and fluid movements had served to give him the appearance of lean brawn, his naked body told quite a different story. In truth, Jake Moran had a rugged frame that was magnificently, powerfully built. Tight, rippling muscles defined his biceps and forearms. His chest was impossibly broad and dusted with a light, downy mist of fine, dark hair. His stomach was washboard flat, his waist and hips lean and narrow. Long, powerfully sculpted thighs tapered down to smooth, round knees and thickly muscled calves.

Her eyes moved reluctantly away from his body to study his face. The cocky smile, ice-blue eyes, and dark, silky hair were no different than before. Yet his striking masculine beauty seemed more oddly compelling now, when he stood before her naked. Annie pondered that discovery in silence. The raw appeal of his natural physical attributes formed a package that was as tempting as sin on a Saturday night. That is, if she were interested in the man. Which, of course, she absolutely, definitely was not. It simply surprised her that the slick-talking gambler wasn't as difficult to look at as she might have suspected.

"You coming out now, darlin', or would you like me to come in and get you?"

His words snapped her out of her reverie. Annie jerked down low in the water, splashing steamy bubbles against her chin. "You stay right there, mister."

Jake tipped back his hat as a slow grin spread across his face. "You planning on staying in there until you prune up?"

Maybe, Annie thought. Given her alternatives, it wasn't such a bad idea. Looking at Jake in all his naked glory hadn't been too hard to stomach. But the thought of him looking at her—now, that was a problem. Unwilling to dwell on that mortifying prospect, she turned her attention to more practical matters. "That low-down thief get away?" she asked.

"With both horses and everything on them. I left my boots and hat over by that rock." he said, gesturing vaguely behind him. "What about you? Anything you want me to look for?"

"My shoes," she answered, pointing toward an outcropping of sagebrush. Everything else she'd worn had been folded and stacked neatly atop her saddle. Jake nodded and turned in the direction she had indicated. As he strode away, she noted the long, muscular lines of his broad back, the lean taper of his narrow waist and hips . . . and the perfectly formed curve of his tight, masculine buttocks.

Annie squeezed her eyes shut, forcing the image out of her mind. With all the problems she currently faced, the *last* thing she needed to think about now was Jake Moran's naked butt.

He returned seconds later, depositing her shoes near the edge of the spring. Annie kept her eyes determinedly lowered, her gaze steadfastly focused on the tips of his boots.

"Well?" he drawled.

"Well, what?"

"Well, what are you waiting for?"

The earth to open up and swallow me, she fumed silently. *Or better yet, for the earth to open and swallow this fancy-pants, too-good-looking-for-his-own-good gambler.* But since that didn't seem likely to happen—her luck had been on a sort of a downswing for the past dozen years or so—the only real alternative was for her to stand up, get out of the spring, and try to track down Dulcie.

Knowing that was one thing; actually doing it was something else altogether.

As Diego might have said, she was *entre la espada y la pared.* "Between the sword and the wall."

Annie took a deep breath and steeled herself. Granted, she'd seen nothing in Jake's personality that would indicate he might come after her, but that didn't mean anything. He was still a man, and that was what counted. He was no different than Snakeskin Garvey. Even Pete Mundy had been charming in his day, a pretty boy with thick blond hair and manners slicker than wet riverbed stone. But when Pete got mad or drunk . . . well, that was something else.

"Turn around," she barked at Jake, funneling her fear into brusqueness.

"Whatever you say, darlin'."

Once his back was turned, Annie scurried out of the spring, grabbed her shoes, and ducked behind a thick grove of blue spruce. She emerged minutes later with her shoes fastened tightly and a long-needled branch held before her like a lofty, oversized fan. She clenched a rock in her opposite fist, using it as a makeshift means of protection and defense. It wasn't much, but it was the best she could do. She nervously cleared her throat, signaling her presence to Jake.

"You better not get any funny ideas, mister."

"Believe me, darlin', there's nothing funny about being stuck out here with—"

Whatever words he might have intended to finish that thought with were lost as he glanced over his shoulder at her. For the first time since she had met him, the cocky expression that had seemed permanently fixed to his features faded away. A quiet intensity darkened his eyes as his gaze traveled briefly over her body. While there was nothing lewd or threatening in his look, Annie was all too aware of what he was seeing. The thick limb screened her breasts, stomach, and the tops of her thighs, but the coverage it afforded was minimal at best. Gaps between the needles and branches did nothing to hide the shadowy curves of her form and various bare expanses of skin.

She shifted uncomfortably as a cool breeze swept over her body. Her legs were completely exposed, as were her arms and backside. Her wet hair clung to her shoulders and drifted down her back in a thick, tousled mass. Night would be falling shortly, but that fact did her little good now. The dusky afternoon light afforded ample opportunity to view nearly every shameful inch of her unclothed figure. She sent up a silent prayer of gratitude that she wasn't given to blushing; otherwise she would doubtless be as red as a berry patch in August by now.

Jake studied her for a long moment in silence, his expression unreadable. Finally he suggested, "Maybe you ought to wait here while I go after him."

She stubbornly shook her head. "That no-account thief got my money, my deed, my horse, and my clothes. I'm going—with or without you."

His familiar grin slowly returned as an expression that looked almost like approval entered his eyes. "You've got guts, darlin', I'll give you that."

Annie brought up her chin and stated the obvious. "I've got nothing left to lose."

*J*ake walked a few paces ahead of Annie, silently studying the ground as he followed the horse thief's tracks. Not only did he feel like a complete jackass, he knew he looked the part. A cursory search of the abandoned mining shed had revealed a pair of moth-eaten red-flannel drawers, which he had gratefully claimed for himself. His entire ensemble now consisted of his boots, underwear (complete with a breezy rear "trapdoor" which was missing half the buttons), and his hat.

For Annie, they'd found an old saddle blanket that was dried stiff with sweat and mud, and torn a slit in the middle. She wore the blanket serape style, draped over her shoulders like a coarse, oversized cape. While the garment didn't cover her completely—her forearms and calves were still openly exposed—it was a hell of a lot better than that old spruce branch.

Jake shook his head at the memory of her stepping out before him outfitted in nothing but a few spiky spruce needles. If the woman had meant to shock him, it had worked. If she'd meant to seduce him, that damned sure would have worked as well. Outlaw Annie had a body that would stop a downhill-running, coal-fired, brakes-busted freight train.

Her breasts were full and round, her waist tiny, her stomach flat, and her hips had a graceful, gentle swell. Her lush figure showed none of the plump, fleshy softness so often seen in barmaids or ladies of leisure. Annie rode hard and played hard, and it showed. Her skin was taut and smooth; her body was sculpted with long, feminine muscles that served as a luscious counterpoint to her fluid curves. Despite the flimsy branch she'd used to shield herself, Jake had had a clear view of nearly every exquisite inch. And what he couldn't see . . . well, he had no trouble imagining.

But seducing him had obviously not been Annie's intention. In fact, just the opposite was true. She had stood before him with the tree limb clutched in one hand and the rock tightly fisted in the other—fully prepared to take out after the thief who'd stolen her horse. All in all, she'd presented an affecting image of courage and an odd, almost belligerent vulnerability. As if she'd known she would lose but was determined to go down fighting. That kind of bravery was rare enough in men; Jake had never seen anything like it before in a woman.

He glanced over his shoulder, watching as Annie stomped along behind him, with Cat trailing at her heels. She didn't voice a complaint even though they had been walking for more than two hours over rough terrain, it was growing bitterly cold, and night was quickly falling. That in itself served to earn her a tiny measure of Jake's grudging respect. But it did absolutely nothing to help their situation.

He drew to a halt and scanned the ground. Light was fading a little more with every passing minute. Reluctant as he was to stop, it was better to wait and push on at dawn than to attempt to track a man in the dark. "Looks like we make camp," he said. "We keep going much longer and we'll lose him completely."

Annie studied the ground and nodded, clearly as adverse to stopping as he had been but equally aware that they had little choice in the matter.

He searched the horizon, looking for a sheltered spot to bed down for the night, when a faint glow in the distance caught his eye. Glancing over at Annie, he noted that her gaze was fixed on the same point. "Any idea what town that might be?" Jake asked.

"Nope."

"Me neither." He studied the distant shimmer of light, thinking. "Hell, I guess it doesn't matter. Let's give it a try."

Annie's brows snapped together. "What are you talking about?" she demanded. "We're staying right here, right on that thief's tracks. I ain't about to risk losing him."

Jake studied her in astonishment, amazed at what he considered her total disregard for reality. "Darlin', have you really *looked* at either one of us lately? Supposing we do catch up with him at dawn—then what the hell are we gonna do? Threaten to beat him up with my boots if he doesn't return our property? We do that and the only chance we'll have of getting away with our lives is if he's laughing too hard to aim properly when he tries to shoot us."

Annie balled her hands into little fists and set them on her hips. "All right, mister, if you're so smart, what's your plan?"

"We go into town, get us both some clothes, some guns and ammunition, and maybe even a horse. It sure as hell beats freezing out here all night, then tracking him unarmed and on foot."

"We don't have any money. You forgetting that?"

Jake tilted his head toward the town. "That's probably some mining camp we're looking at. That means it's going to be nearly all men. And if it's nearly all men, that means there's going to be a saloon."

"So?"

"So if there's a saloon, you can be damned sure there's somebody playing poker." A slow, contented smile drifted across his face. "C'mon, darlin'. It's time to go water the money tree."

*T*he mining town was about what Annie had expected. Main Street was lined on either side with a blacksmith, land office, general mercantile, stable, undertaker, and, just as Jake had predicted, a saloon. Horses and pack mules crowded the hitching posts. The ground was sodden, squashing beneath her feet in a liquid mire of mud and horse manure. Hogs rooted in the street, and chickens walked between the buildings clucking and pecking. A few stray dogs, drunken miners, and a fiery-eyed preacher who stood on a street corner and shouted his sermon of hell and brimstone to random passersby completed the scene.

Annie took that all in stride. But what proved difficult for her to endure were the catcalls, whistles, and shouts that were directed at her and Jake. It seemed as though every man in town flooded outside just to witness the two of them stroll nearly naked down Main Street. Annie clamped her jaw shut and tilted her chin, refusing to pay them any mind. As for Jake, he appeared completely immune to public humiliation. He strode through town as though he'd just been elected mayor, acknowledging every hoot and holler with a grin and a polite tip of his hat.

Finally they reached the saloon and stepped inside. The interior was as rough and crude as the exterior. The furnishings were simple: a hard-packed dirt floor, a makeshift bar comprised of a sheet of lumber balanced atop two hefty beer barrels, a few tables and chairs, and smoky kerosene lanterns hanging from nails in the bare walls. A cast-iron stove tucked in the corner radiated minimal amounts of heat. The place smelled of damp earth, fresh-cut pine, unwashed bodies, and lamp oil.

Roughly twenty men, including the bartender, lounged about inside. Within seconds of their entrance, Jake and Annie were greeted with the same wide-eyed wonder and lewd comments they had received on the street.

"Looks like you lost your britches, mister!"

"Looks like your lady friend lost even more than that!"

"Why don't you come on inside and let us warm you up, sweet thing?"

Jake doffed his hat and gave a deep, dramatic bow, smiling patiently as the bawdy jests continued. Annie stood behind him, unable to emulate his good-natured indifference to the raucous laughter. It was all fine and well for Jake Moran to act the part of the town buffoon, but she wanted nothing to do with it. She was already getting far more attention than she liked from the male population in town.

Once the noise had died down, the bartender asked flatly, "What the hell happened to you two?"

Jake briefly related how their horses, gear, and clothing had been stolen back at the hot springs.

The bartender, a beefy fellow with swarthy skin and dark eyes, nodded in commiseration. "There's a group been rustling cattle all over these parts. Some say they're Mexican banditos, some say they're renegade Apaches. They hide out in the canyons east of town. Damned sheriff's too yellowbellied to put together a posse and go after them."

So they had been on the right path, Annie thought. The trail they had been following led directly toward those canyons.

"How many are there?" Jake asked.

The bartender shrugged. "Four, maybe five. But they're mean sons of bitches, and they've got plenty of ammo."

"Appreciate the warning," Jake said, then turned his attention to the crowd at large. "Gentlemen, despite our recent setbacks, I can't help but feel that this is my lucky night. Anyone here up for a friendly game of poker?"

"We don't play for chits here. You hiding your money in your boots, mister?" demanded a voice from the back of the room.

"Nope. But I reckon they ought to be good for something." Jake sat down and pulled off his finely tooled black leather boots and set them on the bar beside his Stetson. "Those were both custom-made for me out in Denver City. Boots cost me seventy-five dollars, the hat cost fifty. Any bidders?"

"I'll give you ten dollars for both," said the same man who had spoken before. He pulled a bill from his wallet and held it up. "Probably ain't worth that much, but I reckon I can sell 'em in my store."

A miner stood up to counter the offer, but the first man shot him a look that had him sitting back down real quick. Annie knew the man's type. He was big and brawny, with fair hair and tiny blue eyes that reminded her of a pig's. He had the look of a bully written all over him.

"Take it or leave it, mister," he said to Jake, an expression of smug satisfaction on his face. "Looks like that's the best offer you're gonna get."

It was an insulting amount. Jake had to know that as well as she did. But surprisingly he didn't turn it down.

"Why, that's mighty generous, friend," he said instead, smiling politely. If not for the cool, deadly frost that had returned to his eyes, Annie would have thought him completely unaware of how patently he was being taken in.

"I thought so." The big man slapped the bill on the bar and reached for Jake's boots.

Jake caught his arm. "I assume you'll give me the opportunity to buy those back at the end of the night."

"Sure I will. Unfortunately the price just went up. I figure quality items like these oughta sell for about a hundred dollars." He shook off Jake's arm and smiled. "But I tell you what. Since they're secondhand, and you and your friend there have had such a rough night, I'll sell them to you for ninety-five."

A collective hush fell over the saloon as the men who had been lounging about suddenly tensed, waiting for the brawl that usually followed an exchange of that nature. If Annie had had her guns, she would have been tempted to shoot the man's fancy little hat clean off his head. But Jake surprised her by once again exercising a considerable amount of restraint.

He studied the other man in silence, then nodded. "Like I said, you're a real generous fella."

The big man looked almost disappointed. "I'm glad you see things my way," he blustered gruffly. "Name's Connors. You come see me at my dry-goods store when you get the money."

Annie watched as Jake took a seat with seven other men, including Connors, for a game of stud poker. She frowned, mulling over the exchange. She wouldn't have pegged Jake for a coward, but that man had flat-out stolen Jake's boots and hat, and Jake had done nothing to stop him. If someone had tried that on Pete Mundy . . . hell, he'd be resting six feet under by now.

She took a seat slightly to the left and behind Jake's chair, watching the play. Jake raked in the first pot. "Beginner's luck," he said to the group, then called over his shoulder for a glass of whiskey.

The bartender brought the drink and set it down by Jake's elbow. He looked at Annie and scowled, saying to Jake, "Sorry, mister, but I'm afraid your lady friend has got to go. We don't allow no ladies in the saloon—town ordinance." He shot a dark look at Cat, who sat curled up near Annie's ankles, and added, "We don't allow no pets, neither."

Jake glanced away from his cards and handed the bartender a coin for his drink. "Trust me," he said loftily, "any woman who's with me is definitely *not* a lady. She and the cat stay."

Annie stiffened as a low rumble of laughter broke out around the table and she was once again the recipient of the men's rude, speculative stares. "Why, you—" she started, but Jake cut her off.

"You hungry, darlin'?"

As a matter of fact, she was. "Yes."

Jake glanced up at the bartender. "What are you serving tonight?"

"We got fried oysters, fried chicken, fried steak, or refried beans and tortillas. What do you want?"

Annie asked for chicken, while Jake ordered a steak. It seemed a foolish waste of money, considering the fact that they were both close to buck naked and had barely a nickel between them. But if Jake was going to eat, she sure as hell wasn't going to go hungry.

Later, with her belly full and her body warmed, Annie relaxed back into her chair and watched the game. Jake won a hand or two, then lost the next several rounds. For a man who supposedly made his living gambling, it was an unimpressive display. Jake seemed to have no strategy at all. He'd see a whopping raise to stay in a hand, then ask for *four* cards. He'd raise a double eagle on nothing but a pair of twos. All in all, he played like a reckless greenhorn with just a bare knowledge of the fundamentals of poker.

The game seemed to go on endlessly, the soft slapping of the cards nearly lulling her to sleep. Annie's attention wavered until a sudden quiet tension brought her focus back to the game. A huge pile of coins, pouches of silver dust, and federal greenbacks sat in the middle of the table. Connors, who was dealing that round, held the deck tightly in his fist. "You in or out?" he demanded of Jake.

Jake glanced at his cards, then shoved every cent he had into the pot.

A tight, satisfied smile slipped across Connors' face. "'Fraid that's not enough, mister. Looks like the stakes just got a might too high for you to match."

Jake studied him in silence, then tilted his head toward Annie. "What'll you give me for her?"

Annie's heart leapt to her throat. "What the hell are you talking about?" she demanded, bolting up straight in her chair.

Jake lifted his shoulders in a casual shrug, eyeing her intently. "I'm talking about one night with Connors if I lose, or you and I split the pot if I win. What do you say, darlin'? You feeling lucky tonight?"

Connors' lewd gaze traveled hungrily over her body. "Either way, the lady comes out a winner, don't she?" he said, a coarse laugh accompanying his words.

Repulsed, Annie turned back to Jake, searching his face for some sign that would help her decide. His expression, however, was completely blank, stripped of any clue as to the value of his cards. He looked, in fact, totally indifferent. He might be holding a royal flush; or the son of a bitch could just be bluffing. She glanced at his whiskey glass, wondering if he'd had one, two, or twenty. She hadn't been keeping track, and there was no way to tell just by looking at him.

She chewed her bottom lip, wracked with indecision. Connors was a disgusting, arrogant pig, no question about it. If she had to choose between letting him touch her and bathing in a pile of mule dung, she'd pick the mule dung any day. On the other hand, the size of that pot made it a hard bet to turn down. If they won, they would be able to buy clothes, guns and ammunition, and maybe even a horse. Then they could track down those outlaws and get their belongings back. Like Jake had said earlier, going after them on foot and unarmed would be pure crazy. Hell, she'd have a better chance trying to rock a baby to sleep during a buffalo stampede.

She tilted her chin, looking Jake straight in the eye. "Take the bet."

A murmur of excitement shot through the crowd.

Jake nodded. A tiny glimmer of what looked like approval glinted in his steely eyes.

"You heard her, boys, the bet's on," Connors declared. The big man confidently set down his cards. "I've got a straight, seven high. What have you got, mister?"

"Two pair."

Annie's heart sank, then her despair turned to fury. Jake had been bluffing. *Bluffing.* He'd bet every cent he had—and let her risk her own body—on *two pair*! That selfish, cocky, good-for-nothing, no-account, *son of a bitch!*

The other man's face beamed with glee and disgust. "Hell, two pair don't beat nothing," he said, reaching for the pot.

Jake coolly smiled. "It does if they're two pair of queens." He set his cards on the table. "Four ladies, gentlemen, ace high."

Connors' mouth dropped open. "That can't be," he stuttered, staring at the cards as though they had grown horns and a tail. "That can't be." He lifted his gaze to Jake, his pink skin turning purple with rage. "That money's mine, and so's the woman."

"Is that a fact?"

"Damned right, it is."

"Funny, the way I've always played the game, four queens beat your puny little straight any day of the week."

"You cheated, mister. And everybody here saw you."

"You were holding the deck, Connors."

The silence was so thick Annie was sure there wasn't a soul in the room still breathing. While their voices hadn't been raised, both men kept only their left hands on the table. Their right hands hung low and loose by their sides, ready for a quick draw.

But Jake wasn't wearing a gun.

Jake was equipped with nothing but his moth-eaten red-flannel underwear. The realization struck Annie with chilling, crystal clarity—at the exact moment that Connors shoved back his chair and reached for his Colt.

Jake shoved back his chair at the same instant . . . and came to his feet with a gun in his hand—cocked and ready to fire—while Connors was still struggling to bring his Colt into play.

Connors froze, dropping his gun back in his holster. He blinked in disbelief, obviously trying to mentally grasp both Jake's speed and the gun that seemed to materialize in his hand out of thin air. "How the hell did you do that?" he gasped.

Jake tilted his head toward the man who had been sitting next to him. "I borrowed it."

Annie's gaze flew toward the other man, who was studying his holster as though the gun had flown out of it on its own accord. Annie had seen some fast draws in her day, but *nothing* like that. Jake Moran had moved rattler fast and was obviously every bit as deadly.

"Not very sporting of you, was that, Connors?" he asked, making a tsking noise with his tongue. "Drawing on an unarmed man. Why, I'm beginning to believe there's no honor left in this world."

"What the hell would you know about honor, you and that little whore of yours—"

Jake's gray eyes went black. "You apologize to the lady real pretty like, or I'll blow your goddamned head off."

Connors glared at him in silent, bitter refusal.

Jake shrugged. "Hell of a stupid thing to die for, mister, but I reckon that's your choice." He lifted his gun and shoved it in Connors' face.

Connors went white, then turned a sickly shade of green. "Jesus! No! I'm sorry—lady, I'm sorry!"

Jake nodded approvingly. "Very good. Now there's just one more thing." He paused, smiling. "I want my hat and boots back."

"You can have 'em, mister. Just get that gun out of my face."

"Well, that's mighty kind of you. Generous, even. But I intend to pay for them fair and square. Annie," Jake said, his eyes never leaving Connors, "give the man ten dollars."

Annie plucked a bill from the table and shoved it in Connors' shirt pocket.

"Now get the hell out of here," Jake said, pulling back his gun.

Connors backed away, tripping over tables and chairs in his hurry to get out of the saloon.

Jake watched him leave. With a satisfied nod, he returned the borrowed gun. "Next time, pal, keep it loaded, will you?"

The little man who owned the gun gave a nervous, almost hysterical laugh and nodded.

Annie felt a little hysterical herself. Jake's gun had been *empty* the entire time? Her stomach flipped and her knees suddenly went weak. That was crazy. Pure and simply crazy.

Jake nonchalantly gathered up the money and dumped it in his hat. Then he looked around the room at his stupefied audience. "It's a sad shame, ain't it?" he said, shaking his head. "Some folks just take personal offense at losing."

A nervous trickle of laughter echoed across the room. The bartender stepped out from behind the bar and looked at Jake approvingly. "You played a straight game, mister," he announced. "If Connors goes caterwauling to the sheriff, I'll make sure he gets the story right." That said, he gestured over his shoulder with his thumb. "I got a livery out back if you and your friend want to put up for the night."

"That's mighty kind. We'd surely appreciate it."

The bartender nodded. "My pleasure. It's about time somebody took Connors down a peg or two. I'm just glad I was here to see it."

Annie followed Jake out of the saloon and down the back alley, which led to the livery. Her mind whirled as she tried to make sense of what had just happened. "You had that planned all along, didn't you?" she asked. "Using me for the stakes."

"Yep."

"How'd you know he'd take that bet?"

Jake stopped and turned to face her. His gaze slowly traveled over her body, moving from the top of her head to the bottom of her toes. She was once again acutely conscious of her near nakedness and the obvious disarray of her hair.

"There ain't a living, breathing man west of the Mississippi who wouldn't have taken that bet," he said, his voice matter-of-fact.

It was strictly a businesslike appraisal, but Annie felt absurdly flattered nonetheless. "What would you have done if you had lost?"

"Well, I guess that's a risk I was willing to take."

The warm glow she'd felt only seconds ago instantly evaporated. "A risk *you* were willing to take?" she sputtered indignantly. "*You?* Looked to me like it was my fanny that was tossed in the ante."

"Then, I guess it would have been your problem." Jake shrugged. "That, darlin', is why they call it gambling."

Annie simply stared at him, struck speechless by his callous disregard at what might have happened to her. "Why, you, you . . ." she began struggling to find a word strong enough to fit her feelings.

Jake studied her for a long moment in silence. Then

a small, cocky grin touched his lips. "Connors was cheating," he finally said.

She blinked. "What?"

"He was cheating the whole time—and doing a hell of a poor job of it too. He dealt me three queens from the bottom of the deck. I picked up the fourth on the draw."

Annie's eyes widened in a flash of understanding. That was why Connors had been so sure he would win—and so furious when he didn't. His hand had been rigged to beat three queens, not four. Picking up the fourth had been pure luck on Jake's part—or perhaps some sleight of hand that had been his own doing.

In any case, Jake had known what Connors had been up to all along. He had played the part of the tinhorn rube so smoothly he'd even convinced her—just as he had doubtlessly convinced the other players at the table. That accomplished, he had waited until he was absolutely certain he could beat whatever Connors was holding, and then he had bet it all. It was that simple.

"Not bad, mister."

Jake shrugged. "Let's get some sleep."

He continued down the alley and pulled back the broad livery door. Annie peered cautiously into the darkness, adjusting her eyes to the light of the interior. Only a few faint traces of moonlight seeped in through the cracks in the broad plank walls. Two horses were inside, dozing in their stalls. They lifted their heads toward Jake and Annie, snorted their displeasure at having been awakened, then went back to their naps. As the small individual stalls were thick with the stench of manure, Jake moved to the pile of fresh straw that sat in the center of the room. He kicked it a bit to flatten it out into a bed, then plopped down and stretched out.

Annie hesitated, then did the same, making her bed a few feet away from his. The straw was a bit scratchy, but at least it was warm. All things considered, their situation had considerably improved in the past few hours. Their bellies were full and they had money in their pockets and a roof over their heads. Things could have been worse.

She lay in silence for a while, listening to Jake breathe. Above her, through the holes in the roof, a few stars glimmered in an otherwise ebony sky. "You ever think about really making something out of yourself, mister?" she asked. "Not just spending your life traveling from saloon to saloon?"

"Nope."

"You're tired, ain't you?"

"It's late, Annie."

"You know how I can tell? You sound more Southern. It comes out every now and then. Especially when you drink, or when you're tired."

"Does the accent bother you?"

"No. Why, should it?"

"It bothers some folks around here."

"Hmmm." Annie thought for a moment, staring up at the barn rafters. "Well, you might not want to change your life, mister, but I'm gonna change mine. You just wait and see. I ain't planning on being Outlaw Annie forever. Once I get my hotel running, I'm gonna be the grandest lady west of the Mississippi. That'll show everybody."

"Is that a fact?"

"Yep. I'm gonna turn my whole life around. Near as I can tell, there's just one thing it takes to make it in this world, and I've got it."

"What's that?"

"Pluck."

"Pluck?"

"Pluck. That may be all the good Lord gave me, but at least He gave me plenty of it."

"And just what exactly is pluck?" Although she couldn't see his face, his voice sounded distinctly amused.

Choosing to overlook his flippant tone, she answered, "You can't define it, it just is. Some call it grit, others call it sand. But I reckon it amounts to the same thing, man or woman. It means that nobody can ever knock you down, no matter what. It means never giving up, never backing down."

She heard Jake rustling in the straw. "You know what I really wish you had, darlin'?"

"What?"

"Sense enough to go to sleep."

She ignored that. Her mind was racing ahead, too full of thoughts that needed sorting out for her to be still. "You as good with your gun as you look?"

Jake sighed. "I'm still on the right side of the ground, ain't I?"

"Then why didn't you kill that fella?"

"You think I should have?"

"He had it coming, that's for sure."

"We've all got it coming." In the shadowy darkness, a hint of melancholy crept into Jake's voice. "Each and every one of us. And sooner or later, we're all gonna get it. That's about the only thing that's certain in this whole damned world." He pulled his hat down low over his face. "Now go to sleep. We'll be tracking those bandits bright and early tomorrow morning."

Chapter 5

*A*nnie awoke to the feel of coarse, scratchy straw tickling her nose. She sat up and gazed about her in bleary-eyed confusion, feeling as though she had just closed her eyes minutes earlier. Her memory of the night before flooded back as she saw Jake, attired in black woolen pants, a gray flannel shirt, and a full-length oilskin coat—along with his hat and boots—standing a few feet away. A cartridge belt hung low in his hips and two .38s filled the holsters.

He glanced in her direction. "Good, you're awake. Your clothes are by your feet."

She glanced down at a small, neat pile of clothing sitting in the straw. Flipping through the stack of garments, she discovered a pair of navy wool pants, similar to those Jake wore but scaled down to her size, a red and navy checked flannel shirt, a set of thick cotton longjohns, sturdy socks, a honey-colored leather jacket that had been lined with lambswool, and a matching pair of riding gloves.

He frowned as he watched her. "Something wrong?" he asked, sounding slightly impatient. "I know they're not very feminine, but I didn't think it would matter to you."

She shook her head, overlooking the insult. "These are fine, mister, real fine."

"Then, why does your face look like that?"

Annie had no idea what her face looked like. She did know what she felt, however, although she doubted she could put it into words. Growing up, she had worn Pete's old cast-offs while doing her chores around the house. For church, she'd worn cut-down versions of Mrs. Mundy's old gowns. When she had ridden with the boys, she had worn whatever throw-outs she could get her hands on and stitch back together.

She reverently touched the clothing and said simply, "I ain't never worn brand-new, store-bought clothes before." Despite her attempts to rein in her emotions, her voice held all the wonder and awe of a child unwrapping a shiny toy on Christmas morning. "Ain't they something? There isn't a hole anywhere in sight, and they're so clean they're almost shiny."

Embarrassed at the way she was carrying on over clothing that the fancy-pants gambler would no doubt consider mediocre at best, she quit speaking and looked away, wishing she could bury herself under the straw.

"I'm glad you like them," he said after a minute.

Annie forced her eyes up to meet his gaze. If he did think her a bumbling simpleton, she couldn't tell. A strange silvery light had entered his eyes, but she couldn't begin to know how to interpret it. The man had his poker face on once again, and his expression was unfathomable.

"They're fine, mister," she said sincerely. "Real fine."

He nodded. "I'll leave you to change, then. There's a bucket of fresh water in the corner if you want to wash up. We've got a four-hour ride ahead of us. Meet me at the cafe and we'll get something to eat before we head out."

They breakfasted on eggs that had been scrambled up spicy with peppers and onions, thick slices of salted ham, and fresh biscuits drenched in butter and honey. The coffee was hot, and the cook kept it flowing. Annie scooped out a portion of the eggs and set them on a small dish on the boardwalk for Cat to enjoy, then went back to her meal. Neither she nor Jake had much to say to each other, but she was too busy eating for the silence to bother her. She had eaten better during the few days she'd been with Jake Moran than she had in months.

She learned that Jake had made arrangements with the bartender earlier that morning to buy one of the livery horses, an ancient sorrel gelding named Sawdust, and a worn-out saddle. As he hadn't had enough money to buy two horses, they made the journey riding double. Annie had elected to ride in front of Jake on the saddle, with Cat curled up in her lap, rather than sit behind him. Accustomed as she was to riding, a four-hour journey was still a lot of wear and tear on the rear if one spent it bouncing up and down on a horse's rump.

A few miles out, however, she wondered if she hadn't made a mistake. Jake rode confidently, with the reins low and loose in his hands. But that didn't prevent his arms from closing in around her, wrapping her in his heady scent. Nor did it prevent her thighs from occasionally brushing up against his, her back from falling against his chest, or his chin from lightly grazing the top of her head. Annie stiffened her spine and sat up straight, determined to prevent any further contact. But it seemed the stiffer she held herself, the more inclined the horse was to veer into a rut or a gully and knock her against him once again.

"Are you doing that on purpose?" she finally demanded as Sawdust broke from a trot into a gallop and knocked her into Jake's arms.

"Doing what?" he asked, his voice dripping innocence.

"Knocking me around like that on purpose."

"I don't know what you're talking about." He veered sharply left, causing her breast and shoulder to brush softly against his arm.

"Very funny, mister."

Jake's low, masculine rumble of laughter filled her ears. His breath fell warm and spicy on her neck. He adjusted the pressure of his thighs, dropping the gelding back into a smooth, even trot. "Relax, Annie. I won't do it again."

Annie grit her teeth and ignored him, hanging on to the saddle horn with all her might. At least she had her clothes on. Had she made the journey in nothing but that beaten-up saddle blanket she had worn yesterday, the constant teasing contact would have been unbearable.

As she thought about it, a slight frown touched her lips. While the gambler's little game had been vaguely annoying, he hadn't truly frightened her. Jake Moran had been touching her and teasing her, but she hadn't been terrified. For the first time in years, a man had brushed his body against hers and Annie's gut reaction had not been one of pure, blind panic. She had been uneasy, yes. Terrified, no. Astonished at the discovery, she almost wished Jake would veer off course again just so she could examine her reaction to him more closely.

He was true to his word, however, and Annie spent the remainder of their journey relatively unjostled. Eventually the canyons loomed up ahead of them. She scanned the horizon, her gaze caught by the movement of a dark shadow against the red earth of the canyon. Directly behind the shadow, a thin plume of gray smoke drifted up through the brilliant midday sky.

Jake reined the gelding to a stop. "Looks like we found our men."

She peered intently at the canyon wall. "Maybe, maybe not. I reckon we better go find out."

Despite the steadiness of her words, a shimmering excitement that was part fear and part challenge fired her belly. Jake urged Sawdust on, bringing him to a stop at the base of the canyon wall. There the sound of coarse laughter and rough male voices echoed out to meet them.

They dismounted. Jake left the reins loose, not bothering to hitch the animal to a tree. Annie didn't need him to explain the action to her. She and Jake would either come out alive with their own horses and gear, in which case they wouldn't need the worn-out gelding, or they wouldn't come out at all. In either case, Sawdust was old enough and smart enough to find his way home on his own.

Crouched down low, they listened for a moment in silence, judging the voices. Three, perhaps four men, sounding drunk enough to be loud and careless but not drunk enough to pass out anytime soon. Wordlessly Jake gestured toward a rocky path that led partway up the canyon wall. Annie nodded. Tucking Cat into the crook of her arm, she scurried effortlessly up the narrow crevice, halting in a natural alcove created by two boulders. The vantage point gave them a unobstructed view of the camp below.

Three rough-looking men sat hunched around a meager fire. Two Colt revolvers, one hunting rifle, and a pistol lay scattered near their feet. A whiskey bottle passed between them. Their badly soiled clothing, matted hair, and crusted beards spoke of years of harsh living and suggested a distinct aversion to regular baths.

A nervous whinny sent Annie's attention to the left of the camp, where she saw a primitively constructed corral. Five horses stood inside, Dulcie and Weed among them. She mulled the odds over in her mind. Three heavily armed, somewhat drunken, and probably desperate men, versus her and Jake. Not the best situation, but she'd faced worse and come out all right, and she reckoned Jake had as well. "I say we sneak in like this—" she began, but Jake immediately cut her off.

"I go in alone," he said, his voice low and unyielding. His attempt at chivalry was lost on her. She barely spared him a glance, her gaze focused intently on the men below. "Like hell you will. Don't be an idiot."

"I mean it, Annie. Stay out of my way."

That got her attention. Her brows snapped together as her head swung around to face him. "Listen here, mister," she whispered harshly, "I don't trust you any more than you trust me. That's what cost us our horses and gear in the first place, remember? So let's talk plain. If we're gonna dress pretty and wager on cards, we'll do it your way. If we're gonna break up a gang of low-down, thieving outlaws, we do it my way. You got that?"

She could see Jake struggling to hold on to his patience. He shot a sharp glance down below, but the men continued on as before, apparently unaware of the heated argument carried on in fierce whispers in the canyon above them. "We don't have time for this," he snapped. "You just stay out of it, you hear me?"

She brought up her chin. "You just try and keep me out of it. Now, are you gonna give me one of those guns you're carrying or ain't you?"

"Dammit, Annie, there are only three of them. I'll handle it."

"What makes you so sure? How do you know there ain't more of them hiding out someplace else? The bartender said four or five, remember?"

He let out an exasperated breath. "Any fool can see that—"

The unmistakable metallic click of a hammer pulling back a trigger echoed loudly behind them.

"Tell me what a fool can see, *señor,*" a rough voice growled.

Annie froze, then slowly raised her hands and turned around. Beside her, Jake did the same.

A potbellied Mexican giant stood before them, a gun in each hand. One weapon was pointed directly at Jake's gut, the other at Annie's. The outlaw was easily a head taller than Jake and looked to have roughly twice the girth. From what Annie could tell, his weight was distributed in a bulky combination of loose fat and thick, tightly bunched muscles. His clothing was battered and stained, covered with broad splotches of what appeared to be an unsettling combination of grease, blood, and mud.

The Mexican smiled widely, revealing a row of badly rotted gums and darkly stained teeth. "Maybe the lady is right," he said. "How do you know there are not more of us?"

Annie shot a quick look at Jake, watching as he lifted his shoulders in cool acknowledgment of the man's words. "Looks like I made a mistake, doesn't it?"

"*Si, señor.* You made a mistake. A very bad mistake." The outlaw's smile slowly faded. "Keep your hands in the air. Either of you moves and I'll kill you both. *Comprende?*" Shifting the gun that had been focused on Annie, he pointed it skyward, fired off a round, then shouted in Spanish to the men below.

He turned back to Jake. "Hand over your guns, *gringo*. Butt first."

Jake nodded. "Easy, *amigo*. They're all yours."

If Annie hadn't seen for herself what happened next, she never would have believed it. Jake eased his pistols from their holsters and held them out butt forward, exactly as the outlaw had requested. But he kept a finger in each trigger guard. Just as the giant reached for the guns, Jake flicked his wrists and reversed them as quickly and neatly as flipping over a card. That was all there was to it. Just *flip*. In a reversal that took less than a second, suddenly the guns were cocked and pointed in the Mexican's face.

Annie knew the move. It was called the road agent's spin, and it was one of the oldest tricks in the book—for show. Lots of gunmen could do it for show. Annie had even seen Pete do it a time or two—or almost do it, nearly firing off his toes every time he tried it with a loaded gun. But to try it on a man holding a gun on you, well, that was a guaranteed way to get your brains blown out. For Jake to try it on a man like the Mexican outlaw, why, that was more than unbelievable. It was flat crazy.

Maybe that was why it worked.

Or would have worked if Annie hadn't been too damned dumbstruck to move.

Unfortunately the giant recovered from his shock before she did. He grabbed a fistful of her hair and yanked her tightly against him, using her as a shield. The cold steel barrel of his gun ground painfully into her temple.

"Do you want me to kill her, *gringo*?" he hissed, jerking her head back. "I'll kill her right now."

For an endless moment, Jake didn't move. His eyes were flat, coolly calculating. Then he shrugged lightly and dropped his guns.

"Bueno." The giant shoved Annie away from him, sending her stumbling toward a steep path that led down the canyon wall to the outlaw camp. He picked up Jake's guns, tucked them into his waistband, then gave them both a curt order. "Move."

Cursing herself for a complete idiot, Annie glanced over her shoulder, risking a look at Jake. If he was furious with her for ruining their chance to escape, it didn't show. Whatever his inner state might be, his features displayed nothing but calm reserve. His eyes met hers for a fraction of a second before she glanced away. She sensed that there was some communication in his look, something he wanted her to see or know, but she had no idea what it might be. Hoping that they would have a better chance down below, closer to their horses and weapons, she made her way cautiously down the cliff.

She tried to brush Cat away, but the stubborn little beast stayed loyally at her ankles, displaying no more sense to run for cover than Annie had shown earlier. Left with no alternative, Jake followed them down the steep canyon crevice, the Mexican giant prodding his pistol into his back along the way.

Three more men waited for them below, their weapons drawn and ready. The trio consisted of one additional Mexican, an Indian—Apache, she guessed—and one white man whose face bore the scars of a knife battle gone bad. They studied Jake and Annie with indifferent expressions and eyes colder than death itself. A blanket lay at their feet, strewn with bounty that had come directly from Dulcie's and Weed's saddlebags. Annie recognized Jake's watch and clothing, as well as her own book, Bible, and the treasured tintype of her and Catherine.

The smaller Mexican stepped forward, his swaggering demeanor clearly establishing him as the leader. *"Que tenemos aqui?"* he drawled. *"What have we here?"*

Although it was framed as a question, Annie knew as well as anyone there that the answer didn't matter. There was nothing they could say that would change the plain facts: She and Jake had tracked down the outlaws and had been caught. The only question left unanswered was what would happen to them before they died.

Unfortunately it didn't take much brains to figure out what lay in store for her. Not the way the outlaws were looking at her. Their gazes swarmed over her body with the sickening intensity of maggots devouring spoiled fruit. Although she tried to hide it, a slight tremor shook her hands, and her knees knocked against each other like branches rattling in the wind.

Like a wolf stalking prey, the leader smelled her fear. He moved toward her, bringing his swarthy bearded face level with her own. "Who are you?"

Annie tilted her chin, saying nothing.

"I seen her somewheres before, Santo," volunteered the knife-scarred outlaw.

"Deveras?" Santo pondered that bit of information

in silence. Finally he asked, "You and Henry are acquainted, *señorita*?"

She met his question with unflinching, stony silence. Santo's eyes darkened. "Answer me."

"Go to hell, *ladron*."

Santo let out a coarse laugh. "Brave words," he said, tossing a glance over his shoulder at his men. "She calls me a thief. Outlaw scum. The lady is not so friendly, is she?" His smile faded as he took a step closer to Annie. He ran one bony, tobacco-stained finger beneath her chin. "You will get friendly, *señorita*. You will get very friendly before this night is over."

"I'd rather friendly up to a passel of half-starved rattlers."

"We can arrange that," Santo replied with an indifferent shrug. "But not until *after* we are done with you."

"Trail City," Henry burst out excitedly, citing a volatile frontier town that was notorious for its lawlessness and tinderbox instability. "That's where I seen her. Three months ago, buying supplies."

"You saw them both?" Santo inquired, glancing at Jake.

"Not him. I never seen that fella before. The woman was with Pete Mundy and some of his boys." The knife-scarred outlaw paused, swallowing nervously. "She and Pete looked close, Santo. Real close."

The outlaws shifted uneasily as Santo regarded Annie in piercing silence. "Is that so?" he drawled. "*Señorita* Outlaw Annie?"

A cold smile touched Annie's lips. "Pete's killed men just for looking at me," she stated calmly. "I wonder what he's going to do to you."

Santo ignored her threat. "Did the Mundy boys break you in for us, *señorita*?" he returned with a leering smile. "Or will you still rut and buck beneath my men and me like a wild mare?" The outlaw withdrew his pistol and slowly rubbed the barrel along the inside of Annie's leg.

He slid the gun past her thighs, then pressed it up against the juncture of her legs and cocked the trigger. "Let us see how brave your threats are once the night is over."

Jake fought back the urge to drive his fist through the son of a bitch's jaw. Although Annie was trying her best to put up a gutsy front, her eyes had the wild, helpless gaze of a terrified doe who had tumbled into barbed wire. He clenched his jaw as his stomach churned with disgust. No woman deserved to die like that. And he sure as hell hadn't saved Annie from the noose just to abandon her to scum like this.

He studied the men, swiftly debating his next move. As near as he could tell, there was only one way left to play it. Chances were slim that both he and Annie could walk out of there alive, but he might be able to create enough of a distraction for her to slip away.

With that in mind, he forced a cool, friendly confidence into his tone. "I'm afraid you won't have an opportunity to find that out," he said. "The lady and I won't be staying the night."

Santo slowly drew his gun back as his focus shifted from Annie to Jake. "Did you say something, *señor*?"

"I said the lady and I won't be staying the night."

The bandit lifted one dark, bushy brow, studying Jake in silence. "I do not think you understand your situation, *señor*," he finally replied, sounding slightly amused. "You are not in a position to decide."

"Tell you what we'll do," Jake said briskly. "You just give us our horses back and we'll be on our way. We'll forget we ever saw you *hombres*."

The bandit paused, studying him in silence. "Or maybe we keep your horses and kill you both."

A low rumble of laughter sounded among the men.

Jake smiled, waiting for the noise to die down. "You look like a sporting group. Why don't we make a wager for the horses? One on one, winner take all."

Santo matched his smile. "Why would we do that, *señor,* when killing you is so much easier?"

"True enough," Jake agreed easily. He paused a beat, then continued mildly, "I just thought there might be one man among you who isn't too much of a low-life chicken-shit coward to take on an unarmed *gringo* without hiding behind his gun." He lifted his shoulders in a cool shrug. "Then again, maybe I was wrong."

Beside him, Jake heard Annie's sharp intake of breath, but his eyes never left the outlaws. Thick, tension-laden silence hung over the group as the men's faces moved from outraged surprise to ugly, mocking contempt. The silence was finally broken by Santo. He moved toward Jake, studying him with arrogant disdain.

"I am beginning to believe you are a very stupid man, *señor.*"

"Not so stupid that I couldn't track the four of you."

"Si," the outlaw replied, eyeing Jake consideringly. "How did you manage to find our little hideaway?"

"Easy enough. I just followed the birds. The ones above you *hombres* are flying upside down."

Confusion showed in the outlaw's face. *"Que?"*

Jake smiled. "Nothing here worth shitting on."

Fury filled Santo's dark eyes. He glanced over his shoulder at his men. "Manuel, *ven aquí,*" he barked, then his gaze locked once again on Jake's. "The *gringo* has decided he would like to die slowly."

The Mexican giant stepped forward, an ominous look of satisfaction gleaming in his eyes. He shrugged off his coat, removed his gun belt, and passed them both to the Apache. Next he flexed his hands, curling them into tight fists at his sides. His gaze locked on Jake's. "You want to say anything before you die, *hombre?*"

Jake ignored the taunt and turned to Santo. "I win, the woman goes free, *untouched*—and she takes her horse and belongings with her."

The outlaw shrugged. "Perhaps."

"The woman goes free," Jake repeated, his voice flat and uncompromising.

Santo arched one dark brow in mild reproof. "Do you not think we are men of honor, *señor*?"

Once again, the low echo of guttural laughter followed Santo's words.

Jake tipped his hat in a cool, mocking salute. "Undoubtedly your word is as good as mine, *señor*." Turning away from the men, he drew Annie aside and whispered tightly, "Give me ten minutes, then make a break for the horses. Get the hell out of here and don't look back."

Annie gave him an icy stare. "You won't last ten minutes."

Despite the direness of their situation, Jake felt a smile tug at his lips. He took off his coat and passed it to her, then he rolled up his sleeves. "Thanks for the vote of confidence, darlin'."

"I've seen Brahman bulls that weighed less than that fella."

"With any luck, he's got less brains than a bull."

"So have you if you mean to go through with this."

"You have any other ideas?"

Annie's gaze darted toward the outlaws, then back to Jake. "I say we charge 'em," she whispered fervently. "Make a play for their guns. The two of us against the four of them. With any luck, we can both get out of here without getting too shot up."

It took Jake a minute before he realized she was actually serious. "I meant," he said, "do you have any *good* ideas?"

"Listen here, mister—"

"I've had enough of your goddamned help," he said, cutting her off. "I wouldn't be in this mess if it wasn't for you." The thought of what Santo and his men would do to her if his plan didn't work made Jake's voice harsher than he intended. "Just get on your horse and ride. Get the hell out of here."

Anger flashed through her golden-brown eyes. She stiffened her spine and drew herself up, an expression of haughty indifference on her face. "That's fine by me. You want to die, you go ahead. Just don't expect me to thank you for it."

Santo's mocking laughter called their attention back to the men. "Problem, *señor*?" the outlaw drawled. "You change your mind? Trying to convince your woman to fight for you?" Glancing over his shoulder, he issued an order in Spanish to his men.

The giant nodded and stepped forward.

Jake didn't hesitate. He'd discovered long ago that in a game of evenly matched odds, victory generally went to the man who made the first move. Although the odds here were far from even, he figured he could use all the help he could get. With that in mind, he charged the giant, driving his head into the big man's gut. He might as well have tried to push his skull through a meeting-house wall. Not only did the move fail to knock the wind out of his opponent, it barely set the man back a pace. He also left himself in a much more vulnerable position than he had anticipated.

The outlaw drove his knee directly toward Jake's groin.

Jake deftly dodged the thrust, taking the hit in the thigh instead. The blow neatly served to establish the tone for the fight. Quick and dirty, just the way he liked it.

Unable to reach his initial target, the Mexican locked his beefy forearms around Jake's chest and squeezed with all his might, until Jake felt sure his ribs would crack. He finally managed to break the lock and stepped back a pace, giving himself a moment to reassess his opponent. He feinted left, then threw a series of strong right-to-left hooks, smashing his fist into the other man's jaw. The Mexican staggered back a pace but took the hits without flinching. The reaction proved what Jake had initially suspected: the giant was strong as an ox, but he had no speed or finesse.

Jake went in again, but the outlaw caught him off guard, sending a blinding punch crashing against his already tender ribs. Jake reeled from the impact, but it didn't take him down. The two men flew against each other, exchanging a series of cruel, punishing blows.

From the corner of his eye, Jake caught the feminine blur of long golden-brown hair speeding toward the corral. Annie was making her move. He heard a rough shout, the crack of pistol fire, and the high whinnying of startled horses—followed by the thunder of furious hoofbeats echoing off into the distance.

She'd done it. Annie had gotten away, he thought, allowing himself a momentary surge of victory.

But the distraction, welcome as it was, cost him. His opponent let loose a fierce jab aimed at his skull. The sharp hook opened the skin above Jake's left eye, sending a stream of blood gushing down his temple and momentarily blinding him. Seizing the opportunity, the Mexican hooked his foot around the back of Jake's calf, catching Jake off balance and hurling him to the ground. The outlaw dove after him, but Jake managed to roll right, narrowly avoiding the giant's crushing weight.

Jake wiped the blood from his eye and rose unsteadily to his feet, bracing himself for more. Much to his satisfaction, he saw that his opponent looked as bruised and bloodied as he felt himself.

Even better, he noted that the horse pen had been knocked open wide, and that Annie and Dulcie were nowhere to be seen. Although Santo and the Apache remained, both of them looking coldly furious, the knife-scarred outlaw was gone. Probably right on Annie's tail, Jake surmised. While the thought wasn't a pretty one, there was nothing he could do about it right now.

Outlaw Annie was on her own.

His opponent lumbered to his feet, breathing hard.

The giant glared at Jake with a mixture of contempt and grudging respect, then his gaze shifted toward the Indian. The Mexican nodded once.

The Apache tossed the big man a knife.

So much for a fair fight.

The Mexican lunged straight for Jake's heart. Jake, who had learned knife fighting in the bayou country of Louisiana, turned his hip sharply and let the blade slip past him. Unfortunately the outlaw's thrust wasn't a complete miss. Jake felt the piercing sting of the knife's razor-sharp edge as the blade skimmed his chest, slashing open his skin.

The Mexican lunged again. This time Jake grabbed his wrist, pitting his strength against his opponent's as they struggled for control of the knife. The two men strained against each other, battling chest to chest. But despite the pressure he applied, Jake couldn't wrest the knife free. Failing that tactic, he tried another. Stumbling over the ring of stones that edged the outlaw's campfire, he let his knees buckle and hit the ground hard.

Sensing victory, the Mexican's eyes glowed with triumph. His knife slashed through the air as he made a wicked lunge for Jake's throat. But the outlaw only made it partway to his goal. Bringing himself to a half-standing position, Jake wrapped his fist around a rock and drove it into the giant's groin. The outlaw let out a bellow of pain, then fell to his knees and doubled over. The blade slipped easily through his grasp.

Jake grabbed the knife without missing a beat. He plunged it into the giant's belly and jerked the blade upward. The man's eyes dilated wildly and a gurgling sound filled his throat. Blood gushed from his wound and spilled over ground. A shudder tore through him, then his head fell back and he gazed up at the sky, his eyes blank and unseeing.

Jake watched, sickened but resolute. One less man to go after Annie, he thought grimly.

The knife clutched firmly in his grasp, he pulled himself to his feet. Santo and the Apache stood a few yards away, their expressions dark and menacing.

Santo pointed his revolver directly at Jake's chest. "Now it is time to watch your blood spill, *gringo*."

The gunshot blast ripped through the air.

Chapter 6

Jake's hand instinctively flew to his chest, searching for what he knew would be a gaping, bloody wound. Instead he found nothing but a thinly torn line of skin from where the knife had grazed him. Nor did he experience the hot, searing pain he knew would accompany a gunshot wound at close range.

His astonished gaze shot back to Santo.

The outlaw's eyes widened with shock, then a thin trickle of blood emerged from the corner of his mouth. He pitched forward without a sound and landed facedown in the dirt.

The roar of thundering hoofbeats snapped Jake's head around. What greeted him was a sight he would not soon forget. Annabel Lee Foster charged back into camp like a gutsy, glorious, angel of wrath. Righteous intensity filled her eyes, and her small chin was tilted with fierce determination. Her golden-brown hair streamed about her shoulders in wild disarray. She gripped her reins tightly in her teeth; a pair of blazing guns filled her hands.

Jake quickly recovered from the shock of seeing her as the world exploded around him. Thick, acrid smoke filled the air. Bullets tore the sky and ricocheted through the camp. Annie fired at the Apache, while the knife-scarred outlaw—who was hot on Annie's trail—fired at Annie, and the Apache aimed at Jake.

Jake lunged for Santo's gun and joined the melee, sending a lump of hot lead into the knife-scarred outlaw's leg. He fired his remaining shots at the Apache and missed, too hampered by the smoke and confusion to be effective. His gun empty, he yelled for Annie and motioned her toward him. Then he rolled for cover, dodging bullets as he lodged himself behind a dense outcropping of boulders.

Annie spurred her little mare on and raced to join him behind the makeshift shelter. She leapt off Dulcie's back and crouched beside him. Wordlessly she passed him two unfamiliar cartridge belts—probably taken from the outlaw's horses—and a set of holsters and guns that Jake instantly recognized as his own. A temporary calm settled over the camp as the outlaws scurried to find cover.

Jake gave her a cursory once-over. "You hurt?"

"No. You?"

"No."

"What the hell are you doing back here? I thought I told you to ride."

She scowled up at him. "In the first place, you don't tell me what to do. In the second place, I'm not about to have your dead hide hanging over my clean conscience—not when things are finally starting to look good for me."

Jake's brows shot skyward. They had been robbed, cheated, left for dead, and shot at. "This is 'things finally starting to look good' for you?"

She shrugged. "More or less. Anyway, I had to come back." She glanced toward the blanket where their possessions lay scattered about. "I'm not leaving without that deed."

He directed his attention to the opposing cliff, watching the shadowy forms of the Apache and Scar Face as they positioned themselves for the fight. "I hope it's worth dying for."

Annie clicked open the circular chamber of her revolver and grabbed a handful of bullets. "If you're half as good with your gun as you are at flappin' your jaw, I won't have to find out, now, will I?"

A reluctant smile touched Jake's lips. "Now, there's gratitude for you, darlin'. After everything I did for you—"

"Dammit. The chamber's cracked."

Jake glanced at her gun and frowned. He offered her one of his own, fully loaded and ready to fire. "Can you shoot with a .38?"

"I can, but I won't hit anything. It's too big for my hand."

"A .32?"

"Better."

He passed her Santo's gun. She hefted it in her hand, testing the grip, then loaded the chamber. Apparently satisfied with the weapon, she tilted her head toward the outlaw camp. "You think you can cover me while I make a run for that blanket?" she asked.

"You can't be serious."

She tightened her lips in obstinate determination. "I ain't leaving without that deed. I'm going to make a run for it—with or without your help." She twisted up and peered over the top of their rocky shelter, scanning the distance to the blanket. "It's just a few measly feet—"

A well-placed rifle shot seared the air just inches above her ear.

She jerked back down, hitting the ground hard as she landed unceremoniously on her rear.

"Change your mind, darlin'?"

Annie sent him a withering glare, dusted off her clothing, and resumed her crouched position. She stewed in silence for a long moment, finally admitting in a small voice, "I reckon I could use your help, mister."

"Well, I'll be damned."

Her expression darkened, reflecting both embarrassment and mulish obstinacy. "You gonna help me or not?"

"You any good with that gun?" he parried.

"I usually hit what I'm aiming at."

Good enough, Jake thought, mulling over a plan. As near as he could tell, they had three immediate objectives: one, to secure their horses and belongings; two, to kill or wound the remaining outlaws before the outlaws got them; and three, to get away alive. Although he normally preferred subtlety in battle, this situation seemed to call for a direct frontal assault.

"You cover me, I'll go for the blanket," he said.

"Why you?"

"For one thing, I can run a hell of a lot faster than you can while someone's firing a gun at my head. Trust me, darlin', I've had plenty of experience in that area. For another, I need to get near that pen if I want to bust out Weed. We won't make it more than ten miles riding double on Dulcie." He turned and gestured across camp. "The Apache's over there at the base of those cliffs. Scar Face tucked himself away behind that pack of cottonwoods. He's got a slug of lead in his leg. With any luck, that'll take the edge off his aim. I'll move out on three. Any questions?"

Much to Jake's relief and amazement, Annie shook her head without further argument. "On three?"

"Three."

"One, two . . . three!" Jake shoved his hat down tight and leapt out from behind their shelter. Annie jerked to her feet, her gun blazing. A riot of bullets instantly tore up the ground around him, kicking up clouds of dust as the outlaws returned fire. Jake swerved and pivoted, moving in a precarious, zigzagging run as he dodged flashes of lead. He ducked low, and a well-placed bullet nearly tore off his right ear. *Shit!* he thought, jerking left. He had to be stupider than a greenhorn cowhand on his first Saturday night drunk to even *think* about trying this.

After what seemed an infinity, he reached the blanket that held their possessions. He dove for it, grabbed the corners, and rolled. He brought his gun into play at the same time, firing at the base of the cliff as he slid across the dirt. He heard a cry of pain and knew that by sheer luck he had hit his mark. Whether the hit had been disabling was another matter, but he didn't intend to stay around long enough to find out.

Moving from a roll to a crouch, Jake tossed the blanket over his back and broke into a dead run for the pen. He let out a sharp whistle for Weed, sending up a silent prayer of thanks that the outlaws had been too lazy to unsaddle him. He swung onto Weed's back and looped the makeshift blanket bag over the saddle horn. He leaned down low over the bay's neck and spurred toward Annie, relieved to see that she was saddled and ready to ride.

"Move!" he shouted.

She fired a few shots for cover, scattering the horses that had remained in the pen. Then she spurred Dulcie on, urging the mare into a thundering gallop.

The sound of a high-pitched, frightened meow rang shrilly through the air. Jake glanced over his shoulder, spotting a familiar bundle of white fur directly behind them.

He drew in a sharp breath, hoping Annie hadn't heard the cat. Even if she had, he reasoned, she wouldn't be fool enough to—

Annie drew Dulcie to an abrupt stop and whirled around.

"Dammit, Annie, you can't—"

She flew past him without a word, her face intent, her eyes panicked. Just as she bent over Dulcie's neck to pick up Cat, a shot cracked through the air. A shuddering jerk seemed to tear through her frame, and for one heart-stopping moment, it looked as though she'd been shot. But she didn't fall, nor did she stop. Moving with more grace than Jake would have believed possible, she leaned down low and scooped up Cat. Then she whirled around, spurring Dulcie toward him.

Jake dug his heels into Weed's flanks and let her take the lead, firing off a few warning shots behind them as they rode out.

They rode hard and fast, with nothing but silence between them, listening for the sound of men giving chase. The longer they went without hearing anything, the more Jake's mind was eased. Scar Face was wounded, and the Apache might have been hit as well. Even if they were able to give chase, it would take them at least an hour to round up their horses.

He glanced over at Annie. She rode stiffly, staring straight ahead, Cat clutched tightly in her grasp. Delayed shock, he suspected. "You all right?" he called.

Her face was pale when she turned to look at him, her expression drawn and tense. Her words, however, were vintage Annie. "You got my deed?"

Jake nodded. "I've got it."

Her mouth curved in a tight, satisfied smile. "Then I'm fine, mister. I'm just fine."

By mutual unspoken consent, they slowed their pace, moving from a flat-out run to an easy canter. As the hours passed, clouds gathered overhead and a soft, misty rain began to fall. A sudden chill filled the air, leaving them both cold and miserable. But at least the rain would help cover their tracks. They rode on in silence, wanting to put as much distance between themselves and the outlaw camp as they could before nightfall.

Jake soon began to feel every bruise and cut that the giant had left on his body. His muscles were aching, his bones felt brittle, and his skin stung as though it had been rubbed raw. Glancing over at Annie, he saw her face was tight and drawn as well, etched with lines of fatigue and strain.

He surveyed the horizon, looking for a place to stop. Finally he spotted a narrow stream that curved through a dense grove of pine. It was situated atop a mesa of rich red clay earth. The surrounding terrain sloped gently downward, giving them the advantage of miles of visibility. Not a bad spot to camp for the night. The ground beneath them was softly bedded with pine needles and looked every bit as inviting as a goose-down bed lined with satin sheets.

Jake glanced over at Annie. "You feel like resting for a bit?"

In answer, she wearily reined Dulcie to a firm stop.

Jake gratefully eased out of the saddle, biting back a groan as he did.

Beside him, Annie dropped Cat to the ground. The feline arched her back and stretched dramatically, then set out to explore their new camp. Jake watched without much interest as Cat poked about her new surroundings, then sat down to lick herself clean. The mud and dirt from Annie's clothing had rubbed off on Cat, he noted, eyeing the dark stain that coated the animal's fur. *The dark, reddish brown stain . . .*

His gaze shot back to Annie. She carefully slid off Dulcie's back, swaying for a moment as her feet hit the ground. She closed her eyes and grabbed her saddle horn for support.

Jake was at her side in two long strides. "Where is it?"

Annie didn't pretend to misunderstand. "My left side."

He put his hand to her waist, gently probing the wound, but drew back quickly at Annie's sharp gasp of pain. A thick smear of blood coated his palm. He jerked his gaze to hers, fighting back panic and anger. "Why the hell didn't you say something?"

"I figured it was just a scratch." Her lips twisted into a bleak smile. "Imagine that, mister," she said weakly, glancing down at her side. "I ain't never been shot before. Now I finally get on the right side of the law—" She stopped abruptly and swallowed hard. "I think I'm gonna be sick."

Jake wrapped his arm around her shoulders for support. "Easy now, darlin'. It's going to be all right. Everything's going to be just fine."

Annie didn't fight his touch as she usually did but leaned heavily against him instead, a fact that only served to heighten his alarm.

"Let's get you down somewhere so I can take a look at that," he said. He tucked his arm behind her knees and lifted her, feeling the hot, wet smear of her blood against his chest. Her head lolled limply against his shoulder as he carried her toward the grove of pine. A fine sheen of perspiration coated her skin. Her eyes were shut and her lips tightly clamped. Whether she was fighting back pain or nausea, or perhaps a bit of both, Jake couldn't tell.

He set her down, making her as comfortable as he could in the bed of pine. Then he stood and turned to go back to Weed. As he moved, he felt a soft tug at his boot. Jake looked down to see Annie's pale hand holding on to his ankle. She quickly released her grasp, as though embarrassed by the neediness of the gesture and resigned to its futility. She stared up at the sky, blinking hard, clearly fighting to get a rein on her emotions.

"I reckon you're just gonna ride off and leave me here," she said. Her voice was tinged with hard-edged acceptance and weary inevitability.

"No. I'm not going to do that."

Jake waited for her eyes to meet his. Once they did, he saw that her gaze was cloudy with pain and confusion, fear and mistrust. She obviously didn't believe him.

"I'm not leaving you, Annie," he said, schooling his voice to a tone of gentle reassurance. "There are some supplies in my bag that I need. I'll be right back."

He strode quickly to Weed and fumbled through saddlebags until he found his knife, a shirt he could rip apart to bind her wound, a canteen of water, and a flask of bourbon.

He returned to Annie, wrapped his arm beneath her shoulders, and eased her to a half-sitting position. He brought the flask to her mouth and carefully tipped it, swilling a generous portion of the contents down her throat. With any luck, it would be enough to knock her out.

Annie swallowed and coughed, then a shudder ran through her thin frame. "You trying to poison me?"

"That's fine Kentucky bourbon, darlin'. You keep it down, or I'll never forgive you for wasting my good liquor." Jake took a generous swig for himself, then set the flask aside.

Annie's eyes opened and locked on his face, watching his every move. He carefully cut open her clothing, gently prying it away from her wound. Knowing she was watching him, he feigned an expression of calm detachment. But what he saw sent his pulse rocketing and his heart pounding hard against his chest. Blood, and lots of it, staining her pale skin and dropping down her left side. Some of the blood had begun to clot, some of it was still flowing freely. He gently examined the wound with his fingers and found the thick, hard lump where the bullet had lodged beneath her skin.

Annie bit back a gasp of pain at his probing. Her eyes flew to his.

"The bullet is still inside," he said, answering her silent question.

"All right." She clenched her fists as she fought back another spasm of pain. "You reckon you can get it out, mister?" she asked hoarsely.

"I reckon so," he said, forcing a calm assurance into his voice.

"Good." She let out a shallow, bourbon-scented breath as a weak smile touched her lips. " 'Cause I ain't ready to die just yet."

Icy dread lodged tightly in Jake's gut. Panic gripped him, momentarily leaving him paralyzed. But night was quickly falling; best to get it over while there was still enough light to see by. He tilted the flask toward her. "You want another swig?"

Annie shook her head. Her eyes were frightened but disturbingly lucid.

Jake poured a generous stream of the bourbon over blade of his knife.

"That for luck?" she asked.

"I guess." During the War Between the States, he'd seen a few surgeons douse their instruments with alcohol before cutting open a body and then douse the wound itself once the operation was complete. For some reason, those patients seemed to fare better than others. Damned if he—or the doctors, for that matter—knew why.

Jake set the flask aside and wiped the sweat from his palms on his pants. No more stalling. He took a deep breath, bracing himself, then looked his patient straight in the eye.

"You don't have to be brave for me, darlin'. Go ahead and scream if you want."

He lifted the knife and touched the blade to her skin.

Annie ran as fast as she could, terrified. Catherine was ahead of her, but she was seven, three years older than Annie's age of four, and her long, skinny legs carried her much faster than Annie's short, pudgy ones. Mama was going to be furious. She'd warned them to stay away from that beehive, but the honeycomb Papa had brought home had tasted so sweet, they couldn't resist going back for more. Now the bees were everywhere, swarming all around her. She couldn't get away, no matter how fast she ran. They started biting her, driving their sharp, pointed stingers into her side. Her left side . . .

Annie was hot; very, very hot. Mama and Papa and

Catherine were gone. She was in her bedroom in the old, run-down farmhouse by the creek. Doc Mundy was taking care of her. She could hear the low, steady drone of his voice as he murmured soothing words to her. His big, gentle hands brushed lightly against her skin as he rubbed a cool, damp cloth over her body. She would be all right now. Doc Mundy and his wife were good folks, kind and gentle. They were too soft though, especially on their boy, Pete. But she couldn't tell the Mundys that. He was their son, their real kin, not Annie.

Now the Doc and his wife were gone. Pete and the boys were carousing in town, leaving her alone in the cabin in the woods. Except she wasn't alone. Snakeskin Garvey was there. Annie tried to run for the door, but he caught her wrist before she made it. He threw her down on the bed, smothering her with his body. She couldn't breathe, she couldn't move. She watched herself from a distance, frozen in her helplessness and her terror, unable to run or scream. If she could just get to her guns . . .

Annie jerked awake with a start.

Her mouth was dry, her heart pounded in her chest. She instinctively groped for a weapon, then she stopped short, frightened and disoriented. She had no idea where she was or how she had come to be there. All she knew was that she was lying in a grove of pine, a bed of soft, fragrant needles beneath her, and a thick stack of blankets covering her. A small pile of ashes smoldered a few feet away, the remains of what looked to have once been a rather decent fire.

Annie drew herself up to a sitting position. A sharp, blistering pain filled her left side. She sucked in a deep breath and held it, exhaling slowly as the burning ache gradually eased to a dull throb. As she glanced down at her side, her memory came back in a rush. She'd been shot by those no-good, thieving bandits. She searched her mind for more details as to what had followed, but that was the last thing she could remember.

Well, at least one thing was clear: She was all alone now. A deep, woodsy silence enveloped her, and there was no sign of another human for miles. At least that fancy-pants gambler had doctored her up a bit before he'd hightailed it out of there, she thought. Her wound was clean and tightly bound—sore but manageable. She was outfitted in one of her old flannel shirts, loose and big enough to be worn as a nightshirt. Jake must have dressed her before he left. The thought of him seeing her body—of him actually touching her, running his big hands over her bare skin—sent a shiver down Annie's spine. Oddly enough, though, it wasn't entirely a shiver of revulsion. She felt anxious and abashed that he'd seen her like that, yes, but not repulsed.

Annie shook off the thought. By running out on her, at least he had spared her the embarrassment of ever seeing him again. But embarrassment quickly gave way to concern as she glanced around, realizing that he'd made off with everything she owned. Including her horse, her guns, and her deed, she thought in alarm. *Damn him.* The full weight of exactly how vulnerable she was hit home as a threatening rustle filled the scrub brush a few yards from her makeshift bed.

It could be those thieving outlaws, trailing after her for revenge. Or maybe a wolf, half starved and crazy. Or maybe—

Jake Moran stepped through the brush, a load of firewood stacked high in his arms and three freshly killed and tightly bound rabbits tossed over his shoulder. Cat bounded along behind him, hissing and swatting at Jake's ankles as he walked. Relief swelled within her at the sight of them both. So he hadn't abandoned her after all.

He glanced in her direction, then drew to an abrupt

stop, surprise clearly etched on his features. "You're awake."

"Appears so."

He continued toward her, pausing only long enough to set down the wood and the rabbits. Cat bounded toward her and leapt into her lap. Annie winced at the sudden motion, then automatically began to stroke the animal's fur. Cat ran her long, crooked tail beneath Annie's chin, then curled up into a tight ball, emitting a rough, gravelly purr of satisfaction.

Jake watched them both for a moment, then hunkered down beside her, resting his weight on his heels as he intently scanned her face. "How do you feel?" he asked.

"Fine," she answered automatically. She glanced down at Cat, feeling more vulnerable than she ever had in her life. A score of emotions fluttered through her, all too confusing to name.

Never before had Annie felt the way she did at that moment. Jake's presence was inescapable, almost overpowering. His attention was too focused on her, his expression too intimate. She saw none of the haughtiness, the boredom, or the restlessness she had read in his face before. Instead he seemed genuinely concerned. No matter where she looked, she couldn't get away from the odd, indefinable light that filled his silvery-blue eyes. Her stomach swarmed with butterflies and she felt horribly exposed. She was awkwardly conscious of her hands, her hair, her clothing—none of which seemed to be in the right place, or looking as it should.

The moment stretched endlessly between them. Annie was aware that nothing was showing, that her shirt was properly fastened up to her throat, and that her blanket was tucked around her waist and securely covering her legs. But Jake had seen her naked, and that realization seemed to hang in the air between them. Maybe that was what had her so riled up.

Not that she entirely blamed herself for her moment of weakness. Jake was dressed in black pants, snugly fitted to encase his long legs, and a pale-blue shirt that brought out the icy glow in his eyes. The man was simply too virile, too potent, and too damned good-looking to be ignored. Especially when he was sitting so close to her. She shook off the thought, mentally squirming against the intimacy that suddenly weighed so heavily between them.

She forced herself to meet his gaze, truly studying his face for the first time since she had awakened. Upon closer inspection, she noticed a faint, subtle swelling around his jaw and cheekbones, and a scar above his right eye. She glanced at his knuckles and saw that they were raw and bruised as well.

Annie shook her head, letting out a soft whistle. "You look like twenty miles of bad road, mister. I warned you not to go up against that *hombre*."

A slow, easy grin softened Jake's expression of concern. He lifted his hand and placed it palm down against her forehead. "Your fever's broken," he said after a moment.

She swatted away his hand, rebuking the tender act of solicitude. "I suppose you think I owe you now that you doctored me up, don't you?"

He shrugged, his expression unreadable. "You don't owe me a thing, darlin'."

"The way I see it, we're even. I pulled your chestnuts out of the fire, didn't I?"

"Whatever you say."

Annie looked away, uncomfortably aware how churlish and ungrateful she sounded. But she didn't know how to stop herself. There seemed to be only two ways to deal with Jake Moran. She either allowed herself to be drawn toward him, ensnared in his silky web like an unsuspecting fly, or she ran as fast as she could in the opposite direction. If there was a middle ground with him, she sure as hell hadn't found it.

"You gonna see to those rabbits," she asked, "or are you just waiting for the skin to fall off by itself?"

"I take it that means you're hungry?"

"I haven't eaten since yesterday morning."

He rose to his feet and moved to the fire, piling dry twigs on the smoldering embers. "You haven't eaten for three days," he corrected. "That's how long you've been sick."

"Three days?" she echoed in disbelief.

Jake nodded. "The wound wasn't too bad. The bullet lodged just beneath the skin. It came out pretty clean, but you lost a lot of blood."

Annie took that all in. *Three days.* He'd stayed with her and cared for her for three days. She didn't recall any of it. She vaguely remembered dreaming that Doc Mundy had been with her. Thinking that it had been Doc's low, soothing voice gently murmuring in her ear; that it had been Doc's hands touching her body with a cool, soft cloth. Had that been Jake all along, or just a fevered dream? She could ask him, of course, but that would open the conversation to too many other mortifying questions. Better to just let it pass.

In any case, the question she truly wanted answered was why he had stayed with her. Her eyes narrowed as she studied him intently. "Why'd you stick around, mister? You could have taken off with my horse, my deed, my money, and just left me here, but you didn't. Why? Most men I know would have taken everything they could and run."

He held her gaze for a long, steady minute. "Maybe you know the wrong men." He shifted his attention to the fire and slowly stoked the flame. "Then again, maybe I'm just different."

She greeted his statement with a healthy dose of skepticism. "Every dog has fleas."

"Well, now, darlin', that's a fine way to thank me."

He shook his head, clearly more amused than offended. Satisfied with the fire, he lifted one of the rabbits and began skinning their dinner. His long, capable fingers moved with quick, clean strokes as he deftly executed the chore. That finished, he skewered the rabbits and held them over the fire.

Realizing it would be fruitless to pursue the subject further, she turned and scanned the horizon. "Any sign of them bandits?"

Jake glanced up, then shook his head. "Nope."

His hesitation had been slight, but Annie had heard it. Her brows snapped together. "You have any trouble, mister?"

"Nothing that I can't handle," he answered vaguely. "You want to wash up before dinner?"

Annie would have argued further, but she just didn't have it in her. After three days of being ill, she felt bone weary, stiff, and sore. She set Cat aside and rose to her feet. Her fatigue must have shown on her face, for Jake was instantly at her side, supporting her arm as she stood.

"Easy now. It might take you a day or two until you get your legs back."

His breath was a featherlike whisper that tickled her ear, all spicy and soft. She felt the rough fabric of his pants brush against her thigh and realized with a start that she was standing next to him without her britches. The realization jerked her back to her senses. Confident that she had gained enough of her balance to stand on her own, she moved away from him.

"Better let me check that bandage for you," he said.

She shook her head. "It's fine. I feel just fine."

He smiled in that slow, lazy way of his. "What are you afraid of, darlin'?"

You, she thought. Specifically the idea of him brushing his large, rugged hands over her skin. But she'd sooner kiss a grizzly on the lips than admit it. "I appreciate what you done for me, mister, but I can take care of myself from here on out." That said, she instantly felt better. She glanced around the campsite for her belongings. "You hide my bag somewhere?"

He pointed to a path that led down a gently sloping hill. "You'll find everything you need down by the creek at the base of that hill. Dulcie and Weed are tethered there as well." He watched her, frowning as she moved unsteadily away from him. "You want me to help you?"

"I can walk just fine," she answered. "Next thing you know, you'll be wanting to bathe me."

Jake crossed his arms over his chest, eyeing her consideringly. His lips curved into a devilish smile that made his ice-blue eyes shimmer with seductive fire. "Only if you insist, darlin'."

An unsteadiness that had nothing to do with her wound spread through her limbs. She tilted her chin and turned away, trying her best to make a dignified exit. *Bathe me, indeed,* she swore silently to herself. *Keep it up, Annie girl, and he's gonna think you suggested it on purpose.*

Which she absolutely, positively, did not.

Definitely not.

It was impossible to even consider.

Just because the man had eyes that were deeper and more mysterious than any sea, a smile so smooth he could lure the devil himself into church on Sunday, a chest so broad you could fit a map of Texas on it, and tighter hindquarters than a range-ridden stallion—

Annie? she said to herself.

What?

Shut up!

Chapter 7

Jake sat with a fallen log at his back, a whiskey bottle between his legs, and a deck of cards in his hand. Normally he would have been eager to move on, but he deliberately slowed the pace for Annie. A week had passed since she had been shot. She had been unconscious for three days, followed by four days for her to rest and recuperate. Although by all appearances her wound was healing nicely, he didn't want to push her. Too much strain or activity and her side might just open up again.

He was also waiting for a break in the weather. A hazy mist shrouded the trees, enveloping everything in a thick, damp fog. The weather had been like that for days, and the unrelenting dampness was beginning to grate on his nerves. He had hung a few blankets in the branches of the trees above them for shelter, and a low fire was burning, but the effect was still drearily oppressive. A restless inertia settled over him like the fog, leaving him listless and bored.

He glanced across their camp. Annie sat just a few yards away, a book in her hands and Cat in her lap. Judging by her expression, she was growing restless as well. As he watched, Cat peeked out from beneath the folds of Annie's coat. The persnickety feline wrinkled her nose in distaste at the inclement weather and issued an ill-humored hiss at the world in general. She arched her back and stood, her crooked tail cocked haughtily in the air as she trotted off into the woods. Annie watched her go, then surprised Jake by moving to sit across from him. For the most part, they'd spent the past couple of days keeping to themselves. Now he welcomed the distraction of her company, and she was apparently of the same mind.

"How are you feeling?" he asked.

She shrugged her shoulders. "Bored, mostly. Edgy."

Whatever her faults, the woman wasn't one for beating around the bush. "I meant, how's your side?" he clarified. She'd refused to let him check the wound since she had regained consciousness.

"Oh. Feels like a bee sting, that's all."

"Any swelling? Discoloration?"

She shook her head.

"Good. In that case, if you're ready, we'll leave tomorrow morning."

"Fine." She studied him in silence, her brows drawn together in obvious disapproval.

"What?" he said.

"You drink too much."

Jake let out a mournful sigh. "Spare me your lecture on the evils of spirits, will you?"

"I was just stating a plain fact. No need to get so testy."

He brought the bottle to his lips, taking another swig. "All right, then, what do you suggest we do in such God-awful weather?"

"I don't know. I reckon we could just talk to each other."

He arched one dark brow. "What a novel idea."

She frowned. "Were you born talking fancy, mister?"

"I was born, darlin', in a one-room shack in a town that settled itself on a swamp off the banks of the Mississippi and lacked the common sense to move."

"You didn't come from some rich, highfalutin family?" she asked, clearly surprised.

"I'm afraid not."

"Well, I'll be damned." Annie studied him again, as though seeing him in a new light. "What were they like? Your folks, I mean."

Jake shrugged, feeling expansive on the whiskey. He wasn't drunk, he just had a good, warm glow. "My father was a big, brawling riverboat captain who ferried freight along the Mississippi. He taught me to fight, he taught me to drink, and when I was thirteen, he introduced me to my first whore."

Unlike most women, Annie didn't pretend to be shocked. "What about your mother?" she asked.

"She was Cajun," he answered. He twisted the whiskey bottle absently between his palms, losing himself for a moment in his memories. "She was a hot-tempered beauty from an even poorer family than my father's, but she had higher aspirations. She wanted to be accepted by society, and she did everything she could to make that happen. We weren't anything but a bunch of lowly river rats, but with her coaching, a little polish, manners, and the right clothing, we actually passed for a respectable household. Truth is, darlin', people see what you want them to see; rarely do they look beyond the immediate facade."

Annie's eyes flashed with sudden interest. "You think I could do that?"

"Do what?"

"Turn myself around, like you did. Put on airs and make myself some grand, fancy-talking lady. Maybe gussy up real fine in one of them swooshy-skirted dresses, put one of them bird's-nest hats on my head, and carry one of them fancy little lace umbrellas."

"Parasols."

She ignored the correction. "What do you think?" she pressed. "Could someone like me do that too?"

Jake shrugged. It sounded like a complete waste of time to him, but maybe the desire to dress up and play the part of a grand society dame was a universal urge in all women. "Why the sudden craving to fit into high society?"

"It ain't sudden at all," Annie corrected. "If I'm gonna be the new owner of the Palace Hotel, I got to know what's proper and what ain't." She pulled the familiar careworn advertising circular from within her coat pocket and waved it in his direction. "See here? This says the hotel is available exclusively for the use of distinguished ladies and gentlemen. *Distinguished,* it says. The finest resort in the West, it says. I bet they got those crystal chandeliers, fancy paintings, thick carpets, china dishes, velvet drapes on all the windows, four-poster beds with feather mattresses, and the like. Since I'm the new owner, I reckon I got to be as snooty and my manners as highfalutin as the folks that'll be staying there."

"I see you've given it some thought," Jake replied, eyeing her consideringly. Not only was that the most the woman had ever said in one breath, but she appeared to mean every word.

"I've been studying up on it too," she continued proudly. She lifted the slim leather-bound volume she had been reading, allowing him a view of the rich gilt cover. *Winston's Guide to Proper Etiquette and Deportment for Refined Young Ladies of All Ages.*

He nodded, recognizing the book. "You enjoying it?"

Annie made a face. "Not enjoying it exactly, but at least I'm learning the rules."

"The rules?"

"High-society rules. I had no idea there were so many." She opened the book and read aloud, "'A proper lady never speaks to a gentleman to whom she has not been introduced. A proper lady never finishes everything on her plate. A proper lady never laughs too loud or offers an opinion on anything other than sewing or child rearing, even when asked. A proper lady never accepts money from a gentleman under any circumstances. A proper lady never, *ever* mentions her unmentionables.'"

Annie let out an impatient breath and set down the book. "What exactly *is* an unmentionable? And if it's so damned unmentionable, why the hell does he keep mentioning it?"

Jake bit back a smile. "I believe he's referring to a lady's undergarments."

"So if your drawers bunch up too tight or get baggy and start slipping around your ankles, it's better not to mention it?"

"Generally one attempts to refrain from embarking on discussions of that nature."

"Oh." Annie thought for a moment. "Fact is, I might be able to go along with some of his rules if he just explained them a bit. But the way I see it, there's way too much this Winston fella didn't take into account."

"Like what?"

"Well, what if the gentleman tries to steal the lady's horse? You better believe I'm gonna have a few words to say to him—whether we've been properly introduced or not. And if I'm paying my hard-earned money to buy myself some fancy restaurant meal, why the hell shouldn't I eat every bite? What's so proper and refined about wasting good food? And if someone *asks* my opinion, I reckon they want to hear it, don't you, else why would they ask? And what if a gentleman owes a lady money after a poker game, then it's all right to take it, isn't it? Which rules do you reckon oughta come first, the etiquette rules or the poker rules?"

"Maybe this Winston fella lost a lot of money to women in poker games."

Annie immediately brightened. "I hadn't thought of that."

He nodded somberly, managing to keep a straight face. "What other little pearls of wisdom have you gleaned from that book?"

"How to talk as fancy as you do, for one thing." She threw back her shoulders and took a deep breath. In a voice as stilted and forced as that of a child reciting lines in a play, she said: "I have always depended upon the patience and tolerance of those wiser than me for guidance."

"You can't be serious."

She glanced up at him in surprise. "It says here that that's a—" She paused, scanned the page, and read aloud, "'. . . a very proper phrase for a woman, useful in any number of circumstances.' "

"May I?" he asked, reaching for the book. He flipped randomly through the pages and passed it back to her, having reached two conclusions. First that *Winston's Guide* was good for producing nothing but a bunch of nervous, empty-headed females who would know how to set a proper table and stitch a hem a hell of a lot better than they would know what to do with their husbands on their wedding night. And second that Winston himself was a misogynistic, pompous ass.

"That's some book, darlin'," he said, passing it back. "You have all those rules memorized now?"

"Hell, no."

He grinned, wondering which choice words Annie would air once she reached the chapter that prohibited women from swearing.

She studied the book with a petulant frown, then brought up her chin, her eyes shining with obstinate defiance. "I reckon these fancy manners are fine in some parts, but as far as I'm concerned, there's just one rule that any woman needs out West."

"What's that?"

"Shoot first and ask questions later." She arched one dark-blond brow, an impish smile curving her lips. "What do you think ol' Winston would have to say about that?"

Jake matched her smile. "I think he'd have an attack of the vapors and faint dead away."

"Me too."

Laughter bubbled from Annie's lips, as light and fluid as water streaming over rocks in the clear morning sunshine. Jake listened, smiling. The sound of it was deeply satisfying, as though Annabel Lee Foster's laughter were something he had been waiting his entire lifetime to hear.

In the ensuing silence, Annie tilted back her head and studied the sky, as though searching for signs that the light rain would soon ebb. Watching her in that unguarded moment, Jake was once again struck by the beauty of her features. Perhaps it was just the grayness of the day that heightened the rich highlights in her hair, but at that moment, Annie's pale-brown tresses seemed to shine with streaks of pure flaxen gold. A soft mist coated her skin, giving it a fresh, dewy appearance. Steady determination filled her eyes, which today appeared more brown than gold or green. Her brows were a dark blond and delicately arched. Her eyelashes were of the same dark hue, except for the very tips, which were flecked with gold. Her mouth was wide and generous, her lips the delectable pink of a ripe summer melon. Perhaps the only flaw in her face was her chin. It seemed too strong and square for most woman, but it somehow suited her.

Hers wasn't the kind of beauty that hit a man straight on, he realized. Annie's beauty was subtle, more elusive. It revealed itself in different lights and with different expressions. She wasn't the brassy, showy type that a man would notice right off in a crowd, but once he did notice her, he might not be able to take his eyes away. Annabel Lee Foster had the kind of look that drew a man in and kept him there.

He studied her for a moment. "Annabel Lee. Is that your real name?"

She nodded. "It's after a lady in a famous poem. My mama used to read it to me when I was a little girl."

Jake took a swig of whiskey and recited in a deep baritone, rich with equal amounts of alcohol and melodrama, "It was many and many a year ago, in a kingdom by the sea, that there a maiden lived whom you may know by the name of Annabel Lee; and this maiden she lived with no other thought than to love and be loved by me."

Annie stared at him in astonishment. "You know the poem?"

"Edgar Allan Poe. One of the South's finest poets." He lifted his bottle and smiled. "And finest drunks."

"I'd like to be her."

"Who?"

"The lady in the poem."

"She dies."

"I wouldn't mind. Not if I could be loved the way she was loved." She glanced away, clearly embarrassed. "That sounds plum crazy, doesn't it?"

He shrugged. "There are worse things to die for."

"It won't happen, though."

"You won't die?"

"No, the love part."

"Really?" he drawled, studying her curiously. "Why not?"

"I know what menfolk want in a woman, and it ain't me."

"You're beautiful, Annie."

She immediately waved that away. "No, I'm not. I ain't all peachy and soft, the way a man wants a woman to be. And even if I were, that wouldn't matter none. Men want more than just someone pretty to look at. They want someone who's upstanding and obedient, delicate and good. Someone who goes to church regularlike and can raise proper children. Someone who ain't like me."

"So you're turning your life around," he said with a

glimmer of understanding. "You want to be a good woman now."

"Not good, just respectable. I reckon the way I've lived, there ain't a chance in hell of me ever being good." She paused, lifting her shoulders in a light shrug. "Maybe it's just as well. I'd rather be strong than good anyway. I've seen too many good people get knocked flat by this life."

"The meek shall inherit the earth."

"What's left of it," she immediately countered. She hooked her arms around her legs and rested her chin atop her knees. A deep, contemplative expression filled her face. "No, that ain't for me. I'm not the type to wait around and let other folks tell me what I can and can't have. Seems to me that each of us has a responsibility to make our own destiny, to turn our lives into whatever we want."

He looked at her, aghast. "Is life really that simple to you?"

"Of course." She studied his face, surprised at his reaction. "Isn't it to you?"

"No."

Jake looked away, absently staring into the dismal gray horizon. All he knew was what he had seen. Luck either ran for you or it didn't. It wasn't a world of justice or goodwill, a world where the bad were punished and the innocent were loved, cherished, and protected. It was a world of random, utter chance. Anything could happen to anybody, anytime.

"How old are you, mister?" she asked.

"Twenty-nine." He studied her face for a moment in silence. "How old are you?"

"Twenty-two."

"You look younger."

"I feel older."

Jake smiled and took another swig of whiskey. "Don't we all, darlin'. Don't we all."

Annie shifted as a lull fell over their conversation. Cat chose that moment to return from the woods. She pranced up and eyed Jake with that single cocked brow of hers, coolly expressing her feline disdain. She didn't hiss at him as she usually did but simply lifted her lip in a silent snarl, then settled herself on Annie's lap.

"I think she's beginning to like you," Annie suggested, rewarding Cat's ill-tempered behavior by kissing her between her bent ears and gently dragging her fingers through the animal's knotted fur.

Jake disdainfully eyed the shaggy beast. "You can't imagine how delighted I am to hear that."

"It's not you personally—she just don't like men in general."

He let that questionable bit of news pass without comment.

Wisely choosing to abandon that line of conversation, Annie glanced down at the cards he had been dealing when she first approached and, receiving his silent nod of assent, flipped over the hand that lay nearest to her. Four kings and a deuce.

He grinned and arched a dark brow. "Care to make a wager?"

She eyed him suspiciously, then reached for his cards and turned them over. Four aces and an eight. A reproachful frown touched her lips. "I thought you said you didn't cheat."

"That's not cheating, darlin', that's just a little parlor trick. Helps keep me in practice."

In truth, Jake wasn't practicing at all but simply idling away the time. He was as familiar with the feel of a deck of cards in his hands as he was with the feel of the ground beneath his boots. He could tell by the weight of a deck if a card was missing, trimmed, or padded. If a deck was marked, he felt it instantly. His fingers moved automatically to any slightly raised bumps in the center of a card, or pinholes at the edge. He needed none of the

mechanical holdouts, sleeve grips, or bulky devices re-
lied upon by other gamblers. Jake played strictly by instinct. He had a keenness not only for the feel of the deck
but for those around him. He could tell who was bluffing
and when, who was holding back, who held a good hand
and who held nothing.

"You think you can do it again? With me watching?"
Annie challenged.

"I'll try." Jake scooped up the deck and shuffled. The
cards flew through his hands with the whisper of silk,
slapping, parting, sliding in and out, rolling through his
fingers, then coming back together again. He shuffled the
cards slowly, moving at a relaxed, rhythmic pace, then
more quickly, then slowly again. His fingers sorted and
adjusted the deck, until everything fell into just the right
order. "What would you like?" he asked politely.

She thought for a moment, her expression highly
skeptical. "A straight. Ace high."

He offered her the deck. She split it and passed it
back. He performed an easy, one-handed shuffle, then
dealt the cards and set the pack facedown between them.

Annie eagerly picked up her hand. She slapped it
down seconds later with a triumphant smile. She held a
three of spades, followed by a ten, jack, queen, and king
of hearts. "Ha! You missed. I didn't get my ace."

Jake merely cocked one brow. "You planning on
keeping that three? Most folks would discard."

Her gaze moved to the pile of cards that sat between
them. Surprise flashed through her eyes, followed by total disbelief. She reached for the deck and turned over the
top card: a shiny red ace of hearts winked up at her.

An appreciative smile curved her lips as she folded
her cards and passed them back to him. "Is that why you
gamble, mister? Because you're good at it?"

"I suppose." Jake thought for a moment, then
shrugged. "Fact is, there are few things in this life that I
do well. I know how to gamble, I know how to kill, and I

know how to drink. Sins all, but of the three, it seems to me the least shameful way for me to make my living is with cards."

"You like the life?"

"Well enough."

He liked the tension, the uncertainty, the risk. He liked the smoky allure of the saloon, the rowdiness of the mining camps, the sheer bawdiness of the cathouses. Before the War Between the States, he'd plied his trade in elegant floating gambling parlors, listening to the gentle *slish-slosh* of paddle wheelers as they slowly cruised up and down the Mississippi. After the war, he'd played cards to the frantic *clickety-clack* of the steam trains that carried him out to the territories. East or West, it was all the same to him.

"It suits you," Annie announced after a minute. "You ain't the settling-down type, mister."

He smiled. "Is that a fact?" he said, but he didn't argue.

It wasn't that Jake didn't enjoy women. He adored them. A world without them would be a very barren place indeed. He loved the softness of their skin, the gentleness of their touch, their lilting laughter, their flirtatious glances, and their seductively swaying walk. But the women he loved best were the ones who understood the rules of the game. The ones with sophistication, experience, and a strong sensual appetite. The ones who contented themselves after lovemaking with new gowns and diamond trinkets rather than promises of undying love and eternal devotion. Those were promises he had never given and doubted he ever would give.

What it all came down to, Jake thought, was a matter of trade-offs. As far as he was concerned, one of the most appealing things about women was their infinite variety. He had yet to meet a woman who merited forfeiting his freedom in return for the rather dubious reward of domestic bliss. Something about the whole concept of marriage seemed eerily unnatural to him. Rather like watching a trained bear—attired in a pointy hat and matching skirt—get up on its hind legs and dance.

"So what type am I?" he asked.

Annie frowned as she studied him. "The moving-on type. The smooth-talking, fancy-pants type. You use your charm the way a crooked sheriff uses his badge, flashing it to get whatever you want. You snap your fingers and get women, whiskey, money. It's all just a game to you."

Jake arched one dark brow. "Why does that sound suspiciously like an insult?"

She shook her head. "Just a fact, that's all. Folks are different, I guess," she said with a wistful sigh. "Now, me, I ain't much of a gambler. I only gambled one time, with that was with that skunk J. D. Thomas."

"Who's J. D. Thomas?"

"The fella who used to own the Palace Hotel."

"What happened?"

She shrugged. "I went into town one day for supplies, and this Thomas fella recognized me. He started talking real loud, saying as how there wasn't a woman born who could outshoot him. Said there was just one thing a woman was good for, and that firing a gun wasn't it." Annie wrinkled her nose in distaste and looked up at Jake. "You know the kind, mister. Big fella, loud and mean. Jackass brains and a face so ugly it'd scare the skin off a snake. *Más feo que el pecado.*"

Uglier than sin. Jake nodded. He knew the type.

"Normally," she continued, "I'd have let it go. But this J. D. Thomas got me plum riled up. You see, there were other women in the store at the time—real ladies, I mean, not like me. Anyhow, they were getting kinda upset by his talk too. The men there were too scared to interfere, so I figured I oughta take the fella down a peg or two by myself. I told him he could either shut his trap or show everybody just how good he was with his gun."

"What happened?"

"Oh, he started swelling up, got even louder, more cocksure of himself. Said why didn't we make a wager out of it? Nothing fancy, just a regular shooting match: The first one to knock five tin cans off a wall would win. He bet me his deed to the Palace Hotel against my saddle, guns, and Dulcie."

"I take it you didn't have any trouble," Jake surmised.

Annie made a sound of disgust. "The only thing that fella was good at shooting off was his mouth."

He studied her in new understanding. "So that's how Outlaw Annie became the proud owner of the Palace Hotel."

"More or less," she answered. "J. D. Thomas was pretty upset after he lost. He claimed I cheated him and stole away his hotel. But there were too many folks who saw what happened to pay him any mind. I rode out of town with the deed free and clear. He came after me that night to try to steal it back, just like I figured he would. I possumed sleep and let him get real close, then I put a hole through his britches—just to let him know that tin cans ain't the only thing I'm good at shooting. He hightailed it out of there real fast."

Several things struck Jake about her story. First there was the steady nonchalance with which Annie had faced down a potentially deadly killer—not just once but twice. Then there was the fact that that very same man, the crude and belligerent J. D. Thomas, was the owner of the palatial Palace Hotel. Thomas sounded like the kind of man who would run a hard-drinking, fist-brawling saloon, not a glamorous resort. And finally Jake found himself reluctantly touched by the matter-of-factness with which Annie had breezily excluded herself from the category of "real lady"—despite her straightforward and seemingly earnest aspirations to the title.

But above all, Jake's curiosity was piqued. In his

estimation, Thomas had been an idiot to risk his hotel when Annie's skills with a gun were legendary. But exactly how fine a shot was she? Were the rumors that surrounded her pure fiction, or was she as good as people said?

"I heard you could shoot an acorn off a tree limb at forty paces," he said, "standing backward, with your rifle slung over your shoulder."

She shrugged. "That's nothing."

"Can you show me?"

"I ain't practiced it in ages."

"I see," he said slowly. "So you can't really do it."

Annie rose immediately to the challenge. "What do you want to lose, Mr. Fancy-Pants?"

Jake smiled. "Loser cooks and cleans up supper tonight."

She nodded in agreement and stood. "I need a rifle and a tin plate."

He passed her his own rifle, watching as she hefted it in her hands. It was probably a little heavy for her; she most likely preferred a lighter, slimmer carbine. She fired a few shots into the brush, testing the weapon for its weight, balance, and kick. No rifle fired exactly straight, but his was pretty close.

Satisfied, she then turned and scouted their surroundings, finally pointing toward an old oak tree. The tree was ablaze with brilliant fall foliage, with the exception of one stark branch from which the leaves had already fallen. A tiny cluster of acorns hung from the end of the limb. She studied the cluster, as though fixing it in her mind, then turned and marched the requisite forty paces away from the tree. She slung the rifle over her right shoulder, lifted the tin place in her left hand, and squinted into it.

Jake watched her, highly skeptical. He considered himself a fair shot with a rifle, but what she was attempting was impossible, no matter how good the marksman.

Annie took a deep breath and fired.

The acorn cluster snapped off the tree.

She turned and looked at the branch, then swung her gaze to his, her expression smug.

Jake shook his head. "Not bad."

"That's just one of the tricks Diego taught me." She shrugged nonchalantly and set down the rifle. "He's the one who taught me to speak Spanish too, but I never quite got the hang of it. At least not like the way I took to shooting."

That had to be Diego Martinez, Jake thought, mentally reviewing the men who had ridden with the Mundy Gang. But before he had a chance to ask her more about the gang, Annie turned and studied the shallow valley beneath them, her gaze moving restlessly across the horizon.

"Dumb of us to fire a weapon and call attention to ourselves," she said. "You reckon he's still out there?"

Jake hid his surprise. Although he knew they were being trailed, until that moment, he'd had no idea that Annie was aware of it as well. He had first noted the man following them shortly after Annie had been shot. Jake had originally thought it had been one of the bandits they had tracked, coming after them for vengeance. After doctoring Annie, he had ridden down the mesa and back across a range of deep arroyos, attempting to circle around and surprise the man from behind. But whoever the stranger was, he had obviously seen Jake coming. Jake had found nothing but the still-warm ashes of the man's fire. Nor had any of his later attempts to confront the man met with success; the stranger had eluded detection each and every time Jake had tried to corner him.

Returning his attention to Annie's question, he scanned the horizon, but the rain dulled his vision. Shapes and shadows blended in the thick gray mist, twisting and merging. "Could be he's still out there," he replied noncommittally, "could be he veered off and headed someplace else.'

A brief, cynical smile touched Annie's lips. "You believe that, mister?"

"No, but I thought you might."

Annie let out a disdainful breath, then turned and frowned into the distance. "What do you suppose he's after?" she asked after a minute.

"You."

Clearly taken aback by his answer, she swung her gaze around to meet his. "What makes you say that?"

Jake lifted his shoulders in a cool shrug. "If he were one of the *hombres* who stole our horses and gear, he would have made his move by now," he replied. "Instead he's just trailing us—hanging back too far for me to get close to him but close enough to let us know he's there."

"So? That doesn't tell us anything."

"He wants to be seen," Jake countered. "He wants us to know he's there—or rather, to let you know he's there. He hasn't let me get anywhere near him, but odds are he'd let you. That is, if you wanted to."

Her brows snapped together. "What's that supposed to mean?"

"Means I think he's a friend of yours."

"I don't have any friends."

"That so? What do you call the boys in the Mundy Gang?"

Annie tilted her chin, eyeing him coolly. "Dead."

Jake nodded and remained silent, unaccountably disappointed. Up until that point, he had been enjoying her honesty and her frankness. But now he was certain she was lying. He had been on the trail of the Mundy Gang for months and knew their movements as well as any law officer in the territory. If they were dead, he would have heard about it. Obviously Annie was still protecting them. Her loyalty might have been commendable at another time, but not now. Not when it was his neck that was about to be stretched.

He reached into his coat pocket and withdrew the makings for a cigarette. He spilled the tobacco onto a thin square of parchment, rolled it tightly, and licked the paper shut. Scraping a sulfur match against his boot heel, he raised the flame to his mouth, lit the cigarette, and inhaled deeply. A warm stream of smoke curled into his lungs. The taste of tobacco clung to his lips, bitter and sweet at the same time.

Annie watched him in silence. "Maybe it's you that he's tracking," she speculated slowly. "How do I know you ain't a wanted man?"

Jake arched a dark brow. "Would Sheriff Cayne have sent you off with a wanted man?"

She frowned but seemed to accept that reasoning, despite the expression of skeptical distrust that remained etched on her features.

In truth, Jake had initially considered the possibility that the man trailing them was after him. It had been three months since Harlan Becker had been killed in an alleyway in Gunpowder Falls. Plenty of time for the sheriff to print up wanted posters with Jake's name and likeness on them and spread them around town. Plenty of time for a bounty hunter to be on his trail. But a bounty hunter would already have made his move. And he certainly wouldn't shadow Jake in plain sight—why give up the element of surprise unless absolutely necessary?"

"Could be it's some fool who thinks I'll lead him to the money from that stagecoach robbery," Annie suggested.

"Could be," Jake agreed, somewhat surprised she was so forthright about it. "You know where that money is?" he asked.

She shook her head. "I could guess, that's all. The boys had a few spots they liked to hide money away until things cooled down. It might be in one of those spots, might not be. There's no telling."

"For twenty-five thousand, it might be worth looking."

Annie stared him straight in the eye. "That's blood money, mister, and I don't want any part of it. I can't change things that happened in the past, but I can go forward, and that's what I aim to do."

"I'm glad to hear it," Jake answered noncommittally.

He turned and studied the horizon. If Outlaw Annie thought she could walk away from the gang clean, she was obviously mistaken. Someone who was trailing them in plain sight was someone who was trying to make contact—and clearly not with him. A feeling of grim satisfaction took hold. There were hundreds of possibilities, but only one that made sense. After months of tracking them, the Mundy Gang was now on Jake's tail. Just a few more weeks—maybe even within a few days—and he would be face to face with the boys themselves.

It was only a matter of time now. Sooner or later, the Mundy Gang was going to show itself. And Jake was damned sure going to be ready for them when they did. "We'll ride out tomorrow," he said, casually adding, "Chances are, that's the last we'll see of whoever's been following us."

Annie studied the horizon, a small furrow between her brows. "I wouldn't bet on it, mister."

Jake took a final drag from his cigarette and tossed it away. He answered softly, almost to himself, "Neither would I, darlin.' Neither would I."

Chapter 8

The town of Two River Flats had changed so much that Annie almost didn't recognize the place. Originally it had started as a ramshackle mining community, comprised of nothing but tents, crude adobe huts, and mud so deep and thick it was said a man could drown his horse in the puddles that filled the streets. But eventually the gold had played out, the railroad had come in, and the town had finally established itself as a bustling trading post. Main Street now boasted an impressive row of false-front buildings that included a bank, a telegraph office, a hotel, and a mercantile. Glancing around, Annie also spotted one school, a church, several dry-goods stores, a stable, a meeting hall, a blacksmith, and of course, the ever-present saloons.

The town was a little out of their way, but it was worth the trip. What had begun earlier in the day as a gentle mist had developed into a hard, driving rain mixed with icy sleet. The freezing water ran down the back of Annie's collar and sent a chill through her bones. Definitely not a night for camping out if it could be avoided.

The soft glow of kerosene lamps spilled out onto the street from the saloons, the jailhouse, and the hotel. Everything else in town was shut down and dark. They rode up to the hotel and stopped. Jake reached for Annie, but as usual, she ignored his offer of assistance. She tucked Cat under her arm and dismounted on her own, looping Dulcie's reins over the hitching post. Her side was still sore but not sore enough to warrant his help. If she was strong enough to ride, she was strong enough to get off a horse. Besides, there was no call to invite his touch. She was already far too aware of him as it was. Better to stay on the right side of temptation.

Jake didn't appear the least bit offended by her rebuff. Ignoring both the weather and her ill humor, he grabbed their saddlebags and tossed them over his shoulder. Cheerfully whistling "Camptown Ladies," he strode toward the hotel. His boots rang on the boardwalk as his long strides carried him swiftly to the front door. He politely opened the door for her and ushered her inside.

The interior was nearly as rough as the exterior, Annie noted immediately. The walls were stark and barren, the floors consisted of wide, uneven planks. No rugs or pictures graced the interior. The lobby held only a few crudely constructed wooden chairs, one potbellied cast-iron stove, and a large table that held a hotel register.

It was nearly as cold inside as it was outside. A group of five rough, down-on-their-luck miners sat clustered around the stove, soaking up the fire's meager heat. One or two of the men glanced their way as she and Jake stepped into the room. Obviously finding them neither a threat nor interesting enough to hold their attention, the men looked away.

Jake proceeded to the table and rang the tin bell that sat near the register. When no one materialized, he rang it again, louder.

"You're wasting your time," called a surly voice from near the fire. "Sam's gone over to Sheriff Pogue's to file a complaint—some drifter skipped town without paying his bill."

Jake nodded at the man who had spoken. "Much obliged. Any idea when he'll be back?"

"He'll be back when he gets back."

Jake hesitated, his brows drawn together in thought. "Is that Sheriff Walter Pogue?"

"That's the man's name," the miner grumbled in response.

"Well, I'll be damned," Jake muttered beneath his breath.

Annie bit back an impatient sigh. Although she was making a valiant effort not to let her teeth chatter, she wasn't entirely succeeding.

As though reading her thoughts, Jake turned back to her and gestured toward the fire. "Why don't we warm up while we wait?" he suggested.

They moved to the stove, only to be pointedly ignored by the group of miners who had already established themselves before its warmth. Although the men were clearly aware of their presence, they hunched closer to the stove, their backs to Annie and Jake. Undeterred by their lack of welcome, Jake said pleasantly, "I'm sure you men wouldn't mind sharing that fire for just a few minutes."

Stony silence greeted his words.

"Never mind, mister," she said, resigning herself to a long, cold wait for the innkeeper. "It doesn't matter."

Jake shrugged, his features perfectly composed. "Maybe I'll ask just one more time." Before she could guess his intention, he lifted his cartridge belt, removed a fistful of bullets, and tossed them over the men's heads and into the open flames.

All hell broke loose in the tiny belly of the stove. The bullets exploded in a cacophony of sparks and sound. They ricocheted against the inside of the cast-iron stove, buzzing and swarming like a fiery nest of angry hornets. Completely taken by surprise, the miners abandoned their chairs with a flurry of heated exclamations and dove for cover.

The bedlam finally quieted, leaving five vacant chairs

in front of the fire—and five dazed and angry miners peering up from the floor.

Jake contentedly surveyed the room as the men rose stiffly to their feet. "The next time a lady enters a room," he instructed patiently, like a teacher speaking to a group of dull students, "you stand and offer her a chair."

Annie flushed with embarrassment as all eyes in the room swung disbelievingly to her. The miners looked her up and down, obviously taking in her oversize flannels and denim, her rough work boots, and the rain-soaked felt hat that covered her hair.

"Hell," one of the miners said, "how were we supposed to know that she was a gal?"

Jake shrugged. "That's your problem, friend, not mine." He reached into his pocket and fished out a silver eagle, tossing it their way. "If you want to warm yourselves up, try the saloon. First round's on me." The men eagerly accepted the offer and scurried out.

Clearly satisfied, Jake turned next to Annie. With a dramatic flourish, he doffed his hat and held out a chair. "After you, darlin'. Never let it be said that there aren't any gentlemen left in the West."

Annie searched his face, feeling more flustered than ever. He looked absolutely serious, holding out the chair for her with the same stiff formality that men used for ladies at fancy tea dances. It was typical that in her case five disreputable miners had literally had to have been knocked out of their seats in order to make the chair available. But that did nothing to lessen her pleasure at the gesture. Looking into Jake's eyes, she felt an odd stirring within her stomach as an emotion that fell somewhere between tension and warmth seemed to grip her and spread through her limbs.

Recalling *Winston's Guide,* she tilted her chin and moved toward the chair, trying to appear as graceful as possible. *A proper lady never looks behind her but feels the chair against the back of her knees and bends smoothly to sit.* As she followed the instructions as she had so painstakingly memorized, a thought suddenly occurred to her.

She glanced over her shoulder and sent Jake a stern frown. "You ain't gonna pull that chair out from under me when I try to sit down, are you?"

His brows shot skyward at the suggestion. A mischievous twinkle filled his eyes and a slight grin curved his lips. "You have my word as a gentleman."

"Hmmph." All things considered, it wasn't much of a promise, but it would have to do, she supposed.

Jake seated her smoothly, then grabbed a chair for himself. Although the fire was meager, the warmth helped, and soon Annie had banished the chill that had plagued her earlier. Jake hooked his boot around a chair and scraped it across the floor to prop up his feet. Annie followed suit, making herself comfortable as well. Cat jumped up in her lap and curled herself in a tight ball, purring. They sat in companionable silence, enjoying the warmth of the stove.

After a few minutes, she asked, "You know the sheriff here?"

"Maybe. If it's the same Walter Pogue I'm thinking of, then, yes, I know him."

"He throw you in jail for cheating at cards?"

Unoffended, Jake smiled and shook his head. "We fought in the war together."

That caught her interest. "North or South?"

"South."

"Why?"

"I was born in Louisiana," he answered, as if that explained everything. In a way, she supposed it did.

Annie knew little about the War Between the States. She'd followed it as best she could in the Denver City papers, but the battles had all taken place in cities she'd never heard of, places with confusing names like Chattanooga, Chickamauga, and Chancellorsville. The battles of Gettysburg, the Wilderness, and Antietam had all been written up in the papers as well, but the death tolls were simply too large for her to comprehend. Hundreds of thousands of men charging each other with rifles, cannons, and guns. Tens of thousands dying in one day, in one place. So much blood that the nearby rivers ran red for weeks.

She shuddered, trying to picture Jake in the middle of all that. But try as she might, she couldn't see him as a soldier, dressed in butternut and obeying orders, dodging bullets and cannon fire. It didn't fit anything she knew about him, or thought she knew about him. "How'd you do?" she asked.

Jake arched a dark brow, a small smile playing about his lips. "We lost."

"I'm sure nobody blames you for that," she blurted out, feeling a strange and sudden urge to comfort him.

He looked momentarily startled, then he grinned. "Not for the entire war, no."

"So what was it like?"

"The war?" he asked. At her nod, he thought for a long moment. "As close to hell as I ever want to get. Fleas and mud, blood and dysentery, everywhere. Sweltering heat in the summer, icy cold in the winter. Long months of unending tedium and boredom, punctuated by occasional bursts of sheer terror. And the food, hell, that had to be the worst food I ever ate in my life"—he paused, smiling as he finished—"and there was never enough of it."

"Where did you fight?"

"Virginia and the Carolinas, generally. I was cavalry, and we spent most of the war in our saddles."

"Why is it that every Southerner I meet claims to have ridden in the cavalry?"

Jake's smile took on a contented glow. "Because we were the best, darlin'. We were the best."

Annie studied him in thoughtful silence, realizing

how little she truly knew about Jake Moran. Up until that very moment, all she had known about him—all she had thought there was to know—was that he was a gambler, that he was good with his gun, and that maybe he drank too much. Now that those small truths had been expanded, she found herself strangely eager to learn more.

"What was the South like before the war?" she asked.

Jake frowned while he thought. "Rich and lush, coarse and ugly."

"Which one?"

"All of them." He shook his head, sighing. "The South was like a temptress, darlin', one that was full of false promises. Like a beautiful woman that a man eagerly strips bare, only to find her body dirty and bruised beneath the silk and satin of her magnificent gown."

"Are you talking about slavery?"

"I suppose. It should have been abolished years ago."

"But you still fought for the South? I don't understand."

"You ever read the Constitution, darlin'? The men who wrote that gave powers to the states so that men could rule themselves; so that men could run their own governments, their own homes. The people in the South are good, moral people—the same as people in the West, the North, or anywhere else. Given time, they would have come to their own decision to outlaw slavery. But the fundamental question was to allow each state the right to come to that decision on its own terms."

Annie listened but couldn't quite accept his reasoning. "It seems to me that we oughta stay together, that folks can't be running out of the Union just because one state doesn't like what the other states are telling them to do."

Jake nodded. "Preserving the Union versus states rights. That little argument is exactly why we fought the war." He touched his fingers to the brim of his hat. "Congratulations, darlin', you won."

There was a weary bitterness to his tone that she hadn't heard before. She wanted to ask more, but the front door swung open behind them before she had a chance. A man who Annie presumed to be Sam, the owner, stepped inside. He was short and stocky, his features fixed in an expression of sour belligerence. A tall, thin woman dressed in a worn black gown followed him. Her face looked haughty and grim, as though life was constantly failing to meet her impeccable standards. They came to a dead stop in the middle of the room as they spotted Jake and Annie comfortably stretched out before the stove. The owner looked them over and let out a weary sigh while his wife's mouth tightened in an expression that was even more pinched and disapproving.

"You two will want a room, I suppose," the innkeeper stated despondently, as though that were tragic news.

Annie couldn't entirely blame them for their reaction. With their sodden, mud-caked clothing, she and Jake looked like a couple of stray mutts who had been left out in the rain for too long.

Jake stood. "Two rooms," he said.

The innkeeper had to tilt his head back to meet his eyes. Jake's presence once again commanded authority, despite his ratty attire.

"You want them by the week or by the day?" the innkeeper demanded.

"The day," Jake answered.

"That'll be eighty cents a night for a room, *in advance,* twenty cents extra for a bath."

"Fine. Two rooms, and a bath for both of us. The water will be hot, I assume?"

"Two cents extra a bucket for hot. How many buckets you want?"

"None," she answered immediately.

"Five each," Jake replied.

To Annie's surprise, the owner didn't wrangle over the price of towels and soap but simply passed them over. His wife looked Annie up and down, then leaned over and whispered something in her husband's ear. Sam's eyes narrowed as his gaze shot toward Cat. "If you're planning on bringing that mangy beast upstairs, you had better think again. We run a dignified establishment here and don't allow no—"

"The cat stays," Jake interrupted firmly. He reached for their saddlebags and tossed them over his shoulder. "Fetch someone over from the stables," he instructed Sam. "I want our horses brushed, fed, and bedded down for the night." He pulled out a five-dollar bill and set it on the counter. "That ought to cover everything."

Annie opened her mouth to protest the exorbitant fee, but the owner snatched up the bill and pocketed it before she could utter a word.

"Your rooms are upstairs, first two doors on the left," he said with a greedy smile, pushing the keys across the counter.

Jake picked up the keys and tipped his hat. "Pleasure doing business with you, Sam."

Annie followed him upstairs, wondering if the man had ever found himself in a situation he couldn't handle. Whether Jake was aware of it or not, he exuded an air of steely-eyed confidence and natural assurance that worked to his advantage as much as his build and the set of revolvers strapped to his hips. Annie had recognized it the first time she had seen him in Sheriff Cayne's office, and clearly it was just as apparent to everyone else around them. Not once had she seen that cool determination of his fail, whether he was facing down a gang of deadly bandits, a cheating opponent across a poker table, or a surly innkeeper.

She took her key from Jake and opened the door to her room. It was just as spartan as she expected it to be, equipped with nothing but the basics. A narrow bed, a pitcher and basin, a chest of drawers with a looking glass, bare floors, and limp muslin curtains completed the space. A smoky kerosene lamp cast melancholy shadows across the room. Annie plopped down on the bed, noting as she did that the mattress was lumpy and emitted a peculiar pungent yet musty odor. She wrinkled her nose and studied the walls as she waited for her hot water. A cheap print of Jesus looking infinitely sad stared back at her, the room's only adornment.

Through the wall that separated their rooms, she heard Jake moving around. She recognized the sound of his boots as they scraped the floor. Then came the sound of something soft—his jacket?—being tossed across a dresser. A heavier object—his guns?—immediately followed. The bed springs groaned as he sat down. He was probably undressing, she guessed. She imagined him tugging off his boots, his coat, his shirt, his pants . . .

She sprang to her feet, evoking a howl of protest from Cat as the animal was dumped unceremoniously on the floor. The walls were too damned thin, Annie noted crossly, blaming her errant thoughts on the hotel's shoddy construction. She paced restlessly around the room, randomly picking up objects and setting them back down, doing anything she could to distract herself.

Within minutes, she heard a knock next door and the sound of buckets being dragged into Jake's room. The hot water for his bath, she surmised. She heard the sound of water splashing into a tub, followed by the deep, authoritative ring of his voice as he gave instructions to the men who carried the buckets.

Next came a sharp rap at her door. Annie raced to open it, gladly welcoming the distraction. The innkeeper and a young assistant gave her a curt nod in greeting and began lugging in buckets of hot water. They filled the tub and left.

Sam reappeared seconds later, a heavy clay dish in his hands. "Where do you want it?" he asked gruffly.

"That depends." She looked at the dish. "What is it?"

"Cream. The fella next door said I was to bring it for your pet."

Annie bit back a smile and gestured to a corner of the room. "I reckon right there ought be just fine."

Sam set it down where she instructed, then left the room. Annie watched Cat greedily slurp up the cream, touched by Jake's thoughtfulness. Her eyes went next to the steaming tub of water that was waiting for her. She moved eagerly toward it, unable to remember the last time she'd had a real, honest-to-goodness, all-over bath. Setting her towel and soap on a stool beside the tub, she immediately stripped and sank into its luxurious warmth. She scrubbed and soaked, letting out a blissful sigh of pure contentment.

As she leaned back and closed her eyes, she heard the sound of soft splashing coming from next door. The image of Jake sitting naked in his bath instantly lodged itself in her mind. She lifted her arm and gently rubbed the soap over her skin, imagining him doing the same thing. The jaunty sound of "Camptown Ladies," sung rather than whistled, carried through the wall. Jake's voice was surprisingly good, she noted, low and soothing. She tilted her head back and closed her eyes once again, enjoying the steady, lulling rhythm of his voice.

After a minute, her thoughts began to wander. Was his tub the same size as hers? she wondered absently. It was perfectly snug and cozy for her, but wouldn't he be a little crowded? Perhaps he managed it by keeping his arms and knees out of the tub, or by sitting up straight rather than lying back. Was he all slick and soapy, or had he already rinsed off? And what about his skin? Was it bronzed from the sun everywhere, or—

Annie dunked her head underwater, mentally cursing herself. She had doctored the boys for years and seen them in various states of undress, but not once had they stirred her senses the way Jake Moran did. Nor did he make her feel cold and itchy all over when he looked at her, the way Snakeskin Garvey did. When Jake Moran looked at her, she just felt warm and fluttery inside. But oddly enough, she didn't mind it at all.

Searching for a distraction from her thoughts, she splashed water over the side of the tub and watched as Cat chased the bubbles across the wooden floor. Cat darted playfully around the room, immediately intrigued by the new game. Then she hit a slick spot and skidded across floor, landing with a dull thud against the wall that separated Annie's room from Jake's.

Jake's singing abruptly stopped. "You all right in there?"

Annie ducked down into the water until it reached her chin. It was silly, but she couldn't help it. She knew he couldn't see anything, but the idea of talking to Jake while he was completely naked—while he knew *she* was completely naked—didn't hold much appeal. "Fine," she called back.

"What happened?"

"Nothing. Cat slid into the wall."

"You still in the tub?"

"None of your damned business."

She heard Jake's low rumble of laughter from the other side, followed by soft splashing sounds as he resumed his bath.

Annie listened for a moment longer, then stepped gingerly from the tub, careful not to slip on the slick wooden floor. She padded across the room and lifted her clothing from her saddlebags, wishing she had time to wash the garments Jake had bought her. Resigning herself to wait and wash her clothing after their meal, she slipped into her old flannels and denims. She ran her fingers through her damp hair, twisted it into a knot, and tucked it under her battered felt hat. Finally she grabbed her holster from the bedpost and slung it low across her hips, then stepped into her boots.

She straightened and turned, catching a glimpse of herself in a looking glass as she did. The glass was foggy and of poor quality, but it confirmed what Annie had begun to suspect. She hadn't paid much attention to her appearance for the past few years and it showed. No wonder the miners hadn't been able to tell she was a woman. She looked about as feminine and desirable as a desert hen with feather molt. Well, she thought, there wasn't anything she could do about it now.

Jake's knock came just minutes later. She opened the door to find him looking crisp and clean, and even more unbearably handsome than usual. His hair was wet from his bath and curled up at his collar, the smell of soap and shaving tonic clung to his skin. His long legs were encased in snugly fitted black pants, and his black boots were perfectly polished to a high, glistening sheen. He wore a matching, finely tailored black jacket, a crisp white linen shirt, a silk brocade vest of deep cobalt blue, and a silky black string tie knotted beneath his chin. The lines of the garments, simple yet elegant, suited him perfectly.

Annie became even more painfully aware of the poor assortment of rags that she had tossed over her own shoulders. Not knowing what else to do or say, she cleared her throat, immediately assuming the offensive. " 'Bout time you showed up," she said, stepping out into the hall to join him. "I was near starving to death."

Jake grinned. "I take it that means you're ready."

"Don't I look ready?" she bristled.

"You always look ready, darlin'," he agreed, wisely choosing to refrain from commenting on her attire.

The town's regular restaurant was closed due to the late hour, but the cafe adjoining the saloon appeared to be doing a booming business. The food was simple, served steaming hot and in generous portions. They each ordered a thick steak, cooked tender and dripping in its own juices, heaping mounds of fried potatoes and onions, stewed green beans, crisp corn dodgers, and hot coffee. Jake topped his meal off with a thick slice of apple pie. As tasty as the pie looked, Annie was too full to manage another bite and regretfully declined.

As their meal ended, they settled contentedly back into their chairs, relaxed and satiated, neither one ready to return to the hotel. Boisterous shouts and laughter from the saloon drifted in toward them, accompanied by the tinny sound of a badly tuned piano and the high-pitched laughter of the barmaids.

Their waitress sashayed toward them with a pot of coffee in her hand. Her face was pretty, Annie thought, but hard. Generous spots of rouge caked her lips and cheeks, and her skin was buried beneath a thick layer of powder. She gave Jake a coyly flirtatious smile and bent to refill his coffee cup. The woman's top was so low cut, Annie was surprised that her bosoms didn't spill over into the cup along with the coffee.

Ignoring her presence entirely, the waitress straightened and gave Jake a look that was rich with invitation. "You see anything else you want?" she cooed.

"I don't suppose you could rustle up a whiskey for me?"

"Is that all you want?"

He smiled—pleasantly, Annie noted, but coolly. "It all looks mighty good, sweetheart. But I think that's about all I can handle right now."

The woman's lips pulled down in a thick pout. "You let me know if you change your mind."

As she watched her walk away, Annie couldn't help but feel a slight stirring of jealousy at the way the woman had handled herself. There were certain kinds of women who could play up to men just fine, but Annie doubted that she would ever be one of them. While that knowledge had never bothered her before, it was beginning to rub her as raw as a prickly pear caught between her saddle and her britches.

"You liked her, didn't you, mister?" she asked, unable to stop herself.

An expression of surprised amusement flashed across Jake's face. "What makes you say that?"

"Why wouldn't you? I reckon any man would take to a gal who comes siding up to him with her tail up in the air, acting as slick and frolicky as a rain-soaked filly in a bed of fresh grass."

His grin widened. "Maybe I'm a little more discriminating than that. Maybe I don't want just any rain-soaked filly."

They fell silent as the waitress returned and set down his whiskey. Jake nodded his thanks and took a sip, his eyes never leaving Annie. As the waitress sashayed away, he asked, "Would it bother you if I did like her?"

Just like that, he had the drop on her. Annie suddenly felt as though she were standing on the precipice of a great, gaping canyon. One wrong word would send her plummeting over the edge. Faced with a question too complicated to answer, she simply shrugged her shoulders and replied, "I reckon it wouldn't matter to me one way or another."

"I see." His gray eyes drifted over her like smoke. "What about you, Annie? Do men instantly fall under the spell of your beauty?"

Until that point, she had been enjoying their light banter, but her enjoyment immediately came crashing to an end. Hurt by his teasing, she lowered her gaze to examine the edge of the table. "Ain't no call to get nasty."

"I meant that sincerely."

She slowly raised her gaze to meet his. Although she wanted to believe him, the cold, hard truth of the matter was impossible to ignore. "There's a looking glass in my room, mister. I look like something that fell off the back of a rag cart."

"You're a beautiful woman, Annie. I'm surprised no one's told you that before."

She shook her head. "My mother was beautiful," she said after a moment. "But I don't reckon I look anything like her."

"What was she like?"

Relieved to have the subject shift off her looks and move on to a less painful topic, Annie thought for a moment, searching her mind for the distant memories. "Fine and proper. Always telling Catherine and me to mind our manners and act like little ladies. She had the softest voice, and an even softer laugh. She wore fancy, swishy gowns in all the colors of the rainbow, and when she walked, it was like she was floating across the room."

"What happened to her? Where's your family now?"

"I lost them when I was six. My father was a professor back in Philadelphia, but we came west one summer so he could do some research. Our wagon was crossing a stream when a flash flood hit, sending a wall of water down the canyon. I remember feeling the wagon overturn, hearing my mother scream, and feeling that rush of water against my face—but that's all. The next thing I knew, I was on another wagon, part of an Army train headed west. They took me to a fort, and some folks who were passing through took me in."

"The rest of your family died in the accident?"

"Yes." Annie hesitated, wishing she could say more. But she had been young when the accident happened, too young to recall much of anything. All she had left were a few blurry memories of her family, and the tintype, Bible, and etiquette guide that had washed up downstream from the accident. Everything else had been lost forever.

"What about the family that took you in?" Jake asked.

"Doc Mundy and his wife? They were good folks.

They took care of me, sent me to school, fed me lots of decent food, and patched me up when I was sick."

"Doc Mundy and his wife," he repeated slowly. "So that's how you met Pete."

There was an odd note in his voice, but Annie was too absorbed in her memories to pay it any mind. "The Mundys said they had always wanted a little girl, and since Mrs. Mundy couldn't have any more children, they took me in."

"What was it like to grow up with Pete Mundy?"

She smiled. "In some ways, it seemed Pete never grew up at all. He had a wild streak in him a mile wide. Rambunctious, the Doc and his wife called him. He could be ornery as the devil when the mood got on him, and twice as mean." She paused, thinking. "It wasn't that Pete was a bad man, just that he was no good. He wanted things to come too easy. He was sure one day he'd be rich and famous, a feared gunfighter or some such thing."

"Is that why he started the gang?"

"I suppose. After Doc and his wife died, Pete got even more wild. The papers made us out to be a vicious, bloodthirsty group of killers, but we really weren't. Nobody in the Mundy Gang ever killed anybody, you know that, mister? Mostly Pete and the boys just hung around saloons, talking themselves up. Occasionally they'd steal some sickly cow that had strayed off from the herd, or steal gold dust by crawling around the saloon floor, but that was about all of their antics. Just harmless pranks and empty bragging, mostly. At least it was that way in the beginning. Sheriff Cayne was right about that. They were just a bunch of misfits with nowhere else to go."

Jake regarded her steadily. "But that all changed, didn't it?"

She sighed. "I reckon it did. All that outlaw talk just went to Pete's head. He met up with some saloon gal out in Woodbine and fancied himself in love. He was just crazy about that gal. He started running around, happier than a blind dog in a butcher's shop. Pete had never had a mind for details before, but suddenly he was coming up with all sorts of easy-money schemes, bank robberies and whatnot. He wanted to prove what kind of man he was, so he and the boys started pulling bigger and bigger jobs. That's when I decided to leave."

"You just took off?"

Annie bristled. "I didn't run out on them, if that's what you're asking. I made my peace with the boys before I went. I told them they were headed for trouble, but they seemed so cocksure of themselves, so certain that everything was going to be all right that they wouldn't listen." She frowned, shaking her head. "It was like they had some secret that I wasn't in on. Like they were a bunch of schoolboys who had stolen the teacher's answer book."

Jake looked as though he wanted to pursue the subject further but asked instead, "Why did you stay with the gang as long as you did?"

"Those boys were family to me. Good or bad, they were the only family I had. They looked after me, so I reckon it was only right that I look after them." She thought for a moment, then shrugged her shoulders. "Besides, where else could I go? I didn't have any other choice."

Jake eyed her coolly over his whiskey glass. "We all have choices."

"Really? And what exactly were mine?" she demanded. "I ain't saying it was right or wrong of me to stay with the boys, 'specially once they started hurting folks, just that I didn't know where else to go. I couldn't hire on as a teacher, even though I know how to read and do numbers and all. Folks would think I was a bad influence on their youngsters. I figured no one would hire me to work as a store clerk for fear that I might rob the place. I might get work as a saloon gal, but that's no kind of work for me. I ain't got no interest in showing men a good time. The way I see it, men can find that easy enough without any help from me. Besides, there ain't any men out there looking to make sure I enjoy myself, so the hell with them, right?"

A small smile tugged at Jake's lips. "Absolutely, darlin'. The hell with them."

"So can you see why—" Annie began, then stopped short as a slight movement at the bat-wing doors that separated the cafe from the rest of the saloon caught her attention.

She glanced up and immediately froze. Her heart slammed against her chest and her voice lodged in her throat.

Pete Mundy stood only two feet away, staring at her.

He was gone before she could move, before she could utter a word. He simply nodded once, then faded away, stepping back into the rowdy dimness of the saloon.

"What is it, Annie?" she heard Jake ask, his voice coming to her as though from a great distance.

She licked her suddenly parched lips and opened her mouth to speak, but no sound came.

"Annie?"

"What?" she finally asked, unable to pull her gaze from the bat-wing door.

"What is it?"

"Looked like someone I knew, that's all."

"You all right, darlin'?"

"Fine." She turned to face him, forcing a weak smile. "Just ate too much, I guess."

"You want me to fetch a doctor?"

"A doc? Just because I stuffed myself?" She shook her head. *It couldn't have been Pete. It just couldn't have been.* "I reckon ol' Winston was right," she said to Jake. "A lady should leave a little bit of grub on her plate."

Jake tossed a bill on the table and stood. "Let's get out of here."

Despite her protests that she could take care of herself, he insisted on walking her back to the hotel. Not until she was alone in her room did Annie allow her panic to take hold. Maybe it had just been a trick of the light that made the man look like Pete. Or maybe it was their talk of the dead that had brought up old memories that were better left buried. Or maybe she had just flat-out been mistaken.

But despite all her cool, calm reasoning, there was no escaping the plain facts. The stranger had had the same build as Pete, the same color hair, and he stood the same height. He had also been wearing Pete Mundy's clothes. Annie would have recognized that vest anywhere. It was a buff-colored suede with long fringes at the hem, decorated with vines and flowers that she and Mrs. Mundy had stitched on themselves. Pete never went anywhere without that vest. Not only that, the man had been wearing Pete's hat. Made of brown leather with a braided black band—but the brim had been pulled down too low for Annie to clearly make out the man's face.

That was one reason she wasn't sure that it had been Pete Mundy staring at her. The second reason was infinitely simpler: Pete Mundy was dead. She had watched him die herself.

Mindful that Jake could hear every move in her room, she slipped off her boots and began to pace quietly back and forth, her thoughts turning in wild disarray. Hours later, Annie took off her guns and hooked them around the bedpost, keeping them within easy grasp. Her mind still spinning but her body exhausted, she stretched out on the bed, holding the pillow tightly against her chest.

Although she was sure she was too tense to get any rest, sleep must have come at some point, for she soon found herself carried away in a beautiful dream. She was in a grand ballroom at the Palace Hotel, dressed in one of the beautiful silk gowns her mother had been so partial to. A man with sparkling blue-gray eyes and a cocky smile bent over her hand, asking for the pleasure of the next dance. She consented and he pulled her into his arms, whirling her around the dance floor. As he pressed his body tightly against hers, her limbs seemed to melt with pleasure.

He continued to spin her around dance floor. Around and around, until Annie thought she would faint from dizziness. She clung to his arms for support and the dream shifted. The big man with the blue-gray eyes faded away. Suddenly she was being held down, knocked flat by Snakeskin Garvey.

She called for Pete, only to realize too late that Pete was dead. There was no one to help her now. She struggled to get up, but Garvey had her firmly pinned down. She couldn't move, couldn't get away. "You owe me, girl," he panted into her ear. "You owe me."

Annie jerked awake, breathing hard.

Silence and pitch-black stillness surrounded her. She listened intently but heard nothing except the normal nighttime noises. Cat's rumbling snore. Jake's low, easy breathing from the room next door. A gentle cough from down the hall. But the sounds didn't bring her any comfort. She had been too long with the Mundy Gang not to trust her instincts. Something was wrong. Something was terribly wrong.

She stood, lifted her gun from her holster, and moved through the darkness of her room to the window. She parted the curtains and peered outside. A man stood across the street, staring up at the hotel. As if aware that she had noticed him, he dipped his head in cool acknowledgment of her presence. Then he faded silently back into alleyway.

Annie's stomach tightened into knots and her blood ran cold as Jake's words flew through her mind. *He wants you to see him. He wants you to know he's there.*

The sleet that had fallen earlier had finally stopped.

Only the wind still roared. An icy gust of air howled like cold, demonic laughter. The curtains fluttered as a shiver ran up Annie's spine. She felt as though the cold, gray hands of death had just reached out and touched her.

She fought the urge to go and wake Jake. Even if she did wake him, what could she possibly say? That the ghost of Pete Mundy was staring up into her bedroom window? Not likely.

Someone—a living, breathing man—had been trailing them for days. Now he was here, making his presence known in the guise of Pete Mundy. Annie thought hard, searching her mind for who it might be. A chill ran down her spine as an echo of her nightmare came rushing back to her.

Snakeskin Garvey. Garvey had blamed Annie for the fact that Pete had kicked him out of the gang. And he had sworn revenge. "Pete Mundy's not always gonna be there to protect you, girl. That's when I'll come calling again. You just wait and see. We ain't finished yet."

Annie swallowed hard as her fingers traced the cold steel barrel of her gun. It was just like Garvey to lurk in the shadows, hiding out like the yellowbellied skunk that he was, waiting to strike.

So he had come to settle the score, had he? Well, all right, then. She would meet him, but on her own terms. She thought about asking Jake to join her but decided against it. Snakeskin Garvey was her problem, and she would take care of him herself. First thing tomorrow morning.

Chapter 9

When Annie failed to materialize for breakfast the next morning, Jake went to her room and knocked on her door. After repeated knocks went unanswered, he tried the knob. Locked. That didn't surprise him. Nor did it pose much of a problem, however, as the doors were constructed with the same sloppy negligence as the rest of the hotel. Using a thin blade and applying a little pressure at the juncture of the bolt and frame, he forced the lock. The door gave a creak of protest and swung easily open.

He took in her sparse room at a glance. Annie and Cat were gone, but at least Annie's belongings were still there, bundled up neatly at the foot of her bed. So she hadn't gone too far. While that was somewhat reassuring, it didn't solve the question of where she had gone or what she was doing.

Jake exited the hotel and stood outside, unable to shake the vague feeling of foreboding that hung over him. He loitered around the town, wandering up and down the streets. He had no clear goal as to what he was looking for. He was simply operating on his intuition and a vague notion that something was wrong, and he would know what it was when he saw it. But he noticed nothing unusual, or even interesting, happening. Just everyday, small-town business being conducted.

Wagons, horses, pack mules, and buggies flooded the street, splashing mud everywhere. Barking dogs and laughing children raced back and forth. The air was filled with the aromas of baking bread, meat sizzling over cooking spits, and sweet pies and cakes cooling on window ledges. Cool autumn sunshine flooded the streets and storefronts, leaving the town awash with color and energy. Excitement hung in the air, as palpable as the soft breeze that blew in off the San Juans.

The morning stage rumbled down Main Street with the pounding of thundering hooves, creaking leather, and rattling springs. Four men were inside the coach, but only one man disembarked. Nothing interesting there, Jake thought, giving the stranger a cursory glance. The man was unarmed and dressed like a banker or an accountant. He dusted off his clothes, picked up his bag, and headed toward the hotel. Next the driver and his assistant jumped down, each holding leather courier bags. One headed toward the sheriff's office with his bag, while the other moved toward the general mercantile. Weekly mail delivery, Jake assumed.

He made his way to the livery. Weed stood in a corner stall, contentedly munching a bucketful of oats. As he expected, Dulcie was nowhere to be found.

"Can I help you with something, mister?"

He turned to see a boy of about thirteen, dressed in tattered overalls, a bucket and shovel in his hand.

"You see a woman leave here this morning riding a gray mare with spotted hindquarters?"

The stable boy frowned. "A woman who dressed funny, wearing guns?" At Jake's nod, he continued, "She rode out about dawn."

Jake swore silently to himself. It was nearly nine o'clock. That meant Annie had been gone for almost four hours. "She say where she was going?"

The boy shrugged. "Nope. She gave me a nickel for helping to saddle her horse, then she rode out."

He thanked the boy and left the stable, contemplating his next move. While riding after Annie didn't make much sense, not with the lead she had on him, neither did he relish the idea of aimlessly wandering around town waiting for her to return. He glanced down the street, edgy and frustrated with himself for not monitoring her better. Then the sign for sheriff's office caught his eye. Remembering the recent stage delivery, Jake decided to drop in. He was taking a risk, but it was better than doing nothing.

He opened the door to the sheriff's office and stepped cautiously inside. The room was empty, warm, and orderly. A large pane-glass window allowed ample sunlight to enter and gave the sheriff a clear view of the street outside. The main desk was broad and sturdy and showed only a minimal amount of clutter. Two locked cells were adjacent to the main office. Both were swept clean, and the bedding looked reasonably fresh. A cast-iron stove stood in one corner with a tin coffee pot warming on top. All in all, the place looked a hell of a lot more inviting than the hotel where he and Annie were staying.

Jake saw the courier bag lying unopened on the sheriff's desk. He glanced over his shoulder, then pulled the straps apart and flipped open the front flap. He rifled through the contents, moving quickly past news of local elections and the calendar for the territory's circuit-court judge. He stopped when he reached what he had been hunting: a thick crop of wanted posters. He pulled those from the leather satchel and scanned quickly through them.

"You looking for this, Jake?" called a voice from behind him.

Jake froze, then slowly turned, surveying the man who stood in the doorway. Walter Pogue hadn't changed much since Jake had last seen him. He had gained weight after the war, of course, as had every man who had fought for the South. He was out of the battered Confederate uniform that Jake had been so accustomed to seeing him in. His former comrade-in-arms was now garbed in typical western attire, wearing a mixture of leather and wool, denim and flannel—with the notable addition of the shiny tin star that was pinned to his chest. Other than those few changes, Walter still had the same pale-blond hair and hazel eyes, the same soft Virginia accent. He had the look of an innocent, gullible farm boy, but Jake knew him well enough to know that behind that youthful face was a man of shrewd intelligence and uncanny instincts.

He tipped his hat and propped one hip up on Walter's desk. "Nice to see you, Walt."

"You too, Jake."

The pleasantries over, Jake's gaze moved toward the wanted poster that Walter held. "May I?" he asked, reaching for the paper.

Walter silently passed it to him. Jake scanned the sketch that covered two thirds of the poster. The similarity was there, but it was vague at best, he noted with satisfaction. The features sketched were bland enough to be anybody's. He scanned the copy at the bottom of the page. *Wanted for Murder,* it read in large type. *Jake Moran. Gambler. Tall man, strong build, clean shaven. Talks smooth, Southern accent, partial to fancy duds, carries silver watch fob in left pocket. Hair: black. Eyes: devil-blue. Rides bay stallion with black mane and tail. Wears two-gun holster strapped down, Navy Colts with smooth silver grips. $500 reward. DOA.*

DOA: Dead or Alive. Jake set the poster down, irritated at the rather cheap price that had been set on his life.

"When did it come in?" he asked.

"A little over a week ago," Walter answered. "There was a report that came with it. Said you were playing poker with a banker by the name of Harlan Becker out in Gunpowder Falls. Apparently you lost big and got pretty angry. Said you followed Becker into an alley and shot him in the back."

Walter stepped out of the doorway and moved into his office. He reached for the coffee pot and poured two cups, setting them on opposite sides of his desk. He sat down, motioning for Jake to do the same.

Jake sat. The chair was large and sturdy, obviously built for a big man. He reached for the coffee, took a deep swallow, and grimaced. "You still make the worst damned cup of coffee I've ever tasted."

"And you still drink it anyway."

"I don't suppose you'd have any bourbon to warm this up?"

Walter hesitated for a moment, then reached into his desk drawer for a bottle. He poured a generous shot in Jake's cup and put the whiskey away.

Jake took a sip as he looked his friend over. "You look good, Walt," he said, meaning it.

Walter nodded. "Things are going pretty well. Elena and I drifted out West after the war and settled down. The baby just turned three, and we've got another on the way."

"I'm glad to hear it. It suits you."

Silence fell between them. Walter settled back into his chair and took a long swig of coffee, then set the cup down with a sigh. "You want to tell me about it?" he said. It wasn't a question, nor was there any mistaking his meaning.

Jake lifted one brow. "As a friend or as the sheriff?"

"Both."

Fair enough, Jake supposed. "Fact is, I did get into a card game with Becker," he answered bluntly. "I lost pretty bad; about two thousand."

Walter let out a low whistle. "That's a lot to lose."

"I've had worse nights. I left the saloon cool. There were no arguments, no fights. I didn't think Becker was cheating—the man just got lucky, I didn't. It was late by then, after midnight, but I wasn't ready to go back to my hotel. I wandered around town for a while just stretching my legs."

"Anybody see you?"

"I didn't know I'd need an alibi, Walt," Jake returned, unable to keep the edge from his voice.

"All right," he replied evenly. "Go on."

"I was headed back toward the saloon when I saw that a crowd had gathered in the alleyway. It didn't take long to learn what had happened. Becker was dead, he had been shot in the back. A woman who had worked the tables that night said she had heard two men arguing about money just before the shots went off. Naturally they assumed the man Becker had been arguing with was me. I walked right into it. The woman said she saw a man riding north just after the shots were fired and thought it was me, but she must have been mistaken. A couple of men drew on me while someone else went for the law."

"You tell your story to the sheriff?"

Jake lifted a single dark brow. "If some drifter tried to sell you that story, would you have bought it?"

Walter shifted uncomfortably. "I reckon not."

"I didn't think so." Jake shrugged, not blaming him in the least. "I figured the only chance I had to clear my name was to ride north and bring back the other man for questioning. Even if he didn't do it, I thought maybe he had seen something or knew something, hell, I don't know what . . . anything. As you can imagine, I didn't have a real clear plan. All I knew was that I didn't kill Becker. I pulled my guns and convinced the good citizens of Gunpowder Falls to let me ride after him and find out what he knew."

"They just let you go?"

"Pretty much. They put together a posse and tracked me for a day or two. Mostly they just drank and slept and got paid for their time. Probably they decided I wasn't worth the trouble to track down."

"What about the man you were following?"

"That's where things start to get interesting. He wasn't easy to track. I followed him for three months, but I kept missing him by a matter of days, sometimes by just a matter of hours. Then I noticed a pattern. Wherever he showed up, the Mundy Gang followed. Each town he visited was hit by the Mundy Gang within a day or two of the stranger's arrival."

A spark of interest shone in Walter's eyes. "You figure he's connected to the gang?"

"I think the stranger I've been following is Pete Mundy himself," Jake answered. "There's something else you should know. I looked into Harlan Becker's past. He had a lot of cash, and he wasn't shy about throwing it around. Turns out the robberies that the Mundy Gang pulled before Becker died were all payroll robberies—payrolls that had been handled by the bank that Becker used to work for."

"You think this Becker fella was setting up the robberies?"

"I think Becker was working with the Mundy Gang and got greedy, and that's why Pete killed him. It explains why they were arguing about money just before Becker was shot."

Walter was silent for a long moment. "Interesting story, Jake. You got any proof?"

"Not yet."

Walter leaned back in his chair and propped his boots up on his desk, toying with his empty coffee cup. "Heard you rode in last night with another fella."

"You're very good, Walt."

"Just doing what I'm paid to do."

"Then tell your sources to take a better look next time. That's a woman I'm with, not a man. Her name's Miss Annabel Foster."

A thoughtful frown crossed Walter's face. "That sounds mighty familiar. Have I met her?"

"Maybe. She also goes by the name Outlaw Annie."

Walter's boots thunked to the floor as he shot up in his chair. "*Jesus, Jake!* You're bringing the Mundy Gang here, to my town? Why the hell didn't you tell me sooner?"

"I don't know for sure that the gang will show up, Walt. I'm sticking close to her in case they do. But the fact is, I figure we'll have to just wait and see."

"Jesus," Walter repeated, shaking his head. "Last I heard, Outlaw Annie was scheduled to be hanged out in Stony Gulch."

"She *was* hanged. The rope gave out before Annie did." Jake felt a funny twist of pride as he spoke. That was just like Annie. The woman wouldn't let anything beat her down.

Something in his tone or his expression must have given him away, for Walter eyed him consideringly, his keen perception coming into play. "Tell me about her. Is she as wild as I've heard?"

Jake thought it over, wondering how to put into words the bundle of contradictions that embodied Miss Annabel Lee Foster. She could swear, she could shoot, she could ride. She was also headstrong, stubborn, loyal, and fearless. As far as his plan was concerned, Outlaw Annie was simply a means to an end. Yet he was the first to admit that plans often went astray. Something about the woman intrigued him, amused him, and flat-out held his attention. She also brought out a protective streak in him that he hadn't even been aware he possessed.

"She's different from any woman I've ever met," he answered simply. "She seems determined to start over, to build a new life for herself."

"You think she means it?"

"Maybe. I haven't figured that out yet."

"Where is she now?"

"She took off at dawn. Someone's been on our tail for the past week. My guess is that she rode out to pay whoever it is a little visit."

A troubled frown crossed Walter's face. "You think it might be the Mundy Gang out there?"

"Seems likely, doesn't it?"

"I could put a posse together right now and ride out after them."

"You could. You have enough men in town to handle the gang?"

A pained expression crossed Walter's face. "Hell, I don't. Three of my best deputies are up north, hunting down rustlers."

Jake nodded, relieved. He needed to catch the Mundy Gang, but not at the risk of hurting Annie in the crossfire. "All right, then," he said. "We'll play it my way. I'll stick by Annie and see if I can get near the Mundys on my own." He hesitated. "That is, assuming you trust me enough to let me walk out of here and wire you once I get close enough to the gang to bring them in. I reckon that's your call."

Walter propped his boots back up on his desk, thinking for a long moment in silence. "You swear you ain't just bullshitting me in order to get out of this wanted poster?"

Jake arched a dark brow. "Being an officer of the law has made you a mighty suspicious man, Walt."

Walter leveled a long, hard stare at him. "You know what I see, Jake, day in and day out? I see men like us, used-up rebels without a war to fight or a home to go to. They wander aimlessly from town to town, drinking too much and stirring up trouble. After a time, these men start to get bored, then they get angry. They decide to rob a few Northern banks, just to get even. That's how the James Gang got started, and the Daltons too."

Jake had seen the same thing himself. While he couldn't deny the truth of Walt's words, he resented being thrown in with that ilk. "There a reason you're telling me this story?"

"You cross me, Jake, and I'll personally hunt you down myself."

Jake sighed. "I won't cross you, Walt. I've got a hell of a lot more at stake here than you do. You and your men can split the bounty on the gang any way you like. All I want is to clear my name." He set down his coffee mug and stood. "We're headed toward Cooperton. Will that be a problem?"

"No, that ought to work, so long as you give me enough notice. I reckon I can get my men down Cooperton way within a week's time."

"Fair enough." Jake put on his hat and moved to the door. "Remember, as far as Annie knows, I'm just doing a good deed escorting her to Cooperton."

"That's not exactly your style."

Jake grinned. "Funny, that's just what she said." He left Walter's office and stepped out onto the boardwalk, watching the flurry of activity that filled the street. His eyes were drawn to a small gray mare that looked remarkably like Annie's horse, tied to the hitching post in front of the general mercantile.

He strode down the street and found Cat curled up in the center of Dulcie's saddle, contentedly basking in the sun. Although she didn't open her eyes, the fussy feline must have sensed his presence, for she issued a belligerent hiss and swiped one sharp claw his way. "Same to you, darlin'," Jake said breezily, then turned to enter the mercantile.

He stepped inside and was greeted by the mingled scents of peppermint, leather, and tobacco, and the distinct aroma of brine from the pickle barrel. Glancing around the interior, he saw bolts of cloth, cured and dried meat hanging from the rafters, skinned hides, Indian beads, various elixirs and tonics, and a miscellany of kitchen goods. The shop was surprisingly well stocked, its merchandise cramming the aisles in a mass of chaotic opulence. Fancy lace fans were shelved next to cowboy boots and spurs. Rifles and ammunition were juxtaposed against baby bonnets and blankets. There was even a pile of big-city newspapers from back East. Jake glanced at the dates, impressed. Some were as recent as a month old.

Rather than move toward the front counter he stood silently in the back, watching Annie. She wandered aimlessly around the store, wistfully touching a few items, then moving on to another display. Although Annie tried several times to catch the attention of the store clerk, each attempt was blatantly ignored. The shop girl had a fairly steady stream of customers, but not so many that she couldn't have helped Annie find what she needed.

Jake watched for a few minutes, then stepped forward. The shop girl glanced his way, her eyes lighting up as she took in the value of his clothes, hat, and guns. Her mouth immediately curved into a subservient smile. "Good afternoon, sir," she said brightly. "What can I do for you?"

He tipped his hat in polite greeting, coolly returning the clerk's smile. "I believe the lady was here first," he replied, nodding toward Annie.

Annie glanced up at the sound of his voice, clearly surprised to see him there, and sent him a hesitant smile.

The clerk didn't even spare her a glance. "I'm sure she doesn't mind waiting."

Jake's polite expression didn't change, but he added a note of firmness to his tone. "Why don't you ask her?"

The girl glanced back and forth between the two of them, her smile faltering. She looked Annie up and down, her gaze harsh with disapproval, then she moved toward her. "What can I do for you?" she asked tightly.

Annie cleared her throat and straightened her shoulders. "I'd like to buy a dress," she replied, sounding more nervous than he had ever heard her. "I ain't exactly sure what size I need, but I do have a picture of what I had in mind." She pulled *Winston's Guide* from her pocket, opened it on the counter, and pointed toward a page. "Do you have anything like this?"

The clerk glanced at the page and arched a brow in haughty disapproval, her mouth curving in a tight, superior smile. "I'm afraid that went out of style more than twenty years ago."

"Oh." Annie glanced down at the book again, then closed it and tucked it back into her pocket. She glanced at the clerk and shrugged, gesturing at the crisp white blouse and navy skirt the girl wore. "Well, if you ain't got nothing fancy, I suppose something like what you got on will have to do."

Jake bit back a grin as the clerk whitened at the unintended insult. "I'll show you what we have," she said and moved stiffly toward a counter in the center of the store. She motioned to a few bolts of fabric that ranged from thin calicoes and cottons to heavy, coarse wools. "These are sold by the yard; prices vary depending on the cloth."

Annie's brows drew together in a troubled frown. "Am I supposed to stitch 'em together myself?"

"Yes. Or you hire a seamstress to sew them."

"The fabrics are all mighty pretty," she said politely. "Problem is, I need something real quicklike. You got any ready-made dresses?"

"Ready-made?" The clerk grimaced and gestured toward a rack of shabby women's garments hanging off a nail peg, her distaste evident. "These were sold to us by the Widow Porter. Although they're not the quality we usually carry, my father bought them as an act of charity. Perhaps there's something there you'll like."

Jake glanced at the battered garments, ready to reject the clothing outright. But before he could, Annie reverently touched the sleeve of a faded brown calico dress with a tiny lace collar. "You reckon this one will fit me?" she asked the clerk tentatively.

A satisfied smile curved the girl's lips. "I believe it will suit you just fine."

"How much?"

She named a price that seemed outrageous to Jake; not the amount in and of itself but when considering the quality of the dress. It was ugly and old looking, the fabric worn thin in spots. He considered interceding on Annie's behalf but ultimately changed his mind. It was her business, not his.

Annie quickly agreed to the sum, apparently unaware that she was being taken in. A few more minutes were spent in acquiring the suitable undergarments for the dress. Jake allowed the women a modicum of privacy for that business, diverting his attention to the store's stock of guns and ammunition while they carried on their conversation. Once her purchases were complete, he followed Annie out of the store.

She clutched the tightly wrapped bundle under her arm, her eyes sparkling with an almost childlike excitement. "I ain't never bought a dress before," she said. "It's pretty, ain't it? It has a lace collar and everything, real fancylike, you see that? You think brown's a proper color? Should I have bought some gloves to go with it? Maybe I ought to have a hat to wear with it too. What do you think, mister, will the other ladies will be wearing hats?"

"What other ladies?" Jake asked, unable to resist her bright mood. Her cheeks were fresh and rosy from the crisp fall air, and golden excitement danced in her eyes. Looking at her now, it seemed absurd that only minutes ago he had been discussing Annie's involvement with a brutal gang of killers.

"The ones who'll be at the dance tonight. Didn't you hear about it?"

"Not a word."

"The mayor's wife gave birth to twin boys last week," Annie explained. "He's throwing a big party over at the town hall to celebrate. Everyone in Two River Flats is invited."

Jake nodded. That explained the general air of anticipation and excitement that swept through the streets.
Town dances ranked right up there with weddings, hangings, and funerals for small frontier communities looking
for some entertainment.

"I ain't been to a dance in years," Annie went on,
"not since I was a little girl. But I reckon I should start
learning how to fit into high society. I figure knowing
proper manners is like firing a gun. You don't wait until
you need it to start learning. It takes a lot of practice to
get it right. I'll get all gussied up in this new dress and
practice my fancy talk tonight. Why, I'll wager folks
around here won't even know it's me."

They reached Dulcie and stopped. Annie set he bundle on the back of her saddle, eliciting a howl of protest
from Cat for disturbing her sleep. "Oh, hush up, you,"
Annie scolded gently, stroking Cat until the ungrateful
feline settled back down. "You don't mind staying over
another night, do you, mister?" she asked.

"I suppose not," Jake answered easily. They stood on
the boardwalk in companionable silence and watched the
activity near the town hall. Women swarmed around the
hall like bees around a beehive, running in and out with
pies and cakes, arrangements of autumn flowers, festive
lamps, and paper lanterns. A light breeze skimmed the
street, and brilliant sunshine filled the sky. "Nice day for
a ride," he finally commented.

Annie glanced up at him and arched a dark-blond
brow. "I reckon that's your way of asking me where I
went this morning. I wondered how long it would take
you."

He smiled. The woman was quick, no doubt about it.
"You mind telling me?"

"Not that I think it's any of your damned business,"
she replied cheerfully, "but I suppose it won't hurt to say.
I rode out to see if I could find that fella who's been
tracking us."

Exactly as he had suspected. The only thing that surprised him was that she admitted it. "Any luck?" he asked.

Annie shook her head. "If someone was out there, I would have found him. Whoever it was must have ridden out. Probably just some drifter making his way west. Fact is, looks like we were worried for nothing."

Jake glanced at her curiously. Was it just his imagination, or did she sound strangely relieved? "You should have asked me to come along. There could have been trouble out there if you had found him."

"You said yourself it was me he was after. That made him my problem, not yours."

The reply was typical Annie bravado, equal parts fearlessness and foolhardiness. If she was telling the truth and had simply gone scouting, Jake had a strong and sudden urge to shake some sense into her. Reckless courage like that would only get her in trouble one day.

His original scenario seemed far more likely, however. In his experience, life wasn't all that complicated. Things were generally what they appeared to be. Annie had ridden with an outlaw gang for years. She knew exactly who was trailing them and had sneaked out of town for a private meeting. She was still protecting the Mundy Gang, still actively a part of them. He didn't like it, but it fit.

As they stood on the boardwalk, a man walked past them, did a double-take, then slowly approached. Jake recognized him as the stranger he had seen step off the stage earlier that morning. He was in his early thirties and of medium height and build; handsome in an unremarkable way. His facial features were soft and slightly pudgy, set off by dull-brown hair and eyes and a perfectly groomed mustache. His suit pegged him as an Easterner, but the man had been in the West long enough to accent it with a broad-brimmed hat, a wide belt, and rich leather boots.

"Pardon me," he said to Annie, "but you wouldn't be Miss Annabel Foster, would you?"

Annie frowned as she looked the man up and down. "Who's asking?" she demanded gruffly.

The stranger smiled politely and removed his hat. "Allow me to present myself. Peyton VanEste, reporter with *The Philadelphia Gazette*. My card."

Annie glanced at the card, then back at the stranger, looking singularly unimpressed. "How'd you know my name?"

"There's very little about you that I don't know if you'll forgive my saying so," VanEste replied enthusiastically, sending her a dramatic wink. "I can't begin to tell you how very fortuitous this meeting is. I wonder if I might ask for just a few minutes of your time to speak with you privately."

"You can talk right here," Jake said.

VanEste turned to Jake as though noticing him for the first time—something Jake found hard to believe. At six-foot-two and weighing in at over two hundred pounds, he was a hard man to miss.

"And who might you be, sir?" VanEste inquired stiffly.

Jake studied the man long enough to let him know he didn't appreciate the question. "A friend of the lady's," he answered.

VanEste glanced from Annie to Jake and sniffed disapprovingly. "Very well," he said. "I suppose there's no harm in talking here. I don't suppose you're familiar with my work?" he asked Annie, a note of pride in his voice.

"I don't know you from Adam, mister."

"I see. Well, if you'll allow me a moment to present my credentials, Miss Foster, I believe you'll understand why I've approached you. My work is serialized in *The Gazette* every month under the title *Life in the Wild West*. The series is part fiction and part truth, daring little stories and biographies that depict the hardship, the untamed beauty, and the ruggedness of the West. Now that the war is over, my readers need something else to focus on. They're starving for just a taste of the adventure and excitement that you experience every day. I've written profiles on Bloody Bill Anderson, Texas Pete, Eddie Hoyle, and Wesley Hardin—just to name a few."

Jake instantly recognized the work. It was overblown, melodramatic doggerel that bore little resemblance to the truth.

Annie was apparently familiar with the man's stories as well. "I ain't interested," she answered flatly.

"If it's a question of money, I can assure you that *The Gazette* has always been quite generous in compensating subjects for their time."

Jake frowned. "I believe the lady told you that she wasn't interested."

"I see." VanEste haughtily drew himself up. "May I suggest that you take some time and consider my offer, Miss Foster. I can make you not only famous but rich as well. *The Gazette* is in the process of assembling a wild West show that will rival even Hickok's extravaganza. I can make Outlaw Annie the star attraction. People will flock from all around the world just to see you ride and shoot. You'll be a legend in your own time." He paused, nodding politely. "I'll be in Two River Flats for another week. After that, you can reach me through *The Gazette*. Good day to you both."

Annie shook her head as she watched him walk away. "Imagine that," she said softly. "Somebody wants to write a story about me." She glanced up at Jake. "Funny little fella, wasn't he?"

Jake shrugged. "All sorts of characters in the West." There was something vaguely familiar about the man, but he just couldn't place it.

Annie let out a contented sigh. "Well, mister, I reckon I'll get me something to eat and take it up to my room. I got me some more studying up to do."

"Studying?"

"I want to memorize all the rules in *Winston's Guide* before the dance tonight. I know it ain't much of a book, but it's all I got. I might even take me another bath, even though I just took one last night. I'm gonna get gussied up real fine." She grabbed Dulcie's reins and turned away. "C'mon, girl, let's go."

Jake watched her walk away, then saddled Weed and went for a ride, backtracking in the direction from which Annie had come. But he found no abandoned campsites, no signs of other riders, and no clue as to who had been following them. No Mundy Gang. Nothing. Moreover, it *felt* empty. When riding in vast, open spaces, it wasn't uncommon to sense other riders long before they came into view. But Jake experienced none of the prickly sensation of being watched. As darkness began to fall, he reined Weed in and returned to Two River Flats.

He stabled his mount and went back to the hotel. As he passed Annie's room, she opened her door a crack and stuck her head out into the hall. "Psst, mister. C'mere."

Curious, Jake moved toward her. Annie eagerly grabbed his arm and pulled him inside, shutting the door behind him. "What do you think?" she asked, holding tightly to the hem of her new brown dress as she executed a pirouette.

It was perfect, Jake thought, . . . for scrubbing floors. The dress was nothing but a tired, limp old rag. Yet as he studied her, he realized that Annie had somehow managed to give it a fresh breath of life.

The gown fit snugly, displaying an enticing combination of girlish innocence and womanly curves. The buttons that lined the front of the bodice from her waist to her throat were straining slightly at her breasts. Not a lot—just enough to keep a man's eyes centered on her chest, waiting to see which button would pop first. The gown also emphasized her narrow waist and the smooth swell of her hips. It was too short by an inch or two, displaying what would have been a shockingly enticing glimpse of ankle had the effect not been spoiled by her thick, clumsy-looking boots.

Last but not least, Annie added a touch that was uniquely her own: her gun belt was strapped snugly around her hips, her revolvers tucked firmly in their holsters.

At Jake's silence, a worried frown creased her brow. "What's the matter? Don't I look respectable?"

Adorable was the word that crossed Jake's mind, not *respectable.* "You look just fine, darlin'," he said. The words didn't sound like nearly praise enough, but Annie didn't seem to notice.

A relieved smile broke across her face, as though she had just been paid the ultimate compliment. "Do I really?" She let out a soft, excited giggle, then executed another pirouette. "I bet you didn't even recognize me without my britches on, did you, mister?"

He smiled. "I bet you're wrong."

"Really?" she repeated. She nervously ran her hands down her sides. "I figure the Widow Porter must have been a mite smaller than me, but as long as I can squeeze myself into this here gown, I reckon that's what counts."

Without waiting for his comment, Annie turned to the dresser, grabbed up a handful of hairpins, and thrust them toward Jake. "I tried to put my hair up all fancylike, but it keeps slipping out. Would you mind trying? I just washed it, so it's clean and all."

Jake contemplated the shimmering curtain of dark-blond tresses that flowed down her back, glowing with shades of chestnut, wheat, and honey. Annie's hair was straight and thick, with no wave to it. He moved hesitantly toward her, wondering if she had any idea of the intimacy involved in asking him to dress her hair. But she simply studied him with eyes that were wide and trusting, waiting for him to comply with her request.

He turned her to face the mirror and stood behind

her, lifting the long, silky strands in his hands. Her hair slipped through his fingers like a warm breeze, carrying with it the soft, floral fragrance of spring. He tried his best to put it up, but as she had complained, her hair was wantonly unmanageable. It kept slipping free of the pins, cascading about her shoulders in a rich, decadent curtain of dark gold. The scent of her hair and the feel of it in his hands was pure sensual torture, yet Jake couldn't stop himself from running his fingers through the rich, silky strands.

After a minute or two, Annie let out a sympathetic sigh. "You ain't having any more luck with it than I did."

Regaining himself, he dropped his hands and stepped back a pace. "I'm afraid my speciality is letting down a woman's hair, darlin', not putting it up."

A small smile touched her lips. "I reckon that's true." She thought for a moment, then suggested, "Should I just leave it down?"

Jake remembered the paper lanterns that were being hung in the town hall. Annie's unbound hair would glisten like gold beneath their gentle glow, drawing men to her like bees to honey. The thought brought him an absurd stab of annoyance.

"Tie it back," he said curtly.

A slight pout touched her lips. "I don't have nothing pretty for it."

"What about this?" he asked, lifting a strand of pale-blue ribbon from the dresser top.

"Oh, I almost forgot," she exclaimed with an excited smile. "That's for Cat." She lifted her pet and tied the ribbon around her neck, then smoothed down the animal's knotted fur. "There, now," she cooed. "Aren't you a pretty kitty? I reckon you look respectable now too."

That accomplished, she took Jake's advice and secured her own hair with a plain leather strap. Once she had finished, she steadily appraised herself in the mirror. Her expression remained coolly indifferent, blind to the beautiful young woman who gazed back at her. Shrugging her shoulders, she turned to face him.

"Well?"

Jake studied her for a moment in silence. *Tell her she looks fine and walk out the door,* his brain commanded. But he ignored his higher sense, giving rein to a more base emotion. Caution was never a trait he particularly admired in a man, anyway. He moved steadily toward her, his gaze fastened on hers. "There's just one more thing I'd change."

Annie stood poised like a deer, ready to run at the slightest provocation. Yet there was an unmistakable hint of both challenge and curiosity in her eyes. Jake slowly lifted his hands and reached for the buckle on her gun belt.

Her hands immediately came up to rest on the thick leather belt. "Nobody touches my guns, mister." Her voice came out in a low, breathy whisper.

A slight grin curved his lips. "Nobody?"

"Nobody."

Jake make a low, noncommittal sound. Ignoring her protest, he slowly unfastened her gun belt and set it on her bed. "You don't need them, darlin'. When a woman's dressed the way you are, she's got a whole different set of weapons to use against a man."

"Like what?" Her lips were ripe with invitation. The scent of her skin drifted around him, as heady as any home-brewed whiskey and every bit as intoxicating. The air felt heavy between them, thick with sexual curiosity and erotic potential.

Don't do it, his instincts warned. *Find another woman.* But Jake didn't want any other woman. The woman he wanted was Miss Annabel Lee Foster, and she was standing right in front of him, just waiting to be kissed.

He slipped his arm around the small of her back and pulled her to him. "Like this."

His lips descended on hers, barely touching, teasing her mouth softly with his own. He wrapped one hand around the nape of her neck, stroking it sensually, while his other hand gently traced the length of her arm. As she stiffened in reaction to his touch, he forced himself to go slowly, to let her adjust to the feel of his hands on her body, to the pressure of his lips against hers.

But the light, tender kiss left him far from satisfied. He wanted more from Annie than just a soft sweetheart's kiss. He wanted the hot, pulsing thrill of a lover's kiss. He wanted to peel her clothing off piece by piece and touch her, kiss her, stroke her body. He wanted the explosion of pleasure and need that would leave them both breathless and trembling. He knew he could achieve that with her. Annie was the kind of woman who would know instinctively when to be wild in her lovemaking and when, on the nights when the weight of the world seemed to rest oppressively on a man's shoulders, to be gentle.

Jake wanted to find that part of her, the fire that was just waiting to be lit. He increased the pressure of his jaw, coaxing her lips apart. Once he did, he swept his tongue inside her mouth, sensually tasting and probing. He felt a tremor of shock sweep through her as their tongues met. He rubbed his hands along her back in soft, soothing circles, giving her time to adjust to the feeling of the kiss.

But to his amazement, Annie did more than simply adjust to the feel of his kiss. She melted into him, meeting his tongue with her own. Her mouth moved against his with such urgency and naked desire that Jake nearly groaned out loud. She rocked against him, her hips pressed against his, her breasts crushed against his chest, matching the rhythm of his kiss.

Jake brushed his hands down her back, caressing and exploring, learning the feel of every curve of her body. She felt exactly the way he had thought she would feel in his arms. Perfect. The woman had a body that was made for loving. Following his lead, she gently explored his frame with her hands, caressing his shoulders, his back, his buttocks; all while locked in their deep, sensual kiss.

He lifted his hand, gently cupping her breast in his palm. Once again, Annie seemed to recoil—whether from shock or surprise, he couldn't tell. Then, like a skittish colt who was learning to trust, she leaned into him, uttering a soft moan that held both pleasure and acquiescence. He felt her nipple rise against his palm through the thin fabric of her dress as she grabbed his shoulders for support.

Jake let out a low groan as a rush of pulsating desire swept over him. He knew that if he didn't stop now, he wouldn't be able to stop at all. Summoning a self-control he hadn't known he possessed, he reluctantly ended the embrace and stepped back a pace. Annie looked up at him with eyes that were bright with desire, lips that were rosy and swollen from their kiss. She showed neither embarrassment or shame, just the soft, satisfied flush of a woman who had been properly kissed.

Not knowing what else to say, he reached out and tucked a loose strand of hair behind her ear. "You better get going."

Disappointment and relief flicked through her eyes in equal measure. She let out a shaky breath and nodded, taking a step away from him. "You ready to leave, mister? We don't want to be late."

"I'm not going."

"You're not?" She looked surprised, then crestfallen, then hurt. "Oh," she said in a small voice. She turned to gaze out the window. "I guess I just figured you were. *Me das perro,* huh?"

You're giving me the dog, Jake translated mentally, feeling a stab of guilt. Never had he promised to escort her to the dance, yet somehow it seemed as though he had broken his word. "I'm not much for town dances," he said. "I thought I'd see if I could drum up a game of poker over at the saloon instead."

"Oh."

She looked like a little girl whose birthday party had just been canceled. Jake suppressed a sudden ridiculous urge to pull her onto his lap and cradle her in his arms. Or even more absurd, to go with her to the dance. Clearly what he needed to do was to put some time and space between them, before he did something he would really regret.

"Annie, darlin'?"

"What?"

"You'll do just fine on your own." He lifted her gun belt from the bed and passed it to her. "But I've changed my mind about the guns. If anybody else tries to do what I just did, you have my permission to shoot him."

Chapter 10

*A*nnie walked down Main Street and toward the town hall, feeling more at peace with herself than she had in years. As near as she could tell, everything was finally starting to go her way. To begin with, she had found no sign of Snakeskin Garvey when she had gone out scouting earlier that morning. It had probably just been some no-account drifter trailing them, she decided, feeling no end of relief. In the second place, she was all gussied up in her new finery and headed for the first real dance she had been to in ages. And lastly, she was on her way to the Palace Hotel. By her reckoning, they would reach Cooperton in about a week.

The only way things could have been better was if Jake Moran were there beside her. A gentle fluttering filled her belly as her thoughts trailed off to the kiss she had shared with Jake back at the hotel. So now she knew. Kissing Jake wasn't terrifying at all. In fact, it was a hell of a lot better than just about anything she had ever done in her life.

Funny how she had always thought that a man—any man—would feel like Snakeskin Garvey; all hot and rough, crudely smothering her with his body. But Jake wasn't anything like that. She didn't mind the way he touched her, or the way his lips felt against hers. A slight shiver ran up her spine, and a warm glow spread through her limbs as she thought about what it had felt like to be in his arms. Instead of feeling threatened, she had felt delicate and desired. Why, she wouldn't even object if he wanted to kiss her again, she decided, smiling softly to herself.

Annie walked a few more paces, nearly skipping with excitement as she neared the town hall. Bright, glowing light poured out from the windows and spilled into the street. The sound of fiddlers playing a jaunty tune echoed out to her, followed by the sound of voices raised in good cheer. She paused to straighten her dress and check her guns, then smoothed back her hair one last time. Well, she thought, even though Jake wasn't with her, at least she wouldn't have to walk in alone. She had Cat to keep her company.

With that reassuring thought in mind, she took a deep breath and pasted a brave smile on her lips. For the first time in her life, she was going to be a true lady. She lifted her skirts and climbed the steps to the town hall with what she hoped was the proper amount of elegance and dignity, then she stepped inside. The huge room with the tall, grand ceilings was packed to the brim with folks laughing and talking. Couples spun around the makeshift dance floor, whirling in time to the music. A broad table stood against one wall, heavily laden with cakes, pies, cookies, and punch.

Not sure where to go, she stood awkwardly at the entrance, drinking it all in. After a moment, she became aware of a rush of excited whispers traveling through the crowd. Heads shot toward her as bold, curious strangers looked her up and down. The words *Outlaw Annie*, *Mundy Gang*, and *no-good, thieving outlaws* buzzed around the room. Finally the frenzied murmur died down and a sullen hush fell over the crowd. The curious gazes turned decidedly hostile.

Annie swallowed hard and tilted her chin. While she hadn't thought she would be received with open arms, neither did she suspect that just walking through the door would cause this kind of a stir. Her heart beat wildly within her chest as she frantically searched her mind for something to do or say. Unable to bear the silence a second longer, she lifted her skirts and performed what she hoped was a reasonably graceful curtsy. That accomplished, she stared into the sea of angry faces and forced a wobbly smile.

"Howdy, everybody," she said, wincing at the painfully high, nervous tone of her voice.

Blank stares greeted her, followed by a second shocked murmur of voices.

One man made his way through the crowd and walked toward her. The deep echo of his boot steps seemed to fill the hall. He was probably a rancher, she guessed as she watched him approach. His hair was deep silver, but his face had the leathery, bronzed look of a man who spent long days out in the sun. He regarded her with dour disapproval, then said, "We don't allow no guns in the town hall. You can check your weapons, or you can turn around and get out. Which is it, girl?"

Annie stiffened her spine and informed him coolly, "My name is Miss Annabel Lee Foster, not girl." She let that soak in, then unhooked her gun belt and passed it to him. Turning to the crowd at large, she continued, "Thank you for your kind invitation. I believe I prefer to stay." Amazingly, despite the fierce knocking of her knees beneath her skirts, the words came out sounding proud and strong.

The rancher silently accepted her guns and deposited them in a box near the front door. Then, one by one, the townsfolk turned their backs on her and went back to their merriment.

Annie stood alone by the door, feeling as foolish and out of place as a mud-soaked hog wearing a satin sunbonnet. As she looked across the room, she spotted the clerk who had sold her the Widow Porter's dress. The girl stood in a tight knot with several other women of approximately the same age as Annie. Although she and the shop girl hadn't been formally introduced, at least they had spoken before. Not only that, Annie had spent money in the store where she worked—a fact she hoped would count for something.

She caught the clerk's eye and sent her a tentative smile, then lifted her skirts and took a step toward her. The girl returned her smile with a cool smirk, then turned and whispered loudly to her friends. A burst of high, jittery laughter sounded from within the group of women. Their gazes shot toward Annie, then they turned and skittered away like a group of nervous hens. Looking distinctly satisfied, the shop girl tossed her head and walked away with her friends.

Annie stood frozen in mid-step, uncertain how to respond to their barefaced rebuff. A cool draft blew in behind her, finally prompting her to action. She remembered the rule in *Winston's Guide* that instructed a guest to find one's hostess and properly greet her before enjoying the evening's activities. Annie scanned the hall, spotting a woman who was seated with her back against the wall. She held two small squirming bundles that had been swaddled in blue in her arms.

Annie made her way across the room. As she approached, the well-wishers who had been gathered around the new mother backed away, various expressions of fear and distaste on their faces. Ignoring their reactions, Annie nodded at the woman seated before her.

"I reckon you must be the mayor's wife."

The woman nodded coolly. "I am."

Annie gave a brief curtsy. "Pleased to meet you. I just wanted to thank you for throwing this fancy shindig and inviting everyone in town. I ain't never been to a party like this before."

The mayor's wife stared back at her with tight, pinched lips.

Annie nervously cleared her throat and tried again.

Smiling at the squirming bundles the woman held, she said, "Those are two fine little babies, ma'am. I reckon you must be awful proud of—"

Her words were cut short as a man stepped between them, reaching for the infants. "Let me help you, my dear," he said. He passed the babies to a nearby woman, then assisted his wife to her feet. She turned and walked away without so much as a backward glance.

The man, obviously the mayor himself, spun around to face Annie. He drew himself up, gazing down at her with indignant outrage. "I would appreciate it if you wouldn't speak to my wife again. I run a peaceful town here, and I don't need any trouble from your kind. Is that understood?" Having said his piece, he turned and marched stiffly away.

As a flurry of excited voices heaped praise on the mayor for his brave defense of his wife, Annie felt her cheeks burn red with shame. She tilted her chin and walked away, moving blindly across the room. The buzzing rhythm of banjos and fiddles echoed through her head, making it throb. The dancers whirled in circles before her eyes, leaving her dizzy and nauseous. Her smile was stretched so tight she felt sure her cheeks would surely burst. But she wasn't about to give up. Not yet.

Somehow she found herself standing next to the table that had been laden with food. Although she doubted she could swallow past the burning lump that filled her throat, at least getting something to eat would occupy her time. She randomly picked up a plate and nodded to the older woman who stood at the end of the table.

"Could you please tell me what I owe you for the pie, ma'am?"

The woman sent her a haughty stare. She picked up her cash box, slammed the lid shut, and moved wordlessly away.

Blinking hard, Annie set down the gooey slice of pie. Determined not to let the townsfolk see her reaction, she clenched her fists against her sides and moved stiffly toward a chair that had been set out for watching the dancing. She sat down and stared blindly ahead, trying her best to look as though she were having the time of her life.

After a minute, she noticed a group of five rough-looking cowhands standing on the opposite side of the hall. They stood huddled together, passing a flask from man to man. From the tone of their voices and the outrageous glances they sent her way, it didn't take long to figure out that she was the object of their attention. Annie tried her best to ignore them, but their crude leers only became more pronounced.

Finally the group of cowhands ambled over, led by one man whose swaggering belligerence told her that he had been drinking more than the others. "You want to dance?" the man demanded.

"No, thank you," she replied and pointedly looked away.

"I don't think you heard me," he said slowly. Before Annie could anticipate his next move, he reached down, grabbed her by her upper arms, and jerked her to her feet. His hot, whiskey-tainted breath fanned her face. "I said, do you want to dance, outlaw gal?"

She shot him a furious glare. "And I said, no, thank you." She struggled to free herself from the man's grasp, but he was simply too strong.

A lewd smile curved the man's lips as he tightened his grip on her arms. His gaze traveled slowly over her body, then his eyes darted toward the dark alley that was visible through the back exit of the town hall.

She went perfectly still. "I'll give you one more warning. Let go of me."

His grin broadened. "What are you gonna do about it if I don't?" A burst of rough male laughter sounded behind him as his friends crowded in closer.

Annie reached instinctively for her guns—and came

up empty. Only then did she remember that she had turned them in at the door.

$\mathcal{J}$ake leaned back in his chair, his gaze drifting slowly around the saloon. As most of the townsfolk had decided to attend the party at the town hall, the crowd was fairly sparse. As it was, he had only been able to find one man interested in a game of poker. The gambler proved to be nothing but an annoyance, however, making Jake wish that he had accompanied Annie after all. The man was drinking steadily and soon became so drunk it was obvious to even the most casual observer that he couldn't tell the difference between a poker chip and a cow chip.

Stifling a sigh of impatience as his opponent fumbled with his cards, he let his thoughts drift toward Annie, wondering if she was having a good time. By his reckoning, she would probably have at least a half dozen gentlemen suitors crowding around her by now, asking for a dance. And given Annie's innocent enthusiasm, she would no doubt accept each and every invitation. The thought did nothing to improve his mood.

He was painfully aware of how much courage it had taken for her to go alone, and felt a stab of guilt for not accompanying her. He pushed the unwanted emotion away, shaking his head. He was with Annie in order to trap the Mundy Gang, and for no other reason. Kissing her, touching her the way he had done, had been nothing but foolish curiosity on his part. If he had an ounce of brains, he would keep that in mind.

He shifted uncomfortably in his chair. While he could argue all he liked about the impossibility of a match between them, that impossibility was slowly turning into something that looked and felt more like an inevitability. His instincts told him that the kiss they had shared had only been the beginning of something bigger. If there was one thing he had learned in life, it was that there was no sense fighting fate. A man most often met his destiny on the road he took to avoid it.

Jake didn't like to be vulnerable. Nor did he consider himself a sentimental or a mystical man. But there were some things in life that had the power to move him very deeply. Things that demonstrated his own insignificance and showed that there was perhaps a grander vision than his own.

He remembered the first time he had held a newborn babe, a tiny girl barely two days old. He certainly hadn't wanted to hold the fragile-looking, squalling creature. But she had been eagerly thrust into his arms, all pink and wrinkled, her little hands and legs flying, and he had had no choice but to accept her. At first, Jake had felt nothing but fear that he might drop the squirming infant. But his fear had gradually eased as the baby had settled down. For a fleeting moment, their eyes had met, then she had wrapped her little fist around Jake's pinky and held on tight, as though she would never let it go.

He remembered the aftermath of the battle of the Wilderness. General Lee had ridden Traveller through the ranks, his face tight with strain and loss. As he did, a hush had fallen among the men. Men who were hungry and cold, bleeding and sick, and dressed in threadbare clothing had stood and come to attention on no orders but their own, in silent tribute to their beloved leader. They would have walked through fire had General Lee ordered it; often he did.

All of it had touched Jake very deeply. He had no illusions about what he was. A drifter, a cardsharp, a gambler with few morals and even fewer principles. But moments such as those made life a little grander, a little nobler than it really was. They made him aware, for however brief a time, that there was perhaps a greater purpose in life than that for which he had been living.

And for whatever reason, no matter how absurd it seemed, Miss Annabel Lee Foster struck a similar chord in him. Holding her in his arms, kissing her the way he had, had been as dramatic and yet as commonplace as the change of the seasons, filling him with a sense of deep satisfaction. It was an odd sensation for him, and one that he was not entirely comfortable with. Jake was accustomed to feeling lust for women, along with a certain amount of respect and affection—but never before had he experienced what he felt when he held Annie.

Unable to get her out of his mind, he decided to fold his cards and call it a night. No sense hanging around the saloon. He might as well head over to the town hall and see how she was getting on.

"Wait a minute," the drunk slurred indignantly as Jake stood. "You won my money, now you're walking out before I get a chance to win it back?"

"Why don't you sober up a bit, then I'll give you another chance."

"I ain't drunk."

Jake sighed and put on his hat. "You're holding your cards backward, mister."

The drunk looked at his hand in astonishment, then let out a deep bourbon-scented guffaw.

It was at that moment that an angry chorus of shouting and screaming echoed into the saloon from down the street. Less than a second later, a young boy burst in through the bat-wing doors. "Fire!" he screamed, his eyes wild with excitement. "That outlaw woman set the town hall on fire!"

*A*nnie stared into a sea of hostile faces, her heart thumping wildly. The town hall of Two River Flats smoldered and sparkled behind her, glowing an eerie crimson and orange against the ink-black sky. Thick, acrid smoke filled the air. The taste of ash coated her mouth and felt heavy on her skin. At least the screaming and shouting of the townsfolk had quieted down somewhat now that the fire had been put out. Only a few remaining embers hissed and popped.

Her focus, however, was on neither the fire nor the angry townspeople. Instead she looked beyond the crowd, her attention caught by the activity in the northern end of town. For amid the pandemonium, amid the running and shouting, the buckets of water, the creaking timber, and the general melee that followed the conflagration, Annie had heard the distinct, rapid-fire blast of gunshots in the distance. Her ears were attuned enough to the sound of gunplay to recognize it when she heard it. She searched the horizon, her stomach tied in knots, looking for trouble.

Something told her that the night had just gone from bad to worse.

Her suspicion that she was headed for trouble was confirmed with the appearance of a tall man who strode confidently down the street toward her. He was handsome enough in a lanky, blond way. His face was boyishly youthful—except for his eyes. He had the flat, cool, judging eyes of the law. Annie saw no badge beneath his thick wool jacket, but there was no mistaking that he was in charge. He was flanked by a pair of big men with rifles grasped casually in their hands.

A respectful silence fell over the crowd. The sheriff stopped and surveyed the wreckage of the town hall, his expression grim. "Somebody want to tell me what happened here?" he said to the crowd at large.

A flurry of excited voices erupted at once.

The sheriff lifted his hand for silence and pointed to a middle-aged man attired in a snugly fitted three-piece suit. "Parnell. Talk."

The man named Parnell threw back his shoulders and cast a superior glance at the rest of the crowd. He drew himself up and pointed a chubby finger at Annie, his florid face indignant. "That outlaw woman set the hall on fire, Sheriff Pogue, that's what happened."

The entire town seemed to angrily second that opinion. Why, they acted as if she had deliberately charged in, taken a torch, and lit the hall afire. The sheriff listened for a minute, then turned toward Annie and intently surveyed her from head to toe. She knew she looked a mess, with her new dress singed and burned, her hair undone and loose around her shoulders, and ashes coating her skin, but there was nothing she could do about it.

She stood her ground and met the sheriff's eyes, refusing to cower. She would accept part of the blame for the fire, but not all of it. It had been an accident, pure and simple—no matter what the townsfolk said.

"I reckon you must be Outlaw Annie," the sheriff remarked.

Annie tilted her chin and drew back her shoulders. In a manner straight out of *Winston's Guide*, she replied politely, "I prefer Miss Foster, if you don't mind, Sheriff."

"All right," the sheriff replied coolly, his eyes giving nothing away. "You want to tell me your side of the story, Miss Foster?"

"That man there asked me to dance," Annie replied, singling out the rough cowhand who had bullied her. "When I said no, he got real insistentlike and tried to pull me out on the dance floor. I told him to let me go, but he wouldn't listen. We tussled for a little bit, and I reckon Cat saw me wrestling with him and didn't like the look of his mangy hide any more than I did. She jumped on his shoulder and took a swipe at his arm."

"That damned beast near clawed my arm off," broke in the cowhand.

The sheriff coolly waved him to silence. "You hold on a minute, Dwight. You'll get your chance to talk. Go on," he said to Annie.

She shrugged. "That's mostly it. He staggered back, trying to knock Cat off his shoulder, and knocked over a couple of oil lamps instead. That's when the fire started."

The sheriff turned to the cowhand. "That what happened, Dwight?"

Dwight's lips worked in silent, angry willfulness. He spit out a long brown stream of tobacco and wiped the dribble from his chin with the back of his sleeve. "If she didn't want to dance, then what the hell was she doing there?"

Jake Moran's voice carried over the excited murmur of the crowd. "Seems to me that the lady has a right to go anywhere she pleases."

Annie felt an immediate, inexplicable rush of relief at the sound of Jake's voice. She spotted him making his way through the crowd, standing a good head and shoulders taller than most folks there. As his eyes met hers, she no longer felt quite so alone.

"You let me handle this, Jake," the sheriff said.

"You go right ahead, Walt." His tone was friendly enough, but as he scouted the faces in the crowd, there was an underlying firmness to it. "I just don't want to see Miss Foster blamed for something that doesn't appear to be her fault."

"Nobody's getting blamed for anything. At least, not yet." The sheriff turned to face the crowd. "All right, folks, the party's over. Those of you who want to help my deputies clean up are welcome to stay. The rest of you can go on home. And as for you, Dwight, I want to see you in my office tomorrow morning at eight. You don't show, and I'll send my deputies out to Parker's ranch to bring you in and fine you a day's wages for wasting my time. You understand me?"

Dwight nodded glumly and turned away. The crowd broke up and slowly dispersed, grumbling but compliant.

Annie turned to head back to the hotel, but the sheriff's voice stopped her. "If you don't mind, Miss Foster, there are a few questions I'd like answered. Would you follow me to my office?"

The question was framed as a polite request, but the

sheriff's gaze was unrelenting. Annie shot a glance at Jake. He shrugged, and the two of them stepped into line behind Sheriff Pogue. Funny how just a few weeks ago Annie would have bridled at Jake's intrusion. But now his presence felt perfectly natural. They made their way to the sheriff's office and stepped inside. Walter Pogue took a seat on one side of a broad rough-hewn desk, then motioned to two chairs across from him.

Once she and Jake were seated, the sheriff quickly got to the heart of the matter. "Heard you went for a little ride this morning, Miss Foster."

Annie didn't bother to question where he had gotten his information. In a town the size of Two River Flats, nothing went unnoticed. "Any law against that, Sheriff?"

"Depends. You talk to anybody while you were out there?"

"My horse."

Sheriff Pogue steepled his fingers, his expression flat. "I can talk all night if you want me to, Miss Foster. But I reckon you'd like to get out of here, go back to the hotel, and maybe get some sleep. You answer my questions straight and you'll leave that much sooner. You understand me?"

Annie leveled a cool, hard look at him. "I understand you."

"Good." He leaned back in his chair and propped his feet up on his desk. "Then, why don't you start by telling me who you met with when you rode out of town this morning?"

"I didn't meet with anyone."

"Well, you didn't ride out there just to enjoy the view. Who were you looking for?"

Annie hesitated, then reluctantly answered. "Someone's been trailing us the past few days. I thought it might be a fella by the name of Jim Garvey. Folks who know him call him Snakeskin Garvey."

"Snakeskin?"

She nodded. "That's about all he wears. Fancy snakeskin boots, snakeskin belt, snakeskin vest, even the band on his hat is made out of snakeskin."

"Did he ride with the Mundy Gang?"

"Not for long. Pete kicked him out, whopped him so bad he almost killed him. Garvey blamed me for what happened. He swore he'd come back and even the score with me once Pete was gone."

"Why'd Pete kick him out of the gang?"

Annie stiffened, then lifted her shoulders in what she hoped was an indifferent shrug. "He had his reasons."

"I see." The sheriff exchanged a veiled look with Jake, then continued, "You find any sign of this Snake-skin fella?"

She shook her head. "I didn't find anything. I rode back into town about noon."

"All right." The sheriff stood and moved to a cast-iron stove that sat in a corner. He filled three tin cups with coffee and passed a cup to her and Jake. He took a deep sip, studying her for a long moment in silence. "When was the last time you talked to Pete Mundy?"

"Three months ago, the morning he and the boys were killed."

"You mind telling me how it happened?"

She shifted in her chair, fighting back her natural instinct to clam up when talking to the law. These were the same questions Sheriff Cayne had asked her—the same questions she reckoned she would hear over and over again for the rest of her days. She might as well keep answering them until somebody believed her.

"The boys were fixin' to rob a payroll off a train," she said. "Normally I stayed home to wait for them, to see if any of them needed doctoring up. But that morning, I was leaving for good. The gang was getting too rowdy, and the jobs they were pulling were getting too serious for my taste. I didn't want any part of it. But before I left, I followed them out to the train and hung back and waited, just to make sure that none of them were hurt. I guess I figured I owed them at least that much."

"What happened next?" the sheriff asked bluntly.

"It was a setup. The train wasn't carrying a payroll but a boxcar full of lawmen instead. The door slid open, and those lawmen blasted the boys off their horses before they could move or lift their hands in surrender."

Annie fought back a shudder at the grizzly memory. It had all happened in less than a minute, yet it seemed to take forever. She remembered the screeching sound of the railcar door sliding open, then the shock of seeing the armed men inside. It seemed she had been able to hear each individual bullet they fired—and there must have been hundreds of them. She smelled the blood, heard the boys scream in shock and terror, and watched in stunned horror as they writhed in agony, then tumbled from their mounts.

She had been hidden in the woods, too far away to fire her gun or do anything to save them. All she had been able to do was watch the boys die. She hadn't been able to scream or to move, or even to look away. She had sat frozen in her saddle, unable to stop watching, as though she were trapped in a nightmare. But that nightmare had been real.

"You sure they were dead?" Sheriff Pogue asked.

Annie swallowed hard. "I know what dead looks like."

"And the whole gang was there?"

"Yes."

The sheriff frowned. "Let me see if I've got this straight," he drawled. "You're telling me that Pete Mundy, Frank Wade, Neil Abbott, Woodie Harold, and Diego Martinez were all shot down in cold blood by a group of lawmen who ambushed them from a railcar?"

"That's right."

"Didn't it strike you as odd that a group of lawmen

would bring down a gang as notorious as the Mundys and not spread the word—or collect the reward? Didn't it seem awfully strange that the news never hit the papers? That should have been the lead story in the territorial papers for weeks."

"I know what I saw, Sheriff. I can't explain the rest of it, but I know what I saw." In truth, Annie had been bothered by the same thing, but this didn't strike her as the time to air her doubts.

"Where's all this leading, Walt?" Jake asked.

"I'll tell you where," Sheriff Pogue answered, his gaze turning hard and flat as he looked at Annie. "Fact is, I'm not a big believer in coincidences, Miss Foster, and we've got a whole string of them to contend with here. Let me start with what was happening at the northern end of town while you were *coincidentally* causing all that ruckus down at the town hall. Five men rode up and tried to break into the bank."

Annie stiffened. That explained the shots she had heard earlier. And she had a sinking feeling that there was more bad news to come.

"They wore handkerchiefs over their faces, but my men and I saw enough to make a guess at who they were. Would you like to hear it?"

"I'm listening," she managed.

"All right. One man was a Mexican. Medium height, stocky build, and short, curly black hair. He rode a big black mare and had a black custom-made saddle embossed with red crosses."

Diego. Annie listened as the sheriff described three more men who could easily be Frank, Neil, and Woodie.

"The leader of the gang," Walter Pogue continued, "was a tall, slim fella with long blond hair peeking out from beneath his hat. He wore a buckskin vest with long fringes and fancy stitching, and black boots with unusual spurs—looked like little silver arrows. He rode a sorrel gelding with one white sock on its left foreleg. That sound familiar to you?"

Pete.

But it couldn't be. The boys in the gang were *dead*. She'd seen them die herself.

Annie tilted her chin, looking the sheriff straight in the eye. "I don't know who those men are, but they ain't the Mundy Gang."

"Is that so?" Walter Pogue replied, unimpressed.

Jake shifted in his chair, regarding the sheriff steadily. "I thought you and I had an understanding, Walt."

The sheriff glared back at Jake, a scowl on his face. "I'm afraid I've got a bit of a problem there. If folks in town discover that I let Outlaw Annie ride out of town clean as a whistle after the Mundy Gang tried to rob the bank, I'm going to have a damned hard time getting elected next year. Especially when they find out that she set the town hall on fire at the exact moment the boys in the gang were attempting to rob the bank. Folks around here don't like that kind of coincidence any more than I do."

"How much?" Jake asked flatly.

Annie and the sheriff both turned to stare at Jake at the same time.

"How much will it cost to fix it?" Jake repeated.

"It's not just a question of money," the sheriff replied.

Jake smiled thinly. "Everything's a question of money, Walt." He reached across the sheriff's desk for an ink pen and paper, scribbled a few lines, and passed it back. "That's a draft note. Take it to the bank in the morning and have them wire for the funds. That ought to cover the damage and then some."

Jake reached for Annie, took her elbow, and politely assisted her up. "You did your job, Walt. You stopped the Mundy Gang from robbing the bank, got rid of Outlaw Annie, and collected damages for the town hall. I reckon that's a fair night's work by anyone's standards."

Annie listened, flinching at his reference to her as Outlaw Annie. It was painfully clear that Jake didn't believe her any more than the sheriff did when she swore that the boys in the gang were dead. For some reason, his distrust bothered her far more than she would have thought.

Walter Pogue stood, picked up the bank note, and stuffed it into his pocket. He fixed Jake with a look that was so dark it was almost hostile. "I'll expect to hear from you sometime in the next few weeks, Jake."

Jake nodded. "You'll hear."

As they stepped out into the street, Annie glanced up at Jake. "What was that all about?"

"Nothing. Just some business between old friends."

The walked toward the hotel. It was nearly midnight and the town looked deserted. The crisp autumn breezes that Annie had enjoyed earlier that day had turned into frosty gusts that seemed to tear through the thin fabric of her dress. The hotel beckoned in the distance, emitting a soft glow through the windows that promised both warmth and security. She wrapped her arms tightly around her waist and quickened her pace.

They reached the hotel and made their way upstairs. Annie paused at the door to her room, searching for something to say that might lessen the evening's disaster. Pasting a brave smile on her lips, she announced brightly, "Well, mister, at least I made an impression."

Jake stared at her for a moment in silence, then he shook his head. A slight smile curved his lips as he unlocked his door and pushed it open. "Next time, darlin', try to make a good one."

Chapter 11

*T*hey left Two River Flats the next morning just after sunrise. Annie rode hard, driven by an emotion that was part desperation, part fear, and part anger. She didn't examine her feelings, nor did she discuss them with Jake. She simply rode. As far as she could and as fast as she could. All that mattered was getting as many miles between herself and the town of Two River Flats as possible.

Shortly after noon, they stopped at the banks of a river that had swollen to near impassibility as a result of the previous week's rain. Remembering the last time she had ridden through the territory with the boys, Annie mentally calculated the distance to the nearest shallow ford where they could safely cross. It was at least three days' ride away—and then three days back. Almost a week's time lost. They studied the river in silence for a long moment, neither one speaking.

"We'll go around," Jake finally said with a sigh.

"We'll go across," Annie countered, tucking Cat securely inside her coat as she spurred Dulcie on.

"Damn it, Annie! Wait a minute!"

She ignored him. Jake Moran could follow her or not; the choice was his. At that moment, it was all she could do to keep her seat. The banks of the river were thick with mud, and Dulcie spooked as she sank to her knees and tried to find solid footing. Undaunted, Annie spurred the little mare on, urging her into the swift current.

After a moment, she heard Jake behind her. "I'm glad you thought this over," he called as he and Weed plunged into the river.

Annie didn't answer. Icy, muddy water splashed her face and soaked her clothing. The river swirled around her, threatening to suck her under. The water was much deeper than she had anticipated, and the current was much stronger. Dulcie began to swim. Annie slipped off the saddle and clung desperately to one stirrup, attempting simultaneously to keep her own head above water, to prevent Cat from drowning, and to avoid Dulcie's thrashing hooves. The threat of being pulled under by the swirling, rushing current was suddenly a very real thing.

She glanced over her shoulder and tried to catch sight of Jake and Weed, but the effort was in vain. Icy water splashed her face and stung her eyes, totally obscuring her vision. Although she couldn't see him, doubtless he was caught in much the same struggle as she.

Dulcie finally reached the opposite bank and lurched up, snorting and breathing hard. Annie dropped to her knees and scrambled through the mud and brush, thankful just to be back on solid ground. Her hat had been knocked off her head and swept away by the current, and her hair drooped in her face like river weed. At least twenty pounds of mud and silt coated her skin and filled her boots and clothing. On top of that, she had probably lost at least half the contents of her saddlebags. But at least she was alive.

She heard the sound of hoofbeats behind her and turned to see Jake, still atop Weed, looking relatively dry and in control. He studied her and let out a short laugh. "You look like a drowned rat, darlin'."

Annie released a dripping wet and thoroughly unhappy Cat from her coat, then rose to her feet with as much dignity as she could muster. "Thank you very much."

"You ever think things through before you do them?"

"We made it, didn't we?" she shot back, her patience at an end. "And why do you always have to be so damn smug about everything?"

"I'm not smug, just right."

"We saved ourselves six days."

"How are your guns?" he parried.

Annie glanced down, mortified and embarrassed. As she had underestimated the depth of the river, she hadn't taken any precautions with her weapons. Her guns and cartridge belt were soaked through, as was her carbine. In effect, her weapons were now completely useless. Not only had Jake kept his seat, he had shown the forethought to wrap his cartridge belt and holsters across his chest and hold his rifle above his head while he crossed. His guns, saddlebags, and clothing were all still relatively dry.

She, in contrast, was sodden, icy cold, and unarmed. A gust of wind whipped around them, sending a chill down her spine. The fight suddenly went out of her. The strain of the hanging, the bandits, the fire, the reappearance of the Mundy Gang—it was simply too much for her to stand anymore. The emotions she had been keeping so tightly in check bubbled to the surface and overflowed like a pot that had been left untended.

Annie clenched her jaw as a tight, burning ache filled her throat and her eyes swelled with tears. She blinked rapidly and swallowed hard, turning her back to Jake.

She heard him sigh, then dismount. The sound of his footsteps carried toward her as he moved in her direction. He wrapped his arm around her shoulder and pulled her to him, pressing her face against his chest as he gently stroked her hair.

"The hell with it, Annie. Go ahead and cry if you want to."

She took a deep, shuddering breath and clenched her fists tightly at her sides. "I never cry, mister. *Never.*"

"I can tell."

That started her crying even harder.

"Shh, darlin'. It's all right. It's going to be all right." He eased her down until they were both sitting, Jake on the ground, Annie in his lap. He rocked her steadily and let her cry, occasionally murmuring low, soothing nonsense or softly caressing her back. Finally her tears dried up. Annie took a deep, gasping breath and hiccupped, wiping her cheeks on the collar of his jacket.

"Feel better?" he asked, passing her a handkerchief.

She blew her nose. "No."

He smiled and removed a shiny silver flask from within his coat pocket. "Here, have a sip of this. It'll put some hair on your chest."

"I don't want hair on my chest."

"Tough. Drink it anyway."

Annie accepted the flask and took a deep swallow. The liquor burned her throat, but once it reached her belly, it felt warm and strangely comforting. She tipped it back and drank some more.

He removed it from her hand. "That's enough, darlin'. I'd say you're sufficiently recovered."

Annie nodded against his chest and let out a deep, almost contented sigh. His strong arms were wrapped tightly around her, as snug and comforting as a goose-feather quilt. She tilted her chin to meet his eyes at the same moment that he bent his head to look at her. Her heart slammed against her chest as Jake's eyes took on a half-lidded, almost slumberous heat, the same expression she had seen the last time they kissed. She boldly met his gaze, wanting the comfort, the distraction, the thrill of another kiss. Without hesitation, she tilted back her chin and offered her lips to his.

His gray eyes drifted slowly over her. Then, mysteriously, he drew back. "Let's get you in some dry clothes before you catch pneumonia."

Annie nodded and pulled away, feeling flustered and clumsy. Before she could remind him that all of her belongings were as thoroughly soaked as she was, Jake gently set her off his lap and stood. He strode to his saddlebags and pulled out a clean set of woolen drawers, a pair of thick wool socks, two flannel shirts, and denim riding pants. "These will be big on you, but they're dry. You can change behind the bushes while I see if I can find some wood for a fire."

She accepted the clothing with a murmur of thanks and rose to change, Jake's matter-of-fact attitude relieving her of some of her embarrassment. His clothes were far too large on her, just as he had predicted, but they felt vastly better than the freezing, wet garments she had worn earlier. The clothing was not only warm and cozy but smelled of Jake, wrapping her in his heady, masculine scent.

When she stepped gingerly out from behind the bushes, she noted that he had not only managed to start a campfire but had unsaddled the horses and put on a pot of coffee as well. Annie busied herself spreading out her clothing and possessions to dry, then she joined Jake in front of the fire. He passed her a hot cup of the steaming brew, as well as two flaky biscuits filled with ham and cheese, purchased from the cafe before they had left town.

She ate slowly, staring into the flickering flames of the fire. Her gaze moved next to Jake, studying him intently. Were his guns more prominent now than before, or was it just her imagination? He looked perfectly calm and relaxed, but there was a subtle readiness about him, as though he expected trouble at any moment.

"Do you think people come back from the dead?" she asked. "Like ghosts?"

"No."

"Neither do I."

"You're talking about the Mundy boys."

She let out a mirthless laugh and wrapped her arms around her knees, resting her chin on top of them. "Who else? The way I see it, there are only two questions to ask." She let out a sigh and counted off the questions on her fingers. "One, who were those men who tried to rob the bank last night, and why were they dressed up like the Mundy Gang? Or two, why am I lying about the boys being dead?" She studied Jake for a long moment in silence. "Tell me, mister, which question are you asking yourself?"

"Both."

A small, knowing smile touched her lips. "You still haven't decided whether you can trust me or not."

"Do you trust me?" he countered.

Annie studied him for a second longer, then turned and gazed off into the horizon. She thought about the kiss they had shared last night—and the one Jake had avoided just moments earlier by deliberately drawing back. "We're at a funny stage, aren't we?" she said. "Like two dogs sniffing each other, neither one quite sure about the other."

Jake's face split into a broad grin. "I would have put it differently, but yes, I suppose that's true." He thought for a moment, then said, "There is a third possibility, you know. You could be wrong about the boys being dead. Maybe they were shot up pretty bad, but they lived."

She shook her head in instant, vehement denial. "I know what I saw. Those boys were dead."

"All right. Let's say the boys are dead. You think this Snakeskin fella could be behind the robbery? If he knew Pete Mundy and the rest of the gang, it wouldn't be too hard for him to step into Pete's place, would it?"

"Snakeskin?" Annie repeated with a shaky laugh.

"Hell, no. The man never did have that kind of brains. He was nothing but a bully, plain and simple."

A heavy silence fell between them. She thought for a moment, then announced briskly, "It's time we talked straight with each other, mister."

Jake arched a dark brow. "By all means."

"Whoever is out there posing as Pete and the boys will likely come after me. Least it seems that they might, seeing as how they were in Two River Flats at the same time that I was. I agree with Sheriff Pogue. That's just a bit too coincidental for my taste. They come after me, and it might just get rough." Annie paused for a minute, frowning. "Fact is, there ain't no call for you to put your neck on the line. Those men are my problem, not yours. If you want to ride off and just meet up with me in Cooperton, that's fine by me. You can even wire the sheriff and say that you escorted me all the way there and get your roll back. I won't say a word."

Jake studied her for a long moment in silence, his expression unfathomable. "I'm in this for the long haul, remember?"

"You sure?" she asked, hoping her relief didn't show on her face.

"I'm sure."

"All right, then, let's talk about the money I owe you. How much were those damages to the town hall?"

Jake named the figure.

Annie blinked, trying to hide her despair at the sum. "I'll pay you back," she swore. "But I won't have the money until we reach Cooperton. I should be able to borrow at least that much against the Palace Hotel."

"I can wait," Jake agreed. He held her gaze for a long moment, then asked, "Is that what had you so upset a little while ago, the town hall burning down?"

Annie looked away, embarrassed. "Partly. That and everything else that's been going on," she admitted. "As long as those men are out there, robbing banks and stages and claiming to be the Mundy Gang, folks will never accept me, no matter what I do. I'm afraid I won't ever get a chance to make myself respectable."

A look of understanding crossed Jake's features. He poured them both a second cup of coffee, then leaned back against a fallen stump, stretching out his long legs. "Why don't you tell me about last night," he suggested.

She lifted her shoulders in a listless shrug. "There ain't much to tell. Folks just didn't take to me the way I hoped they would."

"Maybe it only seemed that way to you."

She shook her head in vehement denial. "I know it. Trust me, mister. I was about as welcome as a flu bug at a kissing contest."

"What happened?"

"I don't know." She looked up at him, feeling both puzzled and hurt. "I was all gussied up real fine in that new dress and all, but they still looked at me and snickered behind my back. I heard 'Outlaw Annie' and laughing, but the kind of laughing that ain't friendly. 'Specially among the ladies. Truth is, those ladies are a lot meaner than most outlaws I've ever run into. Especially the ones in those fancy hats. You ever noticed that? The fancier the hat, the meaner the lady. I tried to introduce myself, but they just turned their backs on me when I walked up." She paused, shaking her head. "I reckon that maybe I had that coming, since I did run with an outlaw gang and all, but I figure every person deserves a chance to start over, don't you?"

Jake took a sip of coffee and nodded. "I reckon they do."

She mulled that over for a moment, then shrugged it off. "I decided that Cat and I should stay, just to hear the tunes and watch the folks dance." She stubbornly brought up her chin. "And I wanted to show them that they couldn't scare me away. I may not be as highfalutin as some of the folks in there, but at least I got enough manners to return a friendly *howdy* from a stranger."

"How did that Dwight fella get involved?"

"Him?" Annie made a face of disgust. "That happened later, after I'd been there for a while. He swaggered over to me, his friends laughing and hollering and backing him up. He'd been drinking more than the rest. Had that hot, musty smell of whiskey on his breath, and his eyes were sort of glazed over. He had trouble walking too. His legs were bent and wobbly, like they were carrying too full a load."

"He cause any trouble for you?"

"Nothin' that I couldn't handle. He slurred something about wanting to dance with me, but I turned him down." She illustrated her next words by tossing back her shoulders and tilting her chin. " 'No, thank you,' I said, all properlike, just the way *Winston's Guide* says it ought to be done."

"I take it Dwight didn't take no for an answer."

Annie nodded, working herself up as she related her story. "No, he didn't. Maybe the men over in England have all read that book and know proper manners, but here in the West, it seems that a gal's got to use a little more force to get her point across, if you know what I mean."

Jake didn't bother to contain his grin. "Exactly what kind of force did you use?"

"Oh, nothing much," she replied breezily. "He tried to pull me out on the dance floor, so I slugged him in that fat gut of his. Not too hard, mind you, just hard enough to double him over and convince him to let go of me. That's when Cat got into the mix."

As if realizing that she was being discussed, Cat sauntered over and stepped into Annie's lap, circling a few times to stake out her territory before she settled down. She looked at Jake, hissing at him less aggressively than usual. Then she shook her tail, regally giving Annie permission to continue her story. Annie did.

"I reckon Cat thought I was in trouble and decided to help me out," she said, brushing her finger along Cat's back. "She jumped onto that Dwight fella's shoulder. The fool started howling and carrying on like a wolf had grabbed hold of him, not some sweet little kitty. He staggered back and knocked a couple of those fancy party lanterns into a pile of hay, just like I told the sheriff. That's how the fire started."

"I see."

Annie chewed her bottom lip, worried. "You think I acted all right? You don't believe I started that fire on purpose, do you?"

"I think you acted just fine."

She didn't miss the fact that he failed to comment on whether or not he thought she had started the fire deliberately. While that bothered her, convincing Jake of her innocence was only a minor part of what worried her. "But what if something like that happens when I get to the Palace Hotel?" she continued. "How am I supposed to prove that I'm a lady, and not just Outlaw Annie?"

"You don't have to prove a damned thing. A woman is always presumed to be a lady unless she demonstrates otherwise. The burden of proof is never on the lady."

Annie immediately brightened. "Really? Where did you learn that, some fancy law book?"

Jake grinned and shook his head. "That's good Southern upbringing, darlin'. You just keep it in mind."

They sat together in silence, sipping their coffee and mulling over their thoughts. "Who knows?" Annie said after a few minutes. "Maybe those outlaws who are pretending to be the Mundy boys won't come after me at all. Maybe they'll head north, or disappear out West. Could be it has nothing to do with me at all."

"You really believe that?"

She managed a weak smile. "No, but I thought you might."

"Listen, darlin', we'll get to that fancy hotel of yours, and everything will be just fine."

Annie nodded, but she couldn't quite convince herself that it was true.

And deep down, behind his cool gray eyes and cocky smile, she doubted if Jake Moran believed it either.

*J*ake didn't know what to make of Annie's story. He had spent the past few hours turning it over in his mind while they rode, but he came to no definite conclusion. Even now, as they stopped and searched for a spot to make camp for the night, he was still wrestling with it.

The problem was simple. He wanted to believe Annie. Everything he had seen indicated that she was completely sincere in her desire to start her life over again. And because he wanted to believe her, he was actually convincing himself of her innocence. Annie was simply too forthright and direct to fabricate an elaborate lie about the boys being dead. Granted, it was suspicious that she had been gone for hours before the Mundy Gang had tried to make a run at the bank, but that truly could have been a coincidence.

Nothing about Annie suggested the type of woman who would cover for a gang of cold-blooded killers. Looking back, Jake remembered the first time he had seen her, standing with a noose around her neck, staring down a hostile crowd with a mixture of anger and bravado. He remembered her storming in on horseback to face down a gang of deadly bandits, and risking her life for an abandoned alleycat. He remembered her gently reassuring him that it wasn't entirely his fault that the South had lost the war. And finally the image of Annie that was carved most vividly in his mind, that of her stepping out from behind a tree in all her naked glory, her willowy limbs and soft curves concealed by nothing but a pine branch: That was one recollection he would carry with him to the end of his days. While none of those memories directly proved her innocence, they did tend to tip the scales more in that direction.

Jake was also listening to what his instincts were telling him. In his experience, instinct was as valid a tool as any other form of reasoning. The mind absorbed a lot that never came to the surface as organized thought. When he played a hunch, he was simply using knowledge that he had but wasn't able yet to identify or put into words. And that instinct told him that Annie was telling the truth.

"Is this all right?" she asked, interrupting his thoughts as she gestured to a patch of grassy brush surrounded by tall cottonwoods.

He nodded in agreement and dismounted. They still had about an hour or so of daylight left, but he didn't mind stopping early. He had had little sleep last night and was willing to bet that Annie had had even less. He glanced around, examining the campsite without much enthusiasm. What he wanted was a soft bed and a good meal. Maybe a plate of fried chicken, mashed potatoes and gravy, stewed tomatoes, fresh green beans, and a thick slice of chocolate cake for dessert. What he got, however, was considerably less. He rolled his blanket on the cold, hard ground and checked his saddlebags for supplies. Dried venison, apples, and a few pieces of hard maple candy.

He split the provisions between them and settled back to eat. The jerky was hard as leather and twice as salty; the apples were soft and mealy. Annie ate uncomplainingly but quickly, as though eager to have the chore finished. He did the same.

The meal over, he settled back and studied the horizon. At the moment, there was nothing but a light scattering of clouds overhead, clouds as thin and fine as homespun lace. But off in the distance, the sky hung low and black. The storm might push their way, it might not. If Jake remembered right, there was a series of shallow caves carved into the base of the canyon walls to which they could retreat for shelter if they needed it.

He glanced over at Annie, noting that she was using the last bit of daylight to intently study *Winston's Guide*. "How are you getting along with that?" he asked.

She looked up at him and sighed. "All right, I reckon. There's just so much to remember."

"You want to practice some?"

An eager expression entered her eyes. "You don't mind?"

In truth, Jake was bothered by the thought of Annie turning herself into the kind of insipid, tittering female that Winston and society in general seemed to hold as ideal. Granted, she might need some polish, but he didn't want to see her change. Nothing about Annie was quite proper, yet her mannerisms suited her perfectly.

Her laugh, for example. Jake knew how a woman should laugh: high and tinkling, like sleigh bells ringing across a field on a star-filled, snowy night. Annie's laugh was rich and full, like biting into a ripe summer peach. A woman should flirt graciously, flutter her eyelashes and glance away. Annie looked a man straight in the eye. A woman should defer from voicing an opinion. Annie was brash and outspoken. A woman should take tiny steps, subtly swaying her hips beneath her skirts. Annie's hips swayed, all right, but her stride was long and determined, sexy but completely unselfconscious.

But if the Palace Hotel was as fine an establishment as Annie claimed, she would need at least a little coaching before she took ownership.

With that in mind, he suggested, "Why don't we begin with the way you speak?"

Her brows immediately snapped together. "What the hell's the matter with the way I speak?"

"I believe Winston would frown on the use of profanity of any sort."

Her eyes widened. "You mean even *hell* and *damn*?"

"I'm afraid so."

Annie let out a discouraged sigh. "What a pain in the ass."

Jake grinned. "You better forget that one too."

"We keep this up, and I ain't gonna have nothing left to say."

"You mean, 'I'm not going to have anything left to say.' And yes, you will. If I know you, darlin', you'll have plenty left to say. Just try to leave out the vulgarities."

Annie frowned as she considered that. "I read something about that, but I figured Winston meant the real bad stuff. You know, the words a fella might use if he were to get his foot stomped by an angry bronc."

"All of it. No swearing of any kind. Nor is a man ever to swear in front of you. It's your responsibility to make that clear."

"How am I supposed to do that?"

Jake thought for a moment, then suggested, "Anytime a man says or does something you find the least bit objectionable or offensive, you say something like, 'I expected better of you, sir.' "

"I expected better of you, sir," Annie repeated, smiling. "I like that. It's simple, dignified, even. What else have you got?"

"You might also reconsider before you offer your opinion on something."

She frowned, clearly puzzled. "Why?"

"You sound too sure of yourself. Too confident."

"What the hell— I mean, what the heck's wrong with that?"

"Men won't like it."

"Why not?"

"It will make them feel inferior, like they can't control you."

"Is that a fact?" As she thought that over, a small, distinctly devious smile curved her lips. "What else won't men like?"

"Annie . . ." he began warningly.

She brought up her chin. "Seems to me I've put up with plenty of bull from men in my time. If I can throw just a little bit of it back in their faces, why shouldn't I? Forget it, mister. I'll try to cut back on my swearing, and maybe even practice some of them grammar rules that are in the book, but I'll say what I please."

Jake shrugged. "Your choice, darlin'. Either you want to act like a lady, or you don't."

Irritation crossed her face. She opened her mouth, then abruptly closed it, as though distracted. Her eyes landed on a spot just beyond Jake's shoulder, then abruptly moved on. "You reckon we're finished for now?"

"Fine with me."

Her eyes moved back to the spot beyond his left shoulder. "Good, because it looks like our little friend is back."

Jake tensed but didn't turn. He casually removed his tobacco pouch from his pocket and rolled a cigarette. He struck a sulfur match against his boot, turning his body slightly as he did, as though protecting the flame from the wind. He didn't lift his head but simply slanted his eyes from beneath the brim of his hat, looking up in time to see a sudden flash of sun on metal against the steepness of the hillside. It wasn't much, just a splinter of light that hung unmoving amid the confusion of jagged rock and tangled brush.

He lit his cigarette and tossed away the match. "It's a rifle, all right," he said. "We'll take for granted that somebody's behind it."

"Indian?"

"Not if the piece is so clean it shines." He paused for a moment, studying her face. "Snakeskin Garvey?"

"Maybe. I'd damned sure like to find out."

Jake grinned, not bothering to correct her. "So would I, darlin'. So would I." He took a long drag off his cigarette and thought. If they charged the stranger who was following them straight on, they would not only put themselves directly in the line of fire but give the man plenty of advance notice so he could get away. What they needed was a more subtle approach.

"You any good at playacting?" he asked.

"Why?"

Jake briefly outlined his strategy.

She offered only one objection. "Why do you get to go?"

" 'Cause it's my plan, darlin'."

That said, Jake moved toward Weed, catching him by the reins. He led his mount across the small plateau until he reached a spot where it was half-darkened by shadows. Then he pulled off Weed's saddle and set it down in a prominent position where it could easily be seen from a distance. Retrieving a brush from his saddlebags, he casually began grooming his horse. Annie brought Dulcie over and joined him, chatting as though casually continuing their earlier conversation. Jake shifted Weed to accommodate the mare, moving until the gelding was hidden entirely in the shadows.

Once Weed was out of view, Jake mounted him bareback. He slipped away from their camp, moving through the dense brush to the spot where he had seen the rifle glint. Glancing back over his shoulder, he saw that Annie had remained exactly where she had been, effortlessly chatting as though Jake were still beside her.

Satisfied that their farce was suitably believable, he brought Weed around in a broad flanking movement, coming up behind the stranger's position. He crept slowly up the hillside, camouflaged by rocks and brush. Finally he gained the advantage he had been seeking and looked down on the small camp.

The stranger was crouched behind two boulders, a flat-topped Stetson pulled down low over his eyes. He wore a brown shirt, black pants, and dark boots. His horse, a sorrel gelding, was saddled nearby. Jake also noticed the fresh fish the man had sizzling in a pan behind him, and the pot of coffee resting over a stack of hot coals. But most importantly Jake noted his gun.

The man's rifle was trained directly on the spot where he had left Annie.

Jake instantly drew his revolver, ready to give the order for him to drop his weapon. But just as he did, a gunshot rang out from behind him. The man whipped around before Jake could react. He brought up his gun and fired.

The shot missed, but only by inches. Jake was certain he felt the heat of the bullet as it skimmed past his arm. Weed reared in fright, startled by the blast, and threw Jake off his back. Jake slammed his head against a rock as he fell. For a moment, his vision blurred and everything went black. He shook off the fall and rolled for cover, fighting to hold on to consciousness.

Then he heard the stranger cock his rifle for his next shot. Jake raised himself on one knee, lifted his revolver, and fired six shots in rapid-fire succession in the man's general direction. He dropped his gun and drew a fresh revolver from his holster. But the stranger made a run for his mount before Jake had a chance to fire. He leapt into the saddle and took off at a gallop, rapidly receding into the tangled brush of the hillside.

Jake heard another rider approaching from behind him. He whirled around and raised his gun. *Annie.* He let out a breath of relief and lowered the weapon. She leapt from her mount and moved quickly toward him.

"What the hell was that shot?" he demanded.

Embarrassment colored her face. "I dropped my gun."

"You *what?*"

"I was coming up from behind to help you. I pulled my rifle out of the scabbard and . . . I don't know. I just dropped it. I'm sorry."

"Damn it."

Annie placed her hands on her hips, her brows knit together in a stern frown. "It ain't like I meant to drop it."

"I know, I know," Jake agreed with a sigh, waving away her protest. Still, he couldn't quite hide his irritation. Had she followed his plan as he had asked her to, he would have captured the stranger who had been following them. Instead, he'd nearly gotten his damned head blown off.

"What about the fella that was up there?" she asked.

"He got away."

"I can see that. I'm asking if you got a good enough look to recognize him."

"I would have if you had stayed behind like I asked you to."

"Look, mister, I said I'm sorry and I meant it." Her rebuke properly delivered, Annie kneeled over him, gently unfastening the buttons on his shirt.

"What the hell are you doing?" he demanded, clamping his hand over hers.

"Your shoulder's bleeding. So's your head."

"Leave it," he ordered curtly. A sharp crack of thunder boomed in the distance as lightning lit up the sky. A sudden gust of wind whipped around them and tossed his hat in the dirt. Jake stomped it with the heel of his boot before the breeze kited it away, then slapped it against his thigh to remove the dust. A few paces away, Weed and Dulcie skittered nervously. "Let's get out of here," he said, his mood turning fouler by the minute.

"Now, just hold on," she said, calmly ignoring both his words and his tone. "I doctored the boys up whenever they were hurt. I reckon I can do the same for you."

He watched as she pulled the scarf from around her

neck, wet it with her canteen, and expertly applied it to his head. He felt the cool, even pressure of the cloth at the base of his skull, and the dull ache gradually faded. After a few minutes, she drew back her hand and frowned at the scarf. "Why, that ain't nothing but a little scratch."

She reached next for his shirt and pulled it off. Jake would have objected, for in truth the bullet had barely grazed his skin, but he was too busy enjoying Annie's touch. The woman's hands felt amazingly soothing on his bare skin. She leaned over him, her brow furrowed in concentration as she brushed the damp cloth over his shoulder. As she moved, her hair fell softly across his chest, as light and provocative as a sweep of golden silk. A second gust of wind sent her hair rippling across his skin and engulfing him in its light, heady fragrance.

Then Annie leaned in even closer, so close that Jake could feel her warm breath against his ribs. The soft flannel of her shirt gaped slightly open, revealing a tantalizing glimpse of her breasts. It was just a hint, a dazzling reminder of what he had felt before. But that hint was enough to set his blood boiling. Annie shifted and her thigh brushed against his. Jake let out a soft moan.

She pulled back immediately. "That hurt?"

"No . . . go on."

"I'll try to be more gentle," Annie promised.

Jake managed not to smile. "You do that, darlin'."

She continued to softly prod his shoulder. Her touch was making him crazy; stirring his blood, sending his pulse racing, and interfering with his breathing. Another minute more of her gentle torture and he would likely explode.

Some awkward, misguided sense of chivalry had made Jake hold back earlier that day, despite the obvious invitation he had seen in her eyes. He had been comforting her, not seducing her, and the line between the two had gotten a mite too fine for his taste. But that was

enough honor for one day. His mama had raised a gentleman, not a complete fool.

As though his hands were moving of their own will,
Jake gently lifted her hair, letting its silky softness cas-
cade through his fingers. Annie's head snapped up and
her lips parted in surprise. She didn't move or swat his
hand away as he thought she might. Instead, her soft
brown eyes locked on his, wide and doelike. As usual,
her face was a canvas for her emotions. He read shock
and surprise in her expression, as well as something that
looked like pleasure.

Gently, almost experimentally, he stroked his fingers
along the satiny skin between her cheekbone and her jaw,
tracing the delicate hollow of her cheek. Then he moved
moved on, gently caressing her chin, the base of her
neck, and the fragile line of her collarbone. Her skin felt
like satin, unbelievably soft and warm. Annie didn't
move while he touched her. She sat immobile, her eyes
locked on his, as though she were uncertain what to do.
Jake lifted his fingers to her mouth, gently tracing
her lips.

For some reason, that seemed to break the spell that
she had been under. Annie let out her breath in a soft gust
of air that held both surrender and release. A slight, almost imperceptible shudder ran through her. She turned
her cheek into his hand and pressed her lips gently
against his palm. The kiss was soft and feather light, like
a kitten nuzzling his hand.

That sweet, artless kiss broke something in Jake. The
cool aloofness with which he held the world at bay
seemed to melt beneath Annie's touch. For a brief moment, as he held her face, it felt as though the world itself
opened, showing him a thousand possibilities he'd never
imagined. Annie was hope and trust and optimism,
united with an unflagging sense of determination.

Although her warm, eager responses to his touch indicated that she had some experience, Jake knew that she was anything but the experienced sexual sophisticate he preferred. She was far more dangerous. A woman like Annie would give everything she had to give—and demand that Jake give something of himself in return.

As sobering as that realization was, it did nothing to dampen Jake's passion. Annie seemed to blossom beneath his touch. In the steady twilight glow that enveloped them, her lush features ripened to an even deeper beauty. Her hair was more vibrantly golden, her eyes a darker brown, her lips fuller and infinitely more seductive. Even her curves, hidden beneath layers of his own clothing, seemed more pronounced. He noted the gentle swell of her hips, the narrow expanse of her waist, and the round fullness of her breasts. Jake felt his blood stirring with the rapid awakening of hot, sexual desire.

He slanted his mouth over hers, kissing her with all the eager hunger and restless ardor of an untried schoolboy. Coaxing apart her lips, he slipped his tongue into her mouth, delighting in the sweet maple-candy taste of her mouth. He pulled her tightly against him and cradled her in his lap, rocking her back and forth in a steady motion that matched the rhythm of their kiss. Annie wrapped her arms around his neck, meeting his hungry ardor with her own. She kissed him with a passion and intensity that left Jake nearly breathless.

He pulled back, holding her tightly in his arms as he kissed her chin, her cheek, the pearly-pink lobe of her ear, then gently trailed hot, loving kisses down the nape of her neck. Annie gave a gasp of pleasure and tilted back her head, giving him full access to the warm, sensitive skin beneath her ear.

While his lips skimmed lightly over her skin, he moved his hand to her shirt and began to slowly release the buttons, one by one. He pulled the soft flannel garment off her shoulders, leaving Annie in nothing but a plain cotton undershirt. But that plain undershirt was a thousand times more enticing than any piece of frilly lingerie Jake had ever seen. Her breasts strained against the fabric, full, round globes that he ached to hold in his hands. Her nipples stiffened to ripe, tiny peaks, their dark coral color visible beneath the thin garment.

Resisting the urge to immediately take her into his hands, Jake lightly traced his fingers over the tops of her breasts instead. "You're beautiful, Annie. So damned beautiful."

She drew in a sharp breath, then quickly let it out. She watched his fingers move across her skin with an expression of guarded reserve, like she was watching water trickle down a rock. She neither pulled back or encouraged him but simply waited and watched, as though wary and unsure as to what might happen next. Unable to interpret her response, particularly after her kiss had been so hot and inviting, Jake tried a little gentle coaxing.

"Do you like that, Annie?" he asked. "Do you like the way I touch you?"

For a long moment, she didn't speak. Then she admitted in a guilty, almost breathless whisper, "I don't hate it."

"I'm glad." It was faint praise, but at that moment, Jake was willing to take whatever he could get.

"I'm . . . surprised," she said, in a voice that was filled with wonder.

She looked more than surprised, but Jake didn't pause long enough to decipher the emotions reflected in her expressive eyes. A hunger to touch her that was so intense it bordered on greed took possession of him. His mouth covered hers, lightly at first, gently exploring. Annie deepened the kiss, eagerly renewing their passion by thrusting her tongue into his mouth. Jake gave a groan of sweet relief. Yielding at last to temptation, he cupped her breasts in his hands as their kiss exploded into one of wild, unrestrained passion.

Annie rocked against him, matching the rhythm of

their kiss with sweet, uninhibited ardor. She was exactly as Jake had expected her to be, sweet and yielding, wild and exciting, exhibiting the same passion and heat in her sensuality as she demonstrated in her everyday life. She ran her hand up his thigh, over his gun belt, moved lightly along his rib cage, then brought her palm to rest softly on his shoulder. His muscles quivered in response to her touch, aching for direct, skin-to-skin contact.

Slowly, gently he reached for her cotton undershirt and lifted the hem. His hand at last made contact with her bare skin, filling him with a rush of heady yearning. He grasped her shirt, intending to pull it off, when Annie suddenly drew back, stopping him. She squirmed off his lap, turning her face away from his.

Jake stopped, frowning at her in confusion. "What is it, darlin'?"

"Can we slow down a bit?"

"Of course," he agreed immediately, feeling totally inept at so obviously misreading her. "I thought you were enjoying—"

"I was," she rushed to reassure him. "I am. It's just that, well . . . I ain't never done this before."

Had she dumped a cold bucket of water over his head she couldn't have shocked Jake any more. Nor could it have cooled his ardor more quickly. He drew back abruptly, appalled.

"I thought you were . . . that is, I thought you had . . ." he managed to stammer out.

Annie studied his face, her eyes wide and innocent. "Why?"

Partly because her responses had been so hot and eager. Partly because of the life she had led. Living in a hideaway cabin in the woods with five notorious outlaws didn't exactly qualify her for the sisterhood. And finally, partly because it made seducing her that much more conscionable.

Her eyes narrowed as she correctly guessed a portion

of his thoughts. "You thought I had experience because I ran with the gang and all."

"Annie—"

"You thought I was one of them easy women, didn't you?" she demanded.

He flashed her his most seductive grin. "Well, darlin', it seemed likely, didn't it?"

"I see." She regarded him steadily, her tone cool and collected. "Yes, I suppose that was natural to assume."

"Then you don't mind—"

Her fist connected with his jaw before he had a chance to finish his sentence. Jake's head snapped around, then his eyes widened with surprise. "What the hell was that for?" he protested, rubbing his jaw. "I thought you said it was a natural assumption."

She sprang to her feet, her eyes flashing fire and her body quivering with angry indignity. "Just because it's natural to assume don't mean it ain't an insult."

Jake watched her stomp away, then threw back his head and let out a shout of laughter. At least one thing was for damned sure. As long as Miss Annabel Lee Foster was around, he would never be bored.

Chapter 12

$\mathcal{A}$nnie studied Jake from across their camp, trying to sort out what had happened between them. She watched as he tended to their fire with a lean, sparse economy of motions, patiently piling kindling onto the already blazing flame. A stiff breeze kicked up, sending a shower of sparks in her direction. She waved the sparks away and glanced up at the sky, noting the dark, ominous clouds that filled the distant horizon.

"You reckon we ought to find another spot to make camp?" she asked.

Jake glanced up at the sky and shrugged. "The storm might miss us. Looks like it's heading east."

Annie didn't argue. She waited until Jake had resumed his seat, then volunteered softly, "I'm sorry I hit you."

Jake looked up at her and grinned. "Seems to me I had it coming, darlin'."

"Why?"

"For assuming things I had no right to assume. That punch of yours was entirely right and proper, so don't you go giving it another thought."

Annie looked away, unreasonably disappointed in his response. She hadn't wanted Jake to stop entirely—in fact, that was the *last* thing she had wanted. She had just needed a minute or two to collect her thoughts. For up to that point, Annie had been engulfed in a wave of pleasure so vast it had threatened to sweep her away entirely. It wasn't that she hadn't been enjoying it—only that she wasn't quite sure what was expected of her next. She had only wanted to stop, get her bearings, and then move on.

But now that moment was over, gone forever. She had ruined it completely, and she had no idea how to repair the damage she had done.

Jake picked up a stick and began to idly poke the fire. Shadows flickered across his face. "What are you thinking about, Annie?" he asked after a minute.

She gave a small, mirthless smile and shrugged her shoulders. "Chasing rainbows."

He arched one dark brow. "What does that mean?"

"When I was a little girl, my father used to tell me stories about magic elves, unicorns, and pots full of gold that were hidden away at the end of a rainbow. He said that they were all there, all the riches in the world, just waiting for the right little girl to come and find them. I was convinced that I was that little girl. Every time it rained, I would hunt for a rainbow, then grab Catherine by the hand and drag her along with me, running and running trying to reach the end."

Jake smiled softly. "Did you ever find it?"

Annie shook her head. She had never found the rainbow's end, but she had spent plenty of time imagining what she would feel like once she did. She would feel wondrously happy, contented, and secure. She would feel as though she were exactly where she belonged, and everything was right with the world.

She would feel exactly the way she had when Jake Moran held her in his arms.

A few minutes passed in empty silence, then Jake quietly asked, "What do you know about making love, Annie?"

Her startled gaze flew to his. "What kind of question is that?"

"That's the kind of question I need to ask if we're going to finish what we started earlier."

"Oh."

"That is, if you want to finish, darlin'."

Her stomach flipped, then began to flutter, as though a dozen tiny butterflies had just taken wing inside of her. "Do you?" she croaked out.

"Probably more than I've wanted anything in my entire life."

His words, spoken so confidently and unashamedly, had a blunt, undeniable ring of truth. Annie felt flushed with pleasure, unnerved, and embarrassed all at once.

He smiled. "Does that surprise you?"

"I don't know."

"What do you know about making love, Annie?" he repeated.

She searched her mind, floundering for words that wouldn't make her sound too naive or clumsy. She had seen a stallion mount a mare. She had also heard the boys bragging about women, late at night after their visits to local cathouses, when they thought she was asleep. She had heard words like *titties* and *fannies*, and how those women kept begging for more. But both those examples were simply too humiliating to mention, so she simply shook her head in silence.

"Tell me about Snakeskin Garvey."

Annie's eyes shot to his. She hadn't wanted to bring that up, but she wasn't surprised that Jake would ask. He looked neither prying or condemning, but simply as though he were gathering information that might affect both of them. She mentally debated the question for a moment, finally deciding it would probably be best to answer straightaway. Otherwise the specter of Snakeskin Garvey might just linger between them, rising up to haunt her when she least expected it.

"The boys met him in a saloon out in Gentry," she replied. "Snakeskin claimed to be an expert with dynamite, and that's why Pete took an interest in him. At that point, the boys were just starting to pull bigger jobs, and I reckon Pete thought a man who was handy with dynamite might be a good man to have around. But I knew the first time the boys brought him back to the cabin that he was trouble."

"Why?"

Annie shook her head, letting out a sigh. "Well, if that man was a snake, he looked at me like I was mouse fricassee. His eyes were constantly moving over me, all hungry and greedylike, you know what I mean?"

Jake nodded but remained silent, letting her continue.

"Anyway, one day, the boys took off for town. Garvey went with them, but he turned around about halfway, claiming he'd left something back at the cabin. I was inside, getting that night's supper ready. I didn't even know he was there until . . . well, until it was too late. He snuck up on me, just like the snake that he was."

"What happened?"

Avoiding his eyes, Annie picked up a fistful of dirt, watching it stream through her fingers. "He grabbed me and threw me down," she answered, amazed how level her voice sounded, as though she were talking about somebody else. "He had me pinned down with his body, and I couldn't get him off me. I fought and I scratched and I kicked, but that just made him smile even more, like he was enjoying watching me struggle. He started tearing my clothes off, telling me I was gonna be his woman, and that he'd kill me if I told anybody."

She paused for a moment, risking a glance at Jake. Fortunately she saw neither pity nor disgust in his eyes. All she read there was a strange, curious mix of sad understanding and quiet fury.

"Pete came back," she continued, "before Snakeskin could finish what he started. I guess Pete started to get suspicious and decided to come check up on things. He walked through that cabin door and found Snakeskin with his britches pulled down and me screaming and hollering beneath him, trying to get away." She let out a deep breath, shaking her head. "I've seen Pete mad before, but I never saw nothing like that. I thought he was going to kill Snakeskin with his bare hands, right before my eyes."

"He should have," Jake said quietly.

Annie's shocked gaze flew to his. To her dismay, she saw that Jake looked deadly serious. She shook her head, letting out a troubled sigh. "I was more scared and shook up than hurt. No sense making things worse by having a murder hanging over Pete's head. Anyhow, Snakeskin got away from Pete before it came to that. He was bruised and cut up pretty bad, but he could still ride. As he took off, he looked me straight in the eye, real furious-like. He said it was all my fault, and that Pete wouldn't always be there to protect me. He swore he'd be back one day to even the score."

Annie paused, rubbing her hands briskly over her arms as a chill ran down her spine. "He meant it too. I could tell. There was a look in his eyes that was just plum crazy, like he was never gonna rest until he found me again."

"If he does come back, Annie, you just let me know."

Although Jake's tone was perfectly calm, there was a solemn threat beneath his words that she had never heard before. A look of quiet, deadly intensity filled his eyes. In that instant, Annie could easily picture him on a battlefield, charging through an onslaught of cannon and rifle fire to do what he thought was right. God help the man who got in his way.

Jake let out a disgusted sigh. "Hell of a way for you to learn about what goes on between men and women."

Afraid that she had sounded too green, Annie

quickly blurted out, "I know folks ain't supposed to hurt each other. I know it ain't supposed to be like that."

He paused for a moment, studying her intently. "Do you know what lovemaking is for, Annie?" he asked.

Relieved at the change of subject, she nodded her head. "Well, for men," she replied confidently, "it's just for fun. All that rutting around is supposed to make them happier than pigs in mud. And for women, that's the way they get with child, so that's why they do it. But women ain't supposed to like it at all. That's why the painted cats in the saloons have to be paid to do it."

A strange expression, something between laughter and pain, crossed Jake's face. "Annie?"

"Yes?"

"Do you like the way I kiss you?"

She glanced away, feeling flustered and foolish. "Yes," she managed.

"What if I kissed your whole body like that? Slowly, inch by inch. Do you think you would like that?"

She nodded. The image of Jake doing exactly that filled her mind, leaving her unable to speak. Finally she gained her voice. "I like it when you touch me. Even when you pretend it's accidental. Like when you pass me a cup of coffee and our fingers touch, or when you adjust Dulcie's cinch and your shoulder brushes my leg. Or the way you hold my elbow while we're crossing the street, then drop it real quick as soon as we get to the other side, as if it was nothing but a habit that you just couldn't break."

Jake grinned. "You noticed that, did you?"

"Yes."

"You didn't mind? I didn't scare you?"

"No." She stopped and delicately cleared her throat. "No, I didn't mind at all. And you didn't scare me, neither. Fact is, it felt real nice."

"Then, I think we're gonna do just fine, darlin'."

Heat filled Jake's eyes and a slow, seductive grin parted his lips. "I think we're going to do just fine."

It took him less than four long strides to reach her side. She expected him to immediately resume their kiss. Instead, Jake scooped her up and carried her effortlessly back to his bedroll, setting her down gently among his blankets. "Comfortable?" he murmured, spreading out his long body beside hers.

Annie stared into his eyes, feeling more vulnerable than she ever had in her life and yet strangely unafraid. "Will it hurt?" she asked.

A look of regret crossed Jake's face. "Yes, for a moment," he replied. "I'd take the pain away if I could, but I can't." He pressed a light kiss at the base of her throat as he gently stroked her arms.

She nodded, bracing herself for the pain. "All right."

"Not now, darlin'." he quickly reassured her. "I'll warn you before it happens. Right now you can just lean back and let me kiss you the way I've been wanting to for days."

The knowledge that Jake had been wanting her as badly as she had been wanting him filled Annie with a steady sense of reassurance and banished the last vestige of her fear. Nervous tension flooded through her, making her body tremble in anticipation of his touch. He wrapped his arm around her waist and gently pulled her to him, capturing her mouth with his. Her lips, cool at first, quickly warmed beneath the gentle pressure of his kiss. She felt the slight pressure of his jaw against hers as he softly coaxed her into parting her lips. Once she did, he immediately deepened the kiss, exploring her mouth with his tongue.

Stormy desire shot through her as his kiss robbed her of all breath and thought. She felt Jake's hands move over her body as though memorizing her every curve. Hot, quivering yearning spread through her limbs in response to his touch. Annie reacted purely on instinct, moving her body against his in a rhythm that mirrored the heat and passion of their kiss. Her own hands, which had been fumbling at his back in search of a home, locked around the base of his neck, clinging to him for support. She arched her hips and pressed herself tightly against him, aching for more.

Jake drew back, his eyes dark with passion. Annie reached for his shirt, working his buttons free while he performed the same task for her. He moved with an easy, unhurried expertise, quickly stripping her of the unwanted garment. Her gun belt, boots, and pants immediately followed, landing in a careless pile at their feet. Annie leaned back, clothed in nothing but Jake's undershirt and long cotton drawers.

She stared up at him, feeling more exposed than she ever had in her life. But Jake quickly calmed her fears. He brushed his hands lovingly over her body, touching her through the light cotton fabric with an almost reverent urgency. Then, moving with infinite care, he eased the garment over her head and tossed it aside. As the chill of the night air touched her skin, Jake rained gentle kisses on her flesh, warming her arms, her shoulders, and her breasts with his mouth. He eased her drawers off next, warming her thighs, hips, and belly with the touch of his hands. Annie squirmed with pleasure beneath him and closed her eyes. A soft moan that was part laughter and part blissful sigh escaped from her lips.

She felt him go still above her, and opened her eyes to find him staring down at her, his beautiful, rugged face framed by moonlight and storm clouds. His gaze seemed to burn her skin as it traveled intently over her body, but his expression was unreadable. He reached for her wordlessly, lifting her golden hair and setting it cascading about her shoulders, carefully brushing the long, silken strands away from her face.

A rolling boom of thunder sounded in the distance, and a crack of lightning split the sky. Weed and Dulcie skittered nervously. But Annie was too focused on Jake to pay the weather any mind, even as the wind tossed her hair and light drops of rain began to sprinkle her skin.

A sense of modesty she had never known she possessed rose suddenly within her. Did Jake enjoy the way she looked, or was he disappointed? She regarded him anxiously, filled with an unreasonable desire to please him.

"Jake?" she said, uncertain how to interpret his expression.

"You're so beautiful, Annie. Just look how beautiful you are." His voice was low and husky, filled with desire.

Her anxiety quickly evaporated. Emboldened by the compliment, she reached for him, running her hands over his chest. Jake eagerly assisted her, tearing off his shirt, boots, gun belt, and pants. He knelt above her in naked, masculine splendor, giving her a full and complete view of what she had only seen glimpses of before. He showed no embarrassment about his state of undress, nor did he need to. Every inch of Jake's body was corded in sinewy muscle, without a spare ounce of flesh anywhere.

He reached for her, his muscles rippling beneath his satiny skin as he moved. Their bodies locked in an embrace, all wet and slick from the steadily falling rain. Jake's hands moved over her body with wild abandon. He traced the rounded curve of her buttocks, the silky smoothness of her thighs, the gentle curve of her hips, and the tiny span of her waist. He cupped her breasts, brushing his palms over her nipples with a light, teasing touch until they grew hard and firm beneath his hand.

Then he shifted his position and leaned forward, bringing a firm, rosy peak into his mouth. Shock and delight screamed through her. She gasped with pleasure, her body twisting against his. Then, when the pleasure became so great that Annie thought she couldn't stand it anymore, he moved lower, tracing hot, lavish kisses over her ribs, across her stomach and the tops of her thighs.

He covered her body with his mouth, claiming her with a savage hunger that found every sensitive inch of her.

As she glanced down at him, a wave of black, silky hair fell across his forehead. Annie tentatively reached out her hand and brushed it back, combing it with her fingers. "I've always wanted to do that," she admitted.

Jake pressed a soft kiss against her shoulder. "Touch me anytime you want, Annie, darlin'. Anywhere you want."

"Can I?" Thrilled with this new power, she placed her hands on his shoulders and felt his muscles contract beneath her palms in response. His reaction not only amazed her but gave her a quiet sense of power. She moved slowly, taking her time exploring his ruggedly beautiful body. She traced the broad expanse of his chest, the power of his strong shoulders and arms, then let her palms drifted downward, over the flat, rippled muscles that lined his stomach.

Her gaze traveled next to the most intimate part of him, rife with curiosity. Moving with a brazen confidence that was entirely new to her, she reached down and lightly grasped his erection, holding him gently in her hand. The skin there was silkier than any other place on his body but every bit as firm and rigid, and throbbing with life. Remembering the way he had caressed her breasts, she lightly teased the tip of his penis with her fingers as he had teased her nipples with his tongue.

Jake gave a low growl of pleasure and caught her hand.

She drew back, puzzled. "Don't you like that?"

He gave a hoarse, muffled laugh. "Too much darlin', that's the problem."

Annie didn't have time to ponder the meaning of that remark. He pulled her back into his embrace, once again lavishing her body with his kisses as he licked the rain from her skin. Annie echoed his movements, wantonly indulging her every whim and urge. She kissed his shoulder, his chest, his neck, matching his passion with her own. As a second bolt of lightning lit up the sky, she locked her arms around his neck and slanted her mouth over his, unleashing all the fervent, wanton longing that was pent up inside her.

Jake's hand drifted to her thighs. His hand rested there for a moment, then he pushed his fingers through the silky hair at the apex of her legs, cupping her with his palm. She stiffened at his intimate touch and instinctively clamped her legs together.

"Shh, darlin', don't be afraid," he murmured into her hair. Once she had relaxed, he traced the curve of her most private place, enticing another shocked gasp of pleasure from her lips. Then he gently slipped one finger inside of her, sliding it back and forth against her warmth and wetness.

Annie tensed, then hots sparks of desire pulsed through her veins. Heat coiled tightly within her belly and spread. Hunger rose within her, laced with stunning urgency and sweet, possessive fire. Her nails racked against the bunched muscles of his back, and her body molded itself to his, as if begging for more.

Jake drew back and raised himself on his forearms above her, the tip of his erection poised at her entrance. His eyes locked on hers as he slowly inched his way inside her. Annie's eyes grew wide with wonder as she felt her body stretch to accommodate him. She was awed by their union, amazed at the feel of him inside her. So this was what lovemaking was all about. This glorious, intimate union between two people. But just as she adjusted to the feel of Jake inside her, he slowly withdrew. Annie stared at him in confusion, feeling a stab of dismay and abandonment as he lifted himself off her.

"I don't want to hurt you, Annie, but there's no other way," he said hoarsely, his breath fanning her neck.

"It's all right," she said, pulling him back down to her. She had no idea what she was agreeing to. She only knew that she wasn't prepared to stop. Any pain, no matter how great, would be better than stopping now, while desire still raged through her veins and Jake's eyes burned with passion.

Jake withdrew almost all the way and covered her lips with his own. His face harsh with regret, he drove swiftly into her. A sharp, biting sensation tore through her. Annie froze, shocked by the intrusion of pain. Then she let out a sigh of relief as the sting slowly faded away. She glanced up at Jake and found him poised above her, holding himself immobile, as though afraid the slightest movement would hurt her again.

Tenderness poured through her. As the pain ebbed, she reached up and ran her hands over his shoulders, smiling brightly. "I thought you said that was going to hurt," she teased, unwilling to burden him with her pain, however slight.

Jake stared into her eyes, then let out a low, shuddering groan. "Annie," he murmured, capturing her mouth with his own. He rewarded her with a kiss of such heat and passion that Annie felt she could glimpse into his very soul.

Then he began to move. Slowly at first, almost teasingly. Wonder and desire exploded within her as she arched her hips to meet his. With each slow, gentle thrust, her nails bit deeper into the bunched muscles of his shoulders. Her body strained against his, aching for release. Each firm, loving stroke carried her a step closer to what she needed. Jake began to move faster, driving himself more deeply within her. She felt as though she were climbing, stretching, striving to reach a plateau she couldn't define.

Annie caught her breath as ecstacy exploded within her. Sweet, shuddering spasms wracked her body, making her gasp with shock. Every nerve in her body seemed to take flight, her very limbs seemed to melt with pleasure.

Just as she found her release, Jake tightened his arms around her, then drove deeply inside her, a shudder running through his frame as he poured himself into her. Abruptly he collapsed on top of her, emitting a low, satisfied growl as he rolled over, taking her with him.

Annie slowly surfaced from the hot, sweet oblivion. Rain pelted them both as she lay splayed across his chest, breathing slowly and deeply. Jake's heart was pounding beneath her ear, his breath coming in short, shallow gasps. Even now she could still feel the warmth of his intimate caresses on her skin and taste his wildly exciting kisses.

Jake's hands came up, gently caressing her back. "Looks like you were right about the storm," he said. "We better find some shelter."

Annie sighed, reluctant to move and disturb their embrace. "I reckon so, mister."

He gave her a tight squeeze, then pressed a light kiss against her shoulder. "Annie, darlin'?"

"What?"

"I think it's about time you started calling me Jake."

Chapter 13

$\mathcal{A}$nnie counted five days since they had left Two River Flats and turned south, following the twisting, rocky route of the Animas River through the San Juan mountains. Five days of riding all day and making love all night. She should have been exhausted from all the travel and the lack of sleep. Instead, she had never felt happier or more alive.

Never would she have believed that she had so much to learn about her own body, nor could she have wished for a better teacher. Jake was a wonderful lover, by turns patient and giving, then wild and unpredictable. Their nights passed in a blur of passion and laughter, full of erotic surprises and deep contentment. And when she did finally drift off to sleep, invariably she was curled up in Jake's arms, feeling blissfully secure and totally protected.

Her gaze traveled to Jake, watching him as he rode. He didn't ride like most Western men, who fought to control, conquer, and tame their mounts. Nor did he ride like the Easterners she had seen bouncing up and down in the saddle. Jake's style was distinctly his own. He controlled his mount, no doubt about that, but he did it in a way that was almost imperceptible.

Jake rode like he was a part of the horse. Annie could almost feel the natural, companionable trust between the rider and mount; they were beautiful to watch in motion. Weed sped along the trail in a light canter that was a steady, smooth, rolling gait, without one missed stride or a single break in movement. Somehow sensing her gaze on him, Jake drew Weed to a halt and turned to face her. Until that moment, Annie was unaware how much she had let herself fall behind. She spurred Dulcie on and quickly recovered the distance.

"Something wrong?" he asked.

"Just thinking."

Jake removed his canteen and shook it. "What about?"

"The way you handle a horse."

He lifted the canteen to his mouth, took a deep swallow, and arched one brow in silent question.

"You ride like a woman."

He choked on the water and lowered the canteen, his expression conveying various degrees of shock and amusement, horror and indignity. "Excuse me?"

"I meant that as a compliment."

"Do me a favor, darlin'. Don't ever compliment me like that if anyone else is around."

"There isn't anything wrong with being compared to a woman, at least not when it comes to riding," Annie maintained. "I'm just saying that you ride like you're in control, but you do it in a quiet way, letting the horse come around to your way of thinking real naturallike. Almost like it was the horse's idea in the first place, rather than trying to force him into doing something he doesn't want."

He studied her for a long moment in silence. "That's the way a woman controls a horse?"

She brought up her chin, a satisfied smile on her face. "Among other things."

"Is that a fact, darlin'?"

Their eyes met, and Annie was once again shocked by the intimacy that had grown between them. Jake had always been courteous, but in a remote, detached sort of way. Now that detachment was gone. A new awareness seemed to grow between them, intensifying with each passing day. She found herself watching his every movement with a fascination she couldn't explain. Everything Jake Moran did was suddenly wonderful and unique—from the way he rode his horse to the way he drank from a canteen. The man held her completely captivated.

Even now she watched as he took off his hat and ran his fingers through his hair. She studied his features, still accustoming herself to his new appearance. When they had first met, Jake had been attired in the trappings of a slick, fancy-talking gambler. But as a winter chill entered the air, he shed the lighter garments in favor of a thick, butter-colored sheepskin jacket, dark whipcord pants, and an indigo flannel shirt. He had also stopped shaving, allowing a thick stubble to cover his cheeks and chin as protection from the cold. The sparse beard made the hollows of his cheeks appear even deeper and gave his eyes a more brilliant glow. All in all, the changes gave him a slightly dangerous appearance and provided him with an earthy ruggedness that sent her pulse racing.

Annie wondered if she had changed in his eyes. Did he still see her as Outlaw Annie? Or was he able to see beyond her reputation and her past? Did he notice that her grammar was improving and that she wasn't swearing as much? Did he notice that she was constantly smiling and humming beneath her breath, or that her hands seemed to flutter whenever he was near? Perhaps those were all silly, trivial details to him. But to Annie, the changes occurring within her were a matter of grand and profound wonder.

Annie shifted her thoughts away from their deepening relationship and lifted her gaze toward the sky. The rain had stopped days ago, but a front of icy-cold air had taken its place. Just a week before, they had ridden through a grove of birch ablaze with shades of golds and amber, the sky had hung above them as blue and wide as heaven itself, and the air had smelled of smoke and earth. Now, in just the blink of an eye, autumn was over. Frost crunched beneath Dulcie's hooves, the trees were bare and skeletal, and Annie's breath formed puffy clouds when she exhaled.

Jake tilted his head, his eyes locked on a faraway spot on the horizon. "See that ridge over there, the one with the shaggy ponderosas? Abundance is just on the other side. We should make it by mid-afternoon. We'll stop there for the night, then head on to Cooperton. We'll be at the Palace Hotel within twenty-four hours."

"Will we?"

"You don't sound all that excited."

"Of course I am. I can hardly wait to get there."

Annie lifted her gaze to scan the deep-red faces of the cliffs that circled them. Not because she expected to see anything there but because anything was better at that moment than meeting Jake's probing gaze. She was lying, and if he looked into her eyes, he would know it.

Until that moment, she had conveniently managed to avoid thinking about what would happen once they reached Cooperton. Now, however, the question was unavoidable. Unfortunately the answer was just as plain. Jake would wire Sheriff Cayne that they had arrived, collect his money, and ride out of town. Not once had Jake promised otherwise, yet the thought of her life without him in it was suddenly unimaginable. Annie was struck by an aching, almost unbearable sense of loneliness as she imagined Jake riding away and out of her life.

"By tomorrow, you think," she said.

"If we leave Abundance by sunup, we should reach Cooperton by noon."

She nodded, her gaze remaining locked on the horizon. Unwilling to dwell on her dismal emotions, she looked instead at the beauty of their surroundings. It was an impressive view. Against the backdrop of the rugged beauty of the San Juan mountain range was a dramatic red-earth canyon. She watched a hawk rise from its nest among the craggy cliffs and soar in a lofty arch above a grove of blue spruce. A herd of wild mule deer contentedly grazed on the rich field grasses in the valley below. The narrow switchback path they followed carved its way into and out of the canyon, hugging the sheer walls.

Annie's eyes took all of this in at a glance, and something else as well. A man sat crouched behind a boulder above the narrow switchback trail, a rifle at his side. He lifted his hat and signaled to another man who sat a few feet away, crouched in a similar position. From where she sat, Annie had a view clear enough to see that the man had fashioned his kerchief across his mouth and nose, bandit style. Her gaze quickly scanned the cliff side. She counted four men, all of them similarly armed and disguised.

"Jake," she said, her voice tense and alert.

"I see it."

Glancing at him, she saw that his eyes were fixed on exactly the same spot. As they watched, a stage swung into view in the distance, rambling along the narrow switchback trail—heading directly toward the ambush that awaited it.

Beside her, Jake let out a sigh. "I don't suppose you would agree that this is none of our business."

"Nope." Annie's voice was firm. She hadn't been able to deter Pete and the boys from heading down the path of crime or to save them from the brutal fate that had awaited them. That was a guilt she would carry with her for the rest of her days. But right now if there was something she could do to stop innocent people from getting hurt, she damned sure wasn't going to simply look the other way.

Jake sighed again. "I didn't think so."

Annie drew her rifle from its scabbard, intending to fire off a round into the air.

He caught her arm. "Not like that."

"Why not?"

"You'll spook the horses. The driver's got enough on his hands just trying to steer them through the pass."

Realizing that he was right, Annie lowered her gun. She thought for a moment, then pointed to a thick, jutting ledge in the canyon wall. "See that overhang above the trail, the one with the tall maple? You think you can get there before the stage rounds that last bend?"

Jake nodded as she quickly explained her plan. Most likely, the bandits' attention was focused exclusively on the approaching stage. Even if they had glanced toward her and Jake, the trees had probably kept them hidden from view. Their best bet was to position themselves above the outlaws, then wait for the men to stop the stage before they made their presence known. With the worry of controlling the horses gone, the driver would then be in a position to defend himself. With any luck, the passengers inside might be armed and able to resist as well.

He gave her a long, hard look. "You sure you want to do this?"

"I'm sure."

A look of worried reluctance crossed his face. "Where will you be?" he asked.

She pointed to a fat boulder across from his position, then touched her heels to Dulcie's flanks.

He caught her arm. "Annie."

"What?"

"If I were trying to rob that stage and somebody fired at me, you know what I'd do?"

"What?"

"Shoot back."

He paused, his gaze locking on hers. Perhaps no more than a second passed, but in that brief moment, infinity seemed to stretch between them. His expression was unusually somber, stripped of its normal cocky laughter. He lifted his hand and lightly brushed his fingers across her cheek. "Be careful."

Annie nodded, feeling her breath catch in her throat. "You too," she said softly and once again spurred Dulcie on. "Let's go, girl."

She moved into position, whispering a prayer of thanks for Dulcie's surefootedness as they made their way through the tangled brush and rocks. Once she reached her position, she quietly dismounted. Leaving both Cat and Dulcie a safe distance from the line of fire, she crept toward her position behind the boulder. She glanced at Jake, seeing that he too had just arrived at the overhang.

Almost immediately she heard the shouts of the men below and the echo of gunfire as they forced the stage to a stop. The driver complied, remaining in his seat with his hands up. The bandits shouted something unintelligible at the stage. The passenger door slowly began to swing open.

Annie shot a glance toward Jake.

He nodded coolly in return and lifted his gun.

With shaking hands, she lifted her carbine and cocked the safety back.

Their shots exploded at nearly the same instant, spraying up showers of mud and ice at the feet of the men who were attempting to rob the stage.

The outlaws, clearly astonished by the shots raining down on them from above, whirled around to return fire. Unable to detect either Jake's or Annie's position, their shots echoed wildly, aimlessly into the canyon. Annie hadn't quite thought it through, but she had held a vague expectation of what would happen next. The bandits would give up and either turn themselves in or scatter for the hills. Instead, what followed was completely unexpected, and eerily familiar.

Under cover of the rifle fire, the driver leapt down from his seat as the coach door flew open. A group of men poured from the stage, positioning themselves on the ground. Even from her distance, Annie could see the sun reflect off the badges they wore. She could see their weapons raised and the deadly determination that filled their eyes.

Annie's heart slammed against her ribs and bile filled her throat. It was happening again. It was all going to happen again. And once again, she was helpless to prevent it.

The lawmen spewed out volley after volley of hot lead, pumping their shots into the bellies of the would-be stage robbers. The bandits' bodies jerked and twisted, caught in a macabre, contorted dance of death. Blood gushed from their wounds as they screamed out their shock and pain. Finally, one by one, they keeled over. They slipped from their saddles and fell limply to the ground, their bodies twitching in agonized, contorted spasms of death.

It was all so familiar. For one horrible, awful minute, Annie was watching Pete die again, Diego die again, Neil and Woodie and Frank die again. Only this time, she was part of the killing. She sat down in the dirt, closed her eyes, and swallowed hard, fighting back a burst of nausea.

She heard a rustling in the bushes behind her and opened her eyes to see Jake approaching, his expression tight and concerned. He knelt down beside her. "You all right, Annie?"

She nodded wordlessly, unable to speak.

"What is it?"

"I never wanted them to die," she said, her voice nothing but a hoarse whisper.

"Who?"

"Those men down there."

Jake's brows drew together in a confused frown. "What did you think would happen?"

She shook her head helplessly. "I thought we could teach them a lesson. I just wanted them to get scared and run. I thought if they came close to getting caught, they might just give up outlawing and turn themselves around." She let out a sigh, realizing how foolish she sounded but unable to stop herself. "I used to wish that for Pete and the boys. I used to wish that one day they would get a dose of somebody firing back at them—not enough for them to get hurt, mind you, just enough to scare them real good. I thought if that ever happened, they might just give it up." She paused, taking a deep, shuddering breath. "But it never did. It all went so smooth for them, so easy, right up until the very end."

Jake sat down on the ground beside her. "So that's why you wanted to help the stage. I wondered."

She thought for a moment in silence. "Does it ever get easy, watching men die?"

"No, it never does." He let out a weary sigh and set down his rifle. "I'm not sure I ever want it to."

"Hmmm." She tilted her head back and rested it against his shoulder, amazed at the comfort she gained through just that slight contact.

"You! Up in the rocks," a voice boomed from the stage below, "come on out where we can see you."

She managed a weak smile. "You think they'll remember we were on their side?"

"I hope so, darlin'." Jake moved out from behind the boulder and showed himself to the men below. "We're on our way down."

"Take it slow and easy, mister," the voice replied.

Jake lifted Annie's rifle and his own, tucking them both into their respective scabbards on their saddles. Leading Dulcie and Weed behind them, with Cat following alongside, they made their way down the rocky ledge to the lawmen waiting below. They still hadn't put away their weapons, Annie noted, seeing their rifles hanging loosely at their sides. The five lawmen watched them with wary distrust, looked highly unappreciative of what she and Jake had done for them.

Between the lawmen and the stage lay the sprawled

bodies of the men who had attempted the holdup. Annie tore her gaze away from the dead men, unable to bear the sight of them. As she returned her eyes to the lawmen, one man stepped forward. He had an authoritative air about him and the shiny gold star of a United States marshal pinned to his coat. He looked them over carefully and seemed to find them sufficiently nonthreatening to relax his grip on his rifle. He stepped forward and offered his hand, moving first toward Annie.

"Much obliged for your help," he said. "I'm Marshal Locke, Will Locke."

He looked to be in his late forties. He was of medium height and stocky build. A bushy brown handlebar mustache dominated his features, contrasting with the curiously delicate pair of wire-rimmed spectacles that sat perched on the end of his bulbous nose. His dark eyes showed intelligence, caution, and warmth.

Annie delicately placed her hand in the marshal's, deciding it was as good a time as any to practice the proper way to introduce herself. She bent her knees, making a small if somewhat awkward curtsy. "Miss Annabel Foster. How do you do," she said, noting the typical expression of surprise on his face. But at least the marshal was tactful enough not to study her body for evidence that she was a woman, which was a man's usual reaction.

"How do you do, Miss Foster," he replied, bowing slightly in return. If he felt at all out of place using ballroom formality on an isolated trail in the middle of nowhere while four men lay dead in the mud behind him, he didn't show it.

Annie turned to Jake to complete the introductions. "And this here's Mr. Jake—"

"Duquette," Jake supplied, cutting Annie off as he leaned forward to offer the lawman his hand.

Surprise shot through Annie. She closed her mouth

and risked a glance at Jake. His features displayed nothing but bland, mild politeness.

"Mr. Duquette," the marshal said, shaking Jake's hand. "Good thing for my men and me that the two of you were here."

Jake tipped his hat. "Just a couple of good citizens, Marshal. Happy to help out."

"We could use more folks like you in this part of the territory."

A shadow of a smile flickered across Jake's face. "Careful what you wish for."

"What?"

"Nothing." Jake nodded toward the dead men. "You been having trouble?"

"You heard about it?"

"Five heavily armed lawmen don't usually ride shotgun for a stage line unless there's been trouble."

"True enough, I reckon." Marshal Locke gestured to one of the dead men. "That there's Charlie Garvey. Foreman of the Tuttle Mining Company just south of here. The mine's payroll makes this route from Leadville every month. They've been hit a few times now. I figured there was an inside man setting it up, but I never would have guessed it was Garvey." He let out a deep sigh and shook his head. "Stupid son of a bitch. Man's got a wife and two children." He shot a quick glance at Annie. "Beg your pardon, ma'am. I didn't mean any offense."

Annie inclined her head. "None taken, Marshal."

"All right, boys," he called to his deputies, his voice resigned, "let's clean 'em up and get 'em back to town for a proper burial."

Jake held Dulcie's bridle while Annie mounted, then passed Cat up to her. "We'll be heading out now, Marshal."

Marshal Locke took a thick cigar from inside his coat pocket and chomped down on one end but didn't light it. Placing his beefy hands on his hips, he studied

Jake quietly for a moment. "Which way you say you were headed, Mr. Duquette?"

"I didn't."

"Just asking a friendly question."

Jake swung into the saddle in one easy, lithe move. He rested his hands on his saddle horn and studied the man in silence for a moment. "South."

Marshal Locke shrugged. "There's a reward offered by the Tuttle Mining Company for these men. Just wanted to make sure you and your friend there get your share."

"You can send my share to Garvey's widow."

"Well, now, that's mighty generous." He looked at Annie. "What about you, Miss Foster?"

Annie glanced at the dead men and repressed a shudder. "Send her mine as well."

"Mighty generous of both of you." The marshal turned back to Jake, his shaggy brows furrowed in thought. "Funny thing is, I can't help but feel that you look familiar, Mr. Duquette."

"That so?" Jake replied. If Annie hadn't known him so well, she would have missed the tension in his voice. She caught her breath as she saw his hands tighten and move ever so slightly closer to his guns.

"You play cards, son?"

"Some."

"You any good?"

Jake shrugged. "My luck comes and goes, just like anybody else's."

"Hmmm." Marshal Locke thought a minute longer, his frown deepening. "Maybe we played a game together somewheres."

"Maybe."

"We're ready, Marshal," called one of his deputies.

Marshal Locke glanced over his shoulder. His men had worked quickly and efficiently. The dead men's bodies were draped over their mounts, their hands and feet tied together beneath the horses' bellies so they wouldn't slip off.

The marshal turned back to Jake and Annie and smiled. "Feels like snow, doesn't it? You all are welcome to pass the night with my men and me. We got a little line shack just a mile or so north of here. Jones has probably got supper ready by now. The place ain't fancy, but it's a hell of a lot cozier than sleeping out in the cold."

Annie was certain that Jake would decline the offer. But to her surprise, he nodded pleasantly. "That's mighty kind of you, Marshal. We'd be obliged."

A satisfied smile showed beneath the marshal's bushy mustache. "Good. That's the least I can do after what you did for my men and me." He turned and addressed his deputies. "All right, men, we're moving out."

*T*hat was just the way his luck was running, Jake thought. Probably ten stages a week ran the route from Silverton to Abundance, and he had to go and rescue a coach full of lawmen.

He was still uneasy about the way Marshal Locke had been studying him. For a moment there, he had been sure that the marshal had had him pegged. The question was, if Marshal Locke had recognized him from that damned wanted poster, what would he have done? Tried to shoot his way out of that canyon, killing the marshal and a few of his men? Or maybe getting himself or Annie killed? Or would he have let himself be peaceably taken in, tried, and hanged? Not exactly an appealing choice, no matter which way he moved.

Fortunately it hadn't come to that. He had dodged that bullet once again, but he was starting to cut it too damned close for his taste. Sooner or later, his luck was going to run out. And the way things were going, Jake had a strong hunch that it would definitely be sooner rather than later.

Unfortunately he would have called even more attention to himself had he declined the offer to pass the night with the marshal and his men. Marshal Locke looked like the kind of man who would stew over a problem until he had his answer. He knew that Jake looked familiar. He probably also had a pile of wanted posters that he occasionally glanced through before tucking them into a desk drawer. Unless Jake were to spend some time with the marshal and his men—time he would spend assuring them that he was just another law-abiding citizen passing through—the marshal might just take it into his head to go through that stack of wanted posters a bit more carefully. And that was a risk Jake simply couldn't afford to take.

He glanced at Annie. She rode beside him, staring silently ahead. The few times that their eyes had met, she had regarded him with a gaze that was neither condemning nor confused, but simply as though seeing him in a way she never had before. She had said nothing so far, but if he knew Annie, it wouldn't be long before the questions started coming.

As they rounded a curve in the trail, he spotted the line shack the marshal had promised. A small stream and a pocket of blue spruce ran alongside it. Light shone from the windows, and smoke curled out of the chimney. The smell of roasting meat made Jake's stomach growl, and he suddenly realized how long it had been since he and Annie had eaten a hot, home-cooked meal.

The stage driver reined in the horses and called out to the line shack. A man appeared at the doorway, scowling in displeasure. He had long, kinky gray hair that fell halfway down his back, a scraggly beard with bits of food caught in it, and the lost, wild-eyed look of a man who had lived too long by himself. "All right, all right, I hear you," he shouted at the driver. "No need to wake the dead."

The marshal stepped out of the stage as Jake and

Annie dismounted. He ushered them inside. "Get on in and warm yourselves up. My men will take care of bedding down the horses."

They stepped inside the cabin. It consisted entirely of one large rather dark and musty room with a dirt floor, illuminated by a three low-burning kerosene lanterns. A rough-hewn table with a dozen crudely constructed chairs dominated the space. Narrow cots sectioned off sleeping quarters in the back. A potbellied stove sat to the right, near the room's only window. It was flanked by shelves stacked high with bags of flour, cornmeal, onions, and potatoes. Except for a small pile of wood and kindling, a fishing pole, and a few tools and cooking implements, the room was barren. As his eyes adjusted to the dimness of the interior, Jake noted the pot of stew bubbling over a large stone fireplace, and the pan of stove-top biscuits cooking on the wood-burning oven.

The marshal performed the introductions. "Mr. Duquette, Miss Foster, this here's Mr. Jones. Grumble Jones, we call him. Lived his whole life in this part of the country. Best scout the Army ever had. Now he manages the station house for the stage."

"Not for long," Jones muttered. "Getting too danged crowded hereabouts. You're the third group to pester me this month." His eyes, so pale a gray they were almost colorless, narrowed on the marshal. "You find the men who've been robbing the payroll?"

"Charlie Garvey and some others."

Jones snorted. "Figures. I always said that Garvey weren't no good."

"Miss Foster and Mr. Duquette will be staying the night," Marshal Locke said, ignoring the man's surly words.

The man's piercing gaze swept over Jake and Annie. "Reckon I ain't got much say in that," he said and turned away to focus his attention on the pot that bubbled over the fire. "Food'll be ready soon enough."

The marshal's deputies, finished with the chore of bedding down the horses, followed them into the cabin after a few minutes. As the heat from the fire and the stove began to warm them, the deputies began to peel off their coats and hats. Annie followed suit, taking off her battered hat and thick jacket. As she did, Jake noted various reactions of surprise to her looks. The deputies' gazes quickly changed from mild curiosity to outright appreciation.

Jake couldn't blame the men for staring. Annie's hair shone like molten gold in the firelight. Her cheeks were flushed and rosy from the cold, her eyes had a rich chestnut glow, and her lips looked as ripe and inviting as midsummer cherries. Despite the men's obvious gawking, Annie remained unmindful of their stares. She straightened the collar of her worn flannel shirt and smoothed her hand over her hair in an attempt to make herself look more presentable, then settled in at the table with the marshal and his deputies.

"You from around these parts, Miss Foster?" Marshal Locke asked in a tone that sounded more polite than prying.

Annie shook her head. "Not really, but I plan to stay," she answered. "You ever hear of the Palace Hotel?" she asked. "I'm the new owner. I'll be running the place from here on out."

The marshal's eyebrows shot skyward. "Out in Cooperton?"

"That's the one," Annie proudly affirmed. She glanced around the room, her smile fading at the men's various reactions to her news.

Jake was puzzled as well. He had expected surprise, perhaps, given the way he and Annie were dressed, but not outright shock. The men looked away, obviously uncomfortable. They coughed, cleared their throats, and studied the dirt floor as though it were the most fascinating thing they had ever seen. Only the youngest deputy kept his gaze on Annie. He studied her in rapt fascination, as though seeing her in a whole new light.

"I wonder," he said, "that is, do you ever—"

"That's enough, Curtis," the marshal said, cutting him off. He came abruptly to his feet and called over to Jones, "How about that grub now?"

A moment of awkward silence passed as the meal was served, then the men got down to the business of eating. Jake wasn't surprised to discover that Grumble Jones's cooking flair matched his social skills. A thin layer of grease floated over the top of the stew, the meat was tough and stringy. The biscuits were burned on the bottom, raw and doughy inside. That was the downside. The plus side was that the meal was hot and filling, and he didn't have to cook it. That and the fact that the coffee was smooth, rich, and dark. Jones even offered the surprising luxury of sugar to sweeten the brew.

Jake's earlier apprehensions eased somewhat as the evening wore on. Conversation flowed smoothly around the table, running with the ease of talk among men who knew one another well. As usual, the discussion centered on local gossip, politics, and the Indian problem. The deputies couldn't quite understand why the Indians weren't content to stay on the reservations like they had been told to do. Instead, they kept wandering off and creating problems for the good folks who were trying to move in and settle the land. As far as politics was concerned, there seemed to be unanimous dislike for the newly elected Governor Hunt, who was pushing a bill through the territorial legislature which would mandate five hours of schooling a day for children between the ages of six and thirteen—regardless of whether the parent needed that child to work the farm or not.

The meal finished, the talk moved on to ranching, cattle, and horses. "There's a ranch out in Leesville," Jake commented, "owned by a man named Ben Davidson. Best horseflesh I ever saw west of Kentucky."

"You mean Grantsville," the young deputy named Curtis corrected sharply. "That's Grantsville now."

Jake thought about that. He hadn't been out there in a while, but he remembered hearing something about the town changing sides after the war. "I believe you're right," he conceded easily.

"Damned straight I am. That's Grantsville now."

The deputy was perhaps nineteen or twenty, tall and rangy, with a sullen, hotheaded look about him. He glared across the table, studying Jake with an air of blatant hostility. Jake returned his glare with an expression of mild curiosity. "Something wrong, Deputy?"

"You're a reb, ain't you, mister?"

Jake had expected questions from the marshal's men, but that wasn't one he had anticipated. He sensed what was coming next but hoped he was wrong. "I'm from New Orleans, if that's what you're asking."

"You fight in the war?"

"I did."

"Now, you just settle down, Curtis," the marshal warned. "We ain't gonna get into this now."

The boy's face puckered in disgust. "Damned rebels killed my pa and my brother. They both fought with Grant, died at a place called Lookout Mountain."

"I'm sorry to hear it," Jake replied evenly. "Lots of good men died."

"And a lot of stinkin' rebs lived." Curtis fingered the butt of his gun. Shadows from the kerosene lanterns played over his face, making him look far more bitter than warranted by his age. "I been practicing shooting every day since I was ten, you know that, mister?"

"Is that a fact."

"I'm good too. I could of wiped out a whole damned army of rebs all by myself."

"I'm sure you could have."

"You any good with a gun?"

"Slowest man in my company."

Disappointment showed in the young deputy's face. "You want to try me?" he asked anyway.

"Not particularly. I think I'll just sit here and drink my coffee."

"Let it go, Curtis," warned the marshal again.

Curtis ignored him, his eyes intent on Jake. "Let me hear it, mister. I want to hear that rebel yell."

"War's over, son."

"Just once. I want to hear it."

Jake eased back in his chair, leveling a cool, flat stare at the boy. "I better educate you on something here," he said slowly. "Fact is, once a Southerner lets out the rebel yell, a madness gets into him. Especially if he's facing a Yank. He can't see straight, his mind gets all twisted up, and his trigger finger starts throbbing. If I let out the rebel yell, you know what would happen?"

"What?"

"I'd have to kill you."

The boy looked startled while uneasy laughter broke out among the rest of the men.

As the laughter rose, Curtis's face flamed bright red and his lips tightened into a thin line. He leapt to his feet, his fury evident. "Why don't you try me, you stinking reb? No shooting, just draw."

"Dammit, Curtis," broke in the marshal. "I said that's enough."

"You afraid, reb?"

Jake sighed. "Why don't we all just—" he began, but he didn't have a chance to finish. Curtis made a move for his gun. The rest was instinctive. Jake had his gun in his hand—cocked, ready to fire, pointed directly at the deputy's chest—before the boy had lifted his from his holster.

The boy's jaw dropped and his eyes looked like they were about to pop out of his skull. A gasp sounded from the men around them, followed by the scraping of chairs as they shoved back from the table. Only Annie and

Grumble Jones hadn't moved. From the corner of his eye, Jake noted that they both looked distinctly satisfied.

He sent the deputy a cool smile. "That was my problem. I was always the slowest man in my company."

The deputy swallowed hard and slowly moved his hand away from his gun.

"I wouldn't blame him if he shot you," said Grumble Jones. "Serves you right for running off at the mouth like that, boy. You been trying to pick a fight ever since your pa and brother died."

"Now, there's no call for bloodshed," the marshal intervened, his voice cool and authoritative. He came to his feet, wisely choosing not to inflame the situation any further by pulling his own gun.

"You're right, Marshal." Jake flexed his fingers, letting his gun spin downward to point harmlessly at the floor, then he returned it smoothly to his holster. "Like I said, the war's over." He paused, giving the boy a long, hard look. "But there are a few Southerners who still suffer from a throbbing trigger finger. It acts up every time someone calls them a stinkin' reb. You might want to remember that, Deputy."

"I will," the boy croaked out.

Jake nodded. He rose to his feet, shrugged into his coat, and put on his hat. "Excuse me, gentlemen. I think I'll check on our horses." He strode to the door and walked out of the shack, letting the door slam behind him.

The threat of snow that had filled the sky earlier had been just that—a threat. The night was as silent as only a night in the mountains can be. A soft breeze blew in from the west, carrying with it the scent of pine and horses. A crescent moon hung in a slate-black sky that glistened with stars. Jake moved to the corral where the horses were penned. From the line shack, the sound of men's voices drifted toward him. He heard a door open and shut, then turned to see Annie walking across the yard.

She reached his side and leaned against the fence post without speaking. Together they watched the horses frolic and nuzzle in the silvery moonlight. "You all right?" she asked after a minute.

Jake shrugged. "Sure. He was just a hotheaded kid." What bothered him more was that the marshal had seen him draw. But that had been unavoidable.

"That happen often?"

"Often enough."

Jake had been in the West long enough to recognize that rebels weren't overly welcomed. He had once read a fiery editorial in the *Rocky Mountain News* calling Southerners the scourge of the West—flotsam and jetsam from the tide of war. According to the paper, rebels were nothing but the disgraceful wreckage of the war washing up on Colorado's proud shores, as unwanted and offensive as a plague of locusts. Jake didn't take it personally. The way he saw it, a country couldn't lose as many men as had been lost in the war without some bitterness. The wounds were still too raw on both sides.

Annie hooked her boot heel over the fence rail and dug her hands deep into her pockets for warmth. "Why Duquette?"

"It was my mother's maiden name."

She turned to face him, her expression frank and trusting. "I'm not asking where you got it. I'm asking why you used it. There's a reason the marshal thinks you look familiar, ain't there?"

"Isn't there."

Her face tightened. "Not now, Jake," she said. "I've been honest with you. I think it's high time you were honest with me."

Jake was still not used to hearing her use his name. The sound of it on her lips pleased him more than he would have imagined possible. In fact, *everything* about

Annie pleased him more than he would have imagined possible. She was artless and outspoken, sensual and compassionate, generous and amusing. He loved her laughter, her eyes, her body, her warmth, and her courage. He loved the fact that she wore nothing but her socks to bed, and that she fell asleep curled up in his arms.

They had been lovers now for nearly a week. During that time, he had seen nothing that might prove that Annie was still involved with the Mundy Gang. But he couldn't deny that there were too many coincidences as far as she and the gang were concerned. First there was the attempted robbery in Two River Flats. Then there was the shot she had accidentally fired that had warned off the stranger who had been following them.

There was also the matter of the wire he had picked up from Walter Pogue two days ago, informing him that the Mundy Gang had just hit a bank outside of Manitobe—just hours after he and Annie had passed through the town. He hadn't mentioned anything about the robbery to her, nor had he examined his reasons for not doing so. Now, however, he wondered. Was there still a part of him that didn't completely trust her? Or had he simply not wanted to frighten her with the news that the gang was on their trail?

Either way, this didn't strike him as the best time to admit that he was using her to track the gang. He simply couldn't risk it. So he lifted his shoulders and replied, "The marshal and I played cards a year or so ago. As I recall, he lost pretty heavily and didn't take it too well."

"Is that it?" Annie let out a deep sigh of relief. "Hell, you had me worried."

He looked at her, surprised. "Why?"

"We're *cumpleaños*, mister," Annie said matter-of-factly, as though shocked that he hadn't realized that himself by now. "Truth is, you're getting to be my favorite *cumpleaño* ever. You been helping me, I figure it's my turn to help you."

Jake spent a few seconds interpreting her fractured Spanish. He was her favorite *birthday* ever? "You mean we're *caballeros*?" he suggested.

"*Caballeros.* Right, that's it. Diego taught me that. You know what it means?"

He knew the word, although he had never used it before and certainly never had it applied to himself. It ran along the lines of *amigo* but had a more formal, richer meaning. A *caballero* was a man of honor and principle, trusted and respected, a knight of sorts. The word fell heavily on his shoulders, a compliment and a burden at the same time.

"I'm no knight, darlin'."

"You're my friend, ain't you? That's why we've been helping each other. You trust me and I trust you."

Jake felt a sharp stab of guilt tear through him. "You shouldn't give your trust away so freely."

"There's nothing I give away freely. 'Specially not my trust in men. I reckon you ought to know that better than anybody."

"I reckon I do."

Their eyes met in the moonlight. Jake had spent a lot of time mentally wrestling with the question of getting close to Annie. He had tried to be noble and keep a distance between them, but that had been as impractical as trying to dam up the Niagara. Yet, as much as he desired her, the last thing in the world he had wanted to do was to hurt her, this beautiful, vulnerable woman with her bulky, masculine clothes, golden-brown eyes, and clumsy shoes.

But at that moment, an astounding question occurred to him. Would he ever really be able to walk away from her? What would happen to him if he did? The thought of losing her was as unimaginable as the thought of Annie being involved with the gang. Yet both possibilities loomed in his mind, growing larger and more distinct with each passing day.

He wrapped his arm around her shoulders, pulling her tightly against him.

"What's going to happen next, Jake?" she whispered against his chest.

"I wish to hell I knew, darlin'. I wish to hell I knew."

Chapter 14

*A*nnie awoke the next morning to the steady, rhythmic sound of a man chopping wood. She sat up in bed, listening for voices or the shuffling of footsteps. The silence that greeted her told her that she was the only one remaining inside the line shack. Last night Marshal Locke had hung a thick saddle blanket over a rope and partitioned her sleeping cot away from those of the other men. While the privacy had been appreciated, the relative darkness and isolation of her quarters had caused her to oversleep, something she rarely did.

She threw off her blankets, occasioning a surprised howl of protest from Cat, who had been contentedly curled up at her feet. "Sorry, darlin'," she said, surprised and embarrassed to find herself adopting Jake's pet phrase. Annie crossed the room to examine the wash basin, pitcher, and chamber pot. She peered cautiously inside, then sent up a short prayer of thanks that one of the men had been courteous enough not only to empty the chamber pot before leaving it for her but to provide fresh water for the pitcher as well. Her toilet finished, she quickly dressed, braided her hair, then pulled on her boots and hat.

She collected her belongings and stepped outside to a misty, overcast sky. The day was warmer than it had been in over a week. The air was wet and strangely beautiful, like looking at the world through a shroud of gray silk. The sun shone faintly through the mist, its pale-gold beams reflecting off the watery drops that glistened in the trees. Tiny beads of moisture clung to the branches and shimmered like opalescent pearls.

She saw Grumble Jones near the stream, stripped down to his woolen underwear, splitting a tree trunk into firewood with a huge ax. Marshal Locke and his men had apparently already left, as the stage and horses were gone. She found Jake near the corral, just finishing the chore of saddling Weed and Dulcie. Hearing her approach, he turned and flashed her a brilliant smile. Annie felt a warm glow spread through her and smiled in return, quickening her pace.

He strode over to meet her. "Morning, darlin'."

"Morning, Jake." She cringed at her voice, which sounded far too breathless and excited. That was exactly how she felt, but not at all how she wanted to sound.

"Sleep well?"

"Fine," she lied. It was the first time she had slept by herself since she and Jake had become lovers, and the adjustment had not been an easy one for her. She had tossed and turned all night, wishing he were beside her. After a lifetime of sleeping on her own, it was amazing how quickly she had accustomed herself to sleeping in Jake Moran's arms.

She tilted her head back to study his features, wondering if her fascination with the man would ever end. She still couldn't quiet the thrill of excitement that pulsed through her veins every time their bodies touched, or when he looked at her with his half-lidded, sexy gaze, or when he sent her one of his slow, lazy smiles. Even now, standing in the bright, bold light of day, all she could think about was the feel of his skin against hers, the feel of his hands as they slowly caressed her breasts and hips, and the way his lips felt so yielding yet firm against her own.

"You ready?" he asked.

Annie nodded and passed him her bag.

Jake grinned as he took the bag. "Handled like a true lady, darlin'."

It took her a minute to understand what he was referring to. Then it finally dawned on her. Up until that moment, she had always handled her own gear, steadfastly refusing his help. But now it seemed perfectly natural to let him handle the gear, tie the bags, and saddle their horses. She bit her lip, floundering in a sea of worried uncertainty. "You mind, Jake?"

"It would be my honor, ma'am," he replied, affecting his best Southern drawl. He sent her a reassuring grin and offered her his arm. "Allow me to escort you to your mount."

They mounted and said their good-byes to Grumble Jones, who waved them off without bothering to turn around. Soon they fell back into their normal, quiet rhythm of riding. As the morning hours stretched into afternoon, traffic began to increase, and the dirt path they had been following grew broader and broader. They passed three riders, two buggies, a few buckboard wagons, and a mail express stage. After days of isolated canyon travel, the little stretch of road seemed almost unbearably busy.

They crested a hill, and Jake reined in, stopping for the first time since they had left the line shack. He pushed back his black Stetson, then turned to Annie and smiled. "What do you think, darlin'?"

Excitement shot through her as she looked down into the valley below. The large, bustling city of Abundance, Colorado, was sprawled out beneath them, teeming with life and prosperity. Cooperton and the Palace Hotel lay just a half day's ride beyond it. After years of waiting, planning, and hoping, her dream was finally in her grasp.

"That's it, ain'—isn't it? That's Abundance."

"That's it."

"Do you see what I see, Jake?"

"What's that?"

"A rainbow," she answered, although the sky before them was cloudless and blue. "And it looks to me like the Palace Hotel is waiting at the end of it."

Jake peered in the distance and slowly smiled, catching sight of her imaginary rainbow. "I believe you're right."

The excitement that had been simmering within her welled up until she thought she would burst. "Then, what the hell are we waiting for? Let's ride!"

Annie let out a war whoop and dug her heels into Dulcie's flanks. She heard Jake let out a whoop of his own and take off behind her. She galloped down the slope as fast as Dulcie could run, laughing with joy and giddy with anticipation. The wind whipped across her cheeks, knocking her hat off her head and sending her hair flying past her ears. She felt gloriously free and alive, as though all her cares and burdens had miraculously been lifted.

They arrived in town exhilarated and breathing hard, slowing down only when they reached the main thoroughfare. Annie stared around her in undisguised wonder. She had heard that Abundance was the territory's newest boom town, but she hadn't expected what she saw. The local miners hadn't found the gold they had been seeking, but they had found something almost as nice. Silver. Thick, rich veins of silver carved deep within the mountains.

The citizens of the town were clearly anxious to show off their newfound wealth. Abundance was a grandiose testament to the riches retrieved from deep within the earth. It appeared as though the showier the display, the better. Each building seemed to exist for no other purpose than to overshadow the one next to it. She counted two churches, three millinery shops, at least a half dozen land, attorney, and claims offices, four blacksmiths, a billiard hall, two gun and ammunition dealers, a

stable, three banks, and so many saloons and dance halls
that she lost count. Plus the assorted general mercantiles,
bakeries, butchers, and feed stores. There was even an
opera house and a town paper, *The Abundance Advocate*.
Wide glass windows in the room above the boot repair
shop showed men busily at work at the printing presses.

And the construction wasn't finished yet. All around
her, Annie heard the sound of timber falling, saws cutting, and hammers swinging as more buildings were furiously erected. The citizens of Abundance showed an
almost childlike eagerness to please and impress. As was
the case with most mining communities, the town was
growing at a pace that was almost frenzied. Or perhaps
that was due to the fact that the citizens of Abundance
were making a play for the territorial—and eventually
state—capital, trying to wrest control away from the citizens of Denver City, another big mining boom town.

The main thoroughfare on which they traveled,
Silver Avenue, was wide and stately, with a row of tall
cottonwoods dividing the street down the middle to separate incoming and outgoing traffic. Still, Annie and Jake
found themselves jostled between pack mules and
Thoroughbreds, boisterous children, yapping dogs, hogs,
and hens. Ladies in fancy carriages traveled demurely
past farmers hauling oats and hay in buckboard wagons.

As for the homes that sat on the outskirts of town,
there seemed to be two distinct districts. To the east of
town, in what was clearly a poorer section, the houses
were scattered about in random order, facing all direc-
tions, as though they had been swept there by a stiff
breeze. A few tents and crude lumber shacks were num-
bered among the homes. On the opposite side of town, to
the west, she saw tall, formal houses with wide porches,
awnings, and planter boxes. Curtains fluttered at the windows, and brightly painted doors and manicured lawns
welcomed visitors. Elegant buggies traveled up winding

roads to reach the haven of the regal, more prosperous citizens.

She drew her gaze away from the disparate neighborhoods and back to the town itself, sliding a glance at Jake as she did. But rather than surveying the bustling town of Abundance, he was openly watching her.

"Disappointed?" he teased.

Somewhat embarrassed, Annie returned his smile, aware that she had been doing nothing but openly gaping since the moment they had entered town. It was exactly what she had dreamed of—only better. She loved everything about the town almost instantly. "You think Cooperton will be as nice?" she asked.

Jake gave her question some thought. "From what I hear, it's much smaller. Just a couple hundred people." As they neared the center of town, he nodded toward one of the largest, most ornate buildings she had ever seen. "I thought we'd rest up a bit, get a room and a bath, then head for Cooperton in the morning. If you like, we'll eat supper there tonight. Have a little celebration."

Annie cast a dubious glance at the restaurant he had indicated. "It looks awfully fancy."

"You may as well start getting used to it, darlin'. I imagine the owner of the Palace Hotel has a certain reputation to live up to."

"I suppose you're right."

"Something wrong?"

She couldn't help but voice her fear. "You think my calico will be good enough?"

"I think you'll look just fine, darlin'," he assured her.

"All right," she answered, unable to keep the uncertainty from her voice. Her confidence was bouncing up and down like skittish bronc. When the Palace Hotel had been nothing but a distant dream, it had been easier to imagine that everything would just magically sort itself out. But now that she was less than half a day's ride away, her doubts and fears took root. Would she really fit in here? And what would happen between her and Jake after tomorrow?

"Why don't we see about getting a room for the night," Jake said, stopping in front of a two-story hotel with a fancy balcony, tall windows, and an ornamental pediment above the broad front door. They dismounted, looped their reins over the hitching post, and went inside. The interior was even more impressive than the exterior. A grand carpeted staircase led to the upstairs rooms and divided the main level into two sections. To the left was the registration desk, to the right was a large public meeting room. The meeting room was tastefully furnished with graceful curved settees, calico curtains, an assortment of colorful rag rugs, and a mammoth stone fireplace, in which a huge fire brightly blazed.

A young, thin clerk sat at the registration desk working numbers in a ledger. His sleeves were rolled up and meticulously secured with a pair of black garters. He wore a visor on his brow and a pair of thin gold spectacles on his nose. A steamy cup of cinnamon tea sat at his elbow. Upon hearing their approach, he rose and offered them a polite if perfunctory smile. If he was at all disapproving of their travel-weary attire, or the fact that they were only requesting one room and not two, it didn't show. They secured their room with no difficulty and pocketed their key.

"If you want to get that trail dust off you, there's a public bathhouse just two streets over," he informed them. "Easiest way to get there is just to cut through the alley out back. Ladies' building is on the left, men's on the right. Barber I'd recommend is Tom Moss, down by the leather goods store. Keeps his blades fine and sharp; never nicked me once. As for your horses, you probably saw the stable when you rode in."

Jake thanked the boy and handed him a two-bit piece. They left the hotel and returned to the hitching post to see to their horses. As they did, the stage thundered into town. The driver reined his team to a stop in front of the hotel. The driver's assistant leapt down, pulled out the folded steps, and flung open the passenger door. The arrival of a stage was a big event in any Western town, for it brought mail, catalog-ordered goods, and new faces to town. Like most others on the street, Annie and Jake stopped to watch the proceedings as the passengers filed out.

One man in particular caught Annie's attention. He was of medium build and height, dressed in a dapper three-piece navy striped suit and broad-brimmed hat. There was nothing at all remarkable about him other than the fact that he looked vaguely familiar. She watched as he rather fussily brushed the dust from his leather suitcase with a handkerchief.

"Jake," she said after a minute, "isn't that that reporter fella? That what's his name—Vannert?"

Jake leaned back against the hotel column and folded his arms across his chest, studying the reporter curiously. "VanEste."

"Right."

Apparently satisfied that the bulk of the travel dust had been removed from his luggage, VanEste lifted the case and headed straight for the hotel. He glanced up and stopped short upon seeing them but quickly recovered.

"Well, Mr. Moran, Miss Foster," he greeted them jovially. He set down his luggage and politely tipped his hat. "This is quite fortuitous, is it not? It appears as though providence has brought us together once again."

"Appears to me that it was the stage that brought you," Jake replied.

Peyton VanEste bowed good humoredly. "Quite so, sir. That, and a bit of luck on my part."

"You wouldn't be following us, would you, VanEste?"

"Perhaps the two of you are following me—you just took a quicker route," VanEste replied smoothly, sending

Annie a dramatic wink. Then he continued brightly, "The fact is, Mr. Moran, I've come to experience Abundance, Colorado, for myself. My writing covers towns of the West, not just the people. On occasion, towns can have almost as much character as the people who build them. Rumor has it that Abundance will be the next Sutter's Mill. I hear tales of silver pouring in from the mountains like rain falling into a barrel. It's said that any man who can carry a bucket and a shovel and stake a claim will make his fortune within a week. Naturally this is a story my readers back East want to hear."

"Naturally," Jake replied.

VanEste turned his attention to Annie. "You're looking well, Miss Foster."

"Thank you, Mr. VanEste."

"I wired my editor at *The Gazette* that we had met but that you had refused to grant me an interview. As you can imagine, he was quite disappointed. Nearly cost me my job."

"I'm sorry to hear it."

"But here we are, meeting again. As my sweet mother used to tell me, things always happen for a reason. Could the reason for this chance encounter be that you've reconsidered my request to hear all your exploits, Miss Foster?"

"I'm afraid not."

VanEste made a tsking sound with his tongue. "Such a shame. Well, perhaps another time. If you should change your mind, I'd be delighted to speak with you at any time. Good day to you both." He tipped his hat once again, picked up his luggage, and strode briskly past them and into the hotel.

"Why don't you get settled in a bit, Annie?" Jake suggested once VanEste was out of earshot. "I've got some business to take care of this afternoon. I'll meet you downstairs at seven for dinner."

"That sounds just fine," she agreed, anxious to get a closer look at the town.

"Good. Until then." He swung onto Weed's back and turned away, disappearing into the throngs on Silver Avenue.

As Annie watched him ride away, her joy at having at last arrived in Abundance was suddenly diminished. She felt a strange, unfamiliar tightness settle in her throat. *Better get used to that view, Annie girl,* she told herself. *After tomorrow, that's exactly what you'll see.*

Jake Moran riding out of your life.

*J*ake's first order of business was at the telegraph office. Fortunately he found no messages from Walter Pogue waiting for him. He nodded his thanks to the telegraph clerk and stepped out into the street.

His second order of business was a bit more productive. He hadn't missed the worry on Annie's face as she'd asked him about her ugly calico gown. Her wardrobe would definitely need a bit of sprucing up before she took over at the Palace. With that in mind, he walked toward a shop whose discreet sign read simply: *Miss Angelique's Boutique. Finest Quality Fashions for Ladies. Ready-made and Custom Available.* He stepped inside and found the shop empty. That suited him just fine. He needed at least one hour of Miss Angelique's full time and attention.

His purchases completed, he went back to the hotel, hoping to find Annie napping in bed—preferably dressed in nothing but her socks. After spending sixty minutes in a perfumed boutique poring over silks and satins, he was ready for a little more amorous sort of relaxation. Unfortunately Annie was out. He resigned himself to a visit to the bathhouse and barber instead, then returned to the hotel and changed.

It wasn't long before he felt the familiar pull of the saloon calling him. He crossed the street and entered

Happy Tom's, which looked to be one of the better establishments in town. He wasn't disappointed. Rather than the sawdust floor he normally found in saloons out West, Happy Tom's had a hardwood floor—maple, to be exact—and it was polished to a high sheen. The long mahogany bar looked fully stocked, the players were well dressed and orderly, and the waitresses were actually pretty.

He took a seat at a table where a poker game was already in progress. The game progressed smoothly, with no big winners or losers. Just a group of men amiably passing away an idle afternoon. The talk drifted here and there, not settling on any one topic long enough to elicit more than a few light opinions.

A waitress sashayed over and brought him his drink, bending down low enough to offer him a full and unobstructed view of her small, pert breasts. Jake prided himself on having a natural appreciation for all women, but if he did have a type, this barmaid was it. She was exactly the sort of woman he had grown to manhood with back in Louisiana. Tall and slim, with long willowy limbs, dusky skin, dark, almond-shaped eyes, and a full-lipped smile that promised an enterprising knowledge of the many ways to please a man in bed. But there was a selfishness in that smile too, a selfishness that told Jake she could take care of her own sexual needs, that she would be using him as much as he was using her. That had always suited him just fine, excited him even. But looking at her now, he realized he was curiously devoid of any real interest.

He suddenly came to a profound realization, one that was so simple it was almost embarrassing. It occurred to him that he didn't want to spend the evening drinking too much bourbon, playing too many hands of cards, and bedding another saloon girl with flashing eyes, a pretty body, and a name he would forget within a week. He didn't want to wake up the next morning, head to a different town, and do it all over again. The slick feel of a deck of cards in his hands, the soft clatter of poker chips, and the rowdy roar of a saloon weren't enough for him anymore. The dull repetitiveness that had been his life had changed once he had met Annie, and he had no real desire to go back to the way things were.

He had always harbored a vague notion that perhaps in a year or two, once the Reconstruction was over, he would go back home. But now he discarded that thought even as it occurred to him. No one in the South had any money, much less money to gamble with. Except, of course, the Yankee carpetbaggers who swarmed over the land like fleas. While there would be a certain satisfaction in cleaning them out, it was a petty sort of vengeance. The war was over, the South had lost, and it was done. As he had said last night, he had no desire to fight it all over again.

No, his real home was in the West, and that was where he would stay. Once he had straightened out this mess with the Mundy Gang, he and Annie might even have a chance at something permanent. The thought of settling down with her in Cooperton rather than spending the remaining years of his life drifting from town to town held a surprising amount of appeal. He might be giving up a bit of his freedom, but it looked like he stood to gain a hell of a lot more in return.

He set down his cards, collected his money, and nodded to the remaining men at the table. "Time for me to bow out, gentlemen."

A gray-haired man eyed him pleasantly. "Quitting while you're ahead, sir?"

"Indeed."

Chapter 15

Annie stood before the looking glass in her room, staring at her reflection with absolute amazement. The gown she wore was a rich, deep gold, made of the finest wood crepe she had ever seen. The skirt was full and generous, tightly fitted at her waist, then artfully split in the front to reveal an underskirt of pale-ivory damask. The bodice, made of the same ivory damask, fell from her shoulders in a deep scoop, revealing just a glimpse of the tops of her breasts. She wore a tightly fitted, cap-sleeved bolero jacket patterned in a gold-and-ivory stripe over the bodice. Long white gloves encased her hands and arms, and a matching gold-and-ivory-striped reticule dangled from her wrist.

Behind her, Mary, the apprentice dressmaker from Miss Angelique's who had accompanied the delivery, nervously cleared her throat. "Ma'am?" she said tentatively. "If you don't like it . . ."

Annie met Mary's gaze in the mirror. The girl was young, perhaps sixteen or seventeen. She had a round, sweet face and blue eyes that reflected both concern and worry as she looked at Annie. Annie realized then that she hadn't been smiling when she looked in the mirror but simply studying herself in stunned disbelief. Obviously Mary had interpreted her silence as disapproval.

"It's beautiful," Annie assured her sincerely. "It's the most beautiful dress I've ever seen."

Relief showed instantly on Mary's face. "Your Mr. Moran has mighty fine taste. He only wanted to look at the best goods that Miss Angelique had."

Annie nodded, feeling a ridiculous thrill run through her at Mary's reference to Jake as *her* Mr. Moran. She glanced at the boxes that were scattered haphazardly around the room, filled with a profusion of silks and cottons, wools and linens. She felt the same disbelief now as she had when the packages had been delivered to her hotel room door. Her initial reaction had been to insist that some mistake had been made. But Mary had insisted that "Mr. Moran ordered everything just for you. He asked me to stay and help you dress, to make sure you liked it all, and to see to any fittings that might be necessary." A note tucked inside the first box Annie had opened affirmed the girl's words. *Thought you might like something else to wear besides your guns and your calico. J.*

Jake had sent her three gowns, all of them fine wool serges. There was the gold she currently wore, a gown of pale blue, and one of deep emerald. He had sent a riding ensemble as well, which consisted of a crisp white linen blouse, a navy wool jacket, and a matching navy skirt. She had also discovered two everyday skirts made from a fine, heavy cotton and four simple blouses. He had also purchased several sets of sheer cotton undergarments bedecked in ribbons and lace, stockings, and a rich chocolate-brown cloak trimmed in ermine. But her favorite item of all was the pair of ankle-high kidskin boots she currently wore. They were made of a rich buttery-brown leather embellished with a row of tiny pearl buttons that went all the way up to her ankles, and had little heels that clicked when she walked.

Fortunately no elaborate fittings were necessary. The clothing was ready-made but had been ingeniously devised to tailor itself to fit several different body types. A drawstring hidden in the waistbands pulled the skirts in to fit Annie's waistline perfectly. Tiny pleats set in the bodices worked to accommodate a variety of bustlines. As she was of average height, the hems needed no adjustment. Aside from realigning a button here and there, the clothing fit perfectly.

"I didn't know you could buy dresses like this ready-made," Annie commented. "I thought they all had to be special-ordered back East."

"Not in these parts," Mary replied proudly. "Miss Angelique's pretty clever that way. When a miner strikes a vein, he and his wife want to look like they got money right away. They don't want to wait three months to show off. That's why Miss Angelique keeps as much as she can in stock."

"I see," Annie murmured, turning back to study her reflection once again in the looking glass.

Mary had even worked miracles with her hair, getting the thick, long strands to curl. She had brought a remarkable device with her, a narrow metal tube she set in the brick fireplace in the room to heat up. Once the device was hot, she wrapped a few strands of Annie's hair around it, then let them go, to fall about her shoulders in thick spiral curls. Once her hairs was set, Mary piled the thick, golden curls high on Annie's crown, allowing a few soft strands to escape and brush the nape of her neck and her shoulders. The overall effect was better than anything Annie had seen in *Winston's Guide*.

Annie lifted her hand and pinched her cheeks to put color in them, then realized that it wasn't necessary. The eyes that stared back at her in the looking glass glistened with excitement, her cheeks were already flushed and rosy, as though blazing with an internal heat. She felt the same way now as she did the first time she had urged her horse into an all-out gallop. She felt as though she were flying, nervous and filled with giddy joy at the same time, wishing it would ever end.

"Is there anything else you need, ma'am?"

"No. Thank you, Mary. It's beautiful. All of it." She reached for her bag to fetch a coin for the girl.

"No, ma'am, that's all right, Mr. Moran has already seen to it. He's a fine gentleman, isn't he?"

"Yes, he is," Annie answered, stifling an inner sigh as she let Mary out. She supposed that was just something she would have to get used to. Women looked at Jake the way stray cats looked at dishes of cream. That was a fact that probably wouldn't ever change.

Once Mary had left, Annie lifted the small glass vial of French perfume Jake had sent with the clothing. She opened the bottle and breathed in the rich, heady scent, then dabbed the fragrance to her wrists, neck, and between her breasts. She glanced at her reflection one last time, trying to see herself as Jake would. But the woman looking back at her was a stranger: a fine, fancy lady she didn't recognize. A rush of insecurity suddenly filled her. Would Jake be disappointed in how she looked after all the trouble he'd gone to, to send her the clothing?

Annie turned to Cat, who had watched her dress with undisguised curiosity, and decided to let her be the judge of things. She smoothed her skirts, turned and struck a ladylike pose. "What do you think, Cat? Do I look fine and upstanding, like Miss Annabel Lee Foster should, or am I just plain ol' Outlaw Annie, fresh out of the tub and stuffed into a thirty-dollar dress?"

Cat tilted her head to one side, as though giving Annie's question the serious consideration it deserved, then let out a yawn and swished her tail.

"You're right. I reckon that's not up to us to decide, is it?" Annie said. She crossed to the bed and stroked the soft, downy fur beneath Cat's chin. "Be a good kitty," she said. She lifted her reticule, folded her new brown cloak over her arm, and left the room, softly closing the door behind her.

Annie made her way downstairs. She paused at the last step, using the extra height to scan the hotel's public meeting parlor. The room was filled almost entirely with men. They lounged comfortably about on chairs and set-tees, smoking, talking, and drinking, giving the room an air of a private all-male club rather than a public parlor. She hesitated, uncomfortable descending into their midst. Her hand resting lightly on the rail, she scanned the room for Jake.

Her eyes went to one man who was sitting alone on a settee, seemingly engrossed in his paper. His relaxed posture and long-limbed frame told her it was Jake, but his face was blocked by his newspaper. Annie took a step toward him, then hesitated, not wanting to enter the room and approach him for fear that she was mistaken.

The man turned a page of his paper, and as though suddenly alerted to her presence by the silent hush that had fallen over the room, he looked up. Annie breathed a sigh of relief—it was Jake. His eyes scanned the room, then went directly to her. A shocked, frozen expression carved itself onto his features. His gaze traveled slowly from the tips of her shiny new boots to the top of her curled, gloriously swept-up hair. Uncertain what to do or say, she returned his gaze with a soft, hesitant smile.

Jake immediately set aside his paper and stood. He was clad in much the same attire he had worn on the day they had first met, back in Sheriff Cayne's office. A long exquisitely fitted black jacket emphasized the breadth of his shoulders and the strength of his arms and chest. His black pants were finely tailored, his freshly starched shirt was crisp and white, and a black string tie was fastened neatly beneath his chin. His cheeks were shaven, and his dark hair was smoothly slicked back.

But there was one thing about him that was very dif-ferent from the first time they had met. On that day back in Sheriff Cayne's office, Jake's gaze had reflected noth-ing but mild boredom, faint amusement, and a wary, al-most burdened look as he regarded her. Now, however, his silvery-blue eyes shone with a light she had never seen before. As he studied her, his gaze filled with pride, desire, and intense satisfaction.

Annie felt her chest tighten and then expand, as though her heart had suddenly doubled in size and there was too much joy to contain within the walls of her chest. He moved wordlessly toward her and stopped at the bottom of the stairs, holding out his hand for her. Annie effortlessly glided toward him as though she were in a dream. She placed her gloved hand in his as naturally and as coolly as though she had done it a million times.

Smiling up into his eyes, she said softly, "I bet you don't even recognize me without my britches on, do you, mister?"

A warm glow filled his eyes, and a soft smile touched his lips. "I bet you're wrong."

"I don't know how to thank you," she began. "I'll pay you back—"

"No, you won't. It was a gift."

Her heart gave a funny little leap. "I don't deserve dresses this fine, Jake."

"Why don't you let me decide that?" Their eyes met and held for a long moment as a heavy silence stretched between them. "I was hoping you'd choose that gown. It's amazing what the color does for your eyes." He brought her hand to his lips and bowed over it, pressing a light kiss against the back. "You do me great honor tonight," he said, then he reached for her cloak. "May I?"

She turned slightly, allowing him to settle the cape about her shoulders. A slight shiver ran down her spine as his fingers brushed along the nape of her neck and his warm breath tickled her ear. He lifted a few stray curls from beneath her cape, then settled his hands along her shoulders as he turned her to face him. "Hungry?" he asked.

For you, Annie answered silently, shocked to her toes by her wanton thoughts. Her emotions were running so high and so fast she didn't think she could manage a bite, but she nodded anyway.

"Good. Because I want to take you to the fanciest restaurant in town and show you off."

He offered her his arm, and they left the hotel, stepping out into the street. The first snow of the season had begun to fall. Large powdery flakes drifted slowly to the ground, dusting the buildings and streets and crunching softly beneath their feet. There was a magic in the night that Annie could taste in the air. Horses and buggies moved past them at a leisurely pace, accompanied by the jingle of harnesses. Men and women strolled arm in arm, nodding politely to her and Jake as they passed. The night was filled with a rainbow of colors, ranging from the white, glistening snow, to the yellow glow of the lamps, to the inky black of the sky that hung above them. The brick buildings blazed like cinnamon, and the pines were an smoky jade against the mountains.

She would have been perfectly content just to walk and enjoy the night, but they reached the Golden Pheasant all too quickly. Jake opened the wide, intricately carved oak doors and ushered her inside. Annie was suddenly glad that they had come, for the room was like nothing she had ever seen before.

The restaurant consisted of one grand cavernous room, filled with the low murmur of conversation, clinking silverware, the bright ring of crystal, and the melodic drifting notes of distant music. Thick floor-length red-velvet curtains hung from the windows. The dark wood floors were polished to a sheen so brilliant Annie could almost see her reflection within them. Crystal chandeliers sparkled above her, reflecting the dazzling candlelight. Fresh white linens covered nearly every surface, and at each table sat a tall vase of wild daisies. Waiters in black jackets rushed between the diners, moving with the highly skilled precision of dancers executing an intricate waltz.

Her gaze moved upward to study the remainder of the restaurant's decor. A huge life-size portrait of a voluptuous nude reclining in opulent splendor caught her attention. The model sat on a chaise, surrounded by smiling cherubs with wings. The woman was graced with chubby thighs, a rounded tummy, generous breasts, baby soft cheeks, and pert rosebud lips. The model stared down into the crowd with the dark adoring eyes of a basset hound. Her legs were coquettishly crossed, but her back was arched, displaying her plump breasts to full advantage.

The portrait was repeated on each of the restaurant's four walls. The woman's face and body remained exactly the same, but her hair varied, depending on whether one looked north, south, east, or west. Glancing from wall to wall, Annie saw raven-black, rich chestnut-brown, fiery auburn, and luminous golden-blond tresses. In a distinct territorial touch, heads of wild game, including bison, elk, bear, and antelope, were proudly positioned next to the paintings.

Her gaze traveled next to six men who were seated on a podium playing instruments. The music they created was unlike anything Annie had ever heard. It seemed to call for floating across a room rather than stomping around, like most dance tunes. The sound was rich and melodic, filled with measured beats and haunting crescendos.

Catching her gaze, Jake gave her hand an encouraging squeeze. "They're playing Mendelssohn. Do you like it?"

She nodded. "If God ever decides to let me into heaven, I reckon that's the music I'll hear."

A waiter appeared and showed them to their table. They dined on steamed oysters and tender lamb cutlets, creamed spinach, thick slices of broiled squash, quartered new potatoes delicately seasoned with onion and thyme, and chewy sourdough rolls. They drank a bubbly wine Jake introduced to her as champagne. Throughout the meal, Jake was an ever-attentive host, seeing to her every need, nearly drowning her with his devastating charm and appeal.

"You do anything special today?" he asked.

She shook her head. "Dulcie and I just toured the town. I reckon this place is almost as big and fancy as Denver City itself."

Their conversation drifted this way and that, contrasting the town of Abundance with the cities back East. As soon as the dinner service ended, the waiters began clearing dishes and removing a few of the tables. The orchestra, which had provided background music until that point, rose a notch in volume, filling the restaurant with deep, swelling notes. On cue, couples rose and merged onto the newly cleared dance floor.

Jake stood and held out his hand. "Shall we join them?"

Annie hesitated. She knew a few polkas and jigs but not much else. "I don't think I can, at least not to this . . ."

"Trust me, darlin'. I'll show you how."

She placed her hand in his and stood, walking with him to the dance floor. As the band began to play, the restaurant dropped its fancy airs and came alive, hooting and hollering like the mining town dance hall it was born to be. A pair of fiddlers joined the musicians and struck up one lively tune after another. The crowd square-danced and polka'd, two-stepped and reeled.

Annie's favorite dance, though, was something called a Texas waltz. Her skirts flared full and sassy around her ankles as Jake guided her effortlessly through the waltz, pulling her tightly to him then spinning her around. He held her so closely it seemed almost indecent in public, but at that moment, Annie didn't care. Her senses were swimming, intoxicated by the deep, masculine scent of his skin and the arousing feel of his body as he brushed up against hers.

"There," he said, "waltzing isn't that hard, is it?"

"No, it's not hard," she agreed. In fact, dancing came easy. Her feet moved almost effortlessly in time with his. What was difficult was breathing and talking while her head spun with dizzy excitement and joy flooded her limbs.

They danced as long as the band played, twirling around the cavernous room while the coquettish nudes smiled down on them, conferring their blessing. When the musicians took breaks, they sipped rich, dark coffee from fine china cups and nibbled on slices of chocolate cake. Annie was in no rush to leave. The night was a present she wanted to unwrap slowly and linger over.

When the music ended and they at last stepped out of the restaurant, Annie was blissfully content and gloriously happy. The snow had stopped falling, but the town was coated in a fine layer of glistening white dust. The street was quiet, the sound of midnight stillness broken only by the noise of a horse stomping its feet against the cold and the high, tinkering sound of a piano drifting out from a saloon.

They entered the hotel and went upstairs to their room. Jake pulled a sulfur match from his coat pocket, struck it against his boot heel, and held the flame to the wick of a kerosene lantern. Golden illumination lit the room. A breeze fluttered the curtain, and a gust of cold air filled the room.

"I must have forgotten to close it before I left," Annie said, moving across the room to pull it shut. She glanced around. "Cat's gone."

"She'll be fine," Jake assured her, closing the door behind him.

She followed Jake's gaze around the room as he stepped inside, wishing she'd thought to straighten up a bit before she had left for the evening. Boxes and tissue were flung this way and that, and the clothing he had sent her was strewn across her bed in random piles. He removed his hat and set it on a table, then went to the bed and reverently lifted a silky wisp of a camisole, rubbing the lacy garment gently between his fingers.

"Did everything fit properly?" he asked.

"Yes," she managed, imagining his fingers on her skin, touching her the way he was touching that garment. The room seemed to grow almost unbearably hot and shrink in around her, so large and overwhelming was Jake's presence.

He dropped the camisole and returned his gaze to hers. "You looked beautiful tonight, Annie."

She smiled, smoothing her hands over her skirt. "Who would have guessed that I would end up wanting to dress as fancy as you?"

Jake closed the distance between them. "It suits you." He lifted one of her corkscrew curls, weighing it in his palm, then his eyes moved back to hers. "Everything about you suits me, Annie."

Annie felt her breath catch in her chest. Her heart was racing and a slight shiver ran down her spine. She was still amazed at what Jake could do to her with just one heated glance, one light touch. Even though they had been lovers for days, she felt that same thrill of excitement now as she had at their first kiss, that almost unbearable sense of longing, as though her world wouldn't be right again until he pulled her back into his arms.

"What are you thinking about?" he asked.

"You," she answered bluntly. "The way you look at me."

"Oh?" He arched one dark brow in a silent question.

Annie licked her suddenly parched lips and nodded, letting her words and emotions tumble out blindly. "Some men, well, they have a look like they just want to hurry through lovemaking. You can almost see what they would be like by the way they eat: shoving food down their faces like someone was gonna take their plate away. You don't have that look, Jake. You look like the kind of man who takes things slow. Who gives a woman time. You make a woman feel special, beautiful. That's a gift, Jake. Not many men are like that."

A fiery, intense glow entered Jake's eyes. "That's not the way I feel, Annie. Not with you."

"It's not?"

"No." He unfastened her cloak and tossed it over a chair. His own jacket quickly followed.

"How do you feel?" she asked. Jake didn't answer. He was too busy removing her gloves, one finger at a time. Next he removed her bolero jacket, pulling it gently over her shoulders and down her arms. Annie waited for his reply, passively allowing him to disrobe her. "Jake?" she finally prompted.

"Hmmm?" he murmured, clearly distracted.

"How do you feel when you're with me?"

He gently set her down on her bed. Her skirts spread out in a whoosh of wool and crinoline, fanning around her legs. Jake carelessly brushed the jumbled piles of feminine garments off the bed and onto the floor, then sat down beside her. "Like I'm an eager schoolboy again, and you're the first woman I've ever bedded." He brushed a golden curl aside and tenderly kissed her ear. "Like I'm a starving man, and you're all cake and cream, and I want to devour you in one swallow." He bent his head lower, trailing fiery kisses down the nape of her neck and across her collarbone. He glanced up, his beautiful gray-blue eyes shining with an emotion that wavered between passion and surrender. "Like you're the sea, Annie, and I'm a drowning man."

Her throat went dry. Suddenly she wasn't much in the mood for conversation either. "You can rush if you want to, Jake."

"No, I can't. Not with you, Annie." He kneeled

down before her and lifted her foot, tenderly cradling it in his palm. "Where's your hook?"

"My what?"

"Your shoe hook."

"Oh." Annie retrieved the small tool from her bedside table. "I'll do it."

Jake ignored her, taking the hook from her hand. Lifting her skirts ever so slightly, he cradled her foot in his palm as he slowly worked the buttons of her boot free. His fingers felt warm and strong, subtly arousing even through the thin cotton mesh of her stocking. As he removed one dainty boot, he lifted her foot to his mouth and pressed a light, tender kiss against the inside of her arch. Then he took off her other boot and kissed that foot as well.

Next he gently pushed up her skirts, baring her thighs. He untied the slim pink ribbons that held her garters in place and striped them from her thighs. He slowly rolled her stockings down, inch by inch, his lips following the path of his fingers. Annie trembled as she felt the weight of his head press against her lap. She threw back her head, digging her fingers through his hair, sighing with pleasure and longing. She heard herself gasp his name as his lips moved up and down her leg, nibbling and kissing the tender flesh of her inner thighs, her knees, her calves. Her muscles tightened, giving startled little leaps wherever his lips brushed her skin. She felt a rush of heat race to her thighs and a tight, fiery knot fill her belly. She arched her back and grasped his shoulders, whispering with an almost desperate urgency, "I don't want to wait, Jake."

"Easy, darlin'. Slow is better. Slow is much, much better." Abruptly Jake shifted. Moving with lithe, easy grace, he pulled himself up onto the bed beside her. "Turn around for me, Annie."

"Why?"

"So I can unbutton your blouse."

"Shouldn't we turn down the lamp first?"

"I want to see you."

She bit her lip, uncertain. "Is that proper?"

"Probably not, darlin', but let's leave it on anyway."

Whatever resistance she was about to offer faded like stars at dawn under the heat of his roguish grin. Annie nodded and turned, unable to resist his gentle coaxing. His fingers moved steadily along her back as he worked free the tiny, delicate buttons that lined her bodice. His lips tightly traced the column of her spine, then he eased the bodice off her shoulders and turned her around to face him.

Annie clutched the bodice against her chest, overcome by an alarming sense of modesty. Up until that moment, they had made love primarily in the dark, beneath the silvery beams of the moon or in the earthy glow of a campfire. Something about making love in a hotel room, their naked bodies moving in wanton abandon to the bright and shining glow of a kerosene lantern, seemed decidedly brazen and shockingly improper—rather like indulging in an apple-eating contest in Eden. At the same time, however, it was obvious that Jake truly did want to see her. With that in mind, she bravely let her bodice drop, her desire to please him far outweighing her newly discovered sense of propriety.

She held her breath as Jake's gaze moved over her breasts. To her relief, she saw nothing but heightened pleasure in his gaze, combined with burgeoning desire and raw hunger. He lifted his hands and lightly cupped her breasts in his palms. Then he bent his head, his lips once again following the motions of his hands with light, loving kisses. Annie arched her back, giving him greater access. Her nipples stood hard and erect against his palms, straining against the sheer cotton of the camisole. That light, delicate cotton, which had earlier felt so smooth and soft, suddenly felt almost unbearably coarse against the heightened sensitivity of her skin.

Jake pulled the intrusive garment off and tossed it carelessly to the floor, taking one stiff, rosy peak into his mouth. Annie gasped with pleasure as she clung to his shoulders for support. Desperate to feel Jake's own skin beneath her palms, she tugged at his shirt, mindlessly shoving it down off his shoulders and tossing it onto the floor beside her bodice.

Jake rocked back on his ankles, studying her intently. His gaze was dark and smoldering, like the embers of a fire before it erupted into a full-fledged blaze. He reached for her hair and removed the pins that had so artfully kept it in place all night, dropping them one by one. Released from their confines, the thick golden-brown curls tumbled free, cascading over her shoulders and down her breasts. He brushed them this way and that, like an artist would arrange a model for a portrait.

"You're beautiful, Annie. Has anyone ever told you that?"

"Just you."

A pleased, possessive smile curved his lips. He reached for her and tucked a stray curl behind her ear. "Good."

She knew Jake had meant to proceed slowly. That had been her intention as well. But their good intentions were abandoned as a sudden, burning urgency fueled them both. His mouth slanted hungrily over hers. She met his kiss with open, aching yearning, thrusting her tongue against his own, moving her hips to the same hot, ardent rhythm of their kiss. She fumbled with the buttons of his pants as his fingers tugged at the waistband of her skirt. Soon all of their clothing had been discarded, flung randomly across the room.

Annie discovered that there were definite advantages to making love by the glow of a kerosene lamp. Not only could she smell, hear, and taste Jake, she could now watch his reactions to her caresses. And that was empowering indeed. Following his lead, she touched him the way he had been touching her, lightly running her fingertips over his skin and then following the path with her lips. His muscles quivered and jumped just the ways hers had, and his erection grew firmer and harder with each passing second. She kissed him everywhere, from the coarse sunburned skin of his neck to the tight velvety skin of his ribs to the flat rippled lines of his stomach, then on to the powerful, thick muscles of his thighs.

Jake let out a low growl, filled with both approval and satisfaction, then he pulled her tightly against him, pressing her hips against his own. "Mmmm. Where did you learn that, Annie?"

"From you."

"Did you, now?" The gentle praise fell against her skin like an audible caress. "That's good, darlin'. That's very, very good."

He leaned down and nuzzled her neck, then moved lower still, flicking his tongue against the tight pink bud of her nipple until it went hard and stiff against his lips. His narrow hips matched the rhythm of his tongue, moving in a tight circle that ground firmly against her pelvis. Annie writhed beneath him, instinctively arching her back and uttering a soft moan of desire. Her blood raced through her veins like liquid fire. A small cyclone seemed to build within her belly and spread down to her thighs, creating a yearning chasm of need and desire, an aching emptiness that only Jake could fill.

He moved his hand between her legs, cupping her with his palm. He gently traced the tender pebble hidden beneath the folds of her velvety skin, then slipped one long finger inside her. As he stroked in and out, Annie felt herself leaning into his hand, shamelessly thrashing beneath him, wanting more. The sheets tangled beneath her back, and her breath came out in hot, gasping pants against his ear. She dug her nails into his skin, filled with neither grace nor delicacy, just blazing, blinding need.

Jake removed his hand and rose on his knees above

her. He drove into her with a groan of aching satisfaction, his erection hard and thick. Each swift, sure thrust answered the hollow need that had consumed and inflamed her. As she lifted her hips to match the rhythm of his strokes, a quivering tension built in her belly and spiraled through her veins. Need and desire blended into a sense of overwhelming urgency. She pressed her mouth tightly against the nape of his neck, stifling her cries of pleasure. Her hands moved wildly over his back, cupping his buttocks and stroking his thighs, molding her body against his own.

Annie arched her back and gasped. The sparks that had been kindled within her belly suddenly exploded. Hot, driving spasms of pleasure shot up her spine and raced down her legs. She buried her mouth against Jake's shoulder to keep from crying out, tasting the salt and sweat on his skin. His body stiffened above her, then a shudder ran through his frame as with a final, deep thrust he poured himself into her.

His elbows abruptly buckled, and he collapsed on top of her. As Annie roused herself from her dazed, sated wonder at their union, she became aware of several things at once. The way Jake's short, ragged breathing matched her own. The mingled, slick perspiration of their skin and the heady, potent scent of their lovemaking. The tangled mass of sheets beneath her back. The way the kerosene lamp cast odd shadows across the ceiling. And finally the weight—the heavy, rock-solid, pure muscle weight—of Jake's body on top of her own.

"Jake?"

"What?"

"I can't breathe."

"You always so particular, darlin'?" She heard the grin in his voice as he shifted off her.

She rolled onto her side and curled up contentedly in his arms. They lay together in silence for several minutes, listening to the pounding of their hearts. "Why do I feel so good right now?" she asked.

"It's called afterglow, darlin'."

"Hmmm." She thought for a moment but didn't quite agree. What they had shared seemed much deeper than pure physical pleasure. She felt as though Jake had stripped her bare and touched her very soul. To walk away from each other tomorrow and leave everything they had shared behind seemed the worst sort of gratitude for the gift they had been given. With that in mind, she ventured hesitantly, "Jake?"

"What?"

"Can I ask you something?"

He stroked the bottom of her foot with his big toe, then leaned over and planted a soft kiss on her shoulder. "You can ask me anything, darlin'. I'm your humble servant."

"Anything?"

"Anything."

Annie screwed up her courage and, before she could change her mind, blurted out, "You think you'll ever get tired of drifting and maybe want to settle down in one place? Put the past behind you and start over?"

Jake tilted his head down to meet her eyes, a slight smile playing about his lips. "That's the closest thing to a marriage proposal I've ever received."

"I'm not talking marriage," she quickly assured him, although in truth the thought hadn't been far from her mind. "I just thought that maybe you and I could partner up. I'll need somebody to take care of things and watch the tables at the hotel. Someone I can trust. If things don't work out, you're free to go."

"You might already have a game-room manager."

"If I do, I'll fire him," she swore recklessly. "What do you think?"

He let out a weary sigh, gave her shoulders a light squeeze, and closed his eyes. Annie stiffened, bracing herself for his rejection. But Jake stunned her by replying instead, "I think, darlin', that might just be the best offer I've ever had."

She sat straight up, her heart swelling with joy. "You mean you'll do it?"

He opened his eyes, regarding her sternly. "On one condition."

She caught her breath. "What's that?"

He pulled her tightly to him and flipped her on top of his chest.

"I get twenty percent of the take."

Annie's eyes widened in horror. "You'll get five percent and not a penny more."

He let out a shout of laughter. "By God, a woman after my own heart. Ten percent, Annie, and that's final."

"All right, ten percent. But you'd better be worth it."

Jake smiled his slow, lazy smile. "My dear Miss Foster," he said, "I'm worth fifty."

Chapter 16

The sound of bustling wagons, horses racing up and down the street, and men shouting excitedly back and forth woke Jake the next morning. His first thought was that something was wrong, but as he listened more intently, he heard the benign sounds of vendors opening their shop doors, dogs barking, and children laughing and playing as they headed off to school. There was a little extra noise and commotion, but that wasn't unusual. Some towns just started the day louder than others.

He turned his attention to the woman who lay curled up next to him in bed. Annie's back was fitted snugly against his chest, and her derriere was pressed tightly against his hips. Her body was warm and silky soft, her breathing low and steady. Despite the lateness of the hour, she was still fast asleep. Jake couldn't blame her for being tired. They had made love all night, and neither one of them had fallen asleep until just before dawn.

She murmured something in her sleep and shifted slightly against him. As she moved, her long wheat-gold hair spilled over her pillow and swept across his chest. Her bottom pressed warm and inviting against his groin. Jake felt himself grow hard, wanting her almost as badly as he had last night. He traced his fingers lightly over her breasts, contemplating waking her up and making love to her again.

As though sensing his intentions, Annie stirred,

mumbled a word or two, then twisted around and moved slightly away. Jake smiled and softly kissed her shoulder, deciding to err on the side of gallantry and let her sleep.

His gaze moved around the room, which was flooded with brilliant morning sunshine. Annie had clearly been embarrassed last night by the mess, but Jake had liked it. The disarray had provided him a true glimpse of Annie, for the possessions that filled it were uniquely hers. Mixed in with the assorted lace and finery from Miss Angelique's were her worn boots, ragged flannels, and oversized denims. Her new crinoline petticoats sat on a table beside her guns and holsters. On a separate table, her three most cherished possessions were proudly displayed: her copy of *Winston's Guide*, her worn advertising circular for the Palace Hotel, and the old tintype of her and her sister Catherine.

The variety of items showed two distinct sides of Annie, both of which he loved equally.

Loved. The word stopped him flat, even as it casually slipped through his mind. Had he fallen in love with Annie? The realization wasn't as shocking as he might have expected, for in truth, he had been drawn to her from the first day they had met. He loved her guileless beauty, her self-assured femininity, her unconquerable spirit, her reckless independence, and her sweet sentimentality.

He loved the way she made love, the way she melted into his arms with such innocent sensuality. He had had lovers with more practiced expertise, but never had he been with a woman who moved him the way Annie did. She stripped him of all his defenses and cynicism, demanding as much from him as she gave of herself. The finer points of lovemaking could be taught, but not something like that. Miss Annabel Lee Foster was a rare find, indeed.

He thought about the offer she had made him last night, inviting him to run the gaming room in her hotel. He had accepted readily, for the suggestion suited him on many levels. First it was an excellent business opportunity. He could make as much money by taking a percentage of the games as he could earn by traveling from town to town. He would bring in the players and keep the games square: no holdout devices, loaded dice, dealing from the bottom of the deck, or marking cards. Jake had no objection if some fool tinhorn set himself up to be grazed by a professional—as long as the game was honest and he earned a percentage of the action.

Second he would be firmly in position when the Mundy Gang finally did show up. And Jake had no doubt whatsoever that they were going to show up. The gang was sticking too close to their trail for it to be a mere coincidence. He believed Annie truly thought the boys were dead, but that obviously wasn't the case. For whatever reason, they weren't about to let her ride away from them. A day of reckoning was on the way, and by the looks of things, it was going to happen sooner rather than later. And when the boys finally did appear, Jake definitely wanted to be there—preferably with Sheriff Walter Pogue and a band of deputies by his side.

And last, most important, staying on at the Palace gave him a good excuse for staying close to Annie. The thought of spending the rest of his life with her was an amazingly enticing one. If the Palace Hotel was anywhere near as grand as Annie claimed it to be, the resort would likely grow and flourish along with the towns of Cooperton and Abundance. Hell, he and Annie might even add to the population with children of their own one day. His hand moved to Annie's belly. It was flat now, but the thought of filling it with life and watching it swell was undeniably appealing. Annie would make a fine mother, strong and kind. And the thought of holding a squirming, squalling infant of his own seemed surprisingly proper and natural.

Catching the rapidly escalating train of his thoughts, Jake shook his head. It was far too much heavy thinking for a man to do without at least a cup of coffee in his hands.

He placed a light kiss on Annie's shoulder, then eased himself out of bed. He quietly gathered his belongings, dressed, and stepped out into the hall.

"Good morning, Mr. Moran."

Jake turned to see Peyton VanEste, closing and locking the door to the adjoining room. His expression was flat and pleasant enough, but there was a slight leering glint in his eye. VanEste had probably heard every sound they made last night. While Annie had not been loud, neither had she been a silent partner to their lovemaking. The fact that she had purred and moaned with pleasure at his touch had made it all the more exciting for Jake.

On second thought, VanEste looked entirely too pleased with himself, Jake noted. He had instinctively disliked the man before, but now he knew why. Something about him reminded Jake of the hospital rats he had encountered during the war, that cowardly breed of men who were the bane of the Confederacy. They constantly claimed illness or injury and spent as much time as they could moping around in a hospital bed, eating the best of the Army's food, and generally doing whatever they could to avoid putting themselves in the line of fire.

Jake gave the man a cool nod. "VanEste."

"Quite a commotion outside this morning."

"That so?"

"Although I'm sure that neither you or Miss Foster knows anything about it." There it was again, that overblown wink that made Jake want to shoot out VanEste's eye.

"What are you talking about?" Jake asked, his tone as thin as his patience.

VanEste smiled pleasantly. "Why, nothing, nothing at all." He put on his hat and fastidiously adjusted the brim, then nodded in farewell. "Good day, Mr. Moran."

Jake watched him walk downstairs and exit the hotel. Their brief conversation bothered him more than it should have. There was a smug satisfaction in the reporter's attitude, as though he knew something but wasn't letting on.

Jake left the hotel and stepped outside, struck by the level of commotion and excitement that filled the street. A current of energy seemed to sweep through the townspeople, and the air was filled with the buzz of news. Groups gathered and stood in the street, chattering excitedly among themselves. VanEste moved among them, a pencil and pad of paper in his hands, taking notes. Judging by their raised voices and vivid gestures, their conversations were filled with a combination of outrage, indignation, and pure thrill.

Jake glanced toward the jailhouse. The sheriff and a group of six deputies were making a final check of their arms in preparation for saddling up. He strode across the street and joined the group that had gathered around the sheriff and his men, watching as they assembled their posse.

"The sooner we get after those boys, the sooner we'll bring 'em back," the sheriff growled, clearly growing impatient with the deputies, who were lagging behind, wasting time kissing their wives and children good-bye. "Now, saddle up, men, and let's get a move on."

Jake turned to the man beside him. "What happened?" he asked, although he had a sinking suspicion that he already knew.

"The Mundy boys," the old-timer replied. "They plum cleaned out the bank. Rode off with nearly five thousand cash."

"When?"

"Early this morning, about daybreak."

"They bust in?"

"Hell, no, nothing that clean. Them boys are getting mighty dirty. Word is, they found out who the teller was, followed him home, then broke into his house just before dawn. Nice young fella too, with a wife and three little ones at home. Couple of them boys in the gang stayed with the man's wife while the others dragged the teller back to the bank. They told him that if he didn't open the bank and unlock the safe, they'd kill his wife and kids. The teller let them into the bank, of course. What choice did he have?"

"How did he know it was the Mundy Gang?"

"Pete Mundy flat out told him who he was. He held his gun to the teller's face and said, 'You unlock that safe now, mister, or your wife's gonna feel a breeze through her skull. Pete Mundy don't miss when he fires his gun.' Said it just like that." The old-timer shook his head and made a clucking noise with his tongue. "Them boys are getting mighty cocksure of themselves. Mighty reckless. It's one thing to bust in and rob a bank clean, but it's another to hold a gun to a fella's wife and kids. Now, that's downright uncivilized. I wouldn't mind a bit if the sheriff brings them in. Let them get their necks stretched and we'll see how they like it. Maybe that'll teach 'em not to go around robbing banks and threatening folks."

Jake thanked the man and moved away, heading toward the stable to ready their horses. So the Mundy Gang was still on their trail. On their trail? Hell, they were almost riding neck and neck. He considered telling Annie that the gang had hit the town but abruptly decided not to. She was convinced that the boys were dead. Hearing otherwise would only shake her up. No sense worrying her now, when they were just miles away from Cooperton. There would be plenty of time to sort things out once they arrived.

A skinny, long-limbed boy of about twelve with copper-colored hair and a face full of freckles greeted him at the stable entrance. At Jake's request, the boy brought out Weed and Dulcie. Jake tossed his saddle over Weed's back while the boy adjusted his cinch and bridle. Once Weed was ready to ride, Jake turned to Dulcie.

He found the mare pushing her nose into Annie's saddlebags. Jake flipped open the pocket that Dulcie had been poking and discovered that it was filled with a stash of maple candy. He fed a piece to the greedy mare, then turned and passed a piece to the stable boy as well. While the horse and stable boy munched contentedly, Jake heaved the saddle up on his shoulder, then settled it on Dulcie's back. As he did, a slim white piece of paper drifted from the pocket that contained the candy and fluttered to the floor.

The boy picked the paper up and passed it back to Jake. Jake glanced at it and froze. He read it through a second time, just to make sure he hadn't read it incorrectly. Unfortunately the words, although written in a rough, almost illegible scrawl, were quite clear.

Annie, Meet me at Brenner's Mine at 4. Urgent. Pete.

Stunned disbelief swept through him, then quickly turned to cold, razor-edged fury. Annie had been in touch with Pete all along. *Goddamn her!* She had been lying to him the whole time, and he had been idiot enough to believe her.

If Jake had one weak spot, it was women. Although experience had proven time and again that they were far from the helpless, demure, fragile beings his Southern upbringing had taught him to believe they were, some fatal flaw within him caused him to continue to depict them that way in his mind. That was just the way he had seen Annie. Sweet and adoring, brave and loyal. When in truth, Miss Annabel Lee Foster was nothing but a scheming, lying bitch. He should have recognized that from the start.

Once he faced it, the fact that she was still running with the gang made infinitely more sense than any other theory he had been able to come up with. It explained why she had "accidentally" fired the round that had warned off the man who had been following them—a member of the gang, no doubt. It explained the robbery that had occurred in Manitobe just hours after they had passed through. It explained where she was on the afternoons preceding the robberies in Two River Flats and in Abundance. Although she swore that she had spent the entire afternoon yesterday wandering around Abundance, she could easily have ridden out yesterday and met with the gang.

It explained everything except why she had surrendered her body to him, but that wasn't a hard one to figure. She did it to relieve herself from the tedium of the trail. Or perhaps, he thought, growing even more furious, for the thrill of watching him make a full and complete ass of himself, besottedly declaring his love and undying affection for her.

And Jake had come close to doing exactly that. Too damned close.

"Something wrong, mister?" the stable boy asked, his brows furrowed in concern.

Jake folded the note and stuffed it into his coat pocket. "Where's Brenner's Mine?" he asked.

"That ol' worthless hole? It played out a long time ago. Nothing out there now but an abandoned shack."

"Where is it?"

The boy shrugged. " 'Bout a thirty-minute ride south of here, I reckon."

Jake nodded to himself, his fury escalating by the minute. Playing a hunch, he asked, "You know the lady who owns this horse?"

The stable boy nodded.

"Did anybody come around here looking for her?"

The boy dropped his gaze, digging the toe of his boot into a pile of hay. "I don't know."

"Who came looking for her?" Jake demanded flatly.

The boy looked up at him with round, imploring eyes. "I ain't supposed to say. Pa says for me to keep my mouth shut. He says I'm just telling tall tales and trying to make myself look important."

Jake softened his voice and crouched down, looking at the boy eye to eye. "It's important that I know, son. I swear I won't tell anybody what you saw, especially not your pa."

The boy glanced away uneasily, then admitted in a small voice, "A yellow-haired fella came by the stable early this morning looking for her. He was tall and lean, handsome, I reckon, but sort of mean looking. Fella had real slick spurs too. The jangly type, with silver half-moon rowels." The boy looked at the ground, embarrassed. "I told my pa this morning it might have been that bank robber fella himself. Course, Pa didn't believe me, said I was just trying to look like a big man. Said nobody'd be so stupid as to go poking around town after they was to rob the bank."

Jake stood, letting out a deep sigh. "If there's one thing this world's got plenty of, son, it's stupidity."

He was living proof of it. While Annie was riding out to meet with the Mundy Gang, he was in Miss Angelique's Boutique buying her gowns. While Pete Mundy had been in town looking for her, he was lying in bed with Annie curled up next to him, fancying himself in love. His stomach churned with disgust at how easily he had let Annie lead him around. *Well, I hope you enjoyed the ride, darlin',* he thought grimly, *'cause the fun's just getting started.*

He handed the boy a two-dollar piece and led Dulcie and Weed out of the stable. "Take the horses over to the hotel and leave them by the hitching post, would you?"

The boy's eyes lit up at the size of the coin. "Yes, sir."

Jake left the stable and strode directly to the telegraph office. He scrawled out a brief message and handed it to the clerk. *Our friends have arrived. Will expect you in Cooperton. Jake.*

The clerk read it and nodded. "Where do you want this to go?"

"Sheriff Walter Pogue. Two River Flats, Colorado."

*A*nnie stepped out of the hotel and into a bustling street flooded with bright morning sunshine. She hesitated for a moment on the boardwalk, just drinking it all in. She saw people everywhere—talking, shouting, and laughing among themselves. The town was busy and active, the shops thriving with business. The scents of ponderosa pine, horses, newly cut timber, and the smoky fire from the blacksmith's shop filled the air. If she stood perfectly still, she swore she could even smell the sunshine itself. She clasped her arms tightly around her waist, barely able to contain her happiness.

Glancing down the street, she saw Jake walking toward her, his pace measured and even. Her heart swelled with joy at the sight of him, making her so happy she was sure she would burst. Annie loved the way Jake Moran walked—especially when he was walking toward her. His hat was pulled down too low over his brow for her to see his face, but that didn't matter. She knew every inch of his striking profile. She had *kissed* every inch of his striking profile, and more.

He looked so handsome in the bright morning sunlight, so tall and lean and muscular, so filled with strength and purpose. She barely stifled an urge to run to Jake and throw her arms around his neck, sharing her joy at the new day with him. Instead she closed her eyes and said a silent prayer, thanking God for bringing them together. In just four short hours, they would be in Cooperton. Finally, after what seemed like forever, Jake reached her.

"Morning, Jake." Her voice sounded giddy, breathless, and excited.

"Morning." His voice sounded . . . flat. Cold almost, clipped and reserved. Annie stepped off the boardwalk and pressed a chaste kiss against his cheek. Compared to how open and loving they had been last night, the kiss was nothing but a mere peck. Still Annie felt shy and ungainly about it, particularly when Jake didn't reciprocate. Not by pulling her to him, kissing her in return, or touching her at all. In addition, there was a coldness to his stance, a coldness that Annie shrugged off as a reluctance to engage in a public display of affection.

Or more likely, she realized, his impatience with her for making him wait. By the looks of him, Jake was more than ready to ride. The horses were saddled, and probably had been for at least an hour. Annie nervously toyed with her hands, regretting the fact that she had slept in. Once she woke, it had taken her not only longer to dress but longer to pack, what with all the new clothes Jake had given her. In the end, she rolled them all into a bedsheet as neatly as she could, then spent a few extra minutes settling with the desk clerk over the price of the sheet.

"I didn't mean to be so late," she apologized. "Truth is, I was planning on riding out at dawn."

"I'll bet."

At least, he smiled that time. But it wasn't a smile that Annie recognized. It was a cold, chilling, almost cruel smile. Nor did she recognize his eyes. The things she had come to expect when she met Jake's gaze were no longer there. She saw no warmth, no laughter, no kindness. Just a frightening, unwavering glint of cool brilliance. Like sunlight dancing off the polished silver handles of a coffin.

Annie shifted from foot to foot, hurt and bewildered by the inexplicable change in him. But she wasn't at all certain how to confront him, or how to coax him back to the loving, teasing man she had become accustomed to. Remembering how pleased he had been last night to see her in the gown he had given her, she tugged at her riding skirt, waiting for him to notice her outfit.

She wore the navy riding ensemble he had purchased for her yesterday. The garments were finely tailored, constructed of a heavy cloth that would keep her warm during their four-hour ride. In addition, the riding skirt was split in the middle, so she wouldn't have to travel sidesaddle—something Annie had never bothered to learn. Last night's curls had long since fallen out of her impossibly straight hair, so she had simply pulled it back into a ponytail, an effect that she hoped looked simple and refined. A stiff golden-brown leather hat with a round, feminine brim and a pair of matching riding gloves completed her outfit.

"How do I look?" she finally prompted.

"Fine."

His cursory response to her ensemble felt entirely unsatisfactory. Then again, maybe she was just expecting too much. She glanced beyond him and saw that his bags were packed and tied to his saddle. "You ready?"

"Always."

She smiled. "Me too."

"You seem mighty anxious to leave town."

Annie frowned at his tone of voice, then sent him a small, reassuring smile. "Course I am, silly. Why, we'll be in Cooperton in just a few hours. This is the day I've been waiting for."

"Yes. Silly me."

Annie reached down and scooped up recently returned Cat, placing her in her customary position in the saddle. As Jake didn't offer to help her with her bag, Annie tied it on to the back of her saddle herself. She mounted; again, without his help. She was uncomfortably aware of the distance between them but didn't know how to account for it.

"Something wrong, Jake?"

Jake swung onto Weed's back. He looked at her for a long moment, his silvery-blue eyes intense and unfathomable in the early morning sunshine. "Course not, Annie. What could be wrong?"

"I'm not sure. You're acting kinda funny."

"Am I?" Jake gathered his reins in his hand. He gazed off into the distance, as though looking at something only he could see. "How's the trail south of here?"

"I wouldn't know. I've never been on it before."

His lifeless smile reappeared, and an odd, strangely satisfied light entered his eyes. "That's right. That's what you said." He spurred Weed into a gentle trot, leaving her to follow.

Annie stared after him, lost in her bewilderment and distress. Jake's mood seemed so remote and strange, so entirely different from the way he had been last night. Then again, she thought, this was all so new to her, maybe he was acting entirely properly. Maybe that was the way sophisticated people acted after a night of passion. When the sun rose, the lovemaking ended. *Maybe sophisticated women don't come bounding out of a hotel like a puppy who wants its belly rubbed, Annie, girl.*

Her rationalization did little to lighten her mood. As their journey progressed, the joy that had filled her earlier seemed to evaporate. It was as though a cloud had blocked the sun and cast a shadow over her spirits. She felt gray and burdened despite the brilliant blue sky that hung above them. They traveled in uncomfortable silence, with Jake coolly ignoring her every attempt at conversation.

The road they traveled sliced a neat path through the San Juans, following a riverbed that was crusted with ice and snow. Occasionally a hawk flew overhead, or a deer leapt out from behind a pine. In general, however, the woods were hushed and quiet. As they rode, Annie grew increasingly apprehensive. Her nerves were already strung tight, wondering what sort of reception she would receive upon her arrival. Jake made it worse by subtly tensing at every shadow or squirrel that crossed their path, his hand moving instinctively toward his gun as though he expected trouble at any moment.

After what seemed like endless hours, the trail broadened and they reached Cooperton. A quick glance confirmed that the town was everything Annie had hoped for. It wasn't anywhere near as grand as Abundance had been, but it was respectable nonetheless. She counted one church, a school, several law and claim offices, a variety of stores and shops—mostly selling mining equipment and household goods—a jailhouse, a telegraph office, a stable, and a blacksmith. She saw far more men than women on the street, but that was fairly typical for a mining community. All in all, the town looked simple, relatively clean, and relatively prosperous. It wasn't nearly as flashy as Abundance had been, but that suited her just fine.

They drew a few curious glances as they rode down Main Street, and Annie's thoughts immediately went to what she looked like after four hours in the saddle. Anxious to make a good first impression, she self-consciously reached up and patted her hair, stiffened her posture, and smoothed down her riding skirts.

She saw a hotel, and her heart skipped a beat, for she thought at first that it might be the Palace. But she realized almost immediately that the structure wasn't as ornate as her hotel should have been. In fact, it was hardly a hotel at all, just a rooms-for-rent sign hanging above a saloon. She considered reaching for the advertising circular to check the address, but she already knew it by heart. The only information the circular revealed was a description of the hotel and its general location in Cooperton, Colorado. She would have asked Jake for his advice, but given his odd mood that morning, she thought better of it and decided to find the hotel on her own.

She reined Dulcie in next to a stoop-shouldered old

miner and leaned down to ask, "Pardon me, can you direct me to the Palace Hotel?"

The miner halted and looked her up and down with a leer. "You lookin' for a job, sweetheart?"

Assuming the man had mistaken her for a cook or a maid in search of employment, Annie drew herself up and proudly announced, "I'm the new owner."

The man's eyes widened. He slapped his knee and let out a hoot of laughter, revealing a wide gap between his front teeth. " 'Bout time that old wreck got some new blood. It's down the street a ways. Keep going, you ain't gonna miss it."

Annie turned to Jake, her earlier trepidations now doubled. Although he had obviously heard their entire exchange, he looked at her with nothing more than mild interest. She lifted her chin and said politely, "The man says it's down the street a ways."

Jake nodded without a word and lightly touched his heels to Weed's flanks. They made their way silently down the street, moving through the town until they left the buildings and any semblance of civilization behind them. Finally Annie saw the hotel she had been dreaming about for years. Looming ahead of them was a grand two-story structure that stood by itself.

Annie reined Dulcie to a stop a few yards in front of the building and simply stared.

The words she had memorized from the advertising circular rang through her mind. *The West's most elegant resort for distinguished ladies and gentlemen. The Palace Hotel: culture and civilization in the midst of the wild Western frontier.* But the promise of the words in print collided with the reality of the building before her.

The hotel was structurally similar to the one in the flyer. It had the same multi-columned front porch, gabled roof, carved front doors, wide stairs, bay windows, and louvered shutters. It had the same generously sized rooms and wide lawn. Yes, the bare bones of the building were intact, but that was where the similarity ended.

Chipped and badly peeling paint fell in thick strips from the columns. The porch hung low in front, dropping in the middle like a distended belly. Several steps were missing from the flight of stairs or were simply broken and kicked aside. The porch rails had been knocked loose and scattered across the lawn. The shutters swung out of kilter, flapping in the breeze. Both front windows were smashed in and boarded up. In short, the hotel looked like it had been in a brutal fistfight and lost badly.

Annie stared at the decayed structure in disbelief, frozen in shock and horror. There had to be some mistake. This couldn't be happening. Not now, not after years of planning and hoping and dreaming. It simply couldn't end like this.

Yet even as she denied that it was possible, a battered, weatherbeaten sign that dangled crookedly from a bent nail caught her eye. The words were simple and yet as final and depressing as an engraving on a tombstone:

Welcome to the Palace.

Annie dismounted and wrapped Dulcie's reins around a withered hitching post. She didn't look at Jake, although she was dimly aware of him dismounting beside her. She woodenly made her way up the rickety stairs. The hotel was completely still and silent—except for a few pigs that grunted and squealed near the back stoop, greedily devouring the slops that had been tossed out the kitchen window.

As she pulled open the front door, a cowbell affixed above her head clanged loudly, announcing her presence. She stepped inside. The stench hit her like a brick wall, knocking her back a pace. The place reeked of tobacco, sweat, grease, and stale perfume. As Annie adjusted her eyes to the dimness of the interior, she saw that the hotel looked as bad as it smelled.

She scanned a room that might once have served as a grand lobby but was now functioning as a parlor. The hardwood floor was sticky beneath her feet, coated with mud and the residue of countless spilled drinks. The windows were boarded over. Faint traces of the fancy paper that had once covered the walls were now thick with grime. The furnishings were simple: a few settees and rickety tables, arranged in clusters to allow for intimate seating in the large room. A long bar leaned against one wall; a cracked mirror hung above it. A flight of stairs led from the main parlor to the bedrooms upstairs.

A rough notice had been scrawled on a piece of plywood and hung near the bar. If there had been any doubt in Annie's mind what type of establishment she had inherited, the sign instantly dispelled it. *Friendliest girls in the territory. Full figured, loving, and professional. Available by the hour or by the half hour.*

*A*nnie glanced slowly around the room, fighting an overwhelming sense of defeat and despair. Her gaze slowly moved to Jake. He leaned against the bar, his arms crossed casually over his chest, his eyes flat.

"I don't understand," she said.

"It's a whorehouse."

"I can see that," she snapped.

"What did you expect?"

"I thought . . ." she started, then stopped abruptly, realizing how foolish she would sound. He knew what she had expected. She had thought she would find a grand hotel and instantly transform herself into a fancy, respectable lady. Obviously he found those dreams as ridiculous as reality had proved them to be. It was apparent even to her that she had no more sense now than she had had when she was five. She was still blindly running around chasing rainbows.

She had had every sign in the world that she would more likely find a brothel than a hotel, but she had stubbornly ignored them all. First there was the type of man

J. D. Thomas had been: loud and boorish, not the sort
who would run a fine resort. Then there was the reaction
of Marshal Locke and his men when she had mentioned
the Palace. All of them had looked as sheepish, embarrassed, and guilty as ten-year-old boys caught smoking
behind a barn. Finally there was the condition of the
flyer, which indicated that it had been printed years ago.
Even the most feebleminded fool might have assumed
that the hotel had undergone some changes over the passing years. But all that hindsight and self-recrimination
did her absolutely no good now.

"What should I do?" she asked.

Jake stepped behind the bar, lifted a whiskey bottle
and took a sniff of the contents, then set it down in disgust. "Burning the place down would probably be most
expedient."

"Thank you. That's very helpful."

He shrugged. "What do you want me to say,
darlin'?"

"All right." Annie placed her hands on her hips and
sent him a pleasant if strained smile. "Why don't you
start by telling me why you've been acting like such a
pig-skinned, stony-faced, mule-headed jackass ever since
we left Abundance?"

He studied her for a moment in silence. He didn't
raise his voice, but his tone held the chilling warning of a
rattlesnake shaking its tail. "You don't want to start this,
Annie."

"Like hell, I don't. If something's wrong, tell me
what it is. You owe me at least that much."

"I don't owe you a damned thing, darlin'.."

Annie couldn't have been any more shocked had he
slapped her. It wasn't the words that stunned her as much
as the way they were spoken. He sounded so matter-of-
fact, looking right through her, as though she were a
bothersome stranger begging on the street.

She swallowed hard, uncertain how to react to his

ugly mood. "I don't know why you're acting this way, but I swear—"

"If you had one good point, Annie, it was that you never lied to me." He paused, then continued with a bitter smile, "At least, not directly. Why don't we try to keep it at that?"

Understanding finally dawned on her. "You think I knew all along what sort of place the Palace really was, don't you? I didn't know, Jake, I swear it." She looked around the room, feeling absolute despair. "If I had known . . ." she began but let the words dwindle off. If she had known, what would she have done? The question was too large for her to come up with a quick answer.

Jake leaned back against the bar and crossed his arms over his chest. "I find this very tedious, don't you?"

He was bored, Annie recognized with a start. Her world was falling apart and Jake was *bored.* He was looking at her with the pained, impatient expression of a man forced to sit through the last act of a very stale comedy. That's all she had been to him, she realized—a mildly amusing distraction that had come to a dull, rather predictable end.

"Why don't you go straight to hell, Jake Moran?" she said, finally channeling her shock and pain into fury. "You don't want to stay, get out now. I mean it. Get the hell out of here."

Jake regarded her through flat, cool eyes. "How convenient. But you're forgetting one little thing. You owe me five hundred dollars for burning down the town hall in Two River Flats. Or did you think last night was payment in full? It was nice, Annie, but it wasn't five hundred dollars nice. I've had that before; I know the difference."

She drew in a sharp breath. "You son of a bitch."

The thick silence that fell between them was broken by a stranger's voice. "You folks want to fight, take it outside. We don't open until six."

Annie turned to see a woman in her late thirties standing on the stair landing. She was dressed in a tattered purple robe. Her face was attractive but hard, her curvy body rather loose and flabby. Her coarse blond hair was streaked with gray, and her skin was blotched from too much drinking and not enough sleep. She might once have been attractive, but she had obviously let herself go. She faced them now with her bare feet planted firmly on the stairs and a Sharps buffalo rifle in her hands.

"Who are you?" Annie asked.

"My name is Dora and I run the place " the woman answered. "Now, this here's private property, and if you folks don't get out, I'll send you out myself—" she warned, ominously lifting the ancient carbine.

"That won't be necessary," Annie said.

"You leaving?"

"I'm afraid not." Annie tilted her chin and straightened her shoulders. "My name is Miss Annabel Foster. I'm the new owner."

The woman's expression didn't change one iota as she slowly looked Annie up and down. Finally she shook her head and set down the rifle. She pulled a thin cigar from the pocket of her robe, lit it, then blew out a long stream of smoke. "Well, I'll be damned. Outlaw Annie. J. D. wrote us that you were coming."

Choosing to interpret her words as ones of welcome, Annie sent Dora a hesitant smile. "So," she said, her tone overly bright, "this is the Palace."

"Is it everything J. D. promised it would be?"

"Not exactly."

"You know why?"

"Why?"

"'Cause J.D. Thomas ain't nothing but an ornery, cheating, thieving, lying sack of shit."

Annie blinked. "Oh."

"Like most men I ever met," Dora huffed, then she glanced over at Jake. "No offense, mister."

"Actually," Annie put in, deciding right then and there that she liked the woman, "I think you're a remarkably good judge of character."

"That so? Well, then, I guess there's only one thing left to say."

"What's that?"

Dora cracked a wry grin. "Welcome home, sweetheart."

Chapter 17

*A*nnie spent her first night in Cooperton by herself, bawling her eyes out. She felt ridiculous doing it, but she couldn't stop. She cried at her inability to master her emotions as well as her inability to control her life. She cried at Jake's cool indifference to her plight, at J.D. Thomas for lying to her, and at Pete for starting the Mundy Gang in the first place. She cried because the Palace Hotel was nothing but a decrepit, broken-down old whorehouse. But most of all, she cried herself to sleep because the whole day had turned out to be miserable when it should have been the best goddamned day of her entire life.

As silly as her crying jag had felt, it proved to be strangely productive. When she woke the next morning, Annie felt utterly calm and determined. She rose and washed her face, hoping her puffy eyes wouldn't be too noticeable. Then she dressed in one of the plain, service-able blouses and skirts that Jake had purchased for her and headed downstairs. Of the women who lived and worked at the Palace, Annie had only met Dora. She simply hadn't been up to any more yesterday. She had asked Dora to show her to a room and had retired.

Annie had no idea where Jake had spent the night. She assumed he had taken a room somewhere in the ho-tel, for the sound of his voice had occasionally drifted up toward her bedchamber, making her feel even more miserable and alone. She could also make a reasonably intelligent guess as to what went on in the parlor of the Palace while she was locked away in her self-imposed exile. The constant ringing of the cowbell above the front door, followed by the sound of loud male voices and boots stomping upstairs, told her that it had been business as usual.

But that was yesterday, Annie thought, stiffening her spine with firm determination. Today was a new day.

She surveyed the five women who sat in a semicircle before her in the dank, musty parlor. It had taken Dora a full thirty minutes to rouse them from their beds and herd them downstairs. The women sat before her in various states of undress, wearing flimsy lace corsets, gauzy robes, and thick wool stockings. They looked tousled from sleep but sharp-eyed and attentive nonetheless. They studied her with expressions varying from open curiosity to cool distrust. Annie eyed the women one by one, sizing them up. If she could manage one of the territory's most ruthless outlaw gangs, she figured she could manage a group of women living in a dilapidated brothel. She introduced herself and Jake, then asked them to do the same.

Dora was the oldest and clearly the speaker of the group. Next came Belle, a woman in her mid-twenties who had blue eyes, blond hair, plump cheeks, and a generous figure. She seemed jolly and good-natured if somewhat chatty. In contrast, Jennie Mae was quiet and shy and looked just barely old enough to be out of the schoolroom. She had a sweet face and a round, obviously pregnant belly. Carlotta was Mexican, small but endowed with ample, rounded curves, wavy black hair, and the dark, flashing eyes of a seductress. Of all the women present, she wore the least clothing. Francine introduced herself last. She had brown hair and pretty green eyes and projected the proper refined look of a rancher's wife. Despite her appearance, an air of sadness and shame seemed to cling to her. She reminded Annie of river stone—attractive but worn down by time.

Their introductions complete, Dora took charge of the meeting, as was apparently her custom. "We've been running the place by our own rules ever since J.D. took off," she informed Annie. "Things have been working just fine by us, and we figure to keep things going just the way they are."

Annie eyed the women coolly, her gaze moving from face to face. "I see."

Jennie Mae and Belle both averted their eyes, clearly adverse to either a fight or an open challenge. Francine looked worried but not openly hostile. Carlotta smiled and arched one brow, as though daring her to disagree. Dora looked simply matter-of-fact, as though negotiating water rights at a well rather than the rights of working girls at a brothel.

"Would you mind telling me what these rules are that have been working so well?" Annie asked.

"We get at least one night off a week," Dora began. "No more than four different men per girl per night, no matter how crowded the place is. We want the right to refuse any customer, even if he's paying, and that includes serving him too much liquor. We charge three dollars a spin. J.D. used to take half, but we think it's only fair to change that a little since we're the one's doing all the work. We want to keep two dollars for ourselves, to pay for clothes, shoes, and whatnot. And lastly this place is starting to look neglected. We want to hire a woman to come in and clean up, do laundry, and such, twice a month. We reckon we'll split the cost of that right down the middle."

"Anything else?" Annie asked mildly.

Dora cast a triumphant glance at the other women. "No, I suppose that's it."

"All right, then, here's my answer." Annie smiled politely and looked the women straight on. "No."

Dora's smile instantly faded. Her mouth drew tight and pinched, making her look older and harder than her years.

"I told you she'd be no better than J.D.," Carlotta said bitterly.

A low, rebellious murmuring started among the women. From the corner of her eye, Annie saw Jake watching her, his expression conveying nothing but mild curiosity. Annie took a deep breath, hiding her nervousness. She had one chance, and this was it. If she was going to have any credibility at all, it was up to her to look competent and in control.

"I heard you out. Now I'll ask you to hear me out," she said.

"It doesn't sound to me like we've got much say in this," Dora replied, indignantly rising to her feet and wrapping her tattered robe about her frame.

"Please," Annie said. "Just hear me out."

Annie waited until Dora reluctantly resumed her seat, then began. "This place is mine now, and it's all I have. I mean to make it my home. But I don't plan on living in a brothel."

"So you're kicking us out?" Jennie Mae asked in alarm, her hands moving protectively to her belly.

"Not at all. Just the opposite, in fact. I'm asking you to stay—all of you." Annie paused, making direct eye contact with each of the women seated before her.

Dora sent her a cutting glance. "What are you offering, some charity home for wayward women?"

"Not charity, Dora," Annie replied. "I've never taken it myself, and I'm not about to dole it out. What I'm offering each of you is a job. J.D. told me this place was a hotel, and that's what I intend to make it. It looks to me like this town could use something more than a few boarded-up rooms over a noisy saloon. But it'll be work, there's no question about it. Hard work. I'll need someone to help me cook, to wait tables, clean, make the beds, keep the books, register guests, plant flowers and vegetables, keep a pen for chickens and pigs, do the marketing . . . well, you all get the idea. Food and board will be free, and I'll pay you a fair wage besides."

Carlotta tossed her head. "What if we like the way we're living now just fine?"

Annie shrugged. "Fine by me. You just won't do it here, that's all. If that's what you want, I reckon there's plenty of cathouses that'll be glad to have you."

"So you're kicking us out?"

"I'm letting your choose. I won't judge any woman who does what she can to get by. You're free to live your lives as you see fit. But I don't intend to run a brothel. I want to make that clear right now."

"You make it sound like we can snap our fingers and change overnight," Dora said. "It ain't that easy."

"Why not?"

"We've been making our living flat backing for too long. The good folks around these parts know what we are, and they ain't very forgiving, trust me. Even if we do gussy up the place, there's no way we can change who and what we are. We'll likely just make fools of ourselves trying. We'll be about as welcome in town as a pack of rabid dogs at the preacher's Sunday sermon."

So that was it. Annie studied the women with a new understanding. It wasn't that they didn't want to change, simply that they didn't believe that they could. Hoping that she had read them accurately, she took a bold step, pushing her argument further then she normally would have dared.

"So you're going to let the opinions of a few snooty folks hold you down. You're going to keep lying down for the miners and drunks in this town because that's what folks expect of you." She paused for a moment, letting her words sink in. "Or are you going to try and make something better of yourselves while you have a chance?

Fact is," Annie continued, firing all her guns at once, "I'll bet that none of you really likes the way you're making a living. If you did, you'd be doing it in one of those fancy houses out in Abundance or Denver City, not hiding out in some run-down shack in Cooperton."

The women looked stunned. They glanced at one another as though silently conferring, then their gazes moved to Dora. Dora nodded and straightened, looking uncomfortable but resigned. "If you're gonna talk plain to us, I reckon we can talk plain to you."

"I'm listening."

"We all know who you are. Outlaw Annie. We know you run with the Mundy Gang. I reckon everybody in these parts knows that. If we agree to stay with you and try to turn this place around, how do we know we ain't just getting ourselves in worse trouble? How do we know you ain't just planning on turning this into an outlaw hideout? That being the case, it might just be best if we all packed up and left tonight."

"You have my word that that's not what I aim to do. But since none of you knows me, I suppose that doesn't mean very much," Annie stated plainly. "You know who I am, you know what I've done, and you know my reputation. But that's all in the past. My outlaw days are over, I'm telling you that straight. I'm starting new, and I'm offering you the same chance. I can't promise anything but a lot of hard work. You want to go on whoring, you can head out tonight. You want to do something different with your life, you're welcome to stay. I suppose the rest is up to you."

Silence once again hung between them as the women absorbed her words. Annie could almost see their thoughts turning as they mulled over her words. Dora once again assumed the role of leader of the group. "Will you excuse us a minute? I reckon we got some talking to do among ourselves."

Annie stood, feeling nothing but defeat. She had given it her best try, and she had lost, she could read it in their eyes. She nodded politely to the women and exited the room with Jake, shutting the parlor door behind them.

She paced back and forth on the dilapidated porch, wound up as tightly as a cheap clock. She heard snatches of the women's conversation but not a word of it sounded as though it was in her favor. Unable to stand the suspense any longer, Annie quit pacing and whirled around to look at Jake.

"What do you think?" she asked.

"About what?"

Her eyes widened. "Whether they're going to stay or not."

Jake hooked one boot over the bottom porch rail and watched an old man lead a mule down the muddy street. "I have no idea," he replied. He sounded about as interested as if she had asked him to guess the mule's name.

Annie bit back the sharp retort that sprang to her lips and resumed her pacing. There would be plenty of time to pick a fight with Jake later.

The front door opened, and Dora poked her head outside. "Miss Annie?"

Annie turned sharply. "Yes?"

"We got our answer."

Her voice held no promise. Annie's heart sank, then resolution set in. She lifted her chin, determined not to let his dismay show. If the women deserted her, she would find some way to make the hotel work on her own. Her pride was about the only thing she had left in the world, and she damned sure wasn't about to let anybody take that away. She resumed her seat and waited for Dora to speak, her heart pounding in her chest.

"We just have one question," Dora said.

"All right," Annie replied, expecting to be quizzed about the Mundys again, but Dora surprised her by look-

ing at Jake instead, her gaze flicking to the pair of revolvers strapped to his thighs.

"You any good with those guns, mister?"

"Good enough, I suppose," he replied.

"You better be. You have any idea what's gonna happen when those horny galoots get themselves liquored up
and come lookin' for a good time—and we turn them
away?"

The women were staying. For better or worse, they'd
placed their chips with hers.

Annie let out her breath as relief poured through her.
She looked into the faces of the women, seeing in their
expressions the very emotions that were running through
her. She saw hope and cynicism, worry and concern, determination and commitment.

In that instant, she felt as though she knew them and
understood them, almost as well as she knew and understood herself. These were women who didn't give
up, women who fought and lost and got up to fight again.
Women who spoke their minds and handled their guns as
well as they handled their men. Despite their shameful
pasts, they all shared one thing in common: a ridiculous
conviction that if they tried hard enough, tomorrow
would be a better day.

Now it was up to her to make that happen. Annie
clenched her hands in her lap and sent them a trembling,
wholly inadequate smile.

"Thank you," she said.

*A*nnie had meant to spend a few minutes after the
meeting speaking privately with Jake, but she never had
the opportunity. He rode out without saying a word to her
after the meeting had ended. So much for her hope that
she might be able to rectify whatever had gone wrong between them.

Left with no alternative but to put that problem aside

for the moment, Annie spent the rest of the day taking inventory of the Palace's goods. Dora led the tour, dressed in her tattered purple robe and thick wool socks. The results of the inventory did little to cheer Annie's spirits. The kitchen walls were caked with grease and grime, and the shelves were nearly bare, equipped with only a few cracked pots, chipped plates, and glassware.

"J.D. sold most of this stuff, or traded it for liquor," Dora informed her as they moved through the room.

The formal dining room had been shut up for years. The tables and chairs were caked with dust, thick cobwebs hung from the rafters, and the fancy flocked paper on the walls was torn and peeling. A raccoon had nested in the storage closet that housed the linens, destroying everything inside. Dora and Annie moved from room to room, finding a similar state of disrepair wherever they looked. The stuffing was coming out of the sofas, the curtains were stained, and layers of dust and debris covered the furniture.

The upper-floor bedchambers were divided into two wings, one on the east and one on the west. In total, there were thirty rooms, making it about as large and grand a hotel as any Annie had ever seen. Fortunately the upstairs was in relatively better shape than the downstairs. It was dirty and untended, of course, but not too badly damaged. Each room was furnished with a large bed and feather mattress, a washstand and basin, and a dresser of good quality.

As Annie moved through the property, it became increasingly obvious that no expense had been spared in building and furnishing the original hotel, even if it had fallen into disrepair in later years. The doors were constructed of fine hardwoods, rich wainscoting lined the walls, ornamental plaster work graced the ceilings of the public rooms, and intricately carved banisters lined the stairs.

Dora briefly related the hotel's history. "Some flimflam man was traveling out in the plains and hooked up with a buffalo hunt. He met one of them fancy European counts. Count Von Stracklefurt, or some such name as that. Remember back when it was the rage for all those fancy European kings and princes and dukes to come out West? They'd travel around in their fancy coaches and shoot those poor dumb animals by the trainload, just for sport.

"Anyhow, this flimflam fella got a hold of Von Stracklefurt, a fella with a fancy title, loads of money, and about as much sense as a jackass braying at the moon. The flimflam man convinces the count that he ought to buy this property out in Cooperton and put up the money to build a grand hotel for royalty to stay in while they were out killing buffalo and chasing Indians. See, up to that point, they had just been living in tents and painted wagons. Course, there ain't any more buffalo out here than there are elephants, and only a certified idiot would want to go stirring up the Indians, but the count didn't bother to find none of that out. So he gives the flimflam man a boatload of money to fix up this grand hotel. Stracklefurt's Folly, folks around here called it."

"What did the count do when he found out he'd been duped?"

"He never did find out. Died before he ever made it out here."

"What happened to him?"

"Rumor has it that he was murdered in his sleep by one of his own cousins." Dora shrugged. "More likely he just choked to death on a chicken bone, or some fool thing like that. But you know how it is—folks like to make up stories."

Annie nodded. "What happened to the Palace after he died?"

"The flimflam man sold it off. It traded hands at least five times that I know of. By the time it got to J.D., he won it in a poker pot—that's how worthless folks considered it." She shook her head, letting out a sigh. "You ain't the first one to come in and try to make something out of the place. Other folks have come in and spent their money trying to fix it up, but it just never took."

"Things are different now."

Dora thought that over. "We got a lady outlaw and five whores running a hotel," she said, speaking with a straightforwardness Annie had already come to appreciate. "That might get some attention, folks might come just out of curiosity, but that won't be enough to keep us in business."

Annie smiled. "True, but that's not what I was referring to. The territory has changed since J.D. had the run of the place. We have Abundance to the north of us and Santa Fe and Albuquerque to the south. The way I see it, that makes for a natural route folks are gonna take through Cooperton. And if they're traveling through, they're going to be hungry and tired and want someplace decent to stay. The rooms over the saloon were full up, and the stable even had signs posted offering some of their haylofts to sleep in. Looks to me like the business is out there if we really want it. With a little spit and polish, we might just make this the finest hotel this town has ever seen."

"You really mean that, don't you?" Dora asked.

Annie looked at her in surprise. "Of course."

Their tour of the premises ended where it had begun, back in the kitchen. Dora put a kettle on the stove and heated water for tea. Once the tea was ready, she poured them both a cup and took a seat across from Annie at the kitchen table.

Annie sipped her tea, studying the other woman curiously. "If you weren't sure I really meant to make a go of this place, why did you agree to stay on?"

Dora let out a deep breath. "Mostly because of what you said about taking chances, I reckon. The fact is, there's no woman here who really wanted to be a whore. We all got stories of why it happened, but I won't bore you with none of them. Bottom line is, I guess each of us decided it was better to be alive than to be dead, and we decided to do whatever it took to stay that way. Carlotta does all right, and so do Belle and I, but Francine and Jennie Mae were never really suited for this kind of work." She crossed her arms over her chest, pulling her robe tightly around her. "Fact is, I'm getting kind of old for it. Tired. It takes things out of a woman that she can't ever get back."

"Is that why you talked the other women into giving me a chance?"

"I suppose. Most of the girls didn't want to give you a chance. They were all for packing up and taking off. Nothing personal, just on account of you being an outlaw and all. I changed their minds, told them they could trust you. There sure as hell hasn't been anybody else around here offering us a chance to turn ourselves around." Dora hesitated, then looked Annie straight in the eye. "I reckon that means I'm responsible for what happens next. Those women upstairs have had enough hardship in their lives. Don't none of them deserve any more. If I told them wrong, and you are planning on bringing the Mundy boys here, I'd appreciate you telling me straight out right now."

"What I plan on doing is turning this into a fine, respectable hotel."

Dora studied her face, then set down her teacup. There was a finality in the gesture. "All right, then. I reckon we understand each other. We won't talk about this again." She stood and lifted the teakettle off the stove, refilling their cups. "So what are you going to work on first?" she asked as she resumed her seat.

"I don't know. It's all happened so quickly I haven't had a chance to think."

"That's how life works. It's the things you don't see coming that knock you on your ass."

A faint smile touched Annie's lips. "I don't think I've ever heard a truer statement."

Now it was Dora's turn to study Annie curiously. "So tell me about that gambler man you brought with you."

"Jake? He and I are just friends—business acquaintances, really."

Dora cocked one pale-blond brow. "I've been handed a lot of bull in my time, but that's got to be one of the thickest piles of the stuff ever dumped in my lap."

Annie stiffened her shoulders primly. "I don't know what you mean."

"If there's one thing I know in this life, it's men. I've seen the way that fella looks at you, and it ain't like no business acquaintance. Now, are you gonna sit there and expect me to believe there ain't nothing between you two?"

Annie hesitated, running her fingers along the edge of the table. "Well, there was something between us, but now it's over."

"What happened? You get your nose out of joint because he was chasing some other skirt?"

"No, that's not it at all—at least, not that I know of. Why do you ask?"

Dora shrugged. "Just a guess. I see a lot of that in my line of work. My *former* line of work, I should say," she amended with a wry smile. "What with men naturally wanting variety and all. And a man like that gambler man . . . hell, what woman wouldn't want him? A fella like that can get to places the wind can't."

Annie blushed and looked away. Although she didn't mind Dora's blunt, up-front manner, their conversation was rapidly becoming more intimate than she would have liked.

"So you had him, but now you think it's over," Dora summed up. "Do you want him back?"

"It's not that simple."

"You didn't go and get yourself with child, did you?"

Annie felt the color once again rush to her cheeks. "No."

"Good. You're taking precautions?"

"Precautions?"

"Soak a sponge in vinegar, tie it to a string, and wear it while he's inside you—and for a little while afterward, just to make sure his seed don't take," Dora instructed matter-of-factly. "Love may be grand, but the act sure as hell don't last as long as the consequences, if you get my drift."

Annie regarded her doubtfully. "Did Jennie Mae use that?"

"She swears she did, but I doubt it." Dora sighed and shook her head. "She always kept that sponge in her top drawer, dry as a bone. That girl's just aching for somebody of her own to love, and I guess she thinks she's found it in that little baby that's growing inside her."

Annie nodded, filled with a sad understanding.

"But we're talking about you and that gambler man, not Jennie Mae," Dora continued briskly. "Do you love him?"

Annie blinked, startled by the forthright question. "I . . . yes, I think so."

"Think so, hell. Do you love him or don't you?"

"Yes."

"All right, then." Dora thought for a moment. "Have you told him so?"

"That's where the trouble started," Annie admitted. "I didn't exactly tell him I loved him, but I suggested he stay on here at the hotel and make it more permanent between us. At the time, he didn't seem to mind the suggestion at all. But by the next morning, everything seemed to fall apart. Jake acted like someone I didn't even know. When we finally arrived here, he was even worse."

A look of deep understanding crossed Dora's face. "When a man's getting serious about committing himself to a woman, that's when he gets the testiest. He starts looking for reasons to pull back, making them up if he can't find any. The fact is, being with just one woman for the rest of their lives ain't a comfortable thought for most men. The more time they spend looking for reasons to pull away, and the fewer reasons they find, the testier they get."

Annie shook her head miserably. "I owe him money, that's the only reason he's staying."

"Hell, girl, that don't matter to a man like him. There any other reasons you think he might be sticking around?"

"No. At least, not that I know of."

"There, you see?" Dora pronounced decisively. "That settles it. He's staying here for you, and it's making him crazy. You just give him time to come to terms with what he's feeling. He'll come around."

Annie thought for a moment as a tiny kernel of hope blossomed inside her. "Dora," she ventured hesitantly, "exactly how was Jake looking at me?"

"Like he wants you, but he's worried; like he's caught in something he can't control. Trust me, honey, those are all the signs of a man in love. The bigger they are, the harder they fall." She stood, lifted their teacups, and dumped them in the sink. "Now, that's enough chatter. If we're gonna turn this place into a fine hotel, I reckon we better get to work."

Annie passed the afternoon working shoulder to shoulder with the rest of the women, dragging furniture, rags, feather mattresses, and pillows outside to air. The day passed almost too quickly. Soon an evening chill filled the air, and soft, lavender streaks began to color the sky. The women went inside to freshen up before dinner, but Annie remained outside, wanting to accomplish one last task before stopping for the night.

Beneath the formal painted sign that bore the words *The Palace*, a coarser, crude sign reading *of pleasure* had been hung. The work of J.D. Thomas, no doubt. Annie ripped both signs down, feeling an immense sense of satisfaction as she did so. She found a piece of timber, a brush, and a jar of black paint and went to work making a new sign. *Foster's Hotel* soon hung in place of the old signs. It wasn't fancy, but it would do for the time being.

That accomplished, she painted a second sign, reading *Temporarily Closed*, and nailed it up to the front porch. She didn't expect it to do much good when the rambunctious crowds showed up later that evening, but at least she had given them fair warning.

She stepped back and took a good look at her new hotel. A wry smile curved her lips as she studied the rundown structure, which looked every bit as dilapidated as it had before, despite the fresh and optimistic new sign hanging from the eaves. Perhaps the new name ought to be Outlaw Annie's Folly, she thought. At least that fit.

She heard a rider approaching and turned to see Jake. Relief poured through her. He had been gone all day, and with each passing minute, she had become more and more convinced that he had simply ridden away and out of her life without so much as a good-bye. While she knew rationally that that was very unlikely, it did little to calm her nerves. Nor did Dora's earlier reassurances help much. Without realizing it, she had become entirely too vulnerable as far as Jake Moran was concerned.

Annie watched as he dismounted. He strode toward her with that lean, fluid stride of his, looking tall and unbearable handsome. As he moved closer, however, Annie saw that his gaze remained as flat and distant as it had yesterday.

Ignoring that for the moment, she sent him a bright smile and nodded toward the sign. "What do you think?"

"Of what?"

"Why, the sign, of course."

Jake gave it a cursory glance. "You're really going through with this, then."

His voice held no encouragement. He took hold of Weed's reins and led him toward the barn. Annie followed, determined not to give up. The barn smelled of horses and leather and hay, a welcome break from the rank odors of the hotel. Deep twilight shadows filled the stalls, tinting the air with purple and rose, and changing the golden piles of hay to a soft, mellow amber. Jake lit a kerosene lantern and hung it on the wall, softly illuminating the space.

Annie watched the play of his muscles beneath his shirt as he lifted Weed's saddle and set it on a nearby rail. He wordlessly picked up a brush and began grooming his mount, brushing his coat with long, even strokes. Annie knew that touch. It was firm and gentle, soft and soothing. He had once brushed his strong hands over her body in just the same manner as he was brushing Weed. Although Jake was clearly trying to ignore her, Annie knew that he was as aware of her presence as she was of his. The air between them was highly charged, thick and heavy with tension.

The tension wasn't sexual, however. Annie had felt something like it once before in a saloon. Two men had been playing poker when their game had suddenly erupted. The players had slammed down their cards and lurched to their feet, each man calling the other a cheat and a liar. Annie had held her breath and waited, wondering which one would be the first to make a move for his gun.

The same air of stress and nerve-racking anticipation now hung between her and Jake.

The memory of that game gave her the inspiration she needed for approaching him. She moved forward and leaned against the door to Weed's stall. "What would you do if you were dealt a bad hand, and you'd staked everything you owned on the game?" When he didn't answer, Annie bravely continued, "You'd play it out, that's what you would do. That's exactly what I intend to do. This is my home now. It's not what I expected, but I think I can make it work. I'm staying, Jake. I'm through running."

He turned and looked at her for a long minute. "Your choice," he said flatly.

It wasn't what she had hoped for, but it would have to do. "I appreciate your agreeing to stay on."

"For a little while."

His words cut through her. "Right. For a little while." Annie glanced around the stall, avoiding his eyes. Once she had sufficiently composed her emotions, she pasted a smile on her face and said brightly, "Jennie Mae's fixing dinner tonight. Roast chicken and mashed potatoes. It'll be ready in a few minutes if you want to get washed up. I thought it might be a nice chance for us all to get to know one another."

With an abrupt reversal of motion, Jake reached for Weed's saddle and tossed it over the stallion's back. "I won't be here."

"But you just bedded Weed down," she protested.

"I changed my mind."

"Where are you going?"

Jake glanced up, meeting her eyes for the first time that evening. "That, darlin', is none of your damned business."

Annie clenched her fists, watching as Jake led Weed out of the barn. She wanted Jake Moran, she needed him, and she loved him. But not like this. In that realization, she found a strength she had never known she possessed. She followed him outside, clutching her coat tightly against the cool night breeze.

"Jake?"

He stopped, then slowly turned. "What?"

"This is my hotel now. I own it. I might owe you money, but you'll still be working for me. The next time you tell me to go to hell, you're fired."

She turned without another word and made her way inside.

Chapter 18

*J*ake knew he had done nothing wrong. Annie was the one who had betrayed him, not the other way around. Yet, despite everything he knew, he couldn't help but feel uneasy, not to mention guilty as hell. It was idiotic, really, when it was his neck that was about to be stretched. Still the feeling persisted, growing stronger every time he looked at Annie and saw the hurt and confusion in her big golden-brown eyes.

She was good—he'd give her that. She had spun him upside down and inside out and still continued to do so. In his conceit, Jake had imagined that he had enough intelligence—if not just plain old gut-level intuition— to determine who was lying and who was not. Therefore what astounded him most was not Annie's deviousness but his own idiocy. The legendary Outlaw Annie had acted the part of an innocent ingenue, and he had bought it.

He had been as gullible as any greenhorn who'd ever plopped himself down at a poker table, laid down his money, looked at his cards, and asked what beat what. Worse, really, because at least the greenhorn didn't know any better. Jake knew better. And still he had allowed himself to be taken in. Instead of using Annie as a means to an end, he had allowed her to become the end herself. For a short time there, he had thought of settling down with her . . . actually building a home together. He had erred in the most fundamental way, ignoring a rule that was obvious to any man who had ever held a gun: Keep your eye on what you want to hit. He'd allowed his aim to drift off target. Instead of focusing on capturing the Mundy Gang, he had focused his entire attention on Annie.

Well, no more.

And yet, despite his determination, he still harbored seeds of doubt. Annie was part of the gang . . . Annie wasn't part of the gang. His mind seesawed back and forth. Depending on the day, the hour, and the minute, he could sway himself either way. The thought buzzed around his head continually, as annoying and insistent as a fly at a summer picnic. He couldn't get away from it, or from his thoughts of Annie.

Two full weeks had gone by since their arrival in Cooperton. True to his word, Sheriff Cayne had wired Jake the money he had held in trust for him. Walter Pogue and his deputies were on their way. Jake had absolutely no idea where to tell them to find the Mundys once they did arrive, despite the fact that he had spent the past two weeks lurking around the property searching for signs of the gang.

In the two weeks that had passed, Jake had seen nothing to indicate that Annie was interested in anything but fixing up her hotel. In his opinion, the Palace had been beyond hopeless disrepair. It was as forlorn a fleabag as any he had ever had the misfortune to lay eyes on. To his amazement, however, Annie and the other women appeared determined to make a go of it. While Jake had absented himself as much as possible from the hustle and bustle, he couldn't help but notice that Annie had spent every minute of every day working her pretty little ass off. She was still wearing her holsters, but now she was packing a set of hammers in them instead of her guns.

The building had needed soap and water, paint,

carpentry, and a thorough disinfecting. Annie and the women fought fleas, lice, roaches, mud, and tobacco stains. They washed and repaired sheets, restuffed mattresses, beat rugs, mended draperies, restuffed the upholstery, scrubbed and polished the wood floors, replaced windows rotted out by weather and age, cleaned the stove, cleared the chimney of birds' nests, and whitewashed the walls.

From what he had heard, Annie had spent every last nickel of her own savings. When that had run out, she had taken loans from the women who lived there, spending their money as well as her own to fix up the hotel. Although their reception in town had been decidedly cool, the townspeople apparently weren't adverse to taking their money. The women bought new pots and pans from a traveling man and linens from the general mercantile. They contracted with a woman in town for vegetables until their own garden started producing, bought home-baked pies from the preacher's wife, and made arrangements with a local rancher for the delivery of milk and an occasional slaughtered pig or side of beef.

The results had been amazing. Determined to achieve respectability for the hotel and to create a reputation for the saloon, Annie had ingeniously divided the two buildings. She hired a carpenter from town to seal off the inner wall completely, making the saloon and the hotel two distinct and separate entities, each with its own entrance. To distinguish them further, she whitewashed the hotel and painted the doors and shutters an attractive dark green, while she left the walls of the saloon their natural cedar, allowing the wood to continue to weather gracefully. She had christened the saloon the Bella Luna and hung a large crescent moon above the door. A plaque posted on the outer wall read discreetly: *A saloon for gentlemen. Serving the territory's best cigars, whiskey, beer, and bitters. Honest tables.*

Then she hired a bartender, a tiny wizard of a man

named Johnny Dill. He had short, spiky gray hair, a face like a bulldog, and the loyalty to match. He was a good choice. He took over the bar like he had lived there all his life. In the five days that the Bella Luna had been open for business, Johnny had listened to dozens of long-winded, boring stories without a single yawn, had kicked out rowdy drunks before they became destructive drunks, hadn't watered down the whiskey—at least, not so much that any of his customers could tell—and had broken up three fistfights, and he stayed out of Jake's business when it came to running the tables.

The saloon's only connection to the hotel was through a back door that led to the hotel's kitchen. In that way, Annie was able to offer full home-cooked meals to both the patrons of the Bella Luna and the patrons of Foster's Hotel. Jake watched as Carlotta swung through that back door, carrying two plates of ham, eggs, and fried potatoes. She deposited the food and went back to the bar for a round of beer. All in all, Jake thought, glancing around, it was a damned fine saloon. It boasted a long, polished bar with a fine-looking glass above it, shiny wood floors rather than sawdust, comfortable tables and chairs, and wide windows that looked out on the street. It was masculine but welcoming, a relaxing place for a man to settle in and while away a few spare hours.

Not everything Annie had planned had gone as smoothly as she had hoped, however. Although Annie hadn't come to him directly, he had heard through Dora and others of the mysterious accidents that had plagued them during the renovations. They had started out as pranks: cow chips were dumped in a vat of beer purchased for the Bella Luna, a skunk was tossed down the chimney, and sheets that had been washed and hung out to dry were knocked down and dragged through the mud. In time, the pranks became increasingly disturbing and dangerous. A small fire had mysteriously started in the barn. A wood banister gave way, almost sending Annie pitching down the stairs. A large looking glass had been cracked just enough to shatter in her hands when she picked it up.

And when Annie wasn't fighting the anonymous pranksters, she was dealing with rowdy former clients. Jake had been in the middle of a game of seven-card stud when he had heard shotgun blasts coming from the hotel and the sound of women screaming. He had bolted up and gone running next door, his guns cocked and ready, his heart in his throat and his pulse hammering wildly. He had been certain he was about to find either Annie or one of the women lying in a pool of blood. Instead he had found Annie and Dora standing shoulder to shoulder on the front porch, smoke pouring from the barrel of Dora's buffalo gun. Across from them were two drunken miners, dressed in nothing but their red-flannel skivvies. The men were swearing up a storm and demanding to be let inside. A second shotgun blast from Dora's gun had scattered a thick spray of mud at their feet and persuaded them to find their fun elsewhere.

Jake's relief that Annie had not been hurt had been a living, tangible thing. He had let out his breath in a rush, realizing only then that he had been holding it in. His hands had been shaking as he holstered his weapons, and a cold bead of sweat had trickled down his back. Not trusting his voice to speak, he had simply nodded at the women and walked wordlessly back to the Bella Luna.

That was the main reason Jake was so mad at Annie. It wasn't just her lies and deceit. That he could deal with, maybe even understand. He was furious with her because he was so goddamned afraid. If there was one thing in this world Jake hated more than anything, it was being scared. And Annie scared the shit out of him. He was scared that she might be injured by one of the mysterious pranks. Scared that she might be hurt by one of the bordello's former clients. Scared she might be shot dead one day while riding with the Mundy Gang. Scared she might be picked up by the law and hanged.

He felt constantly on guard, ever watchful and wary. Since their confrontation outside the barn two weeks ago, Annie had made herself conspicuously absent, obviously determined to avoid him at all costs. When their paths did cross, she acknowledged him with nothing more than a cool nod and continued on her way. True to her word, she had left the running of the saloon to him, while she had taken over the hotel. She hadn't even so much as set foot inside the Bella Luna—at least, not while he was there.

Which was why it came as an even greater shock to hear the bat-wing doors of the saloon slam open and see Annie storm inside, looking like the wrath of hell. Her boots rapped against the wood floor as she strode purposefully across the room. Her color was high, and her eyes were stormy. Her breath came in short, jerky gasps, reminding him of the last time they had made love. Annie, however, did not look ready to make love. The lady looked like she was spoiling for a fight.

Jake leaned back in his chair, perversely happy to give it to her. "Miss me?" he drawled.

She ignored him and lifted up his coffee cup, taking a quick whiff. "Keeping sober, I see," she announced churlishly as she set the cup down. "What a pleasant surprise."

Jake froze. "Annie, darlin'?"

"What? And don't call me darlin'."

"If you were a man, I'd kill you for that," he said slowly. "You understand me?"

Silence had already fallen over the room at Annie's stormy entrance. Now the four men who sat at Jake's table sucked in their breath and edged back their chairs, staring from Jake to Annie with undisguised fascination.

Annie drew herself up and glanced around the room, as though suddenly aware of their audience. She took a deep breath and sent Jake a tight nod. "I wonder if I might speak to you privately, Mr. Moran?"

He shoved back his chair and stood. "Certainly, Miss Foster."

She spun around and marched out through the saloon's back door. Once they had gained the privacy of the hotel's kitchen, she wasted no time in getting to the point. "I hear you're giving away my liquor."

So much for Johnny Dill minding his own business, Jake thought.

"I hear you passed out free beer and cigars to the men you were playing poker with last night."

"I did."

A note of haughty triumph shone in her eyes. "So you're admitting it."

"Absolutely."

"And just how were you planning on paying for that?"

"I thought running the saloon was my business."

"Not when it comes to giving away my hard-earned liquor."

Jake gave her a long, cold look. "I see. You're giving me completely control—as long as everything I do and say suits you. Is that how it works, darlin'?"

"That's right," Annie affirmed, lifting her chin defiantly. "And if you don't like taking orders from a woman, you can just—"

"How much did that beer cost you?"

"That's not the—"

"How much?"

"Fifteen cents a glass."

"And the cigars?"

"Twenty-five cents each."

"There were five men there, and I bought each of them four glasses of beer, plus a cigar apiece. That comes to a grand total of . . ." He paused for a moment, adding the figures up in his head. "Four dollars and twenty-five cents."

"Which is four dollars and twenty-five cents more than I can afford to give away."

"That's real smart thinking, Annie."

"I'm not running a saloon for shiftless gamblers and no-account drifters. If a man wants a drink at the Bella Luna, he's gonna pay for it. You got that?"

Jake managed to hold on to his temper, but just barely. "Did it occur to you at all that sometimes when a man gets hold of a little liquor and a clean cigar, he starts having a good time? He starts feeling lucky, generous even. He starts feeling thankful for the hospitality and starts betting more. Did you bother to find out that each of those men had been prospecting all summer and most of the fall, and that each of them carried enough silver in his pockets to line Main Street? The house took in over three hundred dollars last night, darlin', and those men had themselves a damn fine time losing it. They'll be back to play again. Now, why don't you show me what you're doing with this grand hotel of yours to earn that kind of money?"

A heavy silence fell between them. The heat and fire that had filled Annie only seconds ago began to slowly drain away. "I'm sorry, Jake," she said quietly. "You're right. I had no call to question you. It isn't your fault that things aren't . . ." Her voice trailed away. She took a deep breath and shook her head, as though clearing her thoughts. "It isn't your fault."

Jake nodded, surprised by the apology. He had expected, and perhaps even wanted, more of a fight. He stood in awkward silence, unprepared for the sudden truce.

After a moment, Annie pulled out a chair and sat down at the kitchen table. She picked up a glass vase and began idly plucking the petals off a bunch of daisies.

Unable to stop it, Jake's gaze moved hungrily over

her, as though he had been starved for just the sight of her. Her hair was gathered up in a loose knot at the crown, with soft tendrils cascading down around her face. She wore the old brown calico she had purchased back in Two River Flats, but it wasn't quite as tight anymore. She had lost weight. Her curves, while still lush and full, weren't as pronounced. He looked at her more closely, noticing things he hadn't seen before. Her skin was pale, and dark violet moons shadowed her eyes. A pinched tightness lingered about her mouth. Her hands were red, chafed raw from scrubbing and hard work. All of which pointed to weeks of work, worry, and very little food or sleep. While Jake told himself that he didn't give a damn, he found that he wasn't quite as immune to her problems as he wanted to be.

"How are you, Annie?" he asked.

She sent him a nervous smile and pushed away the vase of daisies. "Fine, Jake, just fine."

"Do you mind if I sit awhile?"

She hesitated, then shook her head. An awkward silence hung between them as Jake took a seat. He felt the same strange, magnetic pull he had always felt toward her. Sitting as he was, only inches away from her and yet miles apart, he experienced a moment of both aching closeness and agonizing loss.

There wasn't a damned thing in the world about Annie that he would change. Not the color of her eyes, not the silky straightness of her hair, not the soft curves of her body. Nor would he change the way she looked at life: her loyalty and her stubbornness and her determination to do things her own way. Everything about her suited him perfectly. Everything except her involvement with the Mundy Gang.

As he studied her, he was overwhelmed by an almost uncontrollable need to touch her. He wanted to shake the truth out of her once and for all. He wanted to drag her upstairs, turn the lamp down low, and make love to her.

He wanted to massage her sore muscles, kiss away her aches and pains, and ease all her worries. But in the end, he sat exactly where he was, unable to bridge the gap that hung between them.

"Is everything all right here?" he asked.

A thin smile flitted across her lips. "Perfect."

Jake listened, hearing for the first time the echoing stillness that filled the hotel. Glancing through the kitchen door that led to the lobby, he noted that the cubby holes above the front desk that held the keys to the rooms were nearly all full. The restaurant was vacant as well. Obviously the townsfolk weren't taking to the newly remodeled and respectable hotel as easily as they had taken to the saloon. Then again, the saloon had always been a saloon. Annie was struggling to make a fine hotel out of a run-down bordello. And that was a much tougher proposition.

"It takes a little time, that's all," he said.

Annie gave a perfunctory nod. "We've had a few customers check in. And that reporter fella is here too. Remember him, VanEste?" She paused, sending Jake a slightly self-conscious smile. "I finally agreed to do that interview he's been dogging me for. He says that a lady outlaw and five soiled doves running a hotel on their own ought to make a first-class story. He says that with all that publicity, we'll have so many guests, we won't know what to do with them."

"He might be right," Jake agreed.

"Fact is," she continued, "if it weren't for the money you're making in the saloon, I couldn't afford to keep this place open for much more than a month."

"I see."

Annie gave him a startled, embarrassed look. "That don't mean I'm asking you to stay. I know you'd just as soon ride out of town as spend another night here, and I can't say as I blame you. You don't owe me anything . . .

you were right about that. You were right to say it. Just because we . . . well, got closer than we thought we would, that don't mean there are any ties or obligations between us."

"Annie—"

"No, Jake, let me say my piece." She took a deep breath, as though forcing herself to go on. "I won't say that it felt good to hear it, but that doesn't mean that you weren't right. The truth isn't always pretty. I guess what happened between us meant more to me than it did to you. That's not your fault. I had no right to expect anything of you . . . or to imagine there was any tie between us at all. You never made me any promises, so I reckon it was just foolishness on my part to think you might have felt something different than you did."

"Jesus, Annie—" Hearing her ragged confession made Jake feel lower than a kicked dog and doubled his admiration for her. Most women would have been loath to admit that they had given a failed love affair any thought at all, but not his blunt, courageous Annie.

"I'm not claiming any hold on you at all," she rushed on. "I expect you had a right to be mad at me. You took one look at this place, and you thought I had deceived you, or just plain tried to trick your money out of you. But the fact is, Jake, I had no idea that the Palace was a broken-down bordello. I truly didn't. It would mean a lot to me, everything else aside, if you could believe that."

He nodded. "I believe you didn't know this place was a brothel." At least that much was true. As for the rest of his suspicions, Jake supposed they would just have to go on festering inside him.

"Thank you."

"Sounds like you've been doing a lot of thinking on it."

Annie gave him a rueful smile. "Just about every minute of every day." She squared her shoulders, assuming a tone that was brisk and businesslike. "Now that that's said, let's get on with it. You keeping track of the money I owe you, and taking it out of the saloon profits like we agreed?"

"Yes. You want me to account for that on paper?"

She waved the suggestion away. "I trust you," she replied, with such utter and complete faith that Jake once again felt a sharp stab of guilt slice through his gut.

As he searched his mind for what to say next, a beam of weak winter sunlight filtered in through the window behind Annie. The light bounced off tiny shards of glass that had been swept up in one corner. Jake frowned, glancing from the pile of broken bits of glass to the newly bare ceiling. "What happened?" he asked, although he already knew. Looked like they'd had another little "accident."

Annie confirmed it. "That fancy chandelier fell down this morning. Appears somebody snuck in and cut the chain that held it."

"Anybody hurt?"

"No, thank goodness. The room was empty when it fell."

Jake was silent for a moment, coldly furious. The pranks were not only cowardly but growing increasingly more dangerous. Had Annie or any of the other women been in the room when the chandelier had fallen, they could have been seriously injured if not killed. "You have any idea who's behind it—or why?"

She hesitated, then drew a crumpled note from the pocket of her dress and passed it to him. "I found this earlier this morning, just before the chandelier fell."

He opened the note and read the crude missive. *You scart yet, outlaw womin?*

Although Jake's first thought was of the note he had found in her saddlebags, the writing on this was much worse. Obviously they were not from the same person.

For that matter, Pete would have no reason to threaten Annie or try to sabotage her hotel.

"Have you been getting a lot of these?" he asked.

"I've got a whole collection. They started way back with the first little 'accident.'"

"You see anybody suspicious around this morning?"

"No. But I reckon that someone from town is trying to scare us out," she said, confirming exactly what his instincts told him. Stubborn determination filled her eyes. "I'm not going to let them win, Jake. I've never been one to run from a fight, and I'm not running now. We're staying put, no matter what happens."

"You tell the sheriff what's been going on here?" he asked.

"How much protection you think the sheriff would be willing to give Outlaw Annie and a group of washed-up whores? 'Specially during an election month?"

She had a point, Jake conceded silently. It also occurred to him that if she were still part of the Mundy Gang, the sheriff would be the last person she would want sniffing around the hotel.

Annie stared out the kitchen window, then released a soft sigh. "You think I'm a fool to stay on, Jake?"

He studied her in silence. "I guess that depends on what's keeping you here."

She nodded. Her eyes filled with a faraway look. "Dreams, mostly," she finally admitted with a sigh. "I've been dreaming about this place for so long that I reckon I just can't let it go. And the fact is, the place really isn't so bad. I don't think I've ever seen a finer piece of land than the one this hotel is sitting on. Whole herds of deer and elk gather at the watering hole after sundown. There's a field of wildflowers that covers the entire south slope. And the way the sun comes up over the mountains every morning . . . it just takes my breath away. Plus the building itself is in solid shape. It'll take more money and time to freshen it up, but I know I can make it succeed." She turned to face him directly. "You know why?" she asked.

"Why?"

She smiled the first genuine smile he had seen since he had sat down. "Because I've got pluck."

Jake's heart flooded with an aching tenderness. He smiled softly and nodded. "That you do, darlin'. That you do."

For a moment, their eyes met, and the familiar energy that had always simmered between them flared to life once again. If they had shared that look back on the trail, Jake wouldn't have hesitated in pulling her into his arms. But not now.

A look of sad understanding touched Annie's eyes. "It's funny," she said softly, "it seems we've come so far together, but now we're right back where we started. Just a couple of sniffing dogs."

Silence stretched between them once again. While her words held neither accusation or bitterness, they led in a direction Jake didn't want to go. Determined to steer their conversation away from such dangerous ground, he asked, "So what are you going to do now, Annie?"

She let out a sigh, then stood and began to pace the floor. "Well, I certainly can't wait people out," she said. "I'll run out of money before they run out of their mule-headed foolishness. I reckon my only choice is to run at them head-on. Get them to meet the girls and me face to face. We've been posting flyers all around town for the past week, inviting everyone to a fancy shindig here tonight. I figure that way all the townsfolk can come and see for themselves how we've turned the place around. Once they see it with their own eyes, maybe they'll change their highfalutin ways."

As far as he could see, the only thing her plan demonstrated was hopeless naivete. "You really think that'll work?"

A wry smile touched her lips. "If the reception folks

give me back in Two River Flats is anything to judge by, I'd say my chances were a bit slimmer than a blind man's in a shooting contest. So this time I padded the odds a bit. I let folks in town know that if the girls and I weren't good enough to pay a social call on, then maybe our money wasn't good enough either. I sort of let it slip that we could do our buying in Abundance as well as we can do it in town." She gave a light shrug. "Now it's up to them, I reckon."

Jake nodded. Her plan was a bit heavy-handed, but it might just work. If she truly was interested in getting the hotel off the ground, at least, it was a step in the right direction. "Not bad," he acknowledged.

A determined gaze filled her eyes. *"Poco a poco, la hormiga comio el elefante."*

Little by little, Jake translated with an inner smile, *the ant ate the elephant.* "Do you want me to come tonight?" he asked.

A look of eager relief showed on her face. "Would you, Jake? It'd mean a lot to the girls. And bring anybody you can think of—anybody at all. I reckon the fuller the house, the better it'll look."

He nodded and stood. "You're taking a risk, darlin'. Might be that nobody shows up at all. Or maybe you'll just be entertaining the fella who's been leaving those notes."

Annie brought up her chin and stated the obvious. "Maybe, maybe not. Fact is, I've got nothing left to lose."

Chapter 19

*A*nnie contentedly surveyed the front parlor, filled with a sense of stark incredulity—and glorious relief—that her party was going so well. In truth, she'd had more doubts about the wisdom of throwing the party than a goose had feathers, but she had gone ahead with it anyway.

Miraculously it hadn't turned out to be a complete disaster. The parlor had been swept spotlessly clean, the pillows plumped, fresh flowers filled the vases, and a banquet table full of sandwiches, cookies, and pies had been set out for the guests to enjoy. Low lamplight filled the room, giving it a gentle, welcoming glow. In the kitchen, two fiddlers played a series of catchy tunes; the tables and chairs had been pushed back against the walls to make room for anyone who cared to dance.

Of course, the evening hadn't started out so smoothly. Jake and Johnny Dill had closed the saloon and arrived promptly at seven. For a while, it had appeared as though they would be the only guests to attend. They had sat stiffly in the parlor with the women—all of whom were dressed in their best, high-necked, most respectable gowns—and tried with an almost ridiculous earnestness to carry on a polite conversation and not notice that they were being snubbed by the townsfolk.

At seven thirty-five, to the relief of everyone involved, their first real guests arrived. The rancher from whom Annie purchased occasional sides of beef stood in the doorway, his wife by his side. They both had the sulky, resentful air of children who were being unjustly punished. Annie graciously invited them in and took their coats, then made the introductions. No sooner had she done that than the banker who handled the hotel's account arrived, followed by the couple who owned the general mercantile.

As more guests drifted in, the stilted air gradually gave way to a sense of genuine merriment. Jake and Johnny Dill took turns whirling the girls around the dance floor; soon it was crowded with couples from town. The food on the buffet table was quickly devoured and replaced by more home-baked treats. Conversation began to flow smoothly. Annie opened the upstairs and invited her guests to explore the hotel at will, eager to show off the extent of the repairs and renovations she had made.

Although many of the townsfolk came as a direct result of her financial blackmail, a good many of the attendees simply stopped by out of curiosity. Or, more likely, for the same reason they went to see a hanging—for the sheer thrill of watching an ungodly disaster descend upon somebody else. Much to their surprise and Annie's delight, however, they stayed because they were actually having a good time.

As Annie stood talking with Jake and Peyton VanEste, Jennie Mae approached them, carrying a tray of lemonade and cookies. "You gonna put this in your article, Mr. VanEste?" she asked.

VanEste smiled politely as he surveyed the crowd. "I very well may."

"You ought to," Jennie Mae persisted. "Maybe now some of the townsfolk will come down off their high horses and start giving us the time of day. 'Specially the menfolk. Hell, it ain't like they never met us before, if you get my drift. Most of them were here before Miss

Foster changed the place over. They sure enough found their way then, and most of them were dead drunk at the time, with nothing but the moon and the stars and what was 'twixt their legs to guide their way. And I'm not just talking about the lower elements in town. I'm talking about the judge, the sheriff and his deputies, and that little drugstore man with the big—"

"Thank you, Jennie Mae, that'll be all," Annie interrupted shrilly.

"Horse," Jennie Mae finished, looking at Annie with an expression of baffled innocence. She shrugged her shoulders and smiled sweetly, then picked up her tray and sauntered away.

An ornery smile touched Jake's lips, but he remained mercifully silent. Two spots of bright-red color touched VanEste's cheeks as he toyed with his mustache. After a moment, the reporter cleared his throat and said, "Speaking of my article, I'm reminded that you still owe me an interview, Miss Foster."

"I know, and I haven't forgotten you. I simply haven't had a chance to sit down for more than two minutes," Annie explained. "But I promise we'll talk within the next few days."

"I intend to hold you to that promise," VanEste replied. He puffed out his chest importantly, continuing in the staged voice of an overpaid thespian, "Outlaw Annie, broken away from the Mundy Gang, now the owner of a fine hotel and on the path of righteousness and redemption. That's the kind of story my readers clamor for." He sent Annie his overblown, dramatic wink. "I warned you I'd make a legend out of you yet, Miss Foster."

She forced a polite smile. "So you did."

"And now I'm afraid I must bid you both good night. I should retire and jot down a few notes while my thoughts are still fresh." With that, he turned and made his way upstairs.

It wasn't long before the rest of her guests followed suit. Annie bid them good-bye, thanking them all for attending. Although she knew better than to believe that she had totally turned the townsfolk around, at least they left looking pleasantly surprised. They had spent an evening with the dreaded Outlaw Annie and five recently reformed soiled doves, and it hadn't been nearly as bad as they had expected. Granted, she and the women still had a long way to go when it came to earning the townsfolks' trust and respect. But in time, Annie thought, feeling a renewed surge of hope and optimism, they might just win them over.

They gave the parlor a cursory cleaning, gathering all the dirty dishes and carrying them into the kitchen. That was as much as Annie would allow the women to do. It was well past midnight, it had been a long day, and they all looked exhausted. Distinctly pleased and satisfied, but exhausted nonetheless. Ignoring their protests that they wanted to help, she sent them all upstairs to their rooms. Johnny Dill retired shortly thereafter to the saloon, leaving just her and Jake.

He studied her from across the lamp-lit parlor as a stillness settled over the hotel. "Congratulations, Annie. Your party was a success."

She sent him a wistful smile. "It was, wasn't it? Who would have bet?"

A lingering silence hung between them, then Jake reached for his hat. "I guess I ought to go see if Johnny needs any help in the saloon. He probably threw open the doors to any late-night stragglers."

The words were nothing but an excuse for him to leave, and Annie knew it as well as he did. She took a deep breath, fighting back an impulse to ask him to stay. No sense muddying the waters between them more than they already were. "Thank you for your help tonight. It meant a lot that you and Johnny were here."

He gave a quick nod, then ducked out the door.

Annie bit back a sigh as she watched him leave. Pushing away any maudlin thoughts of what might have been, she busied herself with straightening up the parlor. She rearranged pillows, blew out candles, collected a few discarded bits of food before Cat got to them, then turned down the lamps. She moved into the kitchen, intending to pile the dirty dishes into the sink and let them soak overnight.

But she never made it to the sink.

Annie had taken only two steps through the swinging door that led from the restaurant into the kitchen when she felt a rough hand grab her arm from behind. A second hand came around to clamp firmly over her mouth. Her body was jerked against a hard male form. She felt the man's gun brush her leg and his hot breath against her ear, but she couldn't see his face. He held her with her back pinned against his chest, one arm so tightly strapped across her ribs that she could barely breathe.

His voice came out in a low, gravelly pant that filled her ear. "Miss me, Annie, girl?"

Annie's blood ran cold. Although she still couldn't see his face, she would know that voice anywhere. Glancing down, she managed to catch a glimpse of the man's boot. The man's *snakeskin* boot.

"I told you I'd come back for you someday, didn't I?" Snakeskin Garvey rasped in her ear.

She forced herself to stay calm. All she had to do was to free her mouth. One loud scream and the women in the hotel would come running.

As though reading her thoughts, Snakeskin lifted a saw-toothed hunting knife from his belt and pressed it against her throat. "You make so much as one little squeal, girl, and I swear I'll slit you open. You understand me?"

She nodded against his hand. The man was crazy and ruthless enough to do just that. Not only would he kill her, he'd most likely kill any of the women who came down to help her. Annie had to find some way, *any* other way, to get away from him.

He cautiously removed his hand from her mouth, pressing his knife even harder against her throat. Annie felt a slight sting, then a slight trickle of blood ran down her neck.

"That's it," Snakeskin said from behind her. "You want to feel any more of my blade, you just make a noise. Any noise at all and I'll kill you, so help me God."

She shook her head, silently indicating her obedience. As she did, her eyes scanned the kitchen, looking for a weapon. Her gaze halted abruptly on a crumpled note that sat on the kitchen table. *Yer next, outlaw womin.* Next to the note lay a box of sulfur matches and a tin full of kerosene. Apparently she had walked in on him just before he had set their kitchen on fire.

Silent rage filled Annie as she realized that it had been Snakeskin all along who had been sabotaging the hotel and leaving the threatening notes. She should have recognized the cowardly acts as his long before now.

Following the line of her gaze, Snakeskin gave a low, hollow laugh. "You been getting my notes?" he asked. "I told you I'd be back for you one day, and here I am. Now I reckon it's your turn to pay."

His hand moved up from her ribs, roughly grabbing and squeezing her breasts. Annie instinctively jerked away, but he caught her and jerked her up against him once again, running the cool tip of the knife just beneath her ear.

"What's the matter, Annie, girl? I thought you liked ol' Snakeskin." With the blade pressed firmly against her skin, he grabbed the hem of her skirt, slowly inching it up. "Now we're gonna finish what we started. We can do this the hard way, girl, or we can do it easy. You cross me, and you'll find out the difference."

He reached between her legs and pushed apart her thighs. A surge of hot bile filled Annie's throat.

Behind her, Snakeskin fumbled with the buttons of his britches. Annie's gaze desperately swept the kitchen for a weapon.

The kerosene can. She had to try, she thought, slowly lifting her hand. If she could just reach it and hit him hard enough over the head . . .

The sound of the front door opening startled them both. They listened in silence to the sound of a man's boot steps as they echoed across the polished hotel floor.

"Annie? Are you in there?" the man called as he approached the kitchen.

Snakeskin's knife dug into her skin. "Get rid of him. *Now.*"

She swallowed hard and nodded. "Don't come in here, Johnny."

The boot steps abruptly stopped. "Is everything all right?"

"Of course. But I . . . I spilled lemonade everywhere. The floor's a mess."

"All right." There was a moment's hesitation, then he said, "Good night, Miss Foster." The sound of his boots retreating toward the parlor filled the air, then they heard the sound of the front door softly closing.

Snakeskin's breath filled her ear. "You're gettin' smarter by the minute, Annie, girl. Maybe this time I'll let you—"

He never got a chance to finish. Jake hurled himself through the kitchen door and slammed into Snakeskin's back, sending him crashing roughly to the floor. Annie tumbled to the ground as well, knocked free from Snakeskin's grasp. Before Snakeskin could move, Jake flipped him over and pummeled him with his fists, attacking the man in a blind rage.

Annie watched in paralyzed horror until she found her voice. "Jake, *stop*! That's enough!" she shouted. *"Stop!"*

Her cries finally registered. Jake froze, his gaze moving from Annie to the limp body of the man beneath him. Understanding slowly dawned on his features. Snakeskin had never once struck back. He couldn't. The man stared with vacant, glassy-eyed surprise at the ceiling. His mouth hung open in a silent cry of outraged shock and pain. He was already dead. His own knife had pierced his chest when he had been knocked to the floor.

Jake slid off him and moved to Annie, his gaze moving frantically over her body. His mouth tightened to a grim line as he took in the trickle of blood that ran down her throat. He pulled her to him and gently wiped the blood away with his finger.

Then his eyes locked on hers. "You all right, Annie?"

She took a deep breath and nodded. "I wasn't sure you'd catch my hint that I was in trouble."

"I reckon you know the difference between my voice and Johnny's. Either you were in trouble, or you were in here getting drunk all by yourself." A small smile touched his lips. "Either way, I figured I'd better join in."

Annie forced a small, shaky smile in return. "He was the one who's been leaving the notes, Jake. It was Snakeskin all along." She tilted her chin to meet his gaze. "What made you come back to the hotel?"

"I saw a strange horse tethered behind the barn and figured it might be trouble."

A shudder ran down her spine as her eyes moved back to Snakeskin. "You figured right."

He locked his arms around her and ran a soothing hand down her back. "It's over, Annie. It's all over now. He can't hurt you again."

Annie would have been content to stay huddled in his arms like that for the rest of the night. But within what seemed like mere seconds, the sound of thundering footsteps racing down the stairs echoed loudly around them. The kitchen door burst open once again. Dora stood in the entry, her buffalo gun in her hands. Jennie Mae, Carlotta, Francine, and Belle crowded in behind her.

Jake gently released Annie from his embrace. He stood, then offered her a hand up as well. "One of you run over and wake Johnny Dill and tell him to get the sheriff," he said. "Tell him we just took care of the 'accident' problem that's been plaguing the hotel."

*J*ake eased Weed into a light canter as he rounded a bend in the trail that carried him out of Cooperton. He shifted in the saddle, feeling stiff and sore. He hadn't slept all night. It had taken hours to straighten things out with the town sheriff, and even longer to get the blood cleaned out of the kitchen and the women settled down enough to go back to bed. He'd had no time to speak with Annie, no time to do anything but ride out and keep his appointment with Walter Pogue.

He tipped back his hat and scanned the horizon. Scrub brush spread over the ground, threatening to choke out the narrow band of packed dirt that had once been the road. The Old Tabbot Trading Post stood dead ahead. The original outpost had long ago been burned to the ground during a vicious encounter with a renegade band of Apache Indians. A new trading post had been built in its stead but now stood deserted, having fallen victim to the more banal circumstance of too little business—after the Indian attack, the route was rarely traveled.

He eyed the ramshackle trading post and counted the horses in the lean-to. Six. A full posse. He let out a sigh and spurred Weed down the dusty, weed-choked road toward the outpost. Sheriff Walter Pogue greeted him at the door, a cocked shotgun in his hands.

Jake swung out of the saddle and nodded toward the gun. "Nice way to say hello, Walt."

Walter shrugged and set the shotgun down. "Just a precaution. We expected you last night."

"I was busy."

They moved out of the chill air and into the relative warmth of the cabin. Jake glanced around the room, giving his eyes a minute to adjust to the dimness of the interior. The furnishings were sparse. A rough-hewn table, a crude stone fireplace, and a battered stove completed the space. The five men who had accompanied Walter lounged on the floor on their saddle blankets, warming themselves before the fire. They held cards in their hands and had a five-dollar pot between them.

Jake quickly sized them up. Sheriff Walter Pogue had done well in selecting his deputies. They were hard and lean, with the hollow-eyed stares of men who had faced death before. Judging from the weapons they carried, they were not afraid to face it again.

Brief introductions were made, then Walter lifted a whiskey bottle from the table. "You want a drink?"

Jake tilted his head toward the pot bubbling away on the stove. "Coffee'll be just fine."

Walter poured him a cup and sat down, gesturing for Jake to do the same. "I would have been here sooner, but a group of rowdy cowhands came through Two River Flats and roughed up the town a bit. I locked a few of them up, but I didn't want to leave until their sentences were over and they were out of town for good."

"Fine," Jake answered, brushing that aside. Rather than issue a lengthy preamble and waste either his time or Walt's, he cut straight to what he wanted to say. "I don't think Annie's involved."

"What?"

"I don't think she's involved with the Mundy Gang. At least, not anymore."

Walter let out a sigh of disgust and shoved his chair back from the table.

"Jesus, Jake."

"Sorry, Walt."

Walter's face tightened. He nodded over Jake's

shoulder at his men, who obeyed the unspoken command and stood, stepping outside to give the two men privacy.

"I take it that means you bedded her, and now you changed your mind," Walter stated, coming swiftly to a conclusion that was both harsh and accurate. He shook his head and let out a hollow laugh. "Dammit, Jake, I thought you were smarter than that."

"You don't know her," Jake replied, reining in his anger. "She's gone legitimate, I've seen it myself. She's left the gang and turned that hotel of hers around. She's making an honest living."

"You think she's the first outlaw to set up a legal front? You think there aren't any seemingly upstanding ranchers out there rustling their neighbor's cattle any chance they get? You think there aren't any seemingly honest shopkeepers weighting their scales to cheat their customers out of their gold?"

"I know what I've seen, and she's no outlaw, Walt. I'd stake my life on it."

"She sat there and told both of us that the men in the Mundy Gang had all been killed. That they'd been dead for at least three months. But I've got over a dozen witnesses who saw those boys pull a bank robbery out in Abundance just a few weeks ago."

"There's probably a good explanation for that."

"You got one? 'Cause I'll be happy to hear it if you do."

The problem was, Jake couldn't explain a damn thing—not even to himself. He couldn't explain where Annie had been on the afternoons before the robberies, or why a man who fit Pete Mundy's description had been looking for her the morning after the robbery in Abundance, or the note from Pete he had found in her saddlebag. He couldn't explain why she had tripped and fired the shot that had warned off the man who had been following them, or why the town hall fire had been started at exactly the same moment the gang was trying to break into the bank. He couldn't explain any of it.

Walter's eyes narrowed as he studied him in silence. He toyed with his glass for a minute, then suggested coolly, "You're a wanted man, Jake. You don't help me out, I got the legal right to haul you in right now."

"You could try."

A humorless grin touched the sheriff's mouth. "You gonna draw on me, Jake?"

"You gonna lock me up?"

"I should." Walter gave him a dark look. "You stubborn son of a bitch, that's exactly what I should do. I oughta just slap your ass in jail and let a jury sort the whole mess out. At least, then my men and I wouldn't go home empty-handed."

"That's fine. Just keep your hands off Annie."

"*Goddammit,* Jake!" Walter banged his fist on the table, breathing hard. "Do you know who you're protecting here?"

"Annie. And you'd do the same for Elena."

"Bullshit. This ain't about Annie—and you leave Elena the hell out of this. You're protecting a gang of outlaw scum that ain't fit to suck mud out of a cesspool. You know how they got that teller to let them into the bank out in Abundance?"

Jake shrugged. "I heard. They broke into his home and forced him out at gunpoint."

"That ain't all they did. They tied his hands, roughed him up a bit, then sat him in a chair and let him watch while they took turns defiling his wife. They did it just for sport, Jake, just because they could. The teller had already agreed to let them into the bank." He paused and shook his head, looking both disgusted and furious. "That bit of news wasn't exactly public knowledge."

Jake tightened his fists, sickened. "You sure about that?"

"I'm sure. I stopped in Abundance and read the sheriff's report."

Jake silently absorbed the news. Annie couldn't be involved with men like that. It wasn't possible. But was there a side of the boys she didn't know? She had said that Pete was rambunctious and wild. Did her loyalty make her turn a blind eye to his greater faults?

"They're getting rougher every day," Walter went on. "You want to be the one to tell the next batch of widows that we could have brought the gang in, that we could have stopped it all, but you were too busy getting your pecker wet to do anything about it?"

Jake jerked to his feet, knocking the chair over behind him. "Goddammit, Walt, that's enough."

"Sorry, Jake, but some things have to be said. If you didn't want the gang brought in, you shouldn't have dragged my men and me halfway across the territory."

"She wasn't lying about Snakeskin Garvey," Jake said after a moment. "I know at least that much. I killed him last night when he broke into the hotel. Maybe he's the one who's been running with the gang, and not Annie."

Walter sat in silence, studying him carefully. "Maybe you're right. Maybe it was that Snakeskin fella all along, and Annie's as pure and innocent as newly driven snow. But I reckon the only way to find that out is to test her. That's why my men and I are here." He paused for a moment, then finished in quiet, firm tones, "I'm just asking you to do what's right. If Annie's not involved, she'll walk away clean, with no trouble from me or my men, I promise you that."

Jake turned away, staring into the flames of the fire. What it all came down to, he supposed, were the fundamentals. There were three things that any gambler had to decide before sitting down to play: the rules of the game, the stakes, and quitting time. He had known that all along. The rules? Using Annie to lead him to the gang.

The stakes? His own neck. He had been after the Mundy Gang, and now he had them within his grasp. Clearly it was quitting time.

As Jake struggled with his decision, he remembered feeling this way once before, in a small, unrenowned Pennsylvania town called Gettysburg. He had been ordered to lead his men across a bare field toward a small hill known as Cemetery Ridge. As he had looked across that vast, unprotected stretch of land, he had known it was impossible, just as he had known he would do it. Known he *had* to do it; that he had no choice. He had led his men to their deaths as though watching himself from a distance, as though he were an actor in a grossly written, tragic play.

He stared now into the flames of the fire, burdened with the same sense of idiocy, inevitability, and loss. No matter which way he looked at it, he was betraying Annie, pure and simple.

"What did you have in mind?" he finally asked.

"We need you to be with Annie at the hotel around six o'clock tonight. Fella I know works out in the mines in Surreysville. He'll drop by to see you and just happen to mention that the mine changed their payroll date to Wednesday. You just listen and then go about your business. That's all I'm asking you to do, Jake."

"You're setting up the gang."

"Damned right, I am. We've been going at this the wrong way the whole time. We've been waiting for the Mundys to hit someplace, then trying to chase them down. Makes about as much sense as a fool dog chasing his tail. I'd say it's about time we turned that around."

It was a good plan. Jake couldn't fault him for that. "Six o'clock. I'll be there, so will Annie."

"The fella's name is Porter. Bill Porter."

Jake nodded and turned to leave, but Walter's voice stopped him. "I'm sorry you came to care for her, Jake, but that don't change facts. Outlaw Annie has run with that gang all her life. I ain't saying that's her fault, just that it's all she knows. Why, I knew a man once who was out hunting and shot himself a wolf. When he found out that it was a she-wolf with a couple of cubs in her lair, the fella got softhearted and brought the cubs home with him. He gave them names, fed them every day, played with them. Treated them like they were his own children. Then one day, out of the blue, one of them cubs took a wild turn and bit off four of his fingers. The fella was never able to fire a rifle properly again."

"That story got a point, or you just like telling it?"

"You can't domesticate wild creatures, no matter how hard you try."

"Uh-huh." Jake put on his hat, adjusted the brim, and slipped on his riding gloves. "I'll keep that in mind." He strode out the door without another word.

*C*onsidering how difficult it had been for him to make the decision, getting Annie alone at the appointed hour and the appointed place proved relatively simple. Jake found her in the front parlor, going over the hotel's grocery receipts. Despite last night's ordeal with Snakeskin Garvey, she looked relatively calm and composed.

Glancing around the parlor, he saw that the room was nearly empty. A travel-weary young couple with two small children sat at a table near the window, drinking tea and eating cookies. Peyton VanEste sat with Jennie Mae on a settee, furiously scribbling notes in his pad.

Good enough, Jake thought. Knowing that if he hesitated, he wouldn't go through with it at all, he stepped into the parlor and said to Annie, "Sorry to interrupt, but I wonder if you could show me where you keep the ledgers for the saloon. I need to make some adjustments."

Annie ducked beneath the long front counter, retrieved a thick ledger, and placed it between them. "What's the matter, Jake?" she asked.

"What do you mean?"

"Just look at your face. I've seen happier undertakers."

Jake shrugged. "Nothing's wrong, Annie. I've just got a lot on my mind." He turned his attention to the book, making small adjustments to the column of numbers before him.

"If you lost money, don't worry, we'll cover the bets somehow."

Jake looked up to see Annie's soft smile, her eyes sweetly encouraging, and nearly groaned. "I'll remember," he managed to reply.

The door swung open behind him and a voice boomed out, "I thought I'd find you here, Moran. Like I told you before, Bill Porter may be down, but he ain't out. Now, are you going to give me a chance to win back my money or not?"

Jake turned to see a middle-aged man with a salt-and-pepper beard, a jovial grin, and a slight paunch at his belly. "How are you, Porter?"

"Two hundred dollars poorer than I was the last time we met. But I'm feeling lucky today."

"I thought you were cleaned out."

"I was, but the boss moved up our payday. The pay wagon's coming through on Wednesday instead of next Friday. Our regular drivers quit, and there's just one greenhorn kid dumb enough to take on the route. Boss thought if he mixed up the payday, it might give that poor kid a fightin' chance to make it through Drifter's Gap on his own."

There it was. The trap neatly sprung, as relaxed and casual as if they had rehearsed it for days.

"Payday's still a few days off," Jake said. "Why don't you come back then?"

"Are you saying my marker's no good?"

Jake shrugged coolly. "It's not my house. Why don't you ask the lady?"

"All right." Porter directed his gaze toward Annie. "What do you say, little lady? Will you accept my marker until Wednesday?"

Annie glanced up from the ledgers. "What?" she asked, her voice distracted. "Your marker? If it's all right with Jake, I guess it's all right with me."

"Fine, then." Porter clasped his hands together and smiled. "I'm in the mood for a little seven-card stud. Meet you inside, Moran." With that, he turned and strode out of the lobby.

Jake let out his breath in a low rush as the tension he had held inside seemed to evaporate from his body. Annie had listened to—no, *tolerated*—the interruption of their conversation with such complete disinterest that Jake was certain he had been right all along. Annabel Lee Foster was not carrying information back to the Mundy boys. He'd stake his life on it.

Forty-eight hours later, he was glad he hadn't actually made that bet.

Late Tuesday afternoon, one of Walter's deputies delivered a message to Jake at the Bella Luna that proved him wrong. *Bait taken. Members of gang spotted near Drifter's Gap. Looks like our friends are preparing to meet us tomorrow morning. Want to come along for the ride? W.*

Chapter 20

On Tuesday morning, rabbits dug up Annie's newly planted garden, two pies were burned to a crisp, a bucket of tar used for patching the roof spilled on the front porch, and the reverend's wife dropped by for her first official social call. Despite the inconvenience the accidents caused, at least Annie was somewhat reassured by the knowledge that they were truly just accidents, with no maliciousness behind them. Snakeskin Garvey was gone for good.

Tuesday afternoon, Foster's Hotel booked its first real group of guests. The stage from Albuquerque to Denver City lost a wheel just outside of town. The stage's six passengers and two drivers straggled in tired, hungry, and cold. Annie immediately set about getting them fed and settled in. Tuesday night, four drunks showed up, firing their pistols and loudly demanding their favorite girls. She and Dora dispatched them with a few blasts from Dora's buffalo gun, then spent thirty minutes calming their ruffled guests and coaxing them back to bed.

By the time Annie made it to her own bedchamber, it was nearly midnight. As she undressed and prepared for bed, she realized that she had forgotten Peyton VanEste once again. The poor man had been waiting for days for his interview, and she had repeatedly put him off.

Tomorrow, she swore, sinking into bed. She would give him his interview tomorrow.

For the past few weeks, Annie had been too exhausted to dream, but that night, dreams came anyway, despite her fatigue. Almost as soon as her head hit the pillow, images of Pete and the gang sprang to life in her mind. She saw Pete as a young boy, running through snow-covered woods with a shotgun in his hands, blasting away at squirrels and rabbits. She dreamed of Diego teaching her the finer points of swearing in Spanish. She saw Pete and the boys, their bodies jerking under a fusillade of bullets as the men within the cargo train they were about to rob opened fire on them instead.

Although she had played that ghastly scene over and over in her mind, this time there was a twist. Instead of dying, Pete rose from the ground, his body bloodied and torn but not dead. He moved slowly toward her, his hands outstretched, his mouth gaping open with shock and pain.

Annie gasped and bolted upright, blinking into the darkness. To her horror, the nightmare didn't end. In the hazy interval between dream and reality, the figure did not fade away. Instead the man silhouetted in her chamber doorway moved closer. At the foot of her bed, Cat transformed herself from a tightly curled ball of white fluff into a tiny but ferocious beast, her back arched, her fur standing straight up. She hissed and extended one sharp claw toward the intruder.

Annie's eyes darted around the room for her guns, only to realize that she had tucked them neatly away into a dresser drawer. The figure moved closer. "Pete?" she whispered, clutching her sheet tightly against her chest. The name was torn from her throat as terror welled up within her.

"Sorry to disappoint you, darlin'."

"Jake." Annie let out her breath in a rush and let the sheet slip through her fingers.

"You were expecting someone else?" he drawled.

She shook her head, trying to banish the fragments of her dream from her mind. "I thought you were Pete."

"Really? I thought Pete was dead."

"He was. He is." Annie gave a feeble laugh. "It was a nightmare, that's all. I thought you were Pete's ghost."

"Ah. The ghost of Pete Mundy. Funny how he keeps haunting us." Jake moved farther into the room and closed the door behind him. "I wonder how many more times we'll have to kill him before he has the courtesy to remain dead."

A full moon hung in the sky, filling the room with silver beams of light. Annie studied Jake in the shadowy darkness. He was attired in his fancy gambling duds. He wore a finely tailored black jacket, slim black pants, and a snowy-white linen shirt. A pang of yearning and nostalgia tore through her at the sight of him. Even his expression seemed oddly compelling. She saw desire, regret, compassion, and resolve etched on his finely chiseled, beautiful features.

"Is something wrong?" she asked.

Jake shrugged.

"Bad night at the saloon?"

"Not particularly." He moved forward, unbuckled his gun belt, and set his guns on her small nightstand. Then he stepped closer to her, stopping only inches away from her bed. Annie looked up into his face, flustered and excited, dwarfed by his presence.

"What are you doing?" she asked.

"Taking off my guns."

"I can see that. I meant, what are you doing here?"

"Do you want me to leave, Annie?" His voice flowed over her skin like satin, sending a shiver of longing and expectation along her spine.

"That depends," she replied breathlessly. "What are your intentions, Jake?"

He smiled in that lazy way of his. "My intentions? Why, they're as black as my soul, darlin'."

The bedsprings groaned, and the feather mattress sank beneath his weight as he sat down beside her. He took off his hat and tossed it on the table with his guns, then slipped off his boots. He turned to her, studying her intently. Annie felt suddenly self-conscious beneath the heat of his gaze. She was sleepy-eyed, her hair loose and slipping around her shoulders. She was dressed in nothing but a soft cotton camisole and a pair of lacy drawers.

He reached for her and gently smoothed her hair back over her shoulders. "You're wearing that perfume I gave you, aren't you?"

"Yes."

"I like it."

"So do I."

"How does Pete like it?"

Annie stiffened. "I told you, that was just a dream."

"Of course." A sardonic smile touched his lips. He reached forward and fingered the pink satin strap of her camisole. "This is quite pretty, Annie."

"Thank you. You gave it to me."

He stopped her words by brushing his fingers gently along the column of her throat. "You have such a lovely neck, darlin'. So pure and white, so delicate. The rope scars have nearly faded now. It would be a shame to mar it again."

Annie pulled back, frowning. "What are you talking about, Jake?"

"Just reminding you what happened the last time you were involved with the gang."

"I don't need a reminder."

Jake met her gaze, his eyes as cold and hard as steel. "Good."

She tilted her chin, anger beginning to churn inside her. "Why are you here, Jake?" she demanded.

Silence. Endless, undying silence. Finally, "Because I wasn't strong enough to stay away any longer."

Jake's words tore through her. It was exactly what she had dreamed of hearing—an open admission that he was as incapable of ignoring what was between them as she was. Jake Moran was driven by the same demons, the same yearning, the same desire.

"I'm glad," she said.

His gaze burned into hers. He brought his hand toward her once again, this time to lightly stroke her cheek. "'I was a child and *she* was a child, in this kingdom by the sea; but we loved with a love which was more than love—I and my Annabel Lee.'"

She knew he was only reciting the lines and not referring directly to her. But her pulse surged nonetheless, thrilled at hearing the words. For one brief moment, she let herself imagine that perhaps, in some deep, remote corner of his heart, Jake Moran might feel for her the way she felt for him. "It's pretty, isn't it?" she ventured shakily. "The poem, I mean."

He continued, with a look of almost perverse satisfaction, "'The angels, not half so happy in heaven, went envying her and me—Yes!—that was the reason (as all men know, in this kingdom by the sea) that the wind came out of the cloud by night, chilling and killing my Annabel Lee.'"

Annie shook her head. "It doesn't have to end that way."

"Really? It does every time I've read it."

"You're always so dark. Like it's all gonna end."

He lifted his hand and softly, almost reverently, brushed his fingers along the length of her collarbone. "Because it always does, darlin'."

Her breath caught in her throat. He had come to tell her good-bye. Annie stared at him in blank disbelief, letting his words sink in. She had heard about being heartbroken. She had even spent some time imagining what it must feel like. She expected a sharp, piercing ache in her chest—but the truth of the matter was, her heart felt just fine. What she noticed was a funny, sick feeling in her stomach; her lungs felt suddenly closed off, and a loud roar filled her ears. Then a gradual, almost soothing numbness spread through her limbs. She thought she might start to shake or cry, but she did neither one. Instead she just sat there like someone had picked her up and put her in a gray, foggy mist, where nothing would ever be the same again.

Somehow she managed to speak. "It doesn't have to end at all."

A small, sad smile curved Jake's lips. "Everything ends."

Annie couldn't hold back the torrent of words and emotions that flooded through her. "Maybe you could stay, Jake. Together we could make a go of this place, I just know it. We'll build this into a grand hotel, the grandest in the territory. You're already making money in the saloon. It'll just take a few more months, like you said earlier. We can make it work, I know we can." She took a deep breath, then continued urgently, "I know I shouldn't ask it of you, I know it ain't ladylike and proper, but the hell with what's ladylike and proper. I want you to stay, Jake."

His gaze drifted over her like smoke. "It's not that easy."

"Nothing worth having ever comes easy. I'm not a good woman, Jake. If I was, I wouldn't be here. But I am strong, and so are you. If we walk away from each other now, I don't know which of us will regret it more. I'm willing to make mistakes—Lord knows I've already made plenty. But I won't live my life with regrets."

She shook her head, frantically searching for the right words. "I can't define what was between us, but sometimes, when you touched me, it felt like there was magic in the world. It felt like God himself was smiling down on us, giving us a gift that was rarer than gold. There are people who live their lives wishing for ten minutes of what we had. Seems to me it would be a mighty fool thing to throw all that away."

He studied her for a long, unending minute. "You don't make it easy for a man to walk away from you."

"Good, because I'm not trying to."

Jake lifted a stray strand of hair off her neck and played with it between his fingers, then he met her eyes with his. "My brave, stubborn little Annabel Lee. I don't know you at all, do I?"

"I'm not that complicated."

"Oh, yes you are, darlin', yes you are."

"I don't feel complicated," she whispered hoarsely. "I feel naked when I'm near you, Jake. Like you can see right through me. I feel more exposed and vulnerable than I ever have in my life."

"Do you know how I feel?"

Her eyes locked on his. "Show me."

Jake let out a sound that was half moan, half growl. "Jesus, Annie." He drew her tightly to him and reverently ran his fingers through the shiny gold tresses of her hair. Then he leaned forward and pressed his lips to the hollow of her neck. He kissed her lips, her hair, her mouth, her breasts, and her face.

But despite the urgency that seemed to overtake both of them, Annie couldn't help but feel that something was missing. They were strangers in spite of their intimacy. Their passion seemed tinged with unspoken anger, and Jake kept himself a little apart. At first, she despaired, afraid that the walls that had grown between them had become too thick to penetrate. Then she determined to break through his resistance, as he had once broken through hers. She pressed herself against him, touching his body the way she wanted to touch his heart. She ran her hands over the hard, corded muscles of his chest, across his stomach, and down his thighs. She caressed, she kissed, she suckled and stroked, using every weapon at her disposal to break through whatever it was that kept them apart.

Finally the ice that had surrounded Jake's heart started to melt. He responded to her the way he had in the past, wholeheartedly and aggressively, loving her the way she was loving him. They couldn't get enough of each other that night. Their bodies crashed together in an explosion of passion and need. It was as though some dark, foreboding presence hung over them, threatening to sweep them away. They struggled against it with their mouths, their tongues, their bodies.

Annie was dimly aware of her bed creaking and groaning beneath them and her curtains fluttering in the cool breeze. The faint, rosy hue of dawn began to fill the sky outside her window. She must have slept; perhaps exhaustion simply overcame her. When she woke, the sky was blue, and she was snuggled cozily within Jake's arms, her back pressed against his chest.

He kissed the nape of her neck and ran his hands lightly over her ribs. He cupped her breasts gently in his hands, then traced his fingers down her belly. "I want you to give me your word on something, Annie," he murmured softly into her ear.

She snuggled up tightly against him, pressing her bottom against his hips, greedy for more of his touch. "What?" she asked drowsily.

"Promise me you'll stay on the hotel grounds today."

Sleepy and confused, she rolled over and studied his face. "Why?"

"Just swear it, Annie."

It was an odd request, but obviously one that was important to him. She mentally went over her schedule for the day. There was gardening to be done, washing, the fence to mend, the stove to clean, and she had her interview with VanEste. All of which would keep her tied down on the grounds for at least the next twenty-four hours. "All right," she said.

"You swear it?"

"Yes."

A look of immense relief immediately softened his features.

Her brows drew together in a worried frown. "Jake, if something's wrong, tell me what it is."

"Nothing's wrong, darlin'," he replied, lightly stroking her back as he pulled her against him. "Everything's going to be fine. It's going to be just fine."

She fell asleep again, but the next time she woke, Jake was gone. A cold, empty stillness filled her bedchamber. She would have thought the previous night had all been a dream if not for the scent of Jake's skin that clung to her sheets. She rolled over and clutched his pillow against her chest, feeling drained, saddened, and exhilarated all at once. As she remembered last night's lovemaking, a thrill of trembling anticipation began to burn within her belly.

It wasn't over between them. Not yet. Not by a long shot.

*J*ake rode to the appointed ambush with Walter Pogue and his men. The sky that December morning was cold and brooding, and the air tasted like snow. It was funeral weather, Jake thought. All the colors of death. The clouds were black, the sky gray, and the trees brown and skeletal, like life itself had withered away. Even the mountains looked purple and hunched over, as though shielding themselves from a blow.

The lawmen Jake accompanied rode silently, their faces grim and determined. They arrived at Drifter's Gap in the early morning hours, long before the payroll stage was due to pull through. The land was quiet and serene, filled with a deep winter stillness. They traveled into the dense, bushy hills above the gap, dismounted, and ground tied their horses. Pulling their rifles from their scabbards, they took their positions.

Then they waited.

It was the longest wait of Jake's life. The hours passed with interminable slowness. His nerves felt raw and exposed. Every time a squirrel moved in a branch overhead, or a horse stomped its foot and whinnied, or one of Walter's men swirled the water in his canteen, Jake's heart leapt to his throat. This was worse than any battle he had ever faced during the war. Then he had only been concerned about his own life, or the lives of the men around him. Now it was Annie's life that could be in jeopardy, and that was an entirely different matter.

Finally, at the appointed hour, the payroll stage lumbered into view. Jake released his breath in a rush. Walter must have been wrong—in the hours they had been waiting, he had seen no sign of the Mundys. But even as that thought occurred to him, six riders charged out from behind a dense cropping of rocks as the stage rolled past.

Six.

There were five men in the gang . . . and Outlaw Annie. But she wouldn't be riding with the gang—even Walter acknowledged that she had never actually taken part in the Mundy Gang holdups. She might take care of the gang and pass on information, but never had she been party to an actual robbery.

Until now, Jake thought, dread lodging tightly in his belly.

For even as those arguments played through his mind, reality was inescapable. His gaze flew to one particular rider, a rider who was a bit smaller than the others. A rider whose gold-brown hair flew halfway down her back as she rode.

Annie.

Goddamn her, Jake thought, biting back his shock and his fury. She had given him her word that she would stay on the hotel grounds, but obviously she had lied to him once again.

His mind shifted, moving past the flurry of raw emotion that poured through him. He forced himself to focus on a rapid-fire search of his alternatives. The fact that she was part of the gang, that his own neck was on the line—none of it mattered. He couldn't watch Annie die like this. God help him, he might have sent her into the trap, but he couldn't watch her die. He had to warn her somehow, to get her away from the gang and the stage before the shooting erupted. He raised his rifle to fire off a warning shot, but he was too late.

The driver cracked his whip and urged his team into a frenzied gallop. The stage roared beneath them. The Mundy Gang, hard on the heels of the stage, rode directly into the trap Walter and his men had set for them. The road narrowed, allowing only enough room for the six riders to ride two abreast. Once they were neatly penned in, the deputies opened fire. A fusillade of bullets showered down on them.

There was no shout of warning, no chance for surrender, no mercy. The Mundy Gang had been caught in the act, and few would grieve if they were taken in dead rather than alive.

The riders' cries of terror and panic filled the air. The front two tumbled from their horses. The remaining four jerked hard on their reins, blood gaping from their wounds. They frantically jostled against one another, trying to turn their frenzied mounts around within the narrow confines of the road. Annie, Jake saw, was still alive, fighting to control her mount.

He surged to his feet. "That's enough, godammit!" he shouted to the other deputies. "Hold your fire, we'll bring them in alive!"

Beside him, Walter Pogue raised his arm, then abruptly dropped it.

"You son of a bitch!" Jake screamed as a second explosion of bullets filled the air.

He jerked his gaze back to the outlaws only to watch in horror as Annie's slight frame was lifted off the saddle under the impact of the hot lead. Her body jerked sideways, performed a lifeless half twist in midair, then plummeted to the ground.

"No!"

The single word was torn from Jake's throat in an instant of horrified, impotent rage and anguish. Realizing he still had his rifle clutched tightly in his hands, he threw it to the ground and scrambled down the steep bank ahead of Walter and his men. His heart hammered against his chest as he raced across the ravine to the spot where Annie had fallen.

As he ran, a fervent prayer echoed through his mind. *Please, God,* he whispered urgently, *don't let her die. Don't let Annie die.* He skidded to a halt and dropped to his knees beside her.

She lay facedown in the dirt. A pool of blood seeped out from her body, spreading wider and wider with each passing second. With shaking hands, Jake reached out and turned her over, pulling her gently into his arms. He cradled her against him, murmuring soft, soothing sounds that he knew instinctively went unheard. Her head lolled back against his chest. Her body was heavy and limp, unresisting to his touch. Her arms fell numbly to her side and her golden-brown hair tumbled across her face like a curtain of silk. Moving with infinite care, Jake reverently brushed her hair aside so he could see her face.

His heart slammed against his ribs.

The woman stared up at the sky, her eyes wide and unseeing, vacant with death.

Jake lowered her to the ground and let out a deep, ragged breath. Beside him, Sheriff Walter Pogue placed his hand on his shoulder. "I'm sorry, Jake. We didn't have any other choice. You know that."

Jake took another deep breath, then came slowly to his feet. He slammed his fist into Walt's jaw with every ounce of fury and strength he possessed, knocking the lawman flat on his back. Then he strode away without a single word, ignoring the shouts and threats of the deputies behind him. He picked up his rifle, grabbed Weed's reins, and leapt onto his back, riding away at a full gallop.

As he rode, an image of the woman's eyes filled his mind, blinding him to all else around him.

Her lifeless, empty, *soft blue* eyes.

The woman was not Annie.

Chapter 21

*A*nnie left the hotel with Peyton VanEste shortly after their interview. He had requested a tour of the property, and she had reluctantly agreed. The tour would take even more out of her busy day, but she couldn't deny that it was a good idea. As VanEste had said, the publicity garnered by the article would likely be excellent, and the surrounding lands were simply too beautiful not to be included in the story.

They rode across the flat plains and toward the base of the San Juan mountain range, where her property ended. To her surprise, Peyton VanEste rode reasonably well for an Easterner. He had been both amiable and polite, jotting down nearly every word she said in the little note pad of his. He scanned the horizon, as though mentally taking note of the rugged magnificence of the land.

"It's beautiful, isn't it?" Annie asked, a hint of pride in her voice.

"That it is." He pointed to a series of low-lying hills that rose up against the base of the mountains. "What's over there?"

"Abandoned mines, mostly," she replied with a shrug. "I think they were all played out years ago."

"Let's take a look, shall we? It might just add a bit of color to the story." He smiled and sent her a dramatic wink, urging his horse forward.

Annie hesitated, watching him ride away. As long as

they stayed within the hotel grounds, she wasn't breaking her word to Jake. Then again, what harm would it do to simply poke around a few deserted mines? She and VanEste would be back long before dark, and besides, Jake had ridden out without so much as a word of good-bye. Although it was perhaps childish of her to interpret that as a personal slight, his sudden disappearance had bothered her nonetheless. With that in mind, she spurred Dulcie on and quickly caught up to VanEste.

They dismounted and tied their horses, wandering around the abandoned sight on foot. The sky was low and brooding, thick with the promise of imminent snow. As Annie surveyed the dark, gaping mine shafts and squalid cabins, an icy shiver ran up her spine.

"Something wrong?" VanEste inquired.

"It seems so sad, doesn't it?" she replied hesitantly. "Think of all the people who came here, searching for wealth and happiness, only to find nothing but dirt and sweat and pain. What an awful end to their dreams."

VanEste shrugged. "They knew what they were getting into."

"I suppose."

"There's a price to pay for everything. Anyone who tells you differently, who claims not to have known what he got involved in, is lying. Men may deny their own greed when fate turns against them, but whatever befalls a man in this life is his own doing, no one else's. There are no innocents, Annie."

"That's a rather harsh view, isn't it?"

"Just realistic. Take the Mundy Gang, for instance. Do you truly believe Pete Mundy didn't know there was a risk involved every time he set off to rob a train or a stage? Of course he knew. To him, however, the promise of easy wealth and fame was worth the risk." He glanced at her and raised a brow. "You look surprised, my dear. Didn't Pete ever tell you that I interviewed him over a year ago?"

Annie's heart skipped a beat as a wary note of warning took root in her mind. "No," she replied cautiously, "he didn't."

"Funny," VanEste mused, "I would have thought he would have bragged of it to everyone. Then again, perhaps the two of you simply weren't as close as I imagined. Well, I suppose it doesn't matter any longer, now that Pete and the rest of the gang are dead."

An icy knot of dread lodged in her stomach. Until that point, her insistence that the boys were dead had been met with outright doubt and disbelief. Yet VanEste seemed to be as confident as she was that that was the case.

"You still don't understand, do you?" he asked. He smiled pleasantly and lifted his shoulders in an easy shrug. "Who do you suppose had them killed?"

Annie shot a quick glance beyond his shoulder, judging the distance between her and Dulcie. If she took off in a flat-out run, she might just make it.

VanEste lifted a gun from his coat pocket and pointed it directly at her chest. "I wouldn't try it, my dear."

Annie swallowed hard. She thought of her own set of revolvers, which she had lately gotten out of the habit of wearing. They were waiting for her back at the hotel, neatly tucked away in her nightstand drawer.

"What do you want from me, VanEste?" she asked, edging slightly away from him.

"Why, I want the money, of course. The twenty-five thousand from the stage robbery. The money that's been missing since Pete died. It's my money, after all. Who do you think planned all those robberies for Pete?" He glanced at her feet and frowned. "Oh, and Annie?"

"What?" She edged away from him again.

He pulled back the hammer of his gun. "Take another step and I'll kill you."

She froze in place, her eyes locked on his. She

searched her mind frantically for something to say, for some stalling tactic she could use until she was able to think clearly. "Why did you do it? If Pete and the boys were pulling the jobs for you, why did you have them killed?

"Greed," he answered simply, then clarified, "Pete's, of course, not mine. He was anxious to impress some little slut of a barmaid he claimed to have fallen in love with, so he wanted more money. He had some preposterous idea that since the gang was taking all the risk, they deserved more than fifty percent of the take." He shook his head, making a clucking sound with his tongue. "Can you imagine that, Annie? I created the Mundy Gang, I made them who they were, and he wanted more money."

Annie nodded as horrified understanding swept over her. It all made perfect sense. The boys had always been small-time, more inclined to rowdy pranks and barroom brawls than actual robberies. But that had all changed almost overnight. She should have realized sooner that someone else was doing all their planning for them, that someone else was picking their jobs. But she never saw it. Not until now, when it was too late.

"I saw a group of lawmen open fire from that boxcar the boys tried to hold up," she said, struggling to put together the last pieces of the puzzle.

"You saw that, did you?" VanEste looked pleased. "Those weren't lawmen. They were simply the new replacements for the gang, complete with temporary tin stars pinned on their vests. I thought that if one of the original gang should live, that might give him the incentive to get out of town and not look back—especially if he knew the law was that hot on his trail." He shrugged. "As it turned out, the precaution was unnecessary. But it was a nice touch nonetheless."

"So that's why you did it," she said. "Your plan had been working too well to abandon completely. After you killed the boys, you replaced them with another gang—a gang that looked and rode just like the Mundys."

"Of course. After all, I'm the one who made the Mundys the feared outlaws that they were. No sense losing that edge." VanEste sent her a cool smile. "Ingenious, wasn't it? The only mistake I made was in not realizing that Pete would be fool enough to try to hide that twenty-five thousand from the last robbery from me. Unfortunately I didn't discover that until after he was dead. Had I known, I would have killed him for that alone."

As she studied him, the initial surge of fear Annie had felt slowly channeled into fury. Fury at how VanEste had taken Pete's gullible little-boy fantasies of making himself a big man and twisted them to suit his own brutal ends. Fury at how VanEste had so ruthlessly arranged for the cold-blooded slaughter of the men in the gang. Fury at how VanEste had been tracking her and Jake all along, shadowing their every step. He had had every detail of the boys copied, including their saddles, their horses, and their clothing, she realized with a start, remembering the man she had seen in the smoky saloon who had been wearing Pete's vest. No wonder she had never been able to convince anyone that the boys were dead.

"You won't get away with this," she said. "Too many people saw the two of us leave together this afternoon. If I don't return, they'll come after you."

VanEste's smile turned slightly superior. "How very vain, Annie. Do you really think you're that irreplaceable? The fact is, there's a woman who looks very much like you assisting the Mundy Gang rob a payroll stage at this very moment. You see, Annie, you just couldn't stay straight. After you discovered that your hotel was a broken-down brothel, you went back to running with the gang. It's all rather predictable and mundane, isn't it? No one will ask any questions or miss you at all."

Annie licked her suddenly parched lips. "May I sit down?" she requested, her voice a hoarse whisper.

"Why?"

"I think I'm going to faint."

A disgusted look crossed VanEste's face. "You're as spineless as Pete, aren't you? I'm disappointed, Annie, truly I am. I thought you were made of sterner stuff."

Annie let her eyelashes flutter shut and swayed suddenly.

"Oh, for God's sake," VanEste spit out, "sit down."

She sank immediately to the ground, letting her riding skirts whoosh out around her. She allowed her arms to go limp and rested her forehead on her knees, as though struggling to keep from falling into unconsciousness. In truth, Annie had never felt more alert or able minded. Hiding her hands beneath her skirts, she grasped the two weapons she had been edging toward: a sharp chisel used for splitting rocks and a rusty iron spike.

After a moment, VanEste's impatient voice rang in her ear. "Where can I find that money?"

Annie brought her head up, hoping her expression looked sufficiently terrified. "The boys always hid their loot in an old bear cave outside of Black River Canyon," she lied, naming a spot where she and Pete had played as children. "I'll take you there, just don't hurt me, please."

"Get up."

She attempted to rise, then collapsed back down with a cry of despair. "I don't think I can stand."

VanEste let out an oath and lurched toward her, roughly grabbing her by her arm and hauling her to her feet.

Now that the man was close enough to physically hurt, Annie didn't hesitate to do exactly that. Letting out all her pent-up fury, she slammed the chisel against his head with all her might as she simultaneously drove the rusty iron spike into his shoulder. VanEste let out a roar of pain and rage as she took off running. She heard the blast of his gun behind her and felt the breeze of hot lead as it whirled past her ear. At the second blast, she ducked instinctively, stumbling over a pile of rocks.

The stumble cost her too much time. VanEste was behind her almost immediately. He grabbed her arm and jerked her against him. His blood smeared against her clothing, and his breath came in sharp, furious gasps against her ear. He wrapped his fist in her hair and yanked her head back. "I ought to kill you for that."

Annie's eyes burned furiously into his. "You do it and you'll never get your money."

VanEste's eyes darkened. "It might just be worth it."

"It's over, VanEste," a voice called out from above them. "Drop the gun and let her go."

Annie snapped her head up to see Jake standing just twenty feet away, looking both deadly serious and coldly furious. His rifle was cocked and ready, aimed directly at VanEste's head. To his left were Walter Pogue and two deputies. Like Jake, they stood with their rifles ready, their sights trained on VanEste.

"Now," Jake said.

VanEste panicked, swinging his revolver around to aim at Jake. Annie took her chance. She slammed her boot heel against VanEste's instep as she drove her fist into the bloody wound on his shoulder. VanEste gave a sharp cry of pain and wavered slightly. She jerked out of his grasp and hit the ground flat as the sound of rifle fire exploded into the air.

VanEste's body hit the ground only inches away from her own. Annie tensed, waiting. But there were no moans, no cries, no pleas for help. Just a rushed, gurgling sound. She lifted her head to look at him and instantly understood why.

A bullet had sliced through the middle of VanEste's throat.

*   *   *

$\mathcal{J}$ake paced in the front parlor, waiting for Annie. With every anxious step he took, he heaped a mass of fiery self-recrimination upon his head, unable to forgive himself for his blind stupidity. He had relentlessly demanded nothing but the truth from her—truth that she had willingly given him all along, holding nothing back. He, in turn, had not only refused to believe her but had returned her trust with nothing but lies.

Within the past five days, Annie had faced down both Snakeskin Garvey and Peyton VanEste, and he hadn't been there to help her against either man—until it had been almost too late. His suspicions and mistrust had nearly cost her her life.

Although Annie had claimed to be fine, her skin had been ashen as they had ridden back, and she hadn't spoken a word. Upon reaching the hotel, she had immediately gone upstairs to wash VanEste's blood from her skin and change her clothing. Too worked up to sit down, he paced back and forth, waiting for her to return.

The sound of a light footfall behind him made him swerve suddenly and turn around. Annie stood in the doorway, dressed in a fresh pale-blue blouse and navy skirt. Her expression was both hesitant and wary, as though she were reluctant to enter and didn't know quite what to say to him once she did.

He strode immediately to her side. "Are you all right?" he asked, surveying her anxiously.

"Fine," she answered, although a slight tremble filled her voice.

Jake led her to a settee and sat down beside her. "Annie," he began, but she cut him off before he could finish.

"It was VanEste," she said, staring at him as though desperate for him to finally believe her. "He killed the boys in the gang, then started his own gang, using Pete's name and reputation. I know it sounds ridiculous, but—"

"I know, we heard him."

Naked relief filled her expression. "Thank God," she said. A slight, wavering smile curved her lips. "I was afraid I would have to explain it all over again, and no one would believe me."

"I should have listened to you sooner. It would have made things much easier on both of us."

"What do you mean?"

Jake restlessly stood once again, determined to confess the multitude of his sins. Annie would undoubtedly order him out of her life once he did, but he had no choice. She deserved at least that much from him. He paced a bit more, collecting his thoughts, then began. "I was in a poker game about six months back and lost pretty badly. When Harlan Becker, the man who had won, turned up dead, I suppose it was natural to assume that I had killed him." He let out a sigh and turned toward her, meeting her eyes. "That's why I gave Marshal Locke a false name. There's a bounty on my head, Annie. I'm wanted for murder."

She stared at him, clearly stunned. "Did you kill Becker?"

"No, but I had no way to prove it. All I knew was that Becker had been arguing with another man about money shortly before he died. The man Becker had been arguing with took off, heading north. I followed him and noticed that each town he stopped in was hit by the Mundy Gang within a matter of days. I became convinced that it was Pete Mundy I was following, but I couldn't get close to the gang. That's when I rode into Stony Gulch and saw you."

"And you thought if you stuck by me, I'd lead you to the gang," Annie surmised.

"Yes."

"Congratulations," she said hollowly. "Your plan seemed to be working, didn't it? The gang followed us everywhere we went."

"I tried to believe that was all a coincidence, Annie, that you weren't part of the gang at all. Then I found this." He set the crumbled note from Pete Mundy that he had found in her saddlebag on the table next to her.

She picked it up and read it, a mirthless smile curving her lips. "VanEste must have planted it, or had one of the men who was working for him do it." She hesitated for a moment, then asked, "Where did you find it?"

"It fell out of your saddlebag the morning we left Abundance."

"I see. So that's why . . ." Her voice trailed away as she put the pieces together in her head. That's why he'd started acting like a complete son of a bitch, pulling away from her just when she needed him the most, he finished for her. Jake didn't need her to speak to know what she was thinking.

Silence fell between them. She looked up at him, searching his eyes. "I wish you had showed it to me. I could have told you right then that it wasn't from Pete."

"I know." Jake sighed. "You would have told me that Pete was dead, and he couldn't have sent you a note."

"No," she answered slowly, "I would have told you that Pete couldn't write. He never did learn how. The letters got all turned around and twisted up inside his head, and he was too embarrassed to ask for help. No one else ever knew. I did all the reading and writing for the gang."

Unable to frame a suitable reply, Jake studied her profile. He remembered the first time he had seen her with her hat off, her head tilted back to soak up the warmth of the sun. He had thought her beautiful then. Now he reassessed that impression. Miss Annabel Lee Foster had been graced with more then just mere beauty. Her face was filled with strength and courage, daring and determination.

As he studied her, Jake realized with a start that it was senseless to try to memorize her face. Or to try to memorize her laugh or her walk or the stubborn way she tilted her chin. Remembering Annie wouldn't be the problem. The problem would be spending the rest of his life trying to forget her, trying to tear her out of his heart. She had talked to him just last night about living with regrets. Losing Annie was one regret he was sure he would carry with him for the rest of his days. An aching emptiness, combined with an unutterable sense of loss, settled in his chest.

"So what happens to you now?" she asked. "Are you still a wanted man?"

Jake shook his head. "I don't think so. Walter Pogue and his deputies trapped the men who had been posing as the Mundy Gang this morning. We also heard a great deal of what VanEste had been saying to you before he died. There's probably enough evidence to tie VanEste to Becker and clear my name."

"It's all over then, isn't it?" Annie said softly.

"Yes."

She rose to her feet and walked to the window. She stared outside for a long moment, her features perfectly composed. "And everything that passed between us, Jake, that was nothing but a ruse, part of your plan to get me to lead you to the gang."

Jake's heart plummeted. "No. Annie, I swear that's not true." He was at her side in three swift strides. "I never meant to hurt you. If you believe nothing else I've said, please believe that." He paused, taking a deep, ragged breath. "I tried to stay away from you, but I couldn't. I couldn't do it, Annie, no matter how hard I tried. No matter what I believed you were doing, or who you were involved with."

She turned to face him, her golden-brown eyes flooded with pain and confusion. "Why, Jake?"

"Because I fell in love with you," he replied softly. "My beautiful Annabel Lee. I fell so out-of-my-mind in love with you I couldn't think straight. All I knew was that I wanted to be with you, no matter what the cost." It was a selfish confession, but one he couldn't help but make. He stroked his finger lightly across her cheek, feeling as though his heart was being torn from his chest. He continued in a rough, husky whisper. "And I would give anything in the world to take everything back and change the way I acted, but I can't do that. It's too late now."

He also knew, he thought bitterly, that it was too late to ask for her forgiveness. Annie had treated him as both a trusted friend and a cherished lover, she had risked her life for him, and he had rewarded her with nothing but callousness and mistrust.

"I'll move out of my room tonight," he offered stiffly, "if that's what you'd like."

"I think that's for the best."

Jake swallowed hard and nodded tightly. "Fine."

Her eyes locked on his. "You can move your things into my room."

He froze as disbelief coursed through him.

Annie's eyes welled with tears as a crooked, trembling smile curved her lips. "You think you're the only one who fell in love around here, mister?"

Jake let out a low groan and pulled her to him. "How would you feel about hiring somebody permanently to run that saloon of yours?"

Annie gave him a tight squeeze and let out a bubble of laughter. "Depends on who the fella is."

"Anybody you like," he answered breezily. "As long as he answers to the name of Jake Moran and acts like a complete jackass whenever he's around you."

"I know just the man."

His lips slanted hungrily over hers, kissing her deeply and thoroughly, with all the passion and love he possessed. When he finally pulled back, they were both breathless.

He grinned and ran his fingers through her silky hair.

"We'll probably grow bored with each other within a year," he teased.

Annie smiled. "I wouldn't bet on it, mister."

Jake squeezed her tightly against him, running his hands lovingly down her spine, as though memorizing every exquisite, beloved inch of her body.

"Neither would I, darlin'. Neither would I."

Epilogue

Annie smiled as she lifted her tiny son out of his crib. There was no question at all as to who had dressed him that morning. The chubby six-month-old with the silky black hair and brilliant blue eyes wore a ridiculously expensive custom-tailored ensemble that was an exact replica of his father's. Although his clothing was all miniature, it was perfectly styled and stitched. He wore a formal black jacket, long black pants, a crisp white linen shirt—somewhat dampened by drool—and a narrow cobalt-blue string tie fastened securely beneath his chin.

"Look at you, Mr. Fancy-Pants," Annie cooed, lifting him high above her head. "All dressed up and looking so handsome."

The baby waved his tiny fists and gurgled with delight. He uttered a stream of infantile nonsense that made Annie's heart swell with delight. She pressed him tightly against her chest and placed a soft kiss against his downy hair.

"You're a smooth talker too, aren't you? Just like your daddy."

"You ready, Annie?" Jake asked, poking his head inside the nursery.

Annie nodded at her husband and smiled nervously, brushing her hands over the rich emerald of her gown.

His eyes moved slowly over her, his gaze filled with

both tenderness and admiration. "You look beautiful, darlin'."

"So do you." She paused, lifting one dark-blond brow. "That outfit looks mighty familiar."

Jake grinned and moved into the nursery. He brushed his lips against Annie's, then planted a soft kiss on his son's cheek. "I think he likes it too."

"You're ridiculous, Jake. He'll outgrow those in less than a month."

"Then we'll buy him more. This is his first introduction to the general public, and I want to make sure he makes a good impression." He lifted a tiny black Stetson from the crib and placed it on the baby's head, then gently stuffed his son's pudgy feet into a pair of ridiculously small high-heeled black cowboy boots.

Annie had to bite her lip to keep from laughing. They made their way downstairs and through the hotel's broad front door, stepping out into the brilliant June day. It had been exactly a year and a half since Annie had arrived in Cooperton, and in that time, her life had changed completely. She had a husband she cherished, a baby son she adored, and she was surrounded by friends.

As she gazed through the crowd that had gathered for the official christening of the hotel and the party and dancing that followed, she was amazed and thrilled at the number of people who had turned out for the festivities. The mayor and his wife were there, along with the sheriff and a few of his deputies—one of whom was openly courting Jennie Mae and her tiny daughter.

She saw children laughing and playing in the front yard, swiping cookies from the long trestle tables that bulged with food. Groups of women chattered and gossiped, sending Annie a friendly wave as she passed. Dora, Carlotta, Francine, and Belle strolled through the crowd catching more than a few admiring glances from ranchers and miners in search of a wife. Cat haughtily swished her tail at the crowd and curled up in a tight ball on the porch, content to bask by herself in the sun.

Jake looped his hand around her waist and gave her a quick squeeze. "You can look now, Annie."

Annie turned her gaze away from her friends and back to the hotel. The walls were white and freshly painted, the shutters and doors sparkled a deep, rich green. A riot of colorful primrose bloomed in the window boxes. She took all that in at a glance, and one thing more.

Months ago, she had decided to change the name of the establishment from Foster's Hotel to something else, but she hadn't been able to make up her mind what she wanted to call it. Jake had volunteered to handle the chore. He had selected a name and ordered a brand-new, custom-made sign. But until now, he had refused to tell her what it was.

As the crowd watched, the painters proudly tossed off the sheet that had covered their work. The new sign glistened in the sunlight, sparkling with an abundance of rich, beautiful colors.

Her husband gave her waist another gentle squeeze, studying her face intently. "Do you like it, darlin'?"

She nodded tightly and reached for his hand, so full of joy she felt as though her heart would surely burst. "It's perfect."

Jake had named the hotel the Rainbow's End.